The Highlander's Heiress

Highland Heather Romancing a Scot: Castle Brides
Book 2

Collette Cameron®

Copyright © 2017 Blue Rose Romance® LLC
Collette Cameron®
THE HIGHLANDER'S HEIRESS
Enhanced Second Edition
Highland Heather Romancing a Scot: Castle Brides
Book 2

Cover Art: Joanna D'Angelo

All Rights Reserved

Formerly titled *Highlander's Hope*

This publication is entirely human-authored and not AI-generated.

This book is a work of fiction. Names, characters, places, and incidents are the product of the author's imagination or are used fictitiously. Any resemblance to actual events, locales, or persons, living or dead, is coincidental.

All rights reserved under International and Pan-American Copyright Conventions. By downloading or purchasing a print copy of this book, you have been granted the *non*-exclusive, *non*-transferable right to access and read the text of this book. No part of this text may be reproduced, transmitted, downloaded, decompiled, reverse engineered, or stored in or introduced into any information storage and retrieval system, in any form or by any means, whether electronic or mechanical, now known or hereinafter invented without the express written permission of copyright owner.

Please Note: The reverse engineering, uploading, and/or distributing of this book via the internet or via any other means without the permission of the copyright owner is illegal and punishable by law. Please purchase only authorized electronic editions, and do not participate in or encourage electronic piracy of copyrighted materials. Your support of the author's rights is appreciated.

No part of this book may be reproduced or transmitted in any form or by any electronic or mechanical means, including photocopying, recording or by any information storage and retrieval system, without the written permission of the publisher, except where permitted by law. For permission requests, write to the publisher, addressed "Attention: Permissions Coordinator," at the address below.

Disclaimer: AI-assisted tools may have been used for spell checking, copy editing, grammar, and punctuation. However, the plot, characters, dialogue, setting, worldbuilding, themes, prose, and overall creative direction are entirely the work of the author.

NO AI TRAINING: Without in any way limiting the author's [and publisher's] exclusive rights under copyright, any use of this publication to "train" generative artificial intelligence (AI) technologies to generate text is **expressly prohibited**. The author reserves all rights to license uses of this work for generative AI training and development of machine learning language models.

For permission requests, write to the publisher at the address below.

Attn: Permissions Coordinator
Blue Rose Romance® LLC
info@collettecameronbooks.com
eBook ISBN: 9781954307070
Print Book ISBN: 978-1-966087-17-5
collettecameronbooks.com

Praise for...
The Highlander's Heiress

See What Readers Are Saying About
The Highlander's Heiress

★★★★★ "Full of laugh out loud humour, adventure, villains, intrigue, and of course, romance!" ~ *Grammy H*

★★★★★ "...compelling characters, an enticing mystery, and an emotional romance... truly terrific from beginning to end." ~ *Lusty Penguin Reviews*

★★★★★ "From beginning to end, this novel is absolutely marvelous!" ~ *My Book Addiction*

★★★★★ "I heartily recommend this book to romantic readers and adventurous ones, too. I rate it five stars but wish I could make it more. It is a wonderful book." ~ *The Romance Reviews Top Pick*

★★★★★ "Loved it. Loved it. Loved it. I finished this in one sitting, and for me that is the hallmark of a good book. Ms. Cameron is my new favorite romance author. Highly recommended." ~ *Yvonne Griffen*

FREE BOOK!

JOIN MY EXCLUSIVE MAILING LIST
Collette Cameron Newsletter

AND GET A FREE EBOOK!

https://collettecameronbooks.com/freegift

Plus Sneak Peeks, Giveaways, Contests, Exclusive Content, and More... P.S. I promise only good stuff ~ **no** spam!

Acknowledgments

I find it nearly impossible to believe that four years have passed since the first version of **THE HIGHLANDER'S HEIRESS** was published in May of 2013!

As my first book baby goes to press for the second time, I am writing my twentieth book!

This second enhanced version took me down a nostalgic path and made me realize even more how many people have contributed to my success as an author. I've grown so much, and I strive to always be improving.

So I must thank my Beta readers, the reviewers who left thoughtful insightful reviews, fellow authors for all of their tips, sharing, and encouragement, and most especially my immediate family.

They believed in me even those days when I doubted myself.

And to my loyal readers—I thank you!

xoxo

Collette

~

Dedication

For my daughter, my friend,
Brianna Cherise—named for a romance heroine.
With all my love and appreciation for believing in me; for the
precious little girl you were and the amazing woman you've
become.
I love you!

Prologue

April 1817

"Make haste, Yvette. The coach is readied."

"I know, Pippa."

Yvette and her aged nurse scurried around Yvette's bedchamber quickly packing her valise with the barest essentials.

Yvette swept one last look around the room she'd occupied for the past two years, then donned the woolen cloak Pippa held. Bulging bag in hand, Pippa right behind her, Yvette hastened down the corridor.

They met the rest of household at the bottom of the staircase, their dear faces tense, but resolute.

"Everyone knows what to do?" Fairchild—the butler and long-time family friend—met each of their gazes in turn, received confirming nods from everyone. "Very well, then. Let's be about it."

"Wait!" Yvette cried softly, hugging him. "Thank you, I. . ."

The butler encircled her in a fond, fatherly hug and kissed the top of her head. "I know, Evvy."

She offered the others a brave, if somewhat tremulous smile. How could she bear leaving them? She'd no choice. Edgar's abduction attempt tonight, after his previous effort to ravish her, forced this desperate flight. He continued to elude the authorities, and even armed guards hadn't been able to prevent his sneaking into the manor.

"Evvy, we *must* hurry. The ship sails within the hour." Josiah Fairchild's voice rang with concern as he speared his twin an uneasy glance.

Yvette dropped to her knees. She wrapped her arms around her spaniels' necks and buried her face in their soft, dappled fur. "I'll miss you so much, my sweet friends."

"Evvy, you have to go. *Now*," Isaiah, the other twin, urged. "Edgar may be watching the manor."

She nodded as he helped her to her feet. After hugging him, she took a deep breath and squared her shoulders. "I'm ready."

A flaxen-haired maid, snugly wrapped in Yvette's cloak, and Isaiah slipped out the front entrance where a coach awaited them. They'd offered to act as decoys so she could escape.

Blinking away scorching tears, Yvette rushed to the back of the darkened house. Once there, she embraced a distraught Pippa.

"I'll pray for your safety, Evvy. It'll be but a few short weeks until we meet again in England," managed her long-time nurse through her tear-clogged throat.

Attired in a farmer's rough garb, a dirty hat low on his

head, Josiah grasped Yvette's arm and led her to the waiting cart. She crawled in and, sucking in a steadying breath, lay down. After placing her stuffed valise beside her, he covered her with a tarp. A moment later, something soft dropped onto her.

Straw.

Josiah spread it about, concealing her.

The cart dipped and creaked as he climbed onto the seat. And then, with a small jolt, it lurched forward, spiriting her to freedom.

Several minutes passed before they arrived at their destination, and the vehicle rolled to a slow stop. An instant later, the crisp sea breeze whipped across Yvette's face as Josiah assisted her down. Hiding in the buildings' shadows, they edged along the wharf. Yvette feared they'd be stopped at any moment—that Edgar or his henchmen would discover their ruse.

"There she is," Josiah whispered, pointing at a ship.

Hood raised, Yvette cautiously stepped forward and peered up at the *Atlantic Star*. Holding her fear in check, she drew in a deep, fortifying breath. She turned and clasped Josiah tightly. "I'll miss you."

"And I you, minx." He tweaked her nose affectionately. "Now go."

Chin tilted courageously, she crossed the dock and boarded the waiting ship.

In those long moments before night fully yielded her assiduous watch and dawn gradually roused to full awareness, Yvette stood at the ship's rail. Her posture tense and gaze keen, she searched the flickering, shifting shadows along the murky waterfront.

The *Atlantic Star* silently slipped past the other moored

ships, including the *Peaceful Wind*—the ship she was supposed to sail on in two weeks—and glided away from Boston's harbor.

Out to the open sea. To safety.

One

London Harbor

Late June 1817

"Nooo..."

The strangled cry startled Yvette awake.

Chest heaving, she choked on dry, rasping sobs as she clawed beneath her pillow for the sheath containing her folding dagger. Gulping against the lump wedged in her throat, she struggled to draw air into her lungs and calm her stampeding pulse.

Lord, another nightmare about Edgar.

Struggling to see, she peered into the gloom. A sliver of light peeked through the ship's porthole. The silvery moonbeam illuminated the cramped, airless cabin and the occupants of the equally uncomfortable berths. Though meager, the glow allowed her to examine the shadowy interior of her tiny stateroom.

She sagged against the bedding and shut her eyes. She swallowed again. The stranglehold of fear evaporated.

Well, not entirely.

Truth be told, the suspicious deaths of her parents, her own mysterious riding accident, and Edgar's two abductions and physical assaults still haunted her. Although she couldn't prove it, she suspected he might be responsible for the former two incidents as well.

Sticky with sweat from the fuggy air above her upper berth, Yvette kicked off her coarse blanket. Reaching to push a damp curl off her face, she froze mid-movement.

Before the nightmare awoke her, she'd been dreaming of *him*.

Uncanny, but she knew the visitor in her dreams almost as well as if he'd been a flesh-and-blood man. She recognized his spicy, male scent and the feel of his firm lips on hers—his powerful body and his sinewy embrace holding her close, keeping her safe.

She cherished that the most—the safety of his arms.

He'd been kissing her, and she touched her lips, which throbbed yet beneath her fingertips.

Eyes closed, she furrowed her brow and tried to summon his face. Flitting across the fringes of her memory like an elusive phantom, the image lurked beyond the reach of her consciousness. Then...flitted away.

His eyes, though... Oh, yes, she remembered his startling eyes.

Opening hers, she grinned.

The *Atlantic Star* no longer swayed, and the cabin was blessedly silent. For the first time in weeks—no, it had been months now—her obnoxious cabin mate, Mrs. Pettigrove, wasn't rattling the walls and shaking the berths with her resounding snores.

If only another cabin had been available when Yvette

fled Massachusetts in the middle of the night. Her urgent need to quickly escape—in secret—was so great that Fairchild barely allowed her the time to pack a valise and her weapons.

With two guards lying dead and members of the staff injured, quibbling about accommodations was unthinkable. She took the sole remaining available bunk, which meant Pippa couldn't accompany her as planned.

Sharing a cabin with a stranger as difficult and demanding as Mrs. Pettigrove proved beyond taxing. Several of Yvette's smaller belongings, and the pitiful collection of jewels and monies Edgar had missed in his raid, went missing during the voyage. Yvette had found everything but the jewels hidden amongst Mrs. Pettigrove's possessions.

When Yvette confronted her, the dame denied touching Yvette's effects. She claimed a ship's hand must've stolen the items and placed Yvette's possessions with hers to make Mrs. Pettigrove appear the guilty party.

Yvette had taken to sleeping with her reticule lest Mrs. Pettigrove help herself to the few meager coins Yvette still possessed.

No, she couldn't wait to part company with the woman.

Just then, Mrs. Pettigrove rolled over, and the bunks groaned and shook with her labored movement. She grunted, passed a large expanse of wind, and grew silent once more.

Oh, good Lord.

Yvette quickly smashed a pillow across her face as the results of Mrs. Pettigrove's digestive disruptions drifted upward. She removed the pillow almost as fast. The cloying material was intolerable in this heat.

"How can she sleep when it's this blasted hot?" With the back of her hand, Yvette wiped beads of moisture from her upper lip. "I don't remember June ever being this warm."

Did the other passengers suffer as much as she? Or did they somehow manage to sleep in the dreadful warmth? How they could was beyond her. A shiver of unease whispered across her, and she pursed her lips, releasing a slight huff of air.

One of the other passengers, Nigel Collingsworth—tall, muscular, and oozing cool confidence—had caused her no small amount of disquiet during the Atlantic crossing. His shrewd, dark gaze shifted everywhere. Watched everyone. Missed nothing. On several occasions, Yvette caught him staring at her with a peculiar, assessing glimmer in his eyes.

Brows puckered, she frowned. Mr. Collingsworth unnerved her. Thank goodness she'd never have to see the man again.

Hoping to find some relief from the oppressive temperature, she flipped to her side and plopped an arm and knee over the edge of her bunk. The new position didn't provide much respite.

The quiet *slap, slap* of the Thames lapping against the ship's hull reaffirmed they'd reached London and docked during the night. Mrs. Pettigrove slumbered on, now as silent as a newborn babe. The matron hadn't slept this peacefully throughout the entire journey.

Yvette glanced at the porthole.

What time was it?

The sky remained slate without. Still well before dawn, then.

Muted bangs and thumps, and an occasional curse or

shout, suggested the *Atlantic Star*'s crew stirred in preparation for the disembarking of her passengers and unloading of the ship's cargo.

Stretching, she stared longingly at the porthole. The cabin was stifling. Despite the heat, Mrs. Pettigrove, afraid of catching the ague, had insisted the small window remain shut tight.

Did Yvette dare defy the cranky fusspot and crack it to allow blessedly cool air into the cabin? She blew out a breath of frustration. That might awaken Mrs. Pettigrove.

Awaken Mrs. Pettigrove?

A notion took hold.

Perhaps not an altogether unfortunate thing. No indeed, not unfortunate at all. The sooner they'd dressed and packed, the sooner she could call on Papa's solicitor. By noon, she'd have access to her inheritance and be relieved of Mrs. Pettigrove's trying company once and for all.

Yvette tilted her mouth into a wide smile. The idea pleased her no end. She'd never claimed patience as a virtue. Decision made, she scrambled from the berth, banging her toe in the process.

Zounds, it hurt!

Clutching her foot, she hopped about the cabin, determined to put the past, and Massachusetts, behind her.

Just as soon as she could walk again.

Less than two hours later, Yvette stood on London's East India Docks, surveying the chaotic and foul-smelling wharf. She crinkled her nose. The Thames's stench, combined with piles of rotting garbage and decaying fish, reeked.

A smile hovered on her lips nonetheless.

Home at last.

She peered about. Where was Mrs. Pettigrove? They were to share a hackney.

Yvette had reluctantly handed over the last of her coin for the hired conveyance when Mrs. Pettigrove insisted she had no funds and had asked to share Yvette's.

She took a few steps across the scarred planking, continuing to look around.

No Mrs. Pettigrove. No hackney.

Yvette exhaled in exasperation. Bother and blast, the woman had stolen her money.

Serves me right for stupidly trusting her.

She tightened her grip on her valise and strode across the wharf. She wasn't worried. Well, perhaps a mite. She'd heard torrid stories of unsavory things happening to young women on the waterfront. Papa insisted she never visit his offices unaccompanied, and had absolutely forbidden her to set foot on the docks and side streets.

However, one must do what one must. Besides, she carried a gun in her valise and a blade in her reticule—though, truth to tell, she hadn't practiced with either in some time.

Yvette stopped and perused the area. The dock manager's office was...what? Perhaps a half-dozen blocks away? Papa's offices lay a block farther along. Surely someone there would lend her funds to hire a hackney to her solicitor's.

A familiar twinge gripped her.

Papa and Belle-mére.

No, she wouldn't contemplate their deaths. Not now anyway. She was finally home, and joy whispered across her soul despite her grief. In a matter of days, she'd be at

Somersfield, reunited with her cousin Vangie, and safe from Edgar. Once there, she'd consider her future and decide what she wanted to do.

Edgar's attacks had served one useful purpose. They'd strengthened her resolve to lay the course for her own life. She'd never bend to the whim of a man again.

An only child—other than her two stepbrothers, neither of whom she knew well, though Rory was by far the more tolerable of the pair—she'd inherited Papa's entire fortune. Now, she had the financial means to remain independent once she turned one-and-twenty. And although she'd never wanted for admirers, she had no pressing desire to marry just yet.

In Boston, after she'd rebuffed Edgar's attempts to court her, he'd called her a bluestocking and claimed she was overly educated, that she didn't know her place.

Good.

She had no intention of ever knowing her place. Gads, the notion sounded quite boring and oppressive.

True, she'd been highly educated; Papa had insisted upon it. He'd also insisted she be trained in weaponry in order to defend herself. Though grace wasn't her greatest asset, she was passable with a blade and quite skilled with firearms. She grinned. Why, she could even hit a stationary target with some regularity.

Yes, dearest Papa had been most unconventional, though overly protective. Yvette hadn't minded, at least not when she was younger. She'd enjoyed her studies, and her extensive education hadn't seemed to discourage her suitors.

She permitted herself a rueful smile.

Papa's affluence had garnered her many beaus over the years. She'd tried to develop an interest in the gentlemen who began calling five years ago, when she was five-and-ten. Truly, she had.

So, some considered her on the shelf. She lifted a shoulder as she trudged along. The knowledge didn't bother her. None of those men had quickened her pulse. No overwhelming desire to kiss them until she gasped with pleasure ever seized her.

Truth to tell, she had no desire, much less an overwhelming one, to touch them at all. Papa had understood, and he'd never pressed marriage upon her, though every now and again, he'd teased her.

"I'm hoping for a dozen grandchildren, Evvy."

Her determination to select her own husband, and to marry for love, was something of a hindrance. A rather large hindrance, actually. She could never be sure if a gentleman's interest was genuine, or if he feigned love and adoration to gain access to her father's fortune—now her fortune.

Best to trust no men, except dear, doddering Mr. Dehring, Fairchild, and the twins.

Intent on her thoughts, she tripped over a coiled rope and tottered for a moment. Her arm ached from the valise's weight. She shifted it to her other hand and picked her way across another pile of rope.

Traipsing across the dock, she bit her lower lip as she continued ruminating.

She did want children though, lots of them. And there was the corker. She couldn't very well have one without the other. Good Lord, imagine the scandal. Her gaze dipped to her skirts. What would it be like to have four, or five, or six children clinging to them?

She could adopt, she supposed. For certain, orphans enough wandered London's streets. Were unmarried women allowed to adopt? She'd have to ask Mr. Dehring.

Yvette grimaced, her joy fading. Dash it all. Now she'd become a jumble of confused emotions.

As she strode across the wharf's rough wooden planks, an eerie sensation prickled the length of her spine. Slowing her pace, she glanced over her shoulder, and her heart lurched to her throat and lodged there.

Was that man following her?

Two

Yvette gulped past the lump in her throat and quickened her pace. She maneuvered between seamen, crates, overloaded carts, and the occasional steaming pile of horse droppings. After skirting a well-sprung carriage, she slipped into a dingy warehouse doorway. From its depths, the swish of her heart magnified in her ears, she watched the suspicious man.

Did he truly trail her? Should she confront him? She bit the inside of her cheek and glanced down the alley. Papa's offices were but a few blocks away. Should she make a run for it? She peeked at the man again. He was a rough-looking codger.

He had stopped too, and now peered about, clearly aggravated. Yanking off his shabby cap, he wiped his sweaty brow with his forearm. After cramming the hat back on his bald head, he tugged on his ear, turning his head this way and that.

Crouching low, Yvette crept along the end of a barrel-filled wagon. Obscured in the shadows, and staying close to the cooper's building, she darted down another narrow lane. A half-starved cat jumped from a crate beside her head.

"Lord Almighty," she yelped, wincing when the barrel she plowed into crashed to the ground.

A hoarse shout echoed behind her, followed by the thud of running feet. Grasping her skirts in one hand, lugging her valise in the other, she broke into an awkward, lumbering run. She dared to shoot a peek behind her. The man gained on her, and Lord help her, a second man had joined the chase.

Collingsworth.

She knew there was something untrustworthy about that blackguard.

Her bonnet fell forward, blocking her view. Dropping her skirts, she clamped a hand on her hat. Panicked, terrified her pursuers were hired by Edgar, she dashed across the street then sped down the nearly deserted avenue.

Panting for breath, Yvette barged into a well-dressed gentleman before knocking her knees against a bench occupied by a fishwife a few feet farther along.

"I say, miss!"

"Slow down, dearie."

"I beg your pardon," she gasped, without slowing her pace.

A carriage came alongside her, the door thrown open wide. A man's gloved hand emerged.

"Quickly, Miss Stapleton, get in," ordered a deep baritone voice.

He knows me?

An acquaintance of Papa's perhaps?

Careening along, neck or nothing, Yvette veered a glance over her shoulder. The men continued to chase her, except now only a few feet remained between her and them. No help for it then. It was either this stranger or them.

And being in Edgar's clutches again...

The man repeated, "Hurry. Get in."

She had no idea who the ornate carriage belonged to, but she prayed he was better than the blackguards chasing her. He knew her name, and besides, she had her dagger. She released her bonnet, which promptly plopped onto her forehead. She'd rather take her chances with him than risk being captured by any associate of Edgar's.

Doubtful but desperate, she extended her hand.

At once, he clasped it in his strong grip.

Yvette leaped, lurching ungracefully into the carriage. The momentum flung her, arms and legs splayed, across a very stylish, very male lap. Her valise thwacked the occupant alongside his head, toppling his hat to the carriage floor. His grunt of pain muffled her surprised, humiliated squeal.

"Oh."

"*Oomph.*"

Through the black lace edging her bonnet, she glimpsed a tanned, hawkish face and midnight hair. Tangled in her skirts and shawl, she whiffed his spicy scent even as she tried to scramble off him. As she levered upward, she inadvertently pressed her hand against his generous maleness.

Mortification scorching her cheeks, Yvette released her hold on the satchel and flopped onto the floor in an undignified heap. Her gaze flew to his face and darted away again before he looked up.

A low chuckle rumbled throughout the bouncing vehicle.

He laughed at her, the lout. *Who* was he?

Her curiosity and gratitude faded into leeriness.

Perhaps jumping into his carriage hadn't been the better choice. She righted herself, crawling off the floor and onto the opposite seat. Reaching to grasp her bag at the precise moment her rescuer bent to retrieve his hat, Yvette smacked her head on his square chin.

The man grunted in pain for a second time.

Blast it all.

"I'm terribly sorry, sir." Quite cross, she retreated into the shadowy corner of the plush carriage and rubbed her throbbing forehead.

Peeking at him from beneath her lashes, she reached to straighten her bonnet. It hung askew off the side of her head, like a giant, drooping peony. She shoved it into place, but the moment she removed her hand, it flopped over once more.

The stranger's unrestrained laughter filled the carriage.

"Oh, botheration."

Yvette's patience with both her rescuer and the silly bonnet were at an end. She had no choice but to remove the dratted cap to reaffix the thing, but when she lifted the bonnet from her head, several strands of hair tumbled to her shoulders. Suppressing a shriek of annoyance, she placed the hat beside her, then set about securing the wayward curls. As she pinned the last strand in place, her eyes met those of her companion.

She stilled, as did the world around her. The air hung suspended in her lungs, and her eyes widened in disbelief. *Those eyes.* Fringed by thick lashes, the mesmerizing turquoise pools gazing at her sent her senses reeling in recognition. Her mouth dropped open, and she gave a long blink. No, it couldn't be. *Am I dreaming?*

"You exist?" Her voice husky with awe, her stunned gaze remained riveted to his face.

Ebony eyebrow cocked, a flicker of humor softened the nobleman's features. "So it would appear."

His voice, deep and dark as warm chocolate, caressed Yvette's heightened awareness. Her gaze roved across the handsome planes and angles of his features before returning, as if compelled by some unseen force, to his eyes.

Giving a quick shake of her head, she lowered her eyelids for a moment. My, but he'd befuddled her. "Who are you? Have I met you before?"

Her mind raced, sorting through her memories. Her social calendar had been quite full prior to their temporary move to Boston. In fact, her Come Out had been mere weeks before they'd left. Almack's, Vauxhall Gardens, the opera and theatre, balls, routs, soirées... She couldn't recall seeing him at any of the social gatherings she and her parents had frequented.

The man across from her shifted, adjusting his muscled legs. His gaze rose lazily from her lips, and an unhurried smile quirked the corners of his strong mouth. "I'm Ewan McTavish, Laird of Craiglochy."

A Scot? Yvette wrinkled her forehead. "You speak with barely a trace of a brogue."

"Ah, that credit goes to excellent tutors. My entire family can speak the King's English if they choose. And yes, we've met."

"Where?" Surely she would've remembered *him*.

"At your cousin's wedding."

That explained why she couldn't recollect him. Vangie's wedding was an unpleasant, hazy blur. After a horrid scandal, she'd been forced to marry Viscount Warrick. Yvette had been sick with concern for her dear cousin. In fact, she couldn't even recall what she'd worn that awful day.

She bent forward and cautiously searched the street.

The men were nowhere to be seen. "Were you following me?"

"I saw you being chased, and it seemed prudent to rescue you." He looked beyond the carriage window for an instant before returning his gaze to her. "Do you know why you were being pursued?"

Yvette wasn't about to blurt her suspicions to him. He'd think she was given to flim-flam and flummery. She shook her head. "How did you know I'd get in the carriage with you?"

Mr. McTavish grinned. "I didn't, but I hoped you'd recognize me. Now, where can I deliver you?"

His satiny voice, with its nuance of Scot's brogue, washed across her senses again.

"Hmm?" *Did he say something?* "I'm sorry, what did you say?"

He smiled again, a slow, seductive curl of his lips. "What is your destination?"

Should she go to the Banbury Inn first and rid herself of her cumbersome valise or make straightaway for Mr. Dehring's office?

Nibbling her lower lip in indecision, Yvette considered him. Faith, he was handsome. For the first time, she noticed the small, crescent-shaped scar on the left side of his cheek. The disfigurement didn't detract from McTavish's rugged good looks in the least.

But, could she trust him?

True, he had rescued her from Collingsworth and that other man—and God only knew what else. The familiar weight of her dagger pressed against her leg. She fingered the blade through her reticule's thin fabric. He claimed they'd met before, but other than that, she knew nothing whatsoever about him.

Except those eyes. She knew those eyes. She had seen them in her dreams dozens of times.

No, though he stirred her curiosity, she wasn't so short on wits as to tell him where she was lodging. "My solicitor's office on Red Croft Street, please."

Less than ten minutes later, Yvette stood in front of Mr. Dehring's establishment. Smoothing her skirts, she eyed her rescuer from the corner of her eye. He was a powerful man. Though not as tall as Papa, his abundant muscles made him appear larger.

He reached inside the carriage to retrieve her bulky valise, then turned to her. "Allow me to assist you inside."

The timbre of his voice had the hair rising on her nape. He took her by the elbow, and she started as sparks of awareness spread, lingering in the most interesting places. The pleasant warmth sweeping through her couldn't be attributed to the scorching day.

Eyes wide, she stood mute.

"Miss Stapleton?" Amusement crinkled the edges of his eyes.

Good heavens, whatever had come over her? Blinking, she forced a composed smile. At least she hoped it was composed. Her lips were turned upward, of that she was sure. But mayhap she looked like a calf-eyed, leering ninny.

She stopped smiling. "Thank you, but I can manage. It's only a few steps..."

Her words trailed off when she met his eyes. The inexplicable draw of his gaze held a promise, or perhaps a challenge. She wasn't sure which. It didn't matter. The world blurred around her as she examined his features.

Her attention rested on his full lips. They looked warm. And firm. And oh so kissable.

His teeth flashed white against his tanned face, and she

raised her hesitant eyes to his once more. Was that a knowing gleam in his? Could he read her mind?

She crimped her lips. Of course not.

"Miss Stapleton." Mr. Dehring's exuberant greeting ended the sensual connection. McTavish removed his strong hand from her elbow.

Mr. Dehring beamed with fatherly affection. "My dear, I wasn't aware you'd arrived."

"Only this morning, Mr. Dehring."

He nodded at McTavish. "My—"

"Excuse me, I must be off." McTavish tipped his top hat. "I'm late for an appointment."

Yvette turned to him, smiling her gratitude. "Thank you for your assistance. I'm most grateful. I shudder to think what would've transpired if you hadn't happened by."

Raising her gloved hand to his lips, he placed a chaste kiss on her knuckles. "The pleasure was mine."

The honeyed tone of his voice caused her toes to curl in her boots, until Mr. Dehring's discreet cough broke the spell entrancing her once again.

McTavish bowed to her then inclined his head to Mr. Dehring before turning on his heels and bounding into the carriage.

She watched the conveyance until it faded from sight.

Now there was a man who quickened her pulse. Would she ever see him again? The memory of his beguiling smile flashed before her eyes. Did she want to see him again?

Releasing a long sigh, she gave herself a mental shake.

No, she didn't.

If he wasn't a fortune hunter then a man that striking and confident was undoubtedly a rogue and a rake.

Three

Whistling a jaunty tune, Ewan wended his way through the maze of corridors in the musty War Office. Nodding or raising a hand in greeting to numerous acquaintances, he moved with purpose.

He'd patrolled the docks for the better part of a week, awaiting Miss Stapleton's ship. When she didn't disembark the *Peaceful Wind* as expected, he'd sought the ship's captain to discover the reason. Informed of her pre-dawn flight from Boston, Ewan continued to monitor the dockside, awaiting the arrival of the *Atlantic Star*, which should've docked days ago.

It wasn't uncommon for ships to arrive earlier or later than expected. Seamen were at the mercy of both the sea and the Almighty. Storms, headwinds, or lack of wind could delay a ship for weeks, and a strong tailwind could shorten a voyage by almost as much. Such had been the case with the *Peaceful Wind*. She'd made port before the *Atlantic Star*, though she'd sailed a week later.

Ewan was more determined than ever to see Edgar

Marquardt become a permanent resident of Newgate. According to a letter he'd received from his agent in February, Marquardt, the bloody bastard, had tried to abduct and have his way with Miss Stapleton last December.

Ewan turned into another lengthy passage, this one less populated. No wonder visitors often got lost at the War Office—a labyrinth of fusty corridors and gloomy staircases.

He grazed his fingers along his sore jaw, wincing when he encountered the fresh bruise. His grin widened. Miss Stapleton's lack of grace was endearing. His groin yet burned where she pressed her hand against it in her clumsy haste to put some distance between them in the carriage.

Yes, escorting her to Somersfield would be quite enjoyable. The unexpected absence of her chaperone complicated matters, but he'd cross that bridge when he came to it.

Confound it.

He'd been so taken with Miss Stapleton, he'd forgotten to mention the change of plans to her. No matter. He knew where she lodged and could rectify the oversight later. What would she do when she learned of his other title, Viscount Sethwick?

Without knocking, Ewan entered Secretary of War Bartholomew Yancy's office. His boot heels clicking on the elaborate tiled floor, Ewan quickly scrutinized the occupants.

What were Rothingham and Fielding doing here? Had Yancy sent for all the Diplomatic Corps agents presently in Town, or had the two dropped in uninvited as they were wont to do? They were as nosey as a couple of old crones and every bit as gossipy.

Ewan traded nods with the two lords, then addressed the secretary. "Well, Yancy?"

Yancy cocked his head. "One of our—"

"Agents was found floating in the Thames, throat slit." Lounging against the mantel of an enormous, unlit fireplace, brandy snifter in hand, Lord Fielding appeared unaffected.

Ewan furrowed his forehead in annoyance. Fielding was forever interrupting.

The Earl of Rothingham sat in an armchair before the fireplace, smoking. He removed the cheroot from his mouth then flicked the ashes onto the hearth. "We knew his disappearance was suspect."

"And the Regent's furious." Irritation and fatigue edged Yancy's voice.

Surprised at his tone, Ewan faced him.

The exhausted secretary wiped a hand across his eyes. "I had a meeting with Prinny earlier today." He met each of the men's gazes in turn. "When he ordered us to find the traitor who almost cost him the war, he assumed it would be an easy task."

"He would, the pompous twit. Marquardt's been the only easy thing about it. We know he spied for the French." Fielding gave a dark chuckle before taking a sip of his cognac.

"Be that as it may, traitors don't go unpunished under the Regent's watch." Yancy took a generous swallow from his own snifter. "Every time we get close to discovering who gave Marquardt his orders, another agent or informer dies."

After moving farther into the room, Ewan began pacing. "The war may have ended, but the danger to our agents damned well hasn't. How many does that make now?" Brow raised, he looked to Yancy.

"Eight over the past twenty months." Yancy grimaced. "But five in the last six."

Ewan sucked in a sharp breath and shook his head. "Bloody hell. Eight?"

Someone was eliminating loose ends. Someone who'd handed over royal secrets during the war and was desperate to keep his identity a secret. He met Yancy's gaze. "We're getting close to exposing their organizer then."

He traced the small scar on his cheek. The muscles flexed beneath his fingers. He *would* succeed in ousting the spy.

Rothingham exhaled an extended puff of smoke. "I suppose then, until agents and informants stop getting murdered, we cannot let it rest."

"Ye suppose, do ye?" Mockery thickened Ewan's brogue.

Pinching his nose between ink-stained fingers, Yancy cocked his head to the side. Releasing a deep breath, he slouched into the leather wingback chair behind his desk. He seemed to choose his words with care. "Sethwick... exactly how devious is Marquardt? Is *he* capable of murder?"

Ewan stopped pacing and met Yancy's gaze head-on. "Did you know he's Miss Stapleton's stepbrother? Their parents died recently. The circumstances were questionable, and—"

"Bloody hell, Sethwick. You're not suggesting Marquardt killed his own mother?" Fielding interjected. "What about the daughter? Is she safe? Unharmed?"

Brows raised high on his forehead, Ewan studied Fielding's flushed face. "You're acquainted with Miss Stapleton?"

"No. I... uh..." Fielding's gaze shifted to the snifter he held. "I'm concerned for her safety, that's all." He took a deep gulp of his cognac.

After assessing Fielding for a prolonged moment, Ewan resumed pacing. "Actually, Miss Stapleton arrived in London this morning."

He stopped again, choosing instead to rest one hip against the table centered in the room. "My agent in Boston informed me that Miss Stapleton suffered a riding mishap in December, scarcely a month after Marquardt's arrival in Boston. It wasn't an accident. Her father and stepmother died a mite over three weeks later. Their doctor was suspicious, because they'd attended a soirée the day before, yet no one else became ill."

Ewan's gaze roamed the room before resting on Yancy. "An unusual coincidence, don't you think?"

"Poisoned?" Rothingham stretched his legs before him, then lit another cheroot.

Ewan gave one terse nod. "Likely arsenic or nightshade. Both are undetectable."

His cigar clenched between his teeth, Rothingham said, "You think Marquardt's behind the accident and deaths? Why? I can't imagine he'd murder his mother. That's beyond the pale."

"I'm guessing for the inheritance, and I don't believe his mother was the intended victim. Miss Stapleton was." Ewan shifted his position and crossed his ankles.

"Egads, you don't say!" Rothingham took a lengthy pull on his cheroot. "I don't see how money will help him though. He's accused of treason."

"True, but he's not aware we know he's a traitor. There's only one thing that would cause a man to be so desperate for money he'd resort to murder." Ewan straightened and clasped his hands behind him. "Someone's going to kill him if he doesn't pay up. He's—"

"Being blackmailed," Fielding blurted.

"Dammit, Fielding, stop interrupting me!"

"Sethwick?" Yancy's tone gave Ewan pause, and he looked at him. "Might Miss Stapleton be useful in capturing Marquardt?"

Ewan slanted his head and considered the secretary. "How so?"

"Bait. We— Er... You could use her as bait. Lure Marquardt in with the chit." Unhealthy excitement glittered in Fielding's eyes.

"For God's sake, do shut up!" Yancy slammed his fist on the desk. "That's not what I meant at all, you imbecile. I meant she might have information about him we'd find useful."

"I say, Fielding, old chap, poorly done." Rothingham tossed his cheroot in the fireplace.

Ewan leveled Fielding a blistering glare. "You should be horsewhipped."

As should I.

Guilt washed over him. He'd already considered the unsavory possibility of using Miss Stapleton as a lure himself. Sending Fielding another menacing scowl, he faced Yancy. "I have a pressing need to speak with you about another matter."

Rothingham rose and, after stretching, faced Fielding. "What say you and I make our way to White's?"

Lips pressed into a thin line, Fielding nodded. With a terse, barely civil nod to Yancy and Ewan, he followed Rothingham from the room.

"What's so pressing, Sethwick, you couldn't share it with the others?"

Ewan shrugged. "Not so pressing, but I was afraid if Fielding opened his mouth again, I'd plant him a facer. By-the-by, a man matching Marquardt's description was in the Nag's Head."

Sending him a piercing look, Yancy said, "You're certain?"

"Aye, beyond a doubt. One of Marquardt's lackeys, Belvidere, followed Miss Stapleton. Chased her, to be precise. I rescued her off the docks."

Yancy closed his eyes and shook his head. "The devil take it."

Ewan studied his friend. Yancy knew something. Something, by the haggard look on his face, he was reluctant to share.

"Sethwick?"

Ewan canted his head and waited. Yancy would get to what troubled him.

Rising, Yancy raked a hand through his hair before wandering to the multi-paned window dominating the wall behind his desk. "I wasn't exaggerating when I said Prinny was livid. He raged, 'You couldn't see a snake beneath your nose, Mr. War Secretary!'"

Typical Prinny behavior.

Sagging against the sash, Yancy stared out the window. "That's what gave me the idea."

He spoke so quietly, Ewan strained to hear him.

Yancy swung his jungle gaze around to meet Ewan's. "I suspect we've hunted too far abroad for our spymaster. This last death is too coincidental."

The urgent message his stare conveyed caused Ewan to suck in a great gulp of air.

"*Merde!*" Plopping into a chair opposite Yancy's desk, Ewan leaned forward, resting his elbows on his knees. Worry furrowed his forehead. "You mean one of *us*? One of the elite corps—not just a War Office agent?"

Yancy responded with a curt inclination of his head as he returned to his chair.

"The devil you say!" Ewan slammed his fist into his palm, struggling to control his anger, though surely Yancy could see the outrage simmering in his eyes. He felt its scorching heat strumming through his veins. "It stands to reason, though. That's why the ringleader has always been one step ahead—how he's continued to evade us. Why our agents and informants have gone missing. Because the damn fools trusted him."

Yancy nodded once. "As have we all."

He reclined in his chair and closed his eyes.

Unable to stay seated, his emotions and thoughts cavorting out of control, Ewan rose and paced the War Office.

After several moments, Yancy murmured tiredly, "Do stop. You're wearing a path in my expensive Persian carpet."

Ewan waved his hand dismissively, but he slowed his steps. Facing his friend, he didn't mince words. "This," he spread his hands, "stays between us. I don't need to tell you how dangerous this could be if you're proven right. If it's one of us, he has access to the same information we do." Hands fisted, Ewan closed his eyes. "We're all targets. Even the Regent."

"Do your suspicions include Clarendon?"

Exhaling slowly, Ewan opened his eyes and gave a short nod. "For now, I think we must. Clarendon knows his brother is a spy, and he's done much to help us. Still—" He sat opposite Yancy again. "Clarendon's assistance might've been a ruse to keep us off his scent. Every member of the corps has access to the War Office. Until we can eliminate any of us as suspects, we must be diligent. We don't know who may be involved."

"It's possible we're dealing with a powerful government official, Ewan."

"Aye," Ewan rubbed his bruised jaw, "or a peer." He stood, straightening his jacket. "How could I have been so blind?"

"You no more than the rest of us."

Ewan eyed Yancy, relaxing with his eyes closed against his chair. When was the last time he'd slept?

"You know, Yancy, Prinny's really to blame. He's the one who insisted we bring the others on board. What was it he said?" Ewan scrunched his brow. "Ah, I remember. 'We must utilize the talents of all during wartime.'"

Yancy cracked open one piercing green eye. "I know, but I don't dare tell him that. Before the war, when it was the four of us—Warrick, Harcourt, you, and I—there was no question of a traitor in our midst."

"Dammit, we should've brought Marquardt in when we had the chance." Ewan ran a hand through his hair then spread his hands wide apart. "Now, when Prinny's finally agreed we can arrest him, Marquardt's nowhere to be found."

Ewan couldn't contain his frustration. More than once, Marquardt had been within his grasp, and each time, he'd been forced to let the cur slip away.

"I agree, but again, Prinny wanted the spymaster. It's a pride thing with him, you know." Mockery arched Yancy brows. "He can't stand the thought that someone outsmarted him. In any event, his refusal to let us arrest Marquardt has cost us eight good men."

Ewan shook his head in disgust. "I thought to have ousted our spy by now. I'm a fool for not considering it might be someone in the corps."

"Nobody has the ability to unearth a traitor better than you. You brought in dozens during the war."

"Yes, and, blister it, one blasted man continues to elude me."

Stretching his arms overhead, Ewan heaved a hefty sigh then relaxed against his chair, resting both palms on the arms. "I had another purpose for calling. I shall be out of Town for several days. Perhaps a fortnight or more."

"Oh?"

He chuckled softly. "Warrick had an unfortunate encounter with his new stallion that has made riding impossible. He asked me to escort Miss Stapleton to Somersfield in his stead."

Yancy curved his lips into a rakish smile. "An assignment, I assume, you're not distressed to be burdened with? Your social life *has* been rather restricted due to the Regent's constant demands."

"Most assuredly, my old friend, it will not be a burden. As for my social life, you know I prefer the company of the Highlanders over that of the *haute ton*."

"Indeed." Yancy yawned behind his hand. "What of Marquardt?"

Yes, what of Marquardt?

Someone had given him the documents he'd smuggled to the French. Until the man was caught, Yancy wasn't about to accept Ewan's resignation. The Regent wouldn't allow it, and as long as Ewan remained tied to the War Office, he wouldn't be free to marry. None of the specialized agents were married. Prinny claimed it would be a distraction and forbade it.

Ewan scowled.

This from a man whose hedonistic activities left him minimal time to rule effectively.

"I say, Ewan, did you hear me?"

Ewan nodded. "I'll not use Miss Stapleton as an entice-ment, if that's what you're asking."

Not if he could help it, leastways.

Yancy's face darkened. "You insult me."

Frowning, Ewan cupped his nape with one hand. "Aye, my friend, and I do apologize. I meant no offense." He extended his hand, which Yancy immediately grasped.

No indeed, reflected Ewan as he stepped onto the bustling Horse Guards Avenue and put on his hat. A week in Miss Stapleton's company wouldn't be a burden. In fact, he quite looked forward to it. His agent in Boston, as well as Warrick and Vangie, had kept him abreast of her goings-on. Ewan had heard so much about her, he felt he knew her.

She'd been capering about in his mind for two years. It would be most interesting to see how the flesh-and-blood woman compared to what he'd been told of her.

At any rate, he was sick of the War Office and every-thing it represented. A break from intelligence work was overdue, as was a visit to Scotland. He hadn't seen his family in five months—hadn't played the bagpipes in that long, either.

He grinned in anticipation. His keep overflowed with kin: three younger sisters, a scallywag brother, cousins, two uncles, an aunt, his French mother and Scottish stepfather, and a passel of dogs.

Aye, a visit home was in order.

It was time he took his dual seats. One on Craiglocky Keep's dais, and the other in the House of Lords—though, truthfully, he much preferred the Highlands over Parliament.

Mayhap it was also time to pursue other areas of interest. Namely a golden-haired, sapphire-eyed, freckle-nosed, ungainly heiress.

He shook his head. *Stop it, old chap.* Duty first. He daren't think along those lines until the traitor was caught. And that effort might cost him his life.

Besides, Miss Stapleton was the last woman he should be thinking of in those terms. His fascination with her didn't trump his need to exploit her connection to Marquardt. Though loath to admit it to Yancy, Ewan had nearly exhausted his other options.

Four

Yvette rested her head against the hackney's worn, cracked leather seat. The stale air trapped inside the vehicle was intolerable. She tried taking small breaths but only succeeded in becoming light-headed. Or mayhap hunger caused her faintness.

Her last meal had been supper last eve, and noon had long since passed. The light biscuits and tea Mr. Dehring had provided did little to curb the gnawing in her belly, and her stomach rumbled in protest.

Mr. Dehring had assured her he'd have funds available for her tomorrow. He'd paid for this hack and loaned her a few crowns to hold her over until then. Her lodgings were paid in advance, thank goodness.

After Edgar's first abduction attempt, Yvette had been most careful to keep her travel plans a secret. True, he knew she planned on returning to England, but he didn't know where she intended to reside or precisely when she sailed.

A great deal of monies had exchanged hands to keep that information confidential. To ensure Edgar was unable to acquire a ticket and wouldn't know which ship she departed on, Yvette had purchased every available passage on ships sailing for England in April.

The minute word was out that she'd actually sailed, the other captains would pad their pockets by collecting a second fee. Hoping to keep Edgar off her trail for a few days, Fairchild had contrived a plan to make it appear she still resided within the mansion. He and the other servants would follow her to England when the wounded staff had recovered enough to travel.

Instead of opening up the manor in Berkley Square, where Edgar was sure to seek her out, Yvette had written Vangie and asked her to make lodging arrangements for her and Pippa until Ian arrived to escort them to Somersfield. Given the unpredictability of traveling by ship, Yvette had prudently asked that a room be reserved from the middle of June to the middle of July.

She frowned. *Drat*. Pippa's absence complicated matters, for it was most improper for Yvette to stay at the inn without a female companion. But what else was she to do?

Yvette fiddled with the hackney window in a futile attempt to open it. It seemed to be sealed shut, and she sank against the squabs as perspiration trickled between her breasts.

Vangie and Ian knew about Edgar's first attack on her, but they'd no idea of the second. There hadn't been time to get word to them about the assault or inform them Pippa had remained in Boston. Even without her maid, it was far safer for her, as well as the Berkley Square staff, if she took a room at the inn.

Her last letter from Vangie said Ian would travel to Town toward the end of June. Mr. Dehring had already dispatched a messenger to Somersfield in the event Ian hadn't left for London as yet.

Hounds' teeth, the hack was sweltering. Yvette wiped droplets off her forehead with her handkerchief. She had never been this hungry, sweaty, and tired in her whole life. Stifling a yawn, she fanned her flushed face with her ungloved hand. In her haste to leave Boston, she'd not packed a fan, an oversight she now dearly regretted. She closed her eyes against the pangs portending a headache. A hearty meal, other than ship's fare, and a lengthy soak in a tub would be heavenly.

"Tonight, I shall have a room to myself," she declared aloud. "No snoring or wheezing. No listening to Mrs. Pettigrove babble on in her sleep about her husband's bedroom skills."

Last week, Yvette had awoken to moaning and feared the matron had taken ill. Until Mrs. Pettigrove groaned, "Oh, yes, yes, Willard, you're such a stallion."

Inside the scorching cab, Yvette felt her face reddening further. She might be naïve, but she had a strong notion what her former cabin mate carried on about.

She waved her hand even faster.

The hired conveyance slowed, lurching to a bumpy stop. The hack dipped as the lanky driver jumped from the box. A moment later, the door swung open, and she stuffed her gloves and handkerchief into her reticule before hopping from the hackney.

"Thank you." Accepting her valise, she smiled and passed the driver a crown.

Toting her bulging satchel, Yvette climbed the time-worn steps to the inn's entrance. With a swift, uneasy glance behind her, she shoved open the heavy door. Coming from the bright sunlight outdoors, she blinked several times before her eyes adjusted to the dimmer interior. A busy common room opened to the right, and what appeared to be private dining compartments were situated to the left of a narrow corridor leading to a stairway at the rear of the building.

"May I help you?" A woman spoke behind Yvette.

Dragging her attention from the hallway, Yvette smiled at the attractive middling-aged woman with a spotless apron tied at her waist. "Yes, please. I'm Yvette Stapleton. A room's been arranged for me."

The woman's face beamed brighter. "Oh, yes, Miss Stapleton. We wondered how soon you'd arrive. We expected you when the *Peaceful Wind* docked two days ago. I'm Abigail Quimby. My husband Myles and I own the Banbury."

Astonishment rendered Yvette mute and immobile for a moment.

Originally, she was to have sailed on the *Peaceful Wind*, but after Edgar's second attack, she'd fled Boston in the middle of the night aboard the *Atlantic Star* with only an overstuffed satchel and the clothes she wore. Her ship had encountered a storm, and although the gale hadn't been overly fierce, the squall, combined with a persistent head-wind, had extended the voyage nearly a week.

Why hadn't it occurred to her that the *Peaceful Wind*—scheduled to sail a week after she departed—might arrive in port before the *Atlantic Star*? More on point, what if Edgar had traveled aboard the *Peaceful Wind*? There'd been no passages available, but a man as devious and resourceful as he could finagle a way aboard the vessel. When he didn't find her at the Berkley Street manor, he'd make inquiries.

Thank God her travel arrangements had been kept secret. Only Fairchild and Pippa knew where she lodged.

Still, tomorrow it might be wise to seek accommodations elsewhere. She'd consult Mr. Dehring first thing in the morning and ask for his advice. He'd already alerted the authorities about Edgar, though since his abduction attempts had taken place in America, there wasn't much to be done in England in the way of retribution.

Yvette inhaled a deep, calming breath and shifted her valise to her other hand, grateful for the comforting weight of her gun within. Schooling her expression, she approached the desk, her steps hesitant.

"The *Peaceful Wind* made port two days ago?"

"Why, yes." Quill in hand, Mrs. Quimby nodded. "Your trunks arrived yesterday. Myles put them in your room."

Her heart thudding painfully against her ribs, Yvette fought the waves of panic clawing their way up her throat. Forcing a poised countenance, she prayed her alarm didn't color her voice. "Has anyone inquired about my arrival?"

Glancing up from the ledger, Mrs. Quimby considered Yvette. "No, other than the seaman who delivered your trunks. Should we expect someone else? Your companion perhaps?"

The question hung in the air awkwardly, until Yvette remembered that Vangie had arranged for both her and Pippa to stay at the inn.

"Circumstances required me to sail on another ship, and unfortunately, my lady's maid wasn't able to accompany me. I arrived in port only this morning. Pippa must have arranged for my trunks to be shipped on the *Peaceful Wind* after I left Boston."

Mrs. Quimby continued to stare at her, one expectant brow raised. Yvette's mind raced. What had she forgotten?

"I am expecting my cousin's husband, Viscount Warrick, however. He's to be my escort."

That seemed to satisfy Mrs. Quimby. "Yes, her ladyship's letter requesting your accommodations said he'd meet you here."

"Did Lady Warrick say when Lord Warrick would arrive?"

Would Yvette have to wait long for Ian's arrival? The disturbing notion that Edgar might already be lurking about caused a shiver of unease to trot along her spinal column.

At least she had her pistol and dagger, though Yvette's skills weren't what they once were. Truth to tell, Vangie's talent with a blade—and her gift for healing—were the result of time spent with her Romani family, and not Papa's instruction.

"No." Mrs. Quimby pursed her lips. "Only that he'd be here near the end of the month." Her gaze swept Yvette's lone valise. "You sailed on a different ship? Have you other baggage with you then?"

"No. Only my—"

"Miss Stapleton!"

It can't be.

The piercing voice of Mrs. Pettigrove raked, razor sharp, across Yvette's already brittle nerves. Slowly, she swiveled halfway around, blinking in disbelief. Mrs. Pettigrove emerged from the common room, huffing and puffing as she trundled her way to Yvette's side.

"My dear Miss Stapleton, imagine my surprise at seeing you again so soon."

She's here?

Yvette's dazed mind balked, refusing to comprehend what her eyes observed. Was this some kind of cruel joke? And why did Mrs. Pettigrove scowl at Mrs. Quimby?

"I'm afraid you'll find yourself inconvenienced if you think to acquire a room at *this* establishment." Mrs. Pettigrove raised her hooked nose into the air, her chins jiggling with the emphatic statement.

Yvette's gaze swung between Mrs. Quimby and Mrs. Pettigrove. Animosity permeated the air as the women glowered daggers at each other.

Yvette firmed her mouth before looking directly into Mrs. Pettigrove's belligerent gaze. "You took my funds and hired a hackney with them then left me stranded on the docks."

Mrs. Pettigrove sucked in a sharp breath and clutched at her ample bosom. "I did no such thing. Mr. Collingsworth told me to go along—that you had other arrangements."

Yvette eyed her doubtfully, but given Mr. Collingsworth's frightening behavior on the docks, she grudgingly admitted the matron might be telling the truth.

Mrs. Quimby drew herself up, and after giving Mrs. Pettigrove what Yvette presumed was a dismissive glare, turned her full attention to her. "Miss Stapleton, as you have a room reserved, we'd be *delighted* to have *you* stay with us for as long as you wish."

Yvette suppressed her instinctive pity for Mrs. Pettigrove. Her arrival at this particular inn was no mere coincidence. She knew Yvette was staying here. This morning, when Mrs. Pettigrove asked her about her plans, Yvette had naively told her she had a room at the Banbury Inn.

"Oh, you've a room reserved?" Mrs. Pettigrove said in apparent surprise.

Yvette narrowed her eyes.

You know I do.

"I thought I had one too." Mrs. Pettigrove drew in a ragged breath. "But there's been a... a misunderstanding." She spoke haltingly, withering before them.

Angling her head, Yvette scrutinized the matron. Did

she tell the truth? Why hadn't she mentioned she was staying here this morning then? No, something was too smoky by far.

"I'm certain Willard's missive said he had obtained a room for me at the Banbury Inn." Fingering her brooch, Mrs. Pettigrove muttered, "There's a logical explanation, of course."

Yvette worried her lower lip, compassion engulfing her. *Blister it.* This woman didn't deserve her sympathy.

Mrs. Quimby's visage softened. "We only have two vacant rooms. One must be held for an infrequent guest who's not in residence, but has paid in advance."

She scribbled in the ledger before opening a drawer and rummaging about. Her mouth tipped into a compassionate half-smile as she lifted her gaze, meeting the older woman's eyes. "I'm sorry, but I simply cannot permit another to utilize that room." Returning her attention to the drawer's contents, she lifted a shoulder. "The other room is reserved for Miss Stapleton and her companion."

Oh, no!

Yvette jerked her head up, her eyes rounded in growing horror.

From the gasp and swift, contrite glance Mrs. Quimby sent her, she'd realized her gaffe. She closed the ledger with a thump as she hastily lifted a key from the drawer. "Miss Stapleton, no doubt you're exhausted and would like to be shown to your room."

"*Companion?*" Mrs. Pettigrove's voice held a hopeful note.

Cringing, Yvette clenched her teeth.

No, no, no.

This is too much. She'd been a personal maid to that... that... meddling gossip for the past two months. She couldn't possibly bear sharing a room with her again. Not so god-awful soon.

"Miss Stapleton?" Mrs. Pettigrove's voice wavered and tears swam in her nondescript eyes.

Yvette eyed her, empathy warring with self-preservation.

She truly *did not* want to share her room with Mrs. Pettigrove. She wanted a room to herself. Was that too much to ask? She'd been through a great deal these past weeks. And Mrs. Pettigrove was extremely difficult.

Yvette blinked away the sharp sting of tears.

Mrs. Pettigrove laid a plump hand on her arm. "Please? I could act as your chaperone. It would be most improper for you to stay here alone."

Yvette's heart cramped again. Drat, she was too compassionate by far. And Mrs. Pettigrove had a valid point about the chaperonage. Bother it all.

Head bowed, shoulders slumped in defeat, she exhaled a slow, deliberate breath. "The room is intended for two." Relaxing her vice-like grip on the counter's edge, she turned and met Mrs. Pettigrove's watery eyes. Botheration, she didn't want to do this. "Please." Yvette forced herself to say the words. "Share it with me."

Mrs. Pettigrove promptly lost her prior semblance of humbleness and began issuing orders with the efficiency of a general about to take to the field.

"Mrs. Quimby, have my trunks brought above stairs at once. Do you have a laundress on staff? Good. I shall need a note delivered straightaway. I presume my room is supplied with paper and ink? I thought as much. I shall need a maid to assist me with my unpacking, and I must have water for bathing immediately."

Anything else?

She laid a pudgy hand on her stomach. "Might I trouble you for a tea tray? Some seedcake perhaps? And fruit? And some pastries, of course. Oh, and lemon curd and clotted cream if you have them. Crumpets for the curd, and fruit preserves?"

Jaw slack, Mrs. Quimby gaped in disbelief.

Her monologue at an end, Mrs. Pettigrove eyed Yvette. "It's commendable you knew your Christian duty. It speaks of your genteel breeding."

Christian duty? Breeding?

As a fierce wave of hot anger rolled over Yvette, her misplaced compassion evaporated faster than a water droplet on the searing pavement outside.

Mrs. Quimby snorted and mumbled something unintelligible, though Yvette distinctly heard, "More hair than wit, greedy-gut."

Was Mrs. Pettigrove truly so bird-witted?

Yvette clamped her teeth over her bottom lip to dam the sharp retort struggling to escape. She couldn't, however, prevent her foot from tapping a cadence of vexation.

She stole a sidelong glance at Mrs. Quimby.

The innkeeper, her face a mask of composed annoyance, stared hard at Mrs. Pettigrove. "It is past tea time." Satisfaction edged Mrs. Quimby's voice.

A moue of disappointment contorted Mrs. Pettigrove's full lips. "Oh, I suppose I've no choice but to wait until supper is served then. If you're sure?"

"Quite," Mrs. Quimby snipped.

"What time is supper served?" Mrs. Pettigrove's gaze hovered on the entrance to the dining room. "I'm quite famished. I haven't had a bite to eat since luncheon."

Yvette narrowed her eyes once more.

When was that? An entire hour ago?

Mrs. Quimby didn't answer Mrs. Pettigrove but remained silent, pressing her lips into twin lines of disapproval. The innkeeper wouldn't oblige Mrs. Pettigrove without Yvette's consent.

Yvette met Mrs. Quimby's troubled gaze and attempted a smile. "It's all right."

Drawing in a shaky breath, she feared she might burst into tears. It wasn't all right. Not at all. Nothing about this was right. She should have her own room, deserved her own room. It wasn't fair for Mrs. Pettigrove to commandeer her chamber, even if Yvette was in need of a chaperone.

The nasty ache behind her eyes throbbed full on now.

At Mrs. Quimby's doubtful look, she forced her lips to bend upward. Not trusting herself to speak, her throat clogged with unshed tears, she nodded her approval.

"Supper begins at half-past seven." Mrs. Quimby handed Mrs. Pettigrove the room key, her reluctance evident in her set jaw.

Calling for a maid, and a strapping young lad whom she introduced as her son Henry, Mrs. Quimby sent Mrs. Pettigrove on her way.

"That was extremely kind of you." Mrs. Quimby gave Yvette a forced smile.

"I spent the past two interminable months in a tiny cabin with her." Yvette drummed the counter with her fingers and shook her head. "Trust me when I tell you she is not a congenial companion."

"I shall arrange for supper to last longer than usual this evening, so you can have a few minutes to yourself." Mrs. Quimby came around the counter then handed Yvette her room key. "I'll have a bath prepared for you, and a tray of food too. Perhaps wine as well? You look as if you would benefit from a glass of sherry."

"I don't tolerate spirits. They sicken me, but tea would be wonderful."

As she stepped toward the stairs, the hair raised on Yvette's nape. She shuddered and looked over her shoulder into the common room. Had someone been standing in the entrance just then?

"You're quite sure no one inquired about my arrival?"

Five

"No one but the sailors," Mrs. Quimby assured Yvette. "By-the-by, Miss Stapleton, they didn't leave the keys to your trunks."

Yvette patted her reticule. "I have a set, thank you."

Her uneasiness lingering, she followed Henry as he climbed the narrow staircase. Nodding his head at the lone door at the end of the hall, the lad volunteered, "The inn's been busy these past weeks. That'd be the other vacant room. It connects to yer room. The door between the chambers be kept locked though."

Yvette reached for her satchel. "Thank you, Henry."

"Do ye wish to bathe or eat first?" Gaze glued to the floor, he shuffled his feet. "Mam told me to ask."

"Food, please. I'm ravenous."

"Molly'll bring it straightaway then."

Entering the chamber, Yvette stopped cold.

Merciful God in heaven. One bed?

She searched the room from corner to corner again. There was no mistake. The room held but a single bed, and the temptation to revoke her generous offer assailed her.

Either that or share the lone, much-too-small bed with Mrs. Pettigrove's plentiful form. Yvette wouldn't get any sleep.

Could that inadequate a bed even accommodate two people?

~

That had been hours ago.

Yvette was slightly more inclined to be charitable now that she was bathed and her stomach full. After all, she had tolerated weeks with Mrs. Pettigrove in a room far smaller than this. Another night was endurable. Tomorrow, she fully intended to find other accommodations, and she'd have Mr. Dehring reserve them in a fabricated name.

She rather fancied Cordelia Daisywagon.

A giggle escaped her, giving her pause. She hadn't laughed in a long while.

She had another reason for feeling benevolent. Earlier, after unlocking her trunks, intent on finding a lightweight nightgown, she'd discovered a jewelry box. A note in Fairchild's perfect script explained that the jewels, and the cash stuffed atop them, had been inside a safe at Papa's office. Papa must have moved them there after Edgar arrived in Boston. According to the devoted butler, the *Peaceful Wind*'s captain had been paid handsomely to keep Yvette's trunks under lock and key the entire voyage.

Yvette had unabashedly searched Mrs. Pettigrove's possessions in hopes her other missing valuables might be unearthed. No such luck. Her conscience pricked a mite. Perhaps Mrs. Pettigrove had been telling the truth.

Wearing only a light shift, her hair wrapped in a towel, Yvette relaxed against the overstuffed arm chair. She had given herself over to the luxury of her bath, and it had been pure, calming bliss.

Every morsel of her supper had been superb, too.

She licked her lips again. Even now, she could taste the fresh strawberries and clotted cream. She'd eaten every bite of the food Mrs. Quimby had sent, and she didn't regret it one bit. She had not been this full... well, ever that she could recall.

True to her word, Mrs. Quimby had extended supper past the ninth hour. Yvette imagined Mrs. Pettigrove's antics at having her meal delayed so long. She permitted herself a mischievous grin. Patience wasn't a virtue of Mrs. Pettigrove's either—especially when it came to mealtime.

Yvette scooted to the edge of the chair then unwrapped the towel from her head and briskly rubbed her hair. Bending over, she shook her head and fanned out the damp strands. She curved her lips into a half-smile.

Soon she'd be at Somersfield, where Vangie and the babe she carried waited. There Yvette would be safe from Edgar and his relentless attempts to wed her. Ian was a member of the Diplomatic Corps, and in his stables he employed several soldiers who'd had no work when the war ended.

Yvette doubted Edgar even knew she had a cousin. He'd never met Vangie, and she'd only visited London once. Her other visits had always been at Rosewick, Papa's country estate, which Edgar refused to set foot upon. Until he'd arrived in Boston, Yvette hadn't spent more than half an hour in his company, and no conversation had ever arisen about Vangie.

He'd been at university when Papa and Belle-mére married, and afterward, his antics as a man-about-town occupied his time. He'd been hotly opposed to his mother marrying Papa and had kept his distance the first six years of their marriage. Poor Belle-mére had often commented how much she missed her sons, especially after she moved to Boston.

Yvette narrowed her eyes in resolution. *No man* would force her into marriage, no indeed. There was more to marriage than a cracking good match, and most of what she knew about the sacred institution left her cold. Wives were expected to be their husband's shadows, their chattels, and ignore their many indiscretions.

Balderdash and codswallop.

The tales Pippa had whispered about Belle-mére's first marriage haunted Yvette. She shuddered in remembrance at the abuse her stepmother and stepbrother had suffered at the earl's hands. Her heart broke for her stepbrother, Rory, the Earl of Clarendon. His marriage had ended tragically when his wife had died after giving birth to a stillborn son. Worse, with her last breath, she had confessed that the child wasn't his.

Yawning, Yvette stood and ran her fingers through her hair to speed its drying. They caught on a tangle, jerking her scalp, and she winced as tears filled her eyes. Dear Pippa had brushed her hair nightly since she was a small child. But Pippa was still in Boston with the Fairchilds and Yvette's beloved dogs, Apollo and Artemis.

Tears washed over her cheeks.

Lord, she missed them.

Fairchild and his sons, Isaiah and Josiah, had been a part of her life since she was two. After Papa and Belle-mére died, they'd consoled her. They were her family now, and to escape Edgar, she'd been forced to leave them and her pets behind. They would return to England, of course, at the earliest opportunity, but Yvette had no idea how soon that would be.

Fairchild had done his utmost to protect her. He'd reported Edgar to the authorities and had posted guards around the manor. But Edgar was sly and keenly clever. Using the jewels and money he stole from the mansion, he'd hired men to help him. Isaiah had ended up with a cracked skull, three other staff had been wounded, and two of the guards killed in the mayhem.

Edgar would stop at nothing. He wasn't sane. That very night, with only minutes to pack, Yvette had been smuggled from the rear of the manor, while one of the maids had pretended to be her and left through the front entrance.

Overcome by emotion, Yvette threw the towel on the chair, climbed into bed, curled into a ball, and sobbed. She was alone and afraid. She missed her parents and Pippa and Fairchild and his sons. And Artemis and Apollo weren't nestled next to her on the bed. She wept until exhaustion claimed her and, at last, put an end to the tormenting memories.

Not more than an hour later, a tipsy and very noisy Mrs. Pettigrove trundled into their chamber.

Yvette pretended to be asleep, having no desire to hear her litany of complaints about supper. Little good it did her.

Mrs. Pettigrove plowed about the room, banging into things and muttering beneath her breath before stopping beside the bed, breathing heavily.

"Miss Stapleton, are you awake?"

Yvette held her breath.

"Miss Stapleton?" A pudgy finger nudged her.

Yvette didn't move.

Mrs. Pettigrove shook Yvette's shoulder, none too gently. "I need your help undressing."

Botheration.

Yvette sat up, then swung her legs off the edge of the bed. "Let me light the lamp."

It had been no easy task to undress the half-foxed Mrs. Pettigrove and see her tucked into bed. And Yvette wasn't the least bit surprised when rhythmic, grating rattles filled the room mere moments after the dame's head settled on her fluffy pillow.

Yvette wasn't as fortunate.

She lay awake, staring at the flickering moonbeams slanting across the ceiling. Her thoughts shifted to earlier in the day, to Ewan McTavish. Thank goodness he'd happened by when he did. He had saved her from God only knew what, and he disturbed her in the most intriguing way. Even now, thinking of him caused a ripple to whisper across her flesh.

A rude noise rumbled throughout the room, interrupting her fanciful musing.

Wrinkling her nose in disgust, Yvette closed her eyes and sighed. The grittiness beneath her eyelids, and the wooly thickness in her head, were evidence she had cried herself to sleep and had slept but minutes before Mrs. Pettigrove had lumbered into their room.

How she had wanted—*no, needed*—a peaceful night's sleep. She attempted to turn on her side and stopped short. Mrs. Pettigrove lay on her hair.

"Oh, for pity's sake."

Tugging, Yvette managed to extract her hair from beneath the matron's hefty arm. She rose from the bed then eyed the armchairs on either side of the room. They simply would not suffice.

"There isn't even an extra blanket to create a pallet on

the floor," she muttered, her good nature stretched to the limits.

Mrs. Pettigrove rolled to the middle of the bed, threw her arms wide, and released a ponderous expanse of wind.

Yvette swirled away from the bed in fatigued exasperation. A bright reflection caught her gaze. A moonbeam angled through the billowing curtains, pointing its frail finger at the brass handle on the adjoining room's door. The handle, illuminated by the enticing glow, drew her persistently closer.

I couldn't, her conscience chastised even as she reached for the handle. *But... it's far past midnight. If the other guest was going to arrive, wouldn't he have done so by now? Didn't Mrs. Quimby say this room was only used occasionally?*

Yvette bit her lip in indecision. Did she dare?

I haven't heard any movement or sounds from within.

Mrs. Pettigrove snorted, releasing another startling round of thunderous expulsions that echoed grotesquely throughout the bedchamber.

"That tears it."

Before she allowed her conscience to stop her, Yvette seized her dagger then turned the key and twisted the handle. The door glided open.

The room's curtains were parted, and the moon's bright rays bathed the chamber's large, *empty* bed. With a small relieved huff, she released the breath she held. The room was unoccupied. She tiptoed to the window, though why she felt the need to tread softly when an elephant might have danced in half-boots upon the wooden floor and Mrs. Pettigrove would've snored on uninterrupted.

Yvette peeked at the street.

Nothing.

Not a hint of movement. Stepping backward, her decision made, she drew the panels.

Before she changed her mind, Yvette returned to her chamber door and edged it closed. The key rested in its snug lock on the other side. What about the other door? She tried to open it and found it locked, the keyhole empty.

She pressed her ear to the door.

Silence.

Exhaustion wrapped its arms around her, claiming what meagre reason she had left. It wouldn't be too great a sin to sleep a few hours in this unused bed, would it? She'd be perfectly safe here. She had her small dagger, the door was locked from without, and her chamber lay a few scant steps away. She would slip into her room before dawn, and Mrs. Pettigrove would be none the wiser.

Too tired to think, Yvette succumbed to the enticing bed. After folding the weighty coverlet to the end of the bed, she hopped onto the mattress then flopped on her back. "Oh, this is wonderful."

She slid between the cool, satin sheets. Sighing in contentment, she turned to her side and tucked her knife beneath the pillow, keeping her fingertips wrapped around the handle.

Edgar had experienced the end of her blade once. She'd not hesitate to use it on him again.

Ewan closed the door without a whisper, then with measured tread, crossed the carpet to the window and slid the curtains aside. He made short work of opening the window, letting in the bright moonlight and refreshing night air. He inhaled, savoring the tangy coolness.

Standing in the path of the light breeze, he removed his coat.

In short order he removed his boots and clothing, and then stood naked before the window. Habit caused him to survey the deserted street below. With one last lingering look, he padded to the washstand in an alcove illuminated by a smaller uncurtained window.

As always, the washstand was prepared with water, towels, and soap. His garments would be pressed and hung in the wardrobe, and the satin sheets he required would be washed and spread upon the mattress.

Hell's bells, he craved sleep.

Without a doubt, Marquardt was in London. He'd been seen in the less reputable establishments Ewan frequented this evening, but he'd managed to elude Ewan.

That's not to say the evening had been a total loss. A satisfied grin bent his mouth. Belvidere's lair had been uncovered, thanks to a tip from Nighthawk. No one knew who the phantom informer was, but he had been assisting the War Office for over four years.

With the help of Yancy's agents, Belvidere was detained. Yancy and Ewan had spent the past several hours interrogating the spy, who had remained stubbornly close-mouthed about his association with Marquardt.

Ewan heaved a frustrated sigh.

Blister it.

He wanted to be done with this subterfuge. For over six years he'd been at Yancy's beck and call. No, that wasn't fair. He'd been at Prinny's beck and call. Ewan yearned for Craiglocky, his clan, and his kin. His obligation to the crown came first, though. Until he caught the treasonous bastard—he exhaled in annoyance again—the highlands would have to wait.

After splashing water on his face and head, Ewan lathered a bar of soap, and quickly washed. Toweling off, he tied the linen about his waist and cleansed his teeth. He ran a hand across his face. Shaving could wait until morning. He winced when he connected with the tender skin on his jaw. Grinning, he recalled the precise moment his charming passenger had smacked her head on his chin.

He yanked the toweling from his hips, then rubbed the cloth across his hair one more time before turning in the bed's direction. Linen bunched, he lifted an arm to toss it on the nearby chair and froze.

On his bed, sound asleep, lay Miss Stapleton. He'd known she was staying here, Ian had told him as much, but what the devil was she doing in his chamber? In his bed?

Doubting his senses, he shook his head to clear his muddled mind. Had his exhausted brain conjured her image? Or perhaps he hallucinated? Or... had the excess spirits he'd consumed tonight while venturing into numerous pubs, gambling dens, and other hell-holes addled his mind?

With practiced stealth, he approached the bed.

She lay on her back, her shift midway up her thighs. She'd kicked the sheets aside in her sleep. One slender arm curved above her head, and the other lay across her midsection. The moonlight illuminated her golden hair fanned across the pillow and wrapped around one shoulder. A shiny lock curled under one breast.

The rise and fall of her chest held him captive—her full breasts, their dusky peaks barely discernible through the filmy fabric, threatened to spill from the scanty chemise. He secured the towel about his waist before edging onto the bed. Lying on his side, he allowed himself a leisurely perusal. Everything about her enthralled him, from the dark arc of her lashes brushing her cheeks, to her straight, petite nose and full lips.

Magnificent.

Ewan's gaze inched lower.

Her flawless ivory skin glowed in the shimmering moonlight, her long neck flowing into gracefully sloping shoulders. A small mole on her plump left breast peeked from beneath her shift, daring him to touch the spot. He raised his hand halfway before he stopped himself.

His attention gravitated to her small waist, then to her flaring hips, and downward to the tempting length of her thighs. This was a woman whose full curves demanded touching. His hungry gaze lingered for the briefest of moments on the shadowy triangle at the juncture of her legs.

Never in his seven-and-twenty years had a woman stirred him thus.

Yvette shifted in her sleep, rolling closer to him and wedging one of her legs between his thighs, brushing his penis. At the intimate contact, the appendage sprang to rigid attention, and he inhaled sharply. She smelled of honeysuckle and jasmine and spring.

According to Warrick, Yvette was intelligent, well-educated, and a fine equestrian too.

Ewan's conscience twinged and not entirely because of his prurient thoughts.

He'd still use her to get to Marquardt—*if* he couldn't find any other means.

She slipped her arm across his waist, causing another surge of pleasure-pain in his groin, and he clenched his jaw.

Ewan shoved Marquardt to the recesses of his mind, intent on enjoying this moment. He mightn't ever have another. He firmed his lips in self-recrimination. He doubted she'd allow him to call on her if she had an inkling he'd already exploited her connection to Marquardt.

Lowering himself until his head rested on the same pillow she slept upon, Ewan observed her slumber. Inches separated their faces.

She murmured something unintelligible and scooted closer to him, then nestled into the crook of his arm. Her silky head fit perfectly beneath his chin.

Wrapping her in his arms, he snuggled her soft body even closer, until she was cocooned within his embrace.

Closing his eyes, he breathed her in, caressing the gentle curve of her spine with one hand.

Unwise, this.

A few moments more. Then he'd waken her and learn what had brought her to his bed.

Sensation surrounded Yvette.

Muscled arms held her to a wide, hair-covered chest. She wrapped her arms tighter around the comforting, familiar frame of her dream lover, and her nostrils quivered at his scent.

He showered hot kisses atop her head, forehead, nose, and at last, upon her waiting lips. The kiss proved as sweet as any long-awaited, keenly-anticipated homecoming.

He licked the corner of her mouth, even as his thumb pressed against the crease, forcing her lips to part. Though inexperienced, she recognized the suppressed passion in his kiss. It mirrored her own, which had lain dormant and untouched 'til now. He feathered his large hand across the swell of her breasts and nudged the frail material of her chemise aside.

Shifting, she arched into his palm, then breathed out a blissful sigh as his calloused hand closed over one tip. She twisted beneath his weight, his rigid length pressing against her belly. Reaching between their heated bodies, she wrapped tentative fingers around his expanse.

A groan escaped him, a deep rumbling echo, and she smiled against his mouth, relishing this new power. He lifted his midnight head, and the intensity of his sea-green eyes held her captive.

Six

Ewan jolted awake.

"*Merde.*"

He had fallen asleep with Yvette in his arms. Shooting a worried glance at the window, he recognized the first golden blush of daybreak sweeping across the hazy sky.

Sucking in a strangled breath, he gently grasped the inexperienced hand fondling his nakedness.

His blasted towel had come loose while he slept.

"Yvette," he whispered as she showered kisses across his bare chest and neck. Grasping her roaming hands, he ensnared her in his embrace, and raised his voice. "Yvette, wake up."

He gave her a small shake.

Dark lashes trembled, rising to reveal drowsy eyes. A smile lit her face when her gaze met his. She lifted her hand, caressing his face, her fingers lingering on his scar before she raised herself then kissed the mark.

Caught in the powerful spell, Ewan almost forgot himself. He fought the urge to throw reason to the wind and kiss her with the desire he held in check.

"Yvette…"

Stiffening, she came fully awake and issued a faint cry of shocked dismay. She pressed against his chest with both small hands.

He released her, and she scrambled across the bed. She stopped in the middle, and on her knees, faced him. Her hair swirled around her, settling in shiny waves about her hips.

Dawn's glow lit the room, and a concert of expressions flitted over her pale countenance. Shock, followed by bewilderment, then utter horror as she realized the full scope of her situation.

Frightened and befuddled, nearly unclothed, and her head yet muzzy from her abrupt awakening, Yvette knelt in the center of the bed. A bed occupied by a ridiculously masculine, virile naked man—the man from her dreams.

Fully recognizing him, or rather recognizing his eyes, she gulped, her pulse and heart pattering in stunned disbelief.

Dear God in heaven.

Ewan McTavish—the man who had rescued her.

Scanning the room, she took in his discarded clothing, the open window, the door to her chamber, still closed tight. Brows drawn together, she searched her memory. She remembered crawling between the bed's cool sheets.

Then… nothing.

Until a deep-timbre baritone summoned her from an incredibly realistic dream, a dream about him.

Oh, please… It had only been a dream, hadn't it?

Had she touched him *there*?

Attention fixed on the rumpled sheets, she curled her hands into fists as searing heat suffused her.

Dragging in a large breath, she edged backward off the bed and didn't exhale until her feet touched the floor. She firmly kept her focus riveted to the wooden surface. She didn't dare look up, too afraid she'd stare at his powerful, muscled chest. Or, heaven forbid, allow her curious gaze to travel lower, to the vee of curly black hair disappearing beneath the sheets draped casually across his narrow hips.

Mortified to her marrow, Yvette swallowed.

Had she given herself away?

Did he suspect her erotic dream left her tingling from neck to toe? She folded her arms across her middle and peeked up at him through her lashes.

A slight smile arcing his mouth, McTavish retrieved a towel from beneath the bedding and covered his lower body. Head angled, he grazed his beard-stubbled jaw.

"May I ask why you're in my bed?"

His voice soothed Yvette, banishing her fear. She didn't understand why. Mayhap the lilt of his barely discernible brogue calmed her.

"I thought it was empty. My chamber is next door." Voice husky with guilt and embarrassment, she stole a glance at the door separating their rooms.

He stood, and after better securing the insufficient toweling about his waist, he edged nearer. Did he fear she'd bolt?

Not an altogether bad idea, except she hadn't a doubt he'd cut her off before she made it halfway to her chamber door.

Moving inch by careful inch, he approached.

Like an animal caught in a snare, Yvette couldn't move, though her gaze skipped to her door several times. Trying to dislodge the nerves gripping her throat, she swallowed and shut her eyes, striving for the courage to face him.

With his forefinger, he slowly tipped her chin upward.

Startled, she jumped as her eyes flew open and met his mesmerizing gaze.

And here she'd wondered if she'd ever see him again. *Well, I never imagined seeing him naked.* She suppressed an insane urge to giggle.

Holding her chin, he pressed her in that same caressing tone, "If you've a chamber of your own, why are you in mine?"

Why is he being kind?

An enraged shriek rent the early dawn, and without hesitation, Yvette stepped closer to him.

The trusting movement caused something deep and primitive to birth within Ewan. Folding Yvette's hand in his, he rushed to the adjoining door and yanked it open. Inside the chamber, a man fought to free himself from a large woman's grasp. She had a beefy arm around his throat and a hand fisted in his hair.

"Edgar!" Yvette shrank against Ewan.

He shoved her behind him. Damnation. His man watched the inn. How had Marquardt sneaked in?

At their appearance, Marquardt renewed his efforts to free himself from the matron. With a sound blow to her well-padded ribs, he knocked the air from the woman.

"Fiend," she gasped, collapsing on the bed, bum upward. She lay there wheezing, face pressed to the bedclothes.

Ewan lunged for Marquardt.

With a sidelong, venom-laced glance, and a sneer curling his lips, Marquardt bolted from the chamber a hand-breadth ahead of him. Ewan halted, caught short by the cloth slipping from his hips, and the accusing screech of the oversized dame.

"Miss Stap—le—ton!"

He pivoted around to face the women.

Miss Stapleton, her hair spilling to her hips, stood cringing, completely at the overbearing woman's mercy.

The dame sat on the edge of the bed, shaking with outrage. "What's the meaning of this? That horrid man," she flapped her hand toward the empty doorway, "woke me whispering your name." She pointed a stout, accusing finger at Yvette. "Where were you?"

"I..." Veering Ewan a sidelong glance, Yvette fisted her hands in her shift.

The older woman cast a leering glance in Ewan's direction. "In *his* room?"

Chest heaving with indignation, the overwrought woman struggled to stand. She slipped her wrap on, then tied the belt around her podgy waist.

Brow creased, Ewan secured his towel before closing the door. Hands on his hips, he surveyed the scene before him. The devil take it. This was a fine kettle of fish.

The matron never paused in her tirade. "Pray tell why you're coming from the room of a..." She paused to ogle him, her regard lingering at his groin. "A... a naked man?"

Meeting her hungry gaze, he quirked a brow at her bold appraisal.

She finally averted her attention and flopped into one of the armchairs. At the rude treatment, it squeaked in protest.

Ewan's attention gravitated to Yvette.

"Please, Mrs. Pettigrove—" Fighting tears, she clasped her lower lip between her teeth.

How had Yvette come to share a room with this harridan? Was she her chaperone?

No, she couldn't be. Yvette had sailed alone.

Mrs. Pettigrove's gaze traveled over Yvette's scanty attire. "You're good and ruined, young lady."

Mrs. Pettigrove's crass pronouncement commandeered Ewan's attention again.

"Make no mistake." Mrs. Pettigrove's chuffy face scrunched into a deprecating scowl. "When word of this gets out, you'll be branded a ladybird. No, worse. A harlot!"

Yvette's eyes glittered with unshed tears.

Moaning theatrically, Mrs. Pettigrove flung her hand across her chest. "Oh, the scandal, the gossip. What will my sister, the Baronetess Clutterbuck, say? She'll shun me."

Shrewish fussock.

Outrage boiling his blood, Ewan pressed his lips into a thin line.

Yvette remained swaying in the doorway, her body racked with trembles. At Mrs. Pettigrove's spiteful words, she blanched. "Please, let me—"

"And to think, I've been in your company. Shared a cabin." The shrew waved her hand above her head. "And now I occupy this room with you."

Ewan turned his fiercest glower on her. Many a man had curbed his tongue when leveled such a look, but this harpy seemed incapable of halting her self-righteous prattle.

"What will people think of *me*? The scandalmongers will link our names." Mrs. Pettigrove gripped the armchair and bent forward, a sneer distorting her countenance. "Had you no concern for *my* character? How your behavior would reflect upon *my* good name? You're selfishness is beyond the pale, Miss Stapleton."

"You will cease, madam."

Despite her shaken haze, Yvette recognized McTavish's ire. In high dudgeon, his black brows knotted into a fierce scowl, he challenged Mrs. Pettigrove from across the chamber. Even half-naked, he evoked power and authority.

Who was he angry with? Mrs. Pettigrove... or her, for putting him in this dreadful situation?

Yvette didn't react when he marched to the wall, lifted her shawl from its peg, and then strode across the room to wrap the garment about her shaking shoulders. Rooted to the spot, her mind numb with shock, she stared at Mrs. Pettigrove.

What am I to do?

Deep lines of condemnation creased Mrs. Pettigrove's fleshy face. "Who do you think you are, sir, ordering me about? Why, I'll have you know—"

"Madam, allow me to introduce myself." He bowed before Mrs. Pettigrove, the scant bit of linen not quite covering his taut buttocks.

Yvette averted her eyes, though perhaps not as fast as she might have.

He did have such nicely muscled... legs.

"I'm Ewan McTavish, Laird of Craiglochy, and the Viscount Sethwick." He drew Yvette's quaking form to his side. "Miss Stapleton is my intended."

The merest hint of a Scot's brogue flavored his last few words.

Wait. Viscount Sethwick?

Yvette's attention whisked to his face, her eyes opening wide in sudden recognition as memory flooded her.

The phantom lover of her dreams. Her rescuer yesterday. The man at Vangie's wedding. The Viscount Sethwick Vangie had written about. They were the same man.

Another thought stalled her recollection.

Intended? Is he addled?

"And you are?" Head slanted, his lips curved upward a jot, he stared at Mrs. Pettigrove expectantly.

"Mrs. Millicent Pettigrove." Her lips skewed in a disapproving moue. "Intended? You're affianced to her, your lordship?" Her beady stare traveled between him and Miss Stapleton, her expression growing skeptical. "Miss Stapleton hasn't spoken of it. She shared my cabin for weeks and didn't once mention she was betrothed."

Incapable of speech, Yvette forced one steadying breath after another into her constricted lungs. All along, her subconscious had known that Lord Sethwick was the man in her dreams. She folded the shawl tighter across her chest, digging her nails into the silky material.

Stupid, stupid girl.

Why hadn't she realized it before? How could she have been that blind, that oblivious, especially after he told her his name yesterday? That explained why he'd seemed familiar. The arm draped about her shoulders was familiar too—dratted dreams. She shifted her gaze, peeking at him from the corner of her eye.

Despite his state of undress, he appeared composed and devilishly confident. He turned a charming smile on Mrs. Pettigrove. "Mademoiselle."

With reluctant admiration, Yvette watched him work his wiles.

"Mrs. Pettigrove, if you please." She jutted her chins at a haughty angle.

Yvette detected a flinty glint in his eyes, though he tipped his dark head with its sleep-mussed hair in acquiescence.

"Mrs. Pettigrove, one can easily discern you're a woman of great refinement. And of course, you're aware that when one is in mourning, it's gauche to speak of upcoming nuptials."

Oh, he was clever, appealing to Mrs. Pettigrove's vanity. *Well done, your lordship.*

"Miss Stapleton is grieving the loss of her parents, thus we've kept our troth a secret."

He knows about Papa and Belle-mére?

Eyeing her first, then the viscount, Mrs. Pettigrove's dour frown softened the tiniest bit. "It's true one must observe proper mourning protocol. *But* that doesn't explain, or excuse, Miss Stapleton's presence in your chamber."

Yvette restrained a wry smile. Mrs. Pettigrove had grudgingly acknowledged the former while demanding an explanation for the latter.

"You're a most judicious woman," Lord Sethwick soothed.

Yvette's lips twitched again. He was quite the diplomat.

"Eager to take Miss Stapleton to wife, I procured a special license in anticipation of her return to London." He stopped to stare at Yvette, his gaze darkening to the deep blue-green of the ocean during a squall.

Her stomach flipped, and she swallowed, unsure whether tension caused the peculiar lurching in her stomach or something else. Good Lord, one look from those mesmerizing eyes and she was atwitter.

"I'd hoped to persuade her to marry me in a quiet,

private ceremony. And once her bereavement period ended, we'd enjoy a public reception."

The lies roll off his lips with such ease.

As Lord Sethwick spoke, he led Yvette to the other chair.

Her toe caught on the carpet's edge, and she stumbled.

He steadied her before nudging her into the chair. Wrapped in her shawl, she worried her lower lip, puzzled at this turn of events. How could she possibly remedy this dilemma? What on earth had possessed him to make such an outlandish claim?

She dared to meet Mrs. Pettigrove's superior stare.

"Naturally, I shall need proof of the license," Mrs. Pettigrove said. "One can allow certain... ah... indiscretions for those expecting to marry in the *immediate* future." Her focus dropped to the towel hanging low on his hips again, and she licked her lower lip. "*When* did you say you and Miss Stapleton were to be—?"

A pounding on the door drew everyone's attention, and Yvette sighed in relief.

The interruption spared Lord Sethwick from weaving another thread into his web of deceit.

Myles Quimby's worried voice called, "Mrs. Pettigrove, Miss Stapleton, are you well? I heard a scream."

"Mrs. Pettigrove, please answer the door and assure Quimby you're safe. I must leave, but I shall return shortly." His lordship had already reached the door between their rooms as he spoke. Fingers on the, handle, he paused, then retraced his steps.

Yvette plucked at the shawl. What was he about?

"When I return, please allow me to escort you to breakfast. We shall dine in one of the private rooms below." Bowing, despite the scant bit of linen, he raised Mrs. Pettigrove's dimpled hand to his lips and bestowed a chaste kiss upon the back of the plump appendage. "I would be grateful and honored if you'd consent to act as Miss Stapleton's chaperone."

For all of Mrs. Pettigrove's declarations of affection for her misplaced spouse, she leered at Lord Sethwick as if he were a tasty, cream-filled pastry, and she was about to gobble him up.

"*Anything* I can do to assist your lordship would be my utmost pleasure," Mrs. Pettigrove gushed.

Another series of urgent knocks rattled the door, and with some effort, Mrs. Pettigrove shoved to her feet then waddled to the door and unlocked it. She cracked it open two inches.

"Yvette." Lord Sethwick took her hand in his, giving her fingers a small squeeze. "All will be well."

Studying his intent gaze, she discerned his sincerity, even as his eyes revealed something else—an intimate intensity that sent her pulse skittering again.

"Will you trust me?"

His deep, soothing voice penetrated the fog encompassing her. *Trust him?* Not likely. She didn't know him. Casting a sideways glance at Mrs. Pettigrove still at the chamber door, instead of answering him, Yvette whispered, "I left my dagger under one of your pillows."

"Dagger?" Astonishment registered on his face.

"Yes." Yvette nodded and cast Mrs. Pettigrove another wary glance. "Under the pillow."

"Eh, what's that?" After closing the door, Mrs. Pettigrove's scrutiny swung between Yvette and his lordship.

Lord Sethwick flashed her a rakish smile. "Miss Stapleton left an article in my chamber." He looked to

Yvette and gave her the minutest wink. "I'll see that it's returned to you."

"Thank you, my lord."

"Call me Ewan. After all, we're betrothed," he whispered, grinning mischievously.

Yvette's lips turned upward despite her misgivings. Dash it all, but he was a charming rogue.

Raising her hand to his firm lips, Ewan caressed her palm with his thumb. He placed a lingering kiss on her fingertips, and the roughness of his unshaven face sent ripples of pleasure skipping across her flesh.

"Dress and wait for my return, Yvette. Promise you won't leave this room."

"I promise, my lord." She was unable to deny his request, yet hesitant to address him by his given name.

He chuckled and released her hand. "My name is Ewan."

Striding to the adjoining door, he gave her one last penetrating look then left, closing the door behind him.

Miss Pettigrove pried her gaze from the closed door and, mouth pursed, turned her beady stare on Yvette.

"Precisely how long have you and his lordship been affianced?"

Seven

Less than three hours later—three ceaseless hours in which Yvette repeatedly dodged Mrs. Pettigrove's questions about her betrothal to Lord Sethwick— he rapped on their door.

Yvette's emotions fluctuated between bewilderment and crossness at Mrs. Pettigrove's snooping and his betrothal claim. How dare he proclaim them affianced especially to a rumormonger like Mrs. Pettigrove? To be fair, he didn't know she was loose-lipped, yet he had created a fine bumblebroth with his lie.

Yvette was truly piqued. So why couldn't she tear her gaze from him?

He'd shaved and brushed his shiny ebony hair. A chocolate brown cutaway coat stretched across his wide shoulders, and creamy ivory breeches, tucked into gleaming black boots, revealed long, athletic legs. A patterned waistcoat in green hues deepened the color of his eyes to dark teal.

He bowed over Yvette's hand, and she inhaled his now-familiar scent.

She'd dressed with deliberate care, selecting a gown to

boost her confidence, yet appropriate also for mourning. The violet bombazine was one of her favorites. Around her neck, she wore a violet velvet choker, the center adorned with an onyx cameo, and amethyst and onyx earrings dangled from her ears. She'd styled her hair into a simple knot, intertwined with violet ribbon, while leaving several loose curls to frame her face.

"If you're ready, ladies, let's go below stairs and break our fast." Lord Sethwick extended an elbow to each woman.

At the bottom of the stairway, Mrs. Quimby showed them to a private dining compartment where a sideboard displayed an array of tempting food.

"Ladies, please accept my apologies for any distress you were caused this morning. Myles and I want to assure you, we've never had an intruder on the premises before. We always keep the doors and windows securely bolted." Contrite, her eyes shadowed with worry, she met each of their gazes. "The authorities have been notified."

Mrs. Pettigrove astounded Yvette by responding with kind understanding. "Mrs. Quimby, I don't hold you at all responsible for the unfortunate event earlier."

The petty look she darted Yvette suggested the same mercy wasn't, as yet, extended to her. Mrs. Pettigrove, her plate heaped with a liberal portion of food, waddled to the chair Lord Sethwick held for her. Yvette followed, stopping short of the round table. He moved to the chair opposite Mrs. Pettigrove, rather than one positioned on either side of the munching matron.

"Miss Stapleton." He indicated the chair he stood behind.

Yvette lowered herself onto the seat. "Thank you, my lord."

He dipped his head, his breath tickling her ear. "Call me Ewan, Evvy."

Even if his request was only this side of improper, the way he said her nickname—as if savoring the most marvelous, decadent dessert—caused her heart to trip over itself and beat unsteadily for several delicious moments afterward.

His lordship took a seat between the two women, and Yvette considered him from beneath her lashes.

Vangie must have told him her pet name. Yvette attempted to eat a scone, but abandoned the effort when her stomach rebelled. She nibbled a couple of cherries, but they, too, sent her insides cavorting. However, sipping a cup of steaming tea helped steady her nerves.

Idly admiring the teacup's delicate blue rose pattern, she sought answers to the question haunting her. How on earth was she to solve this disaster of the contrived betrothal to Viscount Sethwick?

She made no attempt at conversation, but sipped her tea and listened to Mrs. Pettigrove's on-going prattle. Why did the viscount keep sending Yvette those assessing looks as if attempting to read her mind?

Mrs. Pettigrove blathered on.

Had she no idea how boorish her behavior was? Given the pinched look on his face, her twaddle strained his manners. Yvette bit the inside of her cheek to stop the smile that threatened. *Gads.* Did Mrs. Pettigrove truly think he cared in the least that shellfish gave her a rash and caused her lips to swell like two great sausages?

Yvette cut Lord Sethwick another peek. He stared at Mrs. Pettigrove, his sausage-laden fork halfway to his mouth. Did his lips twitch? The smile Yvette restrained burst forth when his amused gaze drifted to her.

He raised his fork and took a deliberate bite.

Mrs. Pettigrove's grating voice interrupted the moment. "Lord Sethwick, I'm loath to remind you, but you did promise to provide evidence of a special license."

By thunder, did Mrs. Pettigrove's snooping know no bounds? Mortified to be caught in such a flagrant lie, Yvette looked at him. Now what were they to do?

"To be sure, I did indeed." Unruffled, Lord Sethwick patted his mouth with his serviette before laying the linen square beside his plate. He reached inside his coat then removed the document for the intrusive matron's perusal.

He truly possesses a license? How is that possible?

After unfolding the formal looking papers, Mrs. Pettigrove made a pretense of reading them.

Yvette hid a smile behind her serviette. Mrs. Pettigrove couldn't read a word, let alone see the numerous wiry, gray hairs on her chin, without her spectacles. The viscount might have handed her an advertisement to relieve digestive disorders, or baldness, *or eliminate unsightly facial hair*, and the busybody wouldn't have been able to distinguish the difference.

"The date?" probed Mrs. Pettigrove.

Taking another bite of sausage, Lord Sethwick chewed it before answering. "The license was issued May first, well in advance of Miss Stapleton's arrival."

Unable to tear her gaze away, Yvette stared at the license in rapt silence. How had he acquired one so quickly?

Giving a stiff nod, Mrs. Pettigrove handed him the document. "It *appears* to be in order."

Lord Sethwick returned it to his inside pocket.

Yvette wasn't surprised the oversized matron seemed less than enthusiastic with the discovery.

Her mouth full of scone, Mrs. Pettigrove lifted her teacup. "When did you say the marriage will take place?"

What galling persistence. Yvette flashed his lordship a sidelong glance. He wasn't perturbed in the least. She shifted her gaze to his cravat pin, lest he catch her studying him. How would he answer Mrs. Pettigrove's uncouth question?

A sharp rap echoed at the door. Saved by another fortuitous knock, thank goodness. She raised her head and forced her attention from him.

He stared at her intently before calling, "Enter."

"My lord, please excuse the interruption." A deep, vaguely familiar voice greeted the viscount. "It's urgent I speak with you."

Half-turning to inspect the newcomer, Yvette couldn't contain her frightened gasp. She shot halfway out of her chair before Lord Sethwick swiftly reached across the table and grasped her hand, restraining her.

"Ewan?" Panic dried her tongue.

"Miss Stapleton, Mrs. Pettigrove, may I introduce my associate, Trenton Carmichael? You know him as Nigel Collingsworth." Ewan's reassuring smile did nothing to ease the fear trotting on spiky little heels along Yvette's nerves.

And what in the world had happened to Collingsworth's face? Had he been in a fight?

She sat down so hard, her bottom smacked the chair with a stinging thud. Despite the day's promise to be quite warm, she shivered, chilled to the bone. Stunned, she searched his lordship's face. "Your associate? I don't understand. He chased me yesterday."

Mrs. Pettigrove's gooseberry eyes rounded wide as the moon. "Mr. Collings, er, Carmichael chased you, Miss Stapleton?"

No one responded.

Holding Yvette's hand, Lord Sethwick explained, "He wasn't chasing you. Trent was trying to protect you by catching the man who *was* chasing you."

"A different man also chased you? Whatever for?" Envy shaded Mrs. Pettigrove petulant tone.

Everyone ignored her.

Mr. Carmichael addressed Yvette. "I regret frightening you yesterday. I assure you, it wasn't my intent."

Another brisk knock sounded.

Lord Sethwick frowned. "If you must, come in."

Yvette managed not to gawk at the two men sauntering into the private chamber. At least she thought she did. *Faith, what handsome men.* They must be friends of Lord Sethwick's.

Nobility, no doubt.

"Sethwick, you rogue, keeping the arrival of your lovely bride-to-be a secret," teased a tall gentleman dressed in black from toe to top.

～

Ewan suppressed an oath.

What the devil were Yancy and Harcourt doing here?

He directed a disgruntled scowl at Yancy. Ewan had used Yancy's considerable connections to acquire the special license this morning, and Harcourt had been present when Ewan had asked for the favor. He'd bet his favorite hound this was the secretary's idea of a joke.

Nothing for it then.

Scooting his chair back, Ewan rose to make the introductions. "Mrs. Pettigrove, Miss Stapleton, may I present Rochester, the Duke of Harcourt, and Bartholomew, the

Earl of Ramsbury and Britain's Secretary of War?" Ewan raised a peeved brow. "Gentlemen, Mrs. Millicent Pettigrove and Miss Yvette Stapleton. You're already acquainted with Mr. Carmichael."

He avoided addressing Yvette as his bespoken, intending to spare her a degree of embarrassment. His two comrades were having none of it though. The peers descended on her, like vultures on carrion. He'd suspected they would, just to irritate him, but had hoped otherwise.

Harcourt raised her hand to his lips. "*Enchanté*, Mademoiselle Stapleton. Sethwick's a most fortunate man indeed. Alas, if only I'd met you first..."

His dramatic sigh and the way he let his sentence trail off irritated Ewan—precisely why Harcourt had done it.

Not to be outdone, Yancy bent into a flourishing bow. "Please address me as Yancy. I'm still unaccustomed to my title. Sethwick spoke of your beauty, Miss Stapleton, but his humble words couldn't describe such angelic perfection. No wonder he's guarded your identity so fervently until now."

At his friends' flagrant goading, Ewan released a disgusted snort.

Yvette sent a curious look in his direction, and unfamiliar heat crept up his neck to his face.

Blast and damn, now he colored like a moon-eyed swain.

From the sardonic grin twisting Harcourt's lips, he'd noticed.

"*Won't* you join us?" Ewan grudgingly invited, his deliberate glower belaying his words.

"We'd love to, old chap." Harcourt sniggered, looking at Yancy. "Wouldn't we?"

"Indeed we would," Yancy agreed, a smug smile framing his mouth.

Ewan's scowl deepened.

So, they intended to ignore his hint, did they? He'd no one to blame but himself. He'd given them this fodder when he'd rushed pell-mell into Yancy's office earlier, demanding he help procure a marriage license.

From the chamber's corners, Harcourt and Yancy each dragged a chair to the table, but only Carmichael accepted the offer to dine.

Ewan eyed Carmichael's swollen cheek and bruised face. He must've put up quite a fight to get those. At one time, Carmichael had been a professional pugilist.

Mrs. Pettigrove, a smear of marmalade atop her upper lip, actually stopped eating to leer at each of the men in turn. Probably never dined with such an assortment of males, and her desire for the opposite sex took precedence over her voracious appetite for food.

"I say, Carmichael, what happened to your face?" Harcourt's gaze slid to Ewan then traveled back to Carmichael.

"Yes, what *did* happen? I thought you had an *assignment* last night?" Why hadn't Carmichael alerted him to Marquardt's intrusion?

His mouth full, Carmichael's keen gaze swept the table, and a flush stole across his battered face. He swallowed and wiped his mouth with his serviette. "That's why I sought you this morning. I was attacked while on watch." He cast a hesitant glance in the women's direction. "They knocked me out cold. I awoke in the alley next door."

"They?" Ewan frowned.

"Three." Carmichael nodded before turning his attention to his plate once more.

Ewan leaned against his chair's back and crossed his arms, his gaze skimming Yvette.

She crinkled her forehead in an adorable confusion and kept casting furtive, wary peeks at Carmichael.

It would take time for her to trust him.

Ewan forced his attention away to find Yancy staring at him, a mocking grin twitching his mouth, while Harcourt gazed raptly at her.

Irritation tapped a steady beat in time with Ewan's pulse.

Determined to steer the conversation away from his betrothal, Ewan asked the first thing that came to mind. "Harcourt, when did you arrive in Town?"

"Only yestereve, if you must know," Harcourt answered indifferently, his piercing gaze never veering from Yvette.

Yancy hooked an ankle over his knee. "Harcourt arrived at my office at the crack of dawn this morn. It's most fortunate I keep early hours. You never know *who* may arrive unfashionably early with impractical, nearly impossible requests."

Ewan shot him a warning glare.

Her pretty face a mask of puzzlement, Yvette stared at Ewan. *She senses the undercurrent, blast it.* He knew exactly what his chums were about. The louts thought it great fun to pop over and taunt him about his unexpected betrothal.

"So, when *do* the nuptials take place?" Harcourt's gaze flicked to Ewan before sliding back to Yvette, and examining her much too closely for his comfort.

She blushed and averted her sapphire gaze.

"A firm date hasn't been decided upon, just yet." Ewan fiddled with his knife, regretting her discomfort but seeing no alternative except to continue the ruse.

"Were I to have a bride as exquisite as Miss Stapleton,"

Harcourt dared, "I'd commence with the ceremony with all due haste."

Yancy entered the fray, a wide grin lighting his face. "Do tell, Sethwick. When can we expect the bans to be posted? Or do you intend to use the special license you've been toting around for *weeks*, after all?"

Ewan remained silent, shooting daggers at both men with his eyes. He pushed his full plate away, having lost his appetite.

"Course, you could save yourself a great deal of trouble and hightail it to Scotland with your beautiful bride-to-be," the duke hinted. "Gretna Green, mayhap?"

Merde. Insufferable boors.

"Indeed," Yancy agreed. "You Scots make wedding profoundly easy."

~

Scotland?

Yvette took a sip of tea, sending Lord Sethwick another curious look from beneath her eyelashes.

Whatever is going on?

Mr. Carmichael chortled outright, though he attempted to hide his chuckles behind his serviette and feign a choking fit.

Yvette wasn't fooled in the least. The man was laughing, and heartily.

An odd sense of panic blossomed in the corner of her mind. Something wasn't right. Since when did Mr. Collings —Mr. Carmichael have a sense of humor? He hadn't cracked a hint of a smile during their entire Atlantic crossing.

No, something was off, to be sure.

Shifting her regard from his shaking shoulders, she glanced at the duke and earl before settling her gaze on Lord Sethwick. Did he seem a trifle worried? His scar pulsed white above his clenched jaw. No, he was angry again.

Faith, what a dark temper he had.

"Why, Sethwick, Harcourt and I could stand up for you, and Mrs. Pettigrove could act as a witness for Miss Stapleton. What say you? Shall we arrange a quiet ceremony for this afternoon?"

What?

Surely Lord Ramsbury wasn't serious

"I'm amenable to the suggestion." Harcourt drummed his fingertips upon the lace tablecloth. "The only thing that would delight me more would be your beautiful bride throwing you over and agreeing to have me instead."

Was *he* serious?

Lord Sethwick had the most irregular friends, peers or not.

Yvette speared him an alarmed glance.

His features had hardened into stern lines, and his eyes brimmed with annoyance.

"An excellent idea, Your Grace. For the marriage ceremony to take place immediately, that is," Mrs. Pettigrove agreed. She puffed her massive chest upward and batted her eyelashes.

Yvette almost spilled the cup of tea she'd raised to her lips. With a shaky clank, she set the cup in its saucer so hard that tea sloshed over the brim. Folding her shaky hands in her lap, she squeezed them until her fingers numbed.

I must put a stop to this charade.

"Your Grace, my lord, I must confess—"

"As much as it would please me—us—to accept your

generous offer," Lord Sethwick interrupted, agitation thickening his brogue, "I'm afraid we must decline. It's Lady Warrick's greatest wish to be present at her cousin's wedding. It's only fitting as Miss Stapleton attended hers."

Brilliant. And inarguable.

His gaze met Yvette's across the table, and his mouth curved into a lazy smile. "That's where we met."

Returning his smile, she pressed her hand to her middle. Goodness, her stomach was all aflutter.

She averted her gaze before addressing his grace. "Yes, indeed. Vangie has looked forward to my wedding since we were young girls." Her gaze gravitated to Lord Ramsbury. "I couldn't bear to disappoint her."

No lie there.

Yvette plastered a smile on her face. "My cousin was beyond thrilled to learn that Lord Sethwick and I are affianced."

Colossal lie there.

The door vibrated again.

"Come in," Lord Sethwick promptly called.

A half-smile on her lips, Yvette toyed with a cherry on her plate. Lord Sethwick had been a bit too eager to bid entrance. One might think him anxious for a change of subject.

The clattering of utensils, muted by Mrs. Pettigrove's squawk of delight, revealed that Willard Pettigrove had at last been reunited with his wife. Once more, introductions were made, and Yvette breathed a sigh of relief several minutes later as the door closed behind the Pettigroves.

She wouldn't miss the difficult woman. No, not in the least. She flicked the cherry harder than intended, and the miniature red cannonball shot across the table and bounced off Mr. Carmichael's plate before rolling onto the floor. Embarrassed, she swept her gaze around the table.

Four pairs of amused male eyes regarded at her.

Heat stole up her face, and she dropped her gaze.

"Haven't you pressing business to attend to *elsewhere*, Yancy?" Lord Sethwick's pointed look took in his grace and Mr. Carmichael.

Lord Sethwick had ceased to be subtle. Perhaps he was as eager as she to put aright this betrothal tangle.

That Lord Ramsbury understood was clear. He stood and straightened his coat. "Ah, yes, we'll be off then. There is something pressing that I..." He met Harcourt's and Carmichael's amused gazes. "*We* should see to."

Eight

Without further ado, the men took their leave.

At last, Yvette was alone with Lord Sethwick. Odd, she hadn't been nervous in his carriage or chamber, but now, every pore tingled with awareness.

I wasn't bespoke to him then, either.

The sun's bold rays penetrated the lace curtains, hinting at the temperature mounting outside. Inside, a different kind of heat burgeoned. She had much to discuss with his lordship. She toyed with a curl, fidgeted with her choker, then wadded and unwadded her serviette.

All the while, he sat silently, regarding her with those dratted beautiful eyes.

She grew impatient, her apprehension rising with the temperature.

Her mind wouldn't stop replaying this morning's humiliating events, and being alone with him disconcerted her no end. Try as she might, she couldn't keep from recalling those tantalizing moments in his bed. Heat suffused her once more. Pretending to sip her tepid tea, she stole a glance at him.

Lord, but she was full of tea.

Seeking a distraction, she looked about the room, noting the floral wallpaper and *trompe l'oeil* garden, complete with a painted fountain, on one wall. Sighing, she returned her attention to Lord Sethwick.

What was he thinking?

Why didn't he say something? Should she?

She fisted her hand in the poor, abused serviette. Was he trying to find a discreet way to extricate himself from their mock betrothal? Could she blame him? Wasn't she trying to do the same thing?

Smoothing the serviette, trying to subdue her worry, she took a bracing pull of air. "My lord, what shall we to do?"

Her gaze sought his before returning to the cloth. She folded the wrinkled square and placed it on the table. Awaiting his answer, she traced the seam with her pointer finger.

"Do? Why, journey to Somersfield, of course."

Startled, Yvette snapped her head up. "You're to be my escort? What of Ian? Why isn't he accompanying me?" Suddenly anxious, she stopped fingering the serviette. "Are Vangie and the babe well, my lord?"

A smile played around the edges of Lord Sethwick's mouth. "Call me Ewan, Evvy."

She bristled.

He'd ignored her questions, and continuing to call her Evvy was most presumptuous. They were not intimate acquaintances. He assumed far too much.

Piqued, she angled her head and met his bold gaze. In her frostiest tone, she admonished him. "I've not given you leave to address me so familiarly. Only my family and dearest friends may call me Evvy."

There. She'd brought him up to scratch nicely.

Crooking a brow, he chuckled then laughed outright, a deep, pleasant sound that played across her senses. She almost grinned in response. Oh, he was wickedly charming. However, her twitching lips firmed at his next words.

"How much more intimate must we be? We awoke nearly naked in each other's arms mere hours ago. And need I remind you what was taking place prior to *your* awakening?"

Yvette gave a mortified squeak and threw her hands over burning cheeks. The heat of her scalding shame burned her palms.

How could he?

Tears prickled behind her lids.

A moment later, she scooted away from the table, her chair scraping loudly in the too-silent room. She wouldn't let him see her cry. *She wouldn't.* Yvette sprang to her feet, and without saying a word or looking his direction at all, turned toward the door. She'd taken two steps when he leaped from his seat and blocked her path.

Now what?

She needed to escape.

She mightn't ever marry, but she didn't want ruination either. He was a churl to remind her of her foolishness, of entering his room and sleeping in his bed. She could accept spinsterhood—there was no dishonor in it—but a woman with a tarnished reputation, one labeled wanton and fast, or worse?

That life was something different altogether. Yvette didn't know if she could bear the disgrace.

Tears flooded her eyes, and head lowered, she tried skirting round Lord Sethwick, bumping into a chair in her haste. Intent on leaving the room, she shoved it roughly aside. He stopped her again, this time grasping her arms. Keeping her head bowed and her eyes averted, Yvette held her breath against the sobs lodged in her throat.

"Yvette?"

A fat tear dropped onto his boot, balancing for a moment before rolling off the polished toe. Another swiftly followed.

Lord Sethwick won't like his boots being dripped upon.

Yvette almost laughed at the absurdity of her thoughts. But misery, like her tears, dammed any lighter emotion. Regret and embarrassment riddled her. Sniffling noisily, she sucked in a great, watery breath. He wound her into knots of muddled uncertainty. Why didn't he let her leave? He owed her nothing, and she wasn't naïve enough to think he was mad for her.

True, she was attracted to him, but that didn't mean there could ever be anything between them. They'd just met, for pity's sake, and her heart was too full of grief and fear to consider anything else. Besides, she wasn't so bird-witted as to succumb to the first man who stirred her. A man she knew absolutely nothing about.

Lord Sethwick wrapped his strong arms around her.

Now he's being kind?

This was worse.

She wept harder.

He scooped her into his arms, then retreated to the chair he'd vacated. Cradling her across his lap, he ran a comforting hand down her spine. "I'm sorry," he whispered into her hair. "I'm ten times a fool. Forgive me."

Yvette tried to shake her head against his muscled chest,

succeeding only in wetting his coat front. "Not your fault. I oughtn't to have been in your bed. Shouldn't have been touching..." She pressed her face closer to his chest. This was humiliating. Why had she been so impulsive? "Papa would be ashamed. He raised me to be a moral woman."

"You've done nothing to be ashamed of. Our, ah, *interlude,* was quite innocent." His lordship stopped caressing her for a moment. "You can't be held responsible for what you... what happens when you're dreaming." He resumed the comforting movement along her spine. "It's beyond your control."

What he said was true, but she found it difficult to think. Wool filled her head, and no doubt her eyes and nose were swollen and red. Her weeping slowed to an occasional rasping hiccup as the tremors drained from her body. She wiped her damp cheeks with her hands.

Lord Sethwick shifted, and she settled further into his lap, resting her head on his shoulder. She accepted the handkerchief he removed from his pocket.

"Thank you," she snuffled into the starched material. She sniffed the fabric. It smelled of him. She dabbed at her wet face before blowing her nose.

Drawing in a steadying breath, shyness swept her. "Thank you for earlier, in my chamber. I'm not sure what Mrs. Pettigrove would've done if it hadn't been for your quick thinking."

She shuddered anew at the prospect. Mrs. Pettigrove possessed loose lips, always happy and eager to spread the latest tittle-tattle. She wouldn't keep silent about the matter. Once Mrs. Pettigrove told her sister, Lady Clutterbuck—a notorious rattlepate—the whole of London would learn of Yvette's indiscretion.

Lord Sethwick responded by pulling her closer and

tightening his arms about her. She rather liked that. A whisper of a warm touch caressed the top of her head again.

"I can't imagine why I didn't recognize you in the carriage." Relaxing against him, she scrunched the soaked handkerchief in her fist. "Perhaps it was because two years have passed, and I did only dance with you once."

Yvette tried to tilt her head to look at him, but his chin rested on her head, preventing the movement. "And the circumstances were most unusual. The hurried wedding, I mean, and you left right as the dance ended. Why, I don't believe you spoke a single word to me."

Now she prattled on like an empty-headed ninny.

Nestled within the safe haven of Lord Sethwick's embrace, her face pressed to his chest and his heart beating rhythmically beneath her check, she fought a battle.

She ought to remove herself from his person. This was most unseemly. Scandalous, even. But, she found she fit perfectly against him, and having him wrapped around her thusly caused the most intriguing feelings to take root.

What if someone entered the room, though? Yvette had already been caught in one compromising position today.

"My lord?"

"Ewan."

"Ewan, you never answered my question about Vangie and her babe."

His hold tightened for a moment. "When I left Somersfield, Lady Warrick and the babe she carries were in fine health." Laughter shook his shoulders and chest. "Warrick, on the other hand, was a trifle... uh... shall we say, indisposed?"

"Ian isn't...?"

"Never fear." Continuing to chuckle, Ewan elaborated.

"Warrick recently purchased a nasty-tempered stallion. The brute threw him toe over top two weeks past. As he bent to retrieve his crop, Excelsior bit him in the tender region upon—"

"Was the bite serious?" She tilted her neck to look at him, her head resting in the crook of his shoulder. "Will he be all right?"

"He'll be fine. The doctor says there'll be a scar. Two, actually." Ewan's shoulders vibrated with humor again. "He's not permitted to ride until the wound is healed. Thus, I've the privilege of seeing you to Somersfield."

Privilege? He doesn't mind?

"Perhaps you should let me down now."

He bent his lips into a rakish grin, and her heart gave the queerest little flip.

"In a moment." His grip tensed, his expression taking on a reserved edge. "I think we should continue to claim we're bespoke for a time."

"Whatever for?" Confusion knitted Yvette's brow. "Mrs. Pettigrove is gone, and it's unlikely our paths will cross again. Her tongue will wag, of course, but there's little to be done about that."

"If we portray ourselves as happily betrothed, I'm hopeful your stepbrother will leave you alone," Ewan said.

Yvette twisted on his lap to search his eyes. "You know Edgar?"

"We have mutual acquaintances."

Her gaze hovered on the front of his jacket, and she straightened a jot. "And pray tell, how is it you actually possess a marriage license?"

Ewan's chuckle filled the room again as he adjusted his legs beneath her bottom. "Ah, the license." He gave her a knowing wink. "That's why I dashed off this morning. Lord Ramsbury helped me secure one on short notice. Mrs. Pettigrove was determined to have her proof."

Yvette slowly nodded. "But Lord Ramsbury said you'd had the license for weeks."

"Yancy is an old friend, as is Harcourt. Quite simply, the knaves were teasing me. They know full well we're not truly affianced."

One less complication to deal with later.

"Do you really think Edgar will leave me alone if he believes we are bespoke?"

Ewan angled his head and directed his gaze ceilingward before giving a slight shrug. "There's no guarantee, of course, but it's my hope he'll cease his pursuit of you."

Yvette didn't believe for a minute such was the case, but then, he didn't know Edgar like she did. Didn't know how vile and determined her stepbrother could be. Edgar mightn't know where Vangie lived, but a coin or two in the right hand would loosen a reluctant tongue.

Yvette remained silent, mulling over his suggestion. Her gaze dipped to the twisted handkerchief she still clutched. Confound it, she'd made a cake of things. First venturing into his lordship's chamber, then not denying their feigned betrothal.

A thought rudely shoved its way into her mind. *Oh bother.* There'd be no dashing off to Somersfield today.

"I don't have a chaperone. I can't travel with you."

"*Shh.*" Ewan laid a long finger across her mouth. "We'll secure a suitable one before we leave."

The innocent yet intimate contact dammed her words, but also softened her body to the consistency of warm, creamy custard. Summoning strength of will Yvette didn't know she possessed, she forced herself not to pucker her lips against his finger.

Zounds. What in God's precious name had come over her?

"Evvy, playing the role of a couple soon-to-wed will lessen any gossip or damned hum about this morning events."

"But what happens afterward, Ewan?" She wrinkled her brow and pressed two fingers to the bridge of her nose. "How will we explain our deception?"

"Seeing you safely to Somersfield is our priority right now. With Edgar in Town, we should leave this afternoon —" He stopped short. "Do you think Mrs. Pettigrove would agree to chaperone?"

Yvette shook her head, slicing him a censured glance. "Another week of her company? I think not."

Ewan grinned. "Ask Mrs. Quimby if she knows someone then. If not, I'll send a missive to Dehring. Surely he can retain a suitable female."

Nibbling her lower lip, Yvette deliberated his suggestion. If she and Ewan pretended to be a betrothed couple then traveling together with a chaperone was perfectly respectable. She stopped worrying her lip and sighed.

Truth be told, she wasn't the least upset about continuing their ploy. No, playing the role of a betrothed woman would be somewhat of an adventure, but lying about their troth plagued her conscience. However, no help for it now. The seed had been sown, and she'd no choice but to reap the consequences.

"Yes." She lifted a shoulder in acquiescence.

"Yes?"

Smiling, surprisingly relieved, she nodded. "I agree to

continue to act as your betrothed. Only until the need for the deception isn't necessary, of course."

Yvette almost revoked her consent when his mouth slid into a self-satisfied grin, and his eyes darkened in a manner that stalled her pulse. His lordship appeared far too pleased by half.

She drew her brows together. Perhaps she ought to clarify her position.

"You understand, I've only consented to a faux engagement? I haven't agreed to marry you."

He stared at her for an extended, unnerving moment before drawling, "And I haven't asked you to."

Heat coloring her face, Yvette averted her eyes. Of course, 'twas relief caused her hot cheeks, not embarrassment or disappointment.

The sun's rays had grown bolder, filtering through the curtains and bathing Lord Sethwick in amber light. One ray slanted across her fingers. She could almost envision a slender gold band where the beam lingered.

"Have you changed your mind?"

Did wariness tinge his voice?

Yvette met his probing glance, and his gaze bored into hers.

What would be the point?

Chagrined, she lowered her gaze to stare at her hands. She had to get to Somersfield with her reputation somewhat intact, and she required protection from Edgar. Ewan could help with both. She'd made it clear their betrothal was a calculated ruse, and from his succinct response, he obviously echoed her sentiment.

He needn't have been quite so blunt, however.

She sighed and dared to meet his concerned gaze. "I haven't changed my mind."

"Then it's official—almost." His voice dropped to a deep purr.

"Almost?"

Yvette darted her tongue out to wet suddenly dry lips. Her gaze drifted to Ewan's parted mouth, and she glimpsed his square white teeth

He lifted her higher on his lap, his eyes trained on her damp mouth. "A betrothal should be sealed with a kiss, no?"

Nine

"I..." Yvette had no chance to respond.

Ewan lowered his head until his firm lips met hers in a tender, reverent kiss.

He lifted his head a half-inch, framing her jaw with his forefinger and thumb. Her eyelids fluttered closed, and he traced his tongue along the seam of her lip.

Pure bliss.

A sigh parted her mouth, and she sensed his smile.

He licked her lower lip, flicking his tongue inside her mouth, then retreating. Once. Twice. The third time, she met his bold stroke with her own.

Dear God, her bones had turned to liquid—a fiery, molten fluid. She was in danger of sliding off Ewan's lap into a molten puddle at his feet. How could a kiss hold the power to tilt the world?

Ewan continued his sensual foray, raining hot little kisses on her forehead and cheeks before lowering to nibble a scalding trail across her neck.

Yvette clutched his forearms to keep from slithering to

the floor. Of their own volition, her arms found their way to his shoulders then traveled to clinch behind his neck. Breath quickening, she drew his head closer. Their mouths met on a mutual sigh, tentative at first, then deepening as newfound desire pulsed through her. The kiss became voracious, their tongues dueling and slanting across slickened lips. Stars burst behind her eyes, and new sensual awareness coursed through her veins.

Ewan suddenly raised his head and cocked it to the side, listening. He lunged to his feet, setting Yvette on hers at the same time. She could no more stand on her own than a newborn foal. She wavered before he steadied her.

He's chuckling again?

She couldn't think straight, let alone stand, her legs wobbled so, and he laughed at her. *Again.* Beast.

"Tidy your hair and take a seat. I fear we're about to be interrupted." Ewan straightened his coat and neckcloth then smoothed his hair.

Knees weak, Yvette slid onto a chair. She'd barely secured several errant strands when the door burst open. Her lips still pulsed from Ewan's kisses. Would anyone notice? They'd only to look at her flushed face and swollen mouth to know what had transpired.

The Duke of Harcourt, Lord Ramsbury, Mr. Carmichael, several soldiers, and a couple of other well-dressed gentlemen crowded into the dining compartment.

Whatever was going on?

Ewan moved to stand behind her chair and placed a calming hand on her shoulder.

As the moment for discovery passed without detection, she released a slow breath and directed a quizzical glance to Ewan.

He met her questioning gaze, and the narrow line of his mouth curved encouragingly before he turned his attention to their unexpected guests.

"Yancy?" Expectation rang in Ewan's deep voice

Yancy didn't mince words. "Belvidere's dead."

"How?" Ewan tightened his fingers on her shoulder.

Oddly, the secretary ignored Ewan's question. Instead, Lord Ramsbury slanted his head, his green-eyed gaze flinty and direct. "Lords Rothingham and Fielding insisted upon accompanying me here."

Ewan's grip tensed once more.

The Duke of Harcourt ambled to the window, and after shoving aside the lacy curtains, looked in both directions. A goldfinch and his mate hiding in the purple lilac took to wing in frenzied flight. His grace nudged the curtain open farther, searching the bustling street.

She smothered a gasp.

Good Lord, what happened to him?

A dark scarlet splotch marred the base of the duke's head, and telltale blood smattered his pristine shirt.

"Your Grace, have you need of a physician?"

Half-turning away from the window, the duke crossed his arms and rested against the frame. "Thank you, no. It's naught but a bump."

A bump? Not with that much blood.

Her disbelief must've showed on her face.

One side of his handsome mouth tipped into a wry smile. "Truly, I've suffered far worse."

Yvette scrutinized the other men in the room. Such serious expressions—except for His Grace. He appeared bored.

She searched Ewan's eyes. "Who's Belvidere?"

Her soft question hung in the air.

Why did they stare so? The question had been perfectly logical. Clasping her fingers, she crossed and uncrossed her ankles.

Ewan stirred behind her, his hand burning through the light material of her gown. "Gentlemen, if you'll excuse us. I wish to speak with Miss Stapleton in private."

One of the newcomers, a paunchy man with a red-veined nose, voiced his objection. "Here now, Sethwick. Rothingham and I didn't rush over here to be banished like errant schoolboys."

"There's a matter I wish to discuss in confidence with my intended, Fielding." Ewan's voice acquired a harsh edge.

"Eh, wot's that? Your intended?" Fielding's watery gaze darted between Ewan and Yvette. "You're affianced?" He sputtered, his face turning purple. "You cannot be. It's impossible."

What audacity.

Whether Lord Fielding's objection arose from deplorable rudeness or genuine surprise, Yvette couldn't be sure, but she bit the inside of her cheek to mute the sharp retort rising to her lips.

"I wasn't aware you were betrothed," the other gentleman said.

Ewan smiled and winked at her before turning a flinty gaze on Lord Rothingham lounging against the table, calmly taking in the scenario.

Coming to stand beside her chair, Ewan took her hand. "Miss Stapleton and I have just made known our engagement. You're aware of mourning protocol, are you not, Rothingham? She's grieving the loss of her parents."

Lord Rothingham had the decency to look abashed.

"My deepest sympathy, Miss Stapleton. We heard of your unfortunate loss."

He had? How?

Ah, the Earl of Clarendon, no doubt.

Lord Fielding swung to face Mr. Carmichael. "Did you know about this?" Lord Fielding jerked his head in Ewan's direction. "His betrothal to the *heiress*?" He spat the last word.

Mr. Carmichael's gaze met Ewan's before skimming over Yvette. He slouched in his chair, folded his arms across his chest, and smirked at Lord Fielding.

Lord Fielding curled his mouth into a sneer, his hands fisted at his flabby waist. "So, you did know, you filthy wretch."

He wasn't one to let the matter go, though why he presumed it any of his business, Yvette couldn't begin to imagine. Her eyes narrowed as she stifled her rising ire. *Ill-mannered jackanapes.* She clasped Ewan's hand tighter.

Before Mr. Carmichael could respond, Lord Fielding wheeled to face the duke and war secretary. "And you two—"

"Enough!" Raising his hand in an abrupt gesture, Yancy silenced him.

Yvette almost smiled as Lord Fielding's face reddened in frustration.

Leveling him a blistering glare, Yancy snapped, "It's none of our affair, man. We've much more important things to discuss than Sethwick's upcoming nuptials."

Yancy's perturbed gaze met Ewan's head on. "You've ten minutes. Use them wisely. When I return, I have need of a private word with you."

His keen gaze measured Yvette for a moment.

A shiver rippled across her shoulders.

He stalked to the door and surveying the men, jerked his head. "Clear the room."

Not a man to cross.

His boots echoed rather ominously as he stomped from the compartment. Giving Yvette a cocky smile, Harcourt sauntered after him. The other men shuffled out the doorway, but the last red-uniformed soldier, his hand on the latch, paused. His kind gaze swept over Yvette before he bowed smartly, then turned on his shiny black heels, and disappeared from sight, leaving the door gaping behind him.

Ah, propriety even in the midst of chaos.

Yvette smiled at the irony, her focus still glued to the empty entrance.

"Ewan, whatever is the matter? Why are those men here? And who, pray tell, is Belvidere?"

"Yvette..." Ewan hesitated. He'd spare her this ugliness.

At his lengthy pause, she lifted her attention from the door and arched an eyebrow.

Tense, he shifted forward in his chair. "Belvidere is—was—a spy. He was captured last night. He'd been in Boston and just returned to London, within a day or two of your arrival. I believe he was working with, or rather, more likely for, your stepbrother."

Nose crinkled and brow creased, she asked, "With Edgar, my lord?"

He suppressed a smile when she addressed him formally again. He gauged her expression, noting that the smattering of freckles across her nose and cheeks stood out starkly against the ivory of her skin.

How much should he tell her?

"Edgar is a spy, Evvy. We—Yancy, Harcourt, and others connected to the War Office—know beyond a doubt that he committed acts of treason during England's campaign against Napoleon." Ewan crossed his legs and drummed his fingers on his bent knee. "Because we wanted to expose everyone involved, we've allowed him to remain a free man. Someone in the War Office is giving your stepbrother orders."

Damnation, she's already frightened. This will only make her more so. But she needs to understand how serious this is.

With deceptive nonchalance, Ewan relaxed against the chair, giving Yvette time to digest the information. Other than growing slightly paler, she remained poised.

Guileless gaze meeting his, she spoke plainly. "What has this to do with me? Until Edgar came to Boston, I'd no contact with him for over two years, and only on rare occasions prior."

Ewan rose and plowed his fingers through his hair, leaving it disheveled. He sighed, and with measured steps, wandered the room. "He fled to Boston months ago. Something frightened him enough to send him hotfooting it to America. We think he's being blackmailed, possibly by another spy, and that's why he's after your fortune."

Yvette gave a brief nod. "Edgar did act most peculiarly in Boston. And he was at odds with Papa from the moment he arrived. In fact, I interrupted a heated argument between them one day. Later, he tried to court me." She darted Ewan an uncertain glance and wrung her hands in her lap, her distress tangible. "After I rebuffed him, and Papa and Belle-mére died, he assaulted me. Twice."

She whispered the last painful words.

Ewan clenched his teeth. If Marquardt were here, he'd run him through. *Twice*. Stopping across the table from her, Ewan placed both palms flat on the crocheted surface. Leaning forward he prodded, "Twice?"

The ruthless edge to his voice betrayed his controlled fury.

She shook her head, the fair curls framing her face spinning with the motion, and rubbed her palms down her thighs. "The morning he trapped me in the study, he vowed I'd marry him after he... um... after he *finished* with me. He tried to..." The dark blush sweeping Yvette's face revealed what she couldn't voice.

Ewan's breath caught as rage crashed into his gut.

The bloody bastard.

Sucking in a deliberate, controlled breath, he nodded, encouraging her. "Go on."

"I cut him with my dagger before Fairchild, our butler, and his sons broke the door down. Edgar fled through the terrace entrance. The other time, he sneaked into my bedchamber in the middle of the night and said the most peculiar thing."

Though fury thundered in his blood, Ewan forced a calm demeanor. "What did he say?"

Yvette plucked at her skirt then stopped to peer past Ewan, a faraway expression on her face. "Something queer about, how at first he only wanted my money, but now he had to have me too. He intended to abduct me." Her voice wavered before growing a mite stronger. "But my dogs and Josiah stopped him. Edgar escaped again, though, out my bedroom window."

Wiley rat.

Her soulful gaze met Ewan's. "I believe he's completely mad."

Resuming his pacing—it always helped him order his thoughts—Ewan forced calmness into his tone. "Anything else? Even something you mightn't think is important may be helpful."

Shoulders slumped, Yvette regarded her hands. "I fled for England that very night. I was supposed to sail on a different ship, the arrangements were already made, but Fairchild didn't want me to wait. We realized we'd underestimated Edgar. He was..." Yvette raised her gaze to Ewan. "*Is* ruthless and dangerous. It wasn't until that night that Fairchild told me my mare had been shot. She didn't slip on the ice as I'd thought."

Ewan's brows swooped into an angry vee. "Why didn't he tell you before?"

"Papa forbade it."

"Why?"

Her pretty mouth tilted a fraction. "Papa was very protective of me." Her focus sank to her lap again. "Too protective. He nearly smothered me."

Across the room, Ewan ceased his agitated pacing. "Do you think Edgar shot your mare?"

Yvette shook her head. "No. He was with my father when Aphrodite... when I... that day. He couldn't have shot her, but I suspect he might have hired someone to do it. Mayhap even your Belvidere."

Ewan stopped beside her chair. Lord, how he wanted to gather her into his arms and promise he'd keep her safe. That Edgar, the filthy blackguard, would never trouble her again. Only he couldn't make those promises.

"Is there anything else?" Yvette had probably not spoken of her fears or concerns to anyone before now. He tilted her chin upward until her poignant gaze met his. Her haunted eyes had dimmed to a shadowy slate-blue.

Shifting her regard away, she nodded. "Edgar was irate when our parents' wills were read. He expected Papa to leave him an inheritance. A large one, even though he was only his stepson."

She picked at a bead on her dress. "I'd have given him funds, but Papa's will prohibited any such thing. Anyway, Edgar already received an inheritance from his father's estate and continues to receive a generous annual allowance."

Ewan took his seat again. "He needs more—a great deal more. I believe his life depends on it."

Yvette looked to the window, her delicate features awash in renewed sorrow. "And he killed his mother and my father for it."

"What happened?" His gaze caressed her. Bathed in the morning sunlight filtering through the lacy curtain, she appeared lost and forlorn.

"We had attended a soirée. They became sick hours after we returned home. The doctor believed they must've eaten something tainted. Belle-mére died two days later. Papa less than ten hours afterward."

"But," he touched her arm, "you didn't become ill as well?"

Yvette raised her eyes to his. "I was still recovering from my riding accident and had developed a fierce headache. I didn't eat or drink anything that night." She scrunched her forehead in concentration. "In fact, we were preparing to leave when Edgar arrived with two mulled wines. One for me and one for Papa."

Ewan drew his brows together. "But you said you didn't drink anything."

"I didn't. I don't tolerate spirits. Belle-mére took mine. I distinctly remember her telling Edgar they make me ill."

Yvette gasped, her eyes rounding in horror. "Dear God, it was the wine." The color drained from her face, and she clutched at the table's edge. "Edgar poisoned the wine. Belle-mére wasn't supposed to die."

Yvette stared at Ewan, aghast.

"I was."

Ten

Yvette wanted Ewan to deny it, to tell her she had it wrong, but he remained silent. And that silence spoke volumes.

She cut him an indirect glance.

Yes, just as she feared.

Sympathy glinted in his compassionate blue-green gaze.

She sucked in an unsteady breath and shut her tear-filled eyes. Pain and fear, sharp and jagged, tore through her. Several long, silent moments passed before she composed herself.

Ewan grasped one of her hands, his slightly rough thumb caressing her knuckles.

She opened her eyes, mesmerized by the slow, soothing movement. "Yesterday, when I met with Mr. Dehring, I added a provision to my will naming Vangie's children as my beneficiaries—that is, if I never marry."

His hand is so warm and big and brown. He must spend a great deal of time outdoors.

"That would be a dreadful waste."

What?

Yvette searched his unreadable eyes.

"I've embarrassingly deep pockets," she blurted to cover her discomfiture.

He stilled his addictive caresses. "I'm aware of the extent of your wealth."

She couldn't conceal a small start of surprise. Her gaze roved his impassive countenance.

Ewan smiled and squeezed her hand before releasing it. "I made a point of discovering your worth."

"Why?"

He regarded her for a lengthy moment. "I thought it might be helpful in my pursuit of your stepbrother."

How did knowing her worth help with that? The excuse didn't wash at all.

She regarded him, desperately wishing she knew the truth. Ewan had only delved into her financial affairs because of Edgar's suspicious behavior, hadn't he? What other reason did he have to poke about in her private dealings?

Bother it all.

Was she always to be this distrustful?

Yancy's unannounced entrance halted any further conversation. His bland gaze flicked over Ewan, then her. "Miss Stapleton, may I beg a few minutes alone with your *betrothed?*"

Her imagination or had he emphasized the word? For certain neither man missed the tinge of pink that skated up her cheeks.

Their indulgent smiles confirmed her fears.

Dratted men.

Composing herself, she tilted her head and stood. "Of course, Lord Ramsbury," she said as she hurried to the exit.

"Yvette?"

Already at the threshold, she looked behind her. "Yes, Lord Sethwick?"

He came to her and after tucking a stray curl behind her ear, playfully tapped her earring. "Pack and change into traveling clothes. Take only what is essential. I shall ask Mrs. Quimby to see to the rest of your belongings. Yancy will make sure they're sent on to Somersfield."

He raised her hand to his lips, lingering over her fingertips. "Hurry. Show Carmichael what luggage you want to take with you, and he'll see it loaded onto the coach."

A not-so-discreet cough brought her sailing back to awareness.

Yvette issued a breathless, "Yes, my lord," followed by a wobbly curtsy to Lord Ramsbury. Her skirts swished and rustled around her ankles as she hustled from the dining chamber, leaving the door open in her haste to pack.

She must speak to Mrs. Quimby at once about acquiring a chaperone. One that could leave—

Exactly when did Ewan want to leave?

Already halfway across the lobby, Yvette turned on her heel and rushed back to the dining chamber.

"It's most convenient to be betrothed to one so beautiful *and* rich." Lord Ramsbury's voice carried into the passageway.

His words halted her a few steps from the door. Ewan claimed his friends knew they weren't truly betrothed.

"Don't forget intelligent and intrepid."

Ewan's low murmur caused her heart to stutter uncomfortably.

"Is she?" Lord Ramsbury asked. "*Hmm.* I do believe wealth is usually the more desirable asset in a wife. I'd say you've done quite well for yourself, old chap."

A wealthy wife? Done well?

Ewan chuckled. "Jealous, Yancy?"

"Immeasurably."

A sound like a clap on a shoulder resounded inside the compartment.

A chair creaked as Lord Ramsbury spoke. "What of Marquardt? Can she be of help to us in that quarter?"

Help with Edgar?

Whatever did he blather about?

Casting a cursory glance around the deserted entry, Yvette crept a trifle closer. Her crisp skirts brushed against the door frame, and as one, the men looked to the doorway.

Ewan swiftly rose from his chair then strode to the entry, asking softly, "Did you need something?"

"Yes, I..." She cast a glance at Lord Ramsbury, studying the wall's beautifully painted garden. "I meant to ask Mrs. Quimby about a chaperone, but I don't know what time you intend to leave."

Yvette examined his face but found no hint of subterfuge in the beautiful eyes twinkling at her.

Ewan's smile crinkled the edges of his handsome face. "I'll procure a chaperone. You just get packed. I'd like to leave as soon as possible."

"Very well, then. I'll leave you to it." Thoughts a jumble, Yvette turned and made her way to the stairs. Did Ewan have an ulterior purpose in escorting her to Somersfield?

Confusion and anger skimmed over her, and she paused mid-step.

This is all Edgar's fault, damn him to the ninth level of hell.

～

Ewan's gaze trailed Yvette until she disappeared from sight.

Yancy snorted.

Ewan met his amused gaze. "You do understand we aren't actually betrothed? I made that perfectly clear when I asked for your help obtaining the license."

Yancy nodded, amusement dancing in his eyes. "I know, but egad, you're truly good and taken with Miss Stapleton. When was the last time you saw her? Two years ago?" He held up two fingers, a sly smile quirking his mouth. "I say, my dear fellow, have you carried a torch for her all this while?" His mocking gaze raked Ewan. "That explains so much. Indeed it does."

Ewan schooled his features, determined to ignore Yancy's goading. His friend need not know that his speculating mayhap contained a small grain of truth. "The others?"

"Ah, well, as to that, I had a pressing need to be rid of Rothingham and Fielding."

"Pressing need? Do tell." Ewan knew full well Yancy only tolerated Fielding. He tipped his mouth upward on one side when Yancy speared him a scathing look.

"I sent them on an errand to the docks." Waving his hand, Yancy indicated the general direction of the wharf.

"Ah, the docks."

"To seek word of Marquardt."

"Very clever."

"It's a complete waste of their time."

"Indeed."

"But, at least they aren't snuffling 'round annoying me."

"How sensible." Ewan's grin widened when Yancy faced him, legs spread and arms akimbo.

"Are you enjoying your juvenile jeering?"

"Immensely." Ewan waggled his eyebrows.

Yancy threw his hands in the air before stomping to a chair and sitting. He glared at Ewan then shook his head and smiled sheepishly. "I've been duly chastised. No more prying into your, er, relationship with Miss Stapleton. Can we get on with it?"

Ewan cocked his head, unsure he wanted to let the matter go yet. He rather liked the verbal sparring. He found it quite invigorating, though a round in the ring or a bout of fencing would be much more satisfying.

No, a rousing romp in bed was what he really wanted.

A shadow crossed Yancy's face. "We're at cross-purposes here, Sethwick," he said, waving his hand. "What say you? A truce?"

Ewan tipped his mouth upward slightly. "Aye, a truce then. Where's Harcourt?"

"Off to change his clothes."

"What the hell happened after you left earlier?"

"I presume you are enquiring about Belvidere?"

Ewan narrowed his eyes. "What else?"

Angling to his feet, Yancy blew out a gusty breath. "Blast it, someone knew we had the wretch."

Ewan remained silent, waiting for the details he knew were forthcoming.

"After Harcourt and I left you, we went directly to the War Office. I needed to stop by my office, but sent Harcourt ahead to continue interrogating Belvidere."

Ewan walked to the door and stuck his head out. He asked a passing servant to fetch two tankards of ale then closed the door and rested against it.

"I was approaching the south wing when I heard a shout," Yancy said.

Ewan shoved away from the door, strode to the window, and lifted the curtain aside.

"I ran down the stairway, and as I reached the bottom step, a man ran from Belvidere's cell. He wore a floor-length, hooded cloak. Actually, it looked more like a woman's wrap than a man's."

Ewan pivoted to look at Yancy.

Woman's?

A knock halted Yancy's narrative.

"Enter," Ewan bade.

He knew a woman—a hired assassin.

A servant entered, carrying two tankards of ale. He strode to the table and deposited the frothy brews. "Will there be anything else, my lords?"

"No, thank you." Ewan sank heavily into a seat and cut a glance to Yancy, deep in thought. Ewan doubted he even noticed the foamy-topped flagons.

Lines of concentration creased his friend's forehead.

"Here." He handed Yancy a mug and allowed him to take a large pull of the draught before pressing for more information. "What happened then?"

"When I ran into the cell, Belvidere was already dead. He'd been beaten, and from the looks of him, I'd guess tortured too." Yancy tipped his mug again. "Harcourt lay on the floor, but was coming round. He said he'd surprised the murderer."

Ewan took a swallow of his ale. "He's fortunate he only ended up with a crack on the skull."

"Aye," Yancy agreed.

"Yancy, what about the guard? Where was he?"

"Dead. Throat slit. Looked professional."

Unease prickled the length of Ewan's spine.

Professional? Devil take it.

Yancy released a ragged sigh before taking another drink. Resting an elbow on the table, he crossed his legs.

"Other than you and me," he jutted his chin in Ewan's direction, "and the agents who helped us capture Belvidere, no one knew we had him in custody."

Lifting his tankard, Ewan paused. "Well, obviously, someone else knew and wanted to make sure he didn't talk." Taking a deep, contemplative drink, he hoped to God he was wrong about whom he suspected. Matters were complicated enough already. "Did Harcourt notice anything notable about his assailant?"

"Not much. Only that the fellow was quite small.

"Bloody damned hell." Ewan banged his tankard onto the table. "It wasn't a man."

Yancy slanted a skeptical brow. "No?"

Ewan shook his head, agitation thrumming through his veins. "I'd bet Prinny's Pavilion it was Pauline Borghese, the Italian assassin. She's particularly adept with knives."

"Ah, that explains the slit throats." Yancy finished his ale. He placed both his hands on his thighs before blowing out a low sigh and shoving to his feet. "She's collaborating with someone in the War Office then."

Ewan swore inwardly again. The danger had just increased exponentially. He strode to the door, calling over his shoulder, "Find me a chaperone. Someone—*anyone*—reasonably respectable who can leave within the next thirty minutes."

Eleven

Slightly under thirty minutes later, Yvette's valise had been stowed in the boot, and her trunk strapped atop the elegantly-appointed park drag carriage.

For the trip, she'd donned a gray-blue traveling dress. Embroidered blue roses enhanced each of its three ruffled rows. Beneath her bodice, mother of pearl buttons fastened a smart, form-fitting navy spencer with silver silk braiding. Practical low-heeled boots encased her feet, and a straw bonnet covered her curls. A spray of silk flowers peeked over the brim, waving each time she moved her head. In addition to her reticule, she carried a hatbox, and sensibly, given the unseasonable heat, a brisé fan.

Mrs. Quimby had packed them an overflowing basket to tide them over until supper. Surely with such abundance they wouldn't require supper at all. Yvette changed her mind upon discovering their traveling party consisted of two coachmen, Mr. Carmichael, and six uniformed outriders—each of whom carried multiple weapons.

Malcolm, one of the coachmen, assisted Yvette into the conveyance while Ewan inspected the coach-and-four.

No chaperone waited inside.

Where was she?

Yvette bit her lip and tossed a fretful glance out the window.

Surely, Ewan didn't expect her to make the journey without one, did he?

It simply wasn't done. She'd be ruined.

"Sethwick." Lord Ramsbury called, his voice breathless. "I found one. Come along, girl, do stop your dawdling."

Yvette scooted to the end of the seat to peer through the door opening. Lord Ramsbury hurried down the street, a young woman clutching a bundle in tow.

The chaperone?

Why, she couldn't be more than ten-and-fifteen.

Ewan came around the rear of the carriage. His dark brows nearly vaulted to his hat when Lord Ramsbury thrust the girl forward.

"Here she is. Her name is..." He turned to the girl. "What's your name again?"

"Peggy, sir. Peggy Flanders. I be Molly's sister." She slanted her head in the direction of the Banbury Inn.

Yvette breathed a sigh of relief. Though a mere girl, Peggy would suffice for a chaperone.

Barely.

Ewan had yet to speak. Three times his gaze made the circuit between Peggy, Lord Ramsbury, and Yvette hovering in the carriage entrance.

Clearly annoyed, Lord Ramsbury planted his hand on his hips. "Confound it, Sethwick. You didn't give me much time."

"Sorry, gents. I ain't about to get inside that." Peggy pointed at the coach-and-four. "I gets sick, I do. I'd be spillin' me insides on the floor or on you afore we left town."

"Whatever are you talking about? I clearly told you the journey would take several days." Lord Ramsbury's face took on a rosy hue.

"Aye, sir, you did. But when me family goes jauntin' about, we travels in an open wagon." She stepped forward and peeked inside the carriage, then shuddered dramatically. "No ways is I ridin' in there. I be gettin' sick for certain. And I ate kippers this morn."

Yvette winced.

Now what are we to do?

She veered Ewan a panicked glance.

Seemingly unruffled, he winked and smiled, but she didn't smile in return. There was nothing humorous about this situation.

"What about on top?" He glanced at Peggy then the seats atop the carriage. "Could you ride up there?"

Peggy nodded so fast, half her hair came loose and swirled around her thin face. "Coo, sures I could."

A pleased smile did sweep Yvette's mouth then.

Well done, Ewan.

Grinning, he drew Peggy forward. "Miss Flanders, may I present Miss Yvette Stapleton?"

"I'm so very grateful you agreed to travel with us, Miss Flanders." Giddy with relief, Yvette may have been a trifle over exuberant in her greeting.

"Just call me Peg, miss. If'n you calls me somethin' else, I mightn't answer."

"Let's get you on board then." Ewan handed the girl up.

Yvette scooted back inside the already quite warm coach.

After exchanging a few words with Mr. Carmichael and the soldiers, Ewan hoisted himself inside and settled his powerful body opposite her. Thumping the roof, he signaled Malcolm. With a jerk and a creak, the coach rolled away from the Banbury Inn.

They rode in silence for a time, she absorbed in her thoughts, and he...? Well, only God knew what went on in Ewan's keen mind. Yvette pulled her gaze from the scenery and caught Ewan's staid, rather unnerving perusal.

Whatever did he stare at?

Do she have a smudge on her nose? Food caught in her teeth? Had she left her jacket undone? She smoothed the front of her spencer. No, the buttons were done up.

What *was* he gawking at?

She fidgeted with her reticule. Surely, he knew how impolite staring was. She should say something. Anything.

"Your lordship?"

"Yvette, if our betrothal is to be believed, you must learn to call me by my given name."

"But we're alone."

"True. Nevertheless, you must practice in private so that addressing me by my name becomes natural to you. You called me Ewan earlier."

Flipping her fan open, she conceded with a terse nod before fanning herself.

Lord above, but it's stifling.

Due to the carriage's confinement or that disturbing man lounging across from her?

She eyed him over the top of her fan. Exactly why had he agreed to be her escort? She couldn't rid herself of the niggling suspicion he wasn't being completely honest with her.

He removed his coat and slung it beside him on the seat. He stretched his legs before him, and they brushed against her skirt.

Yvette nudged her hatbox aside then scooted a few

inches nearer the door. "I'm sorry. Your legs are much longer than mine. I didn't think to allow you more room."

She fanned herself even faster, seeking some relief from the sweltering temperature inside the carriage. Did she dare remove her outer garment too?

Fluid as a jaguar, and just as fleet, Ewan sprang to sit beside her. He snatched the hatbox, and giving her a teasing grin, lifted it up and down a couple of times. "What's in here? It weighs a stone."

Before she could protest, he placed it on the opposite seat.

"I've plenty of legroom now." He smiled and tapped one of the silk flowers on her hat. "Remove your spencer and bonnet."

She looked at him doubtfully. Most improper. Ladies didn't travel half-clothed.

He winked, that audacious, seductive gesture that turned her insides all wobbly. "No one will know but us, and you'll be more comfortable."

Could he read her mind?

Yvette quirked her mouth then shrugged. "That was my thought too."

Through hooded eyes, he regarded her.

She removed her bonnet and after carefully placing it on her lap, struggled to shrug off the form-fitting jacket in the confined space.

She elbowed Ewan in the chest.

"Excuse me."

And thumped him in the thigh.

"Sorry."

Blister it. There's not enough room.

"Please allow me to assist you." Ewan chuckled and shook his head. "Else I shall be covered with more bruises."

A flush stole up Yvette's neck and face.

He plucked the hat from her lap then tossed it onto the opposite seat. Startled, she gasped as he reached around her and tugged the spencer from her shoulders without waiting for her consent.

"What are you doing?" Yvette spun around on the seat. She'd give him a proper setdown.

At Ewan's look of mock contrition, a smile crooked her mouth.

He *deserves* a setdown.

Or perhaps his naughty schoolboy grin had her lips twitching.

He can't behave so shabbily.

When he waggled his eyebrows and chuckled at his own audacity, she gave up and succumbed to her laughter.

"You, sir, are incorrigible."

"Let's get that thing off you, shall we?"

Once the jacket was removed, Ewan loosened the latch on one window, allowing fresh air into the carriage. The coach-and-four's speed increased as it left the congestion of London behind and headed into the wide-open countryside.

Yvette glimpsed one of the soldiers through the window. "Ewan, do we truly require the soldiers for our journey?"

"Only Carmichael and the coachmen will continue with us after lodging tonight. Yancy believed it wise to present a strong show of force to anyone thinking to follow us. That's why he sent the soldiers."

Yvette had to acknowledge the wisdom in that. Edgar wouldn't dare try anything with this many armed men along.

"They'll return to London." Ewan angled his dark head toward the soldiers. "Though a difficult task, I hope to arrive at Somersfield in four days' time. We shall travel until dusk today in order to put the city, and Marquardt, as far behind us as possible."

Yvette pushed a damp curl off her forehead. "I've only been to Somersfield on two other occasions. I don't recall the route at all."

"We'll stay on the well-traveled roads," he said. "Warrick made arrangements for our accommodations. However, I frequent these inns regularly, and rest assured, they're clean and respectable."

After spending two months in a tiny cabin with Mrs. Pettigrove, *any* private room, no matter how humble, was acceptable to Yvette.

True to his word, Ewan pressed the traveling party relentlessly before stopping for the night. As she descended from the carriage, Yvette surveyed the inn, too exhausted to take more than a cursory glance.

The driver helped an unsteady Peggy from the top. She wavered for a moment. "Lawks, the ground's amovin'."

Taking Yvette's elbow, Ewan guided her across the threshold, directly into the packed common room.

Peggy made straight for a bench paralleling the wall. Her face ashen, she collapsed on the rough seat and rested her head against the plank wall.

A giant of an innkeeper lumbered from behind the counter, extending his hand to Ewan. The mammoth man sent a curious look her way. "Och. Pleased I be to see ye again, McTavish."

"And I you, Fergus."

Yvette surveyed the unnaturally silent taproom. Every patron had turned to stare at her, several of them lewdly. One aged gentleman dared to wink, and another had the audacity to raise his tankard and salute her, a vulgar leer on his otherwise attractive face.

Stepping closer to Ewan, she placed a finger on his arm and attempted to hide her unease.

Ewan tucked her hand into the crook of his elbow. "Fergus, I'd like to introduce you to my betrothed, Yvette Stapleton. Darling, this is an old friend of mine, Fergus MacDowell."

Yvette didn't miss Mr. MacDowell's grizzled red eyebrows flying to meet the equally bright mop of fiery hair at Ewan's disclosure.

Did he suspect Ewan lied?

"Betrothed, ye say? Och, that's cause to celebrate. It's very pleased I be to meet ye, Miss Stapleton." Fergus's brogue thickened with his enthusiasm. Bowing with the aplomb of a knight at court, Fergus intoned, "Welcome to the Rose an' Crown, lass."

She dimpled and dipped a shallow curtsy. "Thank you, Mr. MacDowell."

"Fergus will do, miss."

Mr. Carmichael and the soldiers entered, and the pub resumed its noisy milieu, the curiosity over the newcomers dismissed as quickly as it had begun.

Thank goodness. Relief washed over her, easing the tension from her shoulders, and she loosened her grip on Ewan's arm. From the corner of her eye, she considered the antechamber and the patrons reabsorbed in their brew.

"All is prepared for ye and yer bonnie lass. The others," Fergus jutted his head in the direction of the soldiers, "will bunk in the loft. Except the lass." He pointed to Peggy. "She can sleep with me own daughter. The room be down the hall from yers, Miss Stapleton, if'n ye needs her during the night."

Peggy raised her head and peered at Yvette with bleary eyes. "Miss, might I go straight to bed? Me belly and me head are swimmin'."

"Of course, Peggy."

Fergus motioned with one ham-sized hand. "If ye'll come with me."

Yvette, Ewan, and Peggy followed him up the squeaky flight of stairs. Each step grumbled and moaned in protest as his enormous form ascended the narrow stairwell.

At the top, he opened a door to a stark but spotless chamber. A small table and two chairs stood in the middle atop a braided rag rug. "Do ye wish to eat below stairs or here?"

"Here will be fine," Ewan answered. "After supping, we'll need water for bathing. Please bring our bags up too."

Yvette took in the rest of the small room.

There's but one small bed.

Ewan didn't mean to share this room with her, did he? No indeed, he would not. He'd be sleeping in the loft then as well.

Bobbing his vibrant head, Fergus turned to do Ewan's bidding. "I shall see to it. Yer chamber's yonder, McTavish." He jerked his thumb to indicate a room across from Yvette's. "It's as ye bid afore."

"My chamber, Mr. MacDowell?" A green tinge about her mouth, Peggy swayed.

He pointed to a door farther along the corridor. "Second door on the right, lass."

Peggy shuffled her way to the door, then disappeared into the darkened room.

Trudging down the hallway, Fergus bellowed a lewd ditty about the generous backsides of bonnie Scots lasses.

Yvette released a pent-up breath.

Ewan only meant to dine with her, not sleep in the same chamber. Scandalous enough to be traveling with only a slip of a girl as a chaperone, but sharing a chamber was unthinkable.

Due to the lateness of the hour, Yvette and Ewan partook of a cold repast. While he enjoyed a bottle of wine, she sipped an aromatic blend of Scots tea.

One of the soldiers delivered their bags while they ate, and soon after, Fergus arrived with buckets of warm water followed by a maid toting soap and towels. "Ye be needin' anything else, Miss Stapleton, laird?"

Yvette smiled and shook her head. "No, thank you."

"Aye. Guidnight then." He crossed to the door.

"Fergus, wait." Ewan stood. "I'll go with you. I need to speak with Carmichael."

Yawning, Yvette rose from her chair, then lifted her valise onto the bed. Once she'd opened the clasp, she rummaged around inside, occasionally placing various items on the bed. She muttered, "Where is it? I know I packed it."

"Yvette, I'll check with you before I retire." Ewan followed Fergus out the door. He paused on the threshold. "Lock the door, and whatever you do, don't open it for anyone but me."

Twelve

Not quite an hour later, attired in a chaste white nightgown and robe, Yvette sat brushing her hair. She'd finally found her brush at the bottom of her valise. A knock rattled the chamber door, and she paused mid-stroke. "Who is it?"

A familiar chuckle echoed beyond the door. "Well done. Now open up. I need a moment with you."

Setting the hairbrush on the table, Yvette stood. Barefoot, she padded to the door, tying her robe more securely before turning the key. Opening the door a fraction, she peeked at Ewan.

"Vixen." Lifting a brow, he slanted his handsome mouth into a sardonic grin. "I've no intention of conversing with you through *that* gap. Let me in. I need to speak with you." He winked. "I promise to behave."

She retreated a step as he pushed into the room, leaving the door ajar. His hair was damp, no doubt from bathing, and the stubble darkening his face earlier had been shaved. Feet bare, wearing only buckskin breeches and a shirt unbuttoned to the waist, he resembled a pirate.

A dangerous. Rakish. Sinfully handsome pirate.

She sucked in her breath.

He oughtn't to be here, but he'd said he wanted to speak to her. And he had promised to behave.

Yvette's gaze traveled the path of silky hair from his chest until it disappeared into his waistband, and her stomach flip-flopped.

Why didn't he say something?

She pressed her hands to her frolicking middle.

A distraction.

That was what she needed. She escaped to the lumpy bed where she'd flung her clothing before bathing. After folding and packing the garments into her valise, she set it on the floor beside her trunk. Bending to retrieve her bath towel from the floor, she peeked side-ways from the corner of her eye.

Ewan hadn't moved. What was he about?

Grabbing the towel, Yvette glanced downward and froze. The candles to her left bathed her in a stream of light, and she could clearly see the outline of her legs. Her night-wear was almost translucent in the candlelight and gave him a shadowy view of—*dear God*—nearly everything.

No wonder he hadn't moved, the rogue.

Standing upright, she clutched the towel to her middle and faced him. "Enjoying the view, your lordship?" she snapped.

"Immeasurably."

Ewan rested a shoulder against the doorframe, his expression unreadable, but alarming nonetheless.

Her anger gave way to nervousness. His relaxed posture contrasted sharply with the predatory gleam in his eyes. She tried a different tack. With calmness she was nowhere near feeling, she said, "You said you wished to speak with me?"

"Indeed, I did." He remained motionless except for his eyes, which burned a scorching path from her neckline to her toes and slowly upward again, lingering on her arms folded across her breasts.

She tapped her bare foot in annoyance. "Well?"

He straightened, then closed the door. His long strides made short work of the distance between them.

Yvette scooted around to the other side of the bed. Better to have something between them with *that* glint in his eye. Why had she been so foolish as to let him in?

Because he promised to behave, fool.

Her mouth sagged when he didn't stop, but came around the bed, advancing slowly and sinuously, until his thighs were pressed against her quaking ones. His chest scant inches from hers, he plucked the towel from her shaking hands.

And that gleam in his eyes?

She'd seen that look before.

In Belle-mére's cat's eyes.

Right before it pounced on an unsuspecting butterfly— and gobbled the poor thing up.

Sucking her lower lip into her mouth and nibbling it in her confusion, Yvette peered at Ewan

He most definitely was *not* behaving.

She didn't have much experience—any experience, truth to tell—with half-clothed men in her bedchamber, but the smoldering look in Ewan's eyes was unmistakable. Spellbound by the mesmerizing promise in the depths of his eyes, she couldn't speak. Her senses sprang to life, whispering a cautious warning.

In a rush, she blurted, "Your lordship, it's most improper for you to be in my chamber. I'm not suitably attired."

A wicked smile curved his mouth. "I've seen you in less."

The husky timbre of his voice rippled over her flesh, raising the hairs. He had, but he was a boor for reminding her.

The whispering increased, transforming into a shrieking alarm in her head. Merciful God, his eyes devoured her.

No indeed, this *was not* good behavior.

He moved an inch closer.

Not acceptable behavior by *any* measure.

His hard groin pressed against her soft womanhood. Arching away from him, Yvette became frantic. She wasn't sure she could resist his advances. And more terrifyingly, did she want to?

"Lord Seth—"

With lightning speed, Ewan encompassed her in an embrace of velvet iron. He didn't attempt anything other than holding her in his arms, stroking her back with one hand. Nevertheless, she struggled against the steely band, more afraid of herself, of her response to him, than anything he might do.

"Ewan," she gasped, levering her arms between them.

She searched his eyes, and all the while, he gently caressed her.

He bent and kissed her on the nose. "I adore your freckles."

You do?

She went squashy inside.

"Don't be afraid," he whispered.

The strong hand caressing Yvette's spine calmed her, erasing her uneasiness, and she relaxed against him. So great was her relief, and so wonderful Ewan's touch soothing away her tension, she almost purred in contentment.

Sighing, she closed her eyes and pressed closer to him.

"*Ma belle?*" He spoke against her hair. Actually, he nuzzled her head in the most delicious way.

Tilting her head, she recognized the hunger in his eyes. Her breath hitched. He wanted to kiss her, yet hesitated. He was letting her choose.

Chin tilted, she offered him her mouth.

Lowering his head, Ewan hovered over her lips as if in anticipation, then captured her mouth in a scorching kiss. The fierceness of the sensual assault stunned her, trapping her in a swirling kaleidoscope of passion, the torrent of sensation stripping away her defenses.

She returned his kiss with a longing she hadn't known she possessed.

He eased her onto the mattress, continuing his tender assault on her overwhelmed senses. Rendered incapable of resisting, she could only feel, respond, and savor these delightful new sensations.

Yvette had bewitched Ewan.

His logical, controlled mind had been taken over by his desire for the woman in his arms. Yvette's innocent responses added fuel to his passion's fire. Rubbing his face alongside her soft neck, he inhaled her floral scent, and nuzzled the tender skin.

"So soft. You smell good."

She moaned, arching against him.

Relishing her pleasure-flushed face, he smoothed his

hand over the indentation of her waist, drawing the silky material of her gown up, up, up, until the luscious curve of her satiny hip lay exposed to him.

Her robe fell open at the waist, exposing the fullness of her breasts above her nightgown.

Her nails bit into his shoulders.

Ewan trailed his fingers along the supple swells and claimed her mouth in a searing, promising kiss as he skimmed his hand along her hip.

"Ewan," she groaned against his lips.

An intoxicated reveler bellowed his drunken displeasure beneath the chamber's open window.

Yvette stiffened, twisting her mouth free of his.

"Stop." She pushed at her nightgown, forcing his hand from her. "I... We can't do this. It's wrong."

Ewan ceased his loving ministrations. Raking in ragged gulps of air, he rested his forehead against hers, trying to curb the lust raging through his body. He willed his labored breathing to return to normal, even as he commanded his body to resist the temptress lying beside him.

Drawing back, he searched her face, then silently cursed.

Unshed tears glittered in her luminous blue eyes, and her lips trembled from her effort not to cry.

He raised onto his elbows and with one hand, swept her silky hair away from her face. With his forefinger, he caught the solitary salty bead escaping from the corner of her eye.

Yvette squirmed from beneath him, then scooched across the saggy feather tick where she sat, regarding him with mournful eyes. Shifting her tearful gaze away, pale cheeks dashed crimson, she whispered, "I'm sorry. I..." She picked at the lace trim of her gown. "I believe such intimacies are meant for... should be saved for marriage."

"You've no need to be sorry."

"I don't know what happened to me." She released a shuddery sigh. "You kissed me, and I remembered naught. I've never... What I mean is, I don't... No man has..."

Her words trailed off as he crept the distance between them. Bit by bit, so he wouldn't alarm her, Ewan reached out and took her hand in his. "It's I who should be begging your forgiveness."

Pressing her hand to his heart in a simple gesture, but solemn with meaning, he vowed to her, "I promise, I'll strive to never put you in a compromising position again. I too forget all else when you're in my arms."

She peeked at him from beneath her spiky lashes. "We're not married. We shouldn't have."

"We did naught but kiss." He released her hand, and she tucked it beneath her thigh. "There's much more to completing the... ah... intimacy between a man and woman."

"Truly?" Hope brightened her tone and eyes.

Grinning, he tweaked her nose. "Truly, minx." His heart tumbled over his ribs as he gazed into her sapphire eyes. He hopped off the bed then cocked his head to one side, eyeing her. A tuft of hair fell forward on his brow, and he brushed it aside. "I suppose if I'm to keep my word, I must leave you."

Ewan strode to the door and contorted his mouth into a silly, lopsided smile. "*Bonne nuit, bien-aimée.*"

She graced him with a beatific smile. "Goodnight, Ewan. Sleep well."

Sleep? Not bloody likely.

Instead of seeking his own bed, he made his way to the icy stream behind the inn. Stripping naked, he plunged into the frigid water.

A movement in the shadows caught his eye.
He stiffened.
Animal or human?

Thirteen

Yvette veered Ewan a sideways glance.

More than once today she'd caught him observing her with an assessing glint in his eyes. He stared out the window of the coach, apparently watching the passing scenery. A muscle ticked in his jaw, revealing some hidden agitation. Surely, he'd prefer to ride —she would've—yet he kept her company in the cramped coach.

Poor Peggy had been most reluctant to take her seat atop the coach this morning. Still a trifle pale, she'd muttered, "Blimey, me insides are still achurnin' from yesterday." She eyed the coach, her distaste apparent. "How many more days?"

"At least three more," Yvette said sympathetically.

Peggy's face turned a shade greener. "Three? Blast and bugger me."

Angling her head to better view Ewan, Yvette smiled. She rather liked his hawkish profile. Her focus fell to the small scar on his face. How had he come by it?

As if alerted to her scrutiny, Ewan turned his head and

caught her perusal. The smoldering smile he bestowed on her sent the mild fluttering in her middle into a frenzied vortex, but only for an instant. She hadn't forgotten the scene at Banbury Inn, and he'd made it clear theirs was a temporary arrangement.

Again, her gaze swept over Ewan, now reabsorbed in the passing landscape.

She knew next to nothing about him. Was he a rake as she had first suspected? A fortune hunter? She worried her lower lip. Would he use her physical attraction to him to manipulate her—to entice her into his bed?

Yvette sank further into the corner, trying to ignore her tumultuous thoughts.

The soldiers parted their company that afternoon, and the next two days of travel proved uneventful, and thankfully much cooler. They passed through villages and towns, some barely large enough to boast a pub, and others offering amenities of every sort.

Ewan had lowered one of the windows, and a light breeze caressed her.

"I'm grateful it has cooled to a more tolerable temperature." Gazing out the window, Yvette fanned herself. The breeze wafting along the road ruffled the tall wispy grasses, tickled dangling viridian leaves, and spun rainbows of wildflowers into languid pathways of streaming color. "Isn't it beautiful?"

"Aye, it's something to behold," he agreed.

His tone drew her attention into the carriage.

He stared at her with a look she had begun to recognize. *Desire.*

She smiled, though color bathed her cheeks, and squirmed at the tingling that began in her belly before creeping lower.

Lord, what he did to her with those eyes.

She sought to divert his attention. "I've not purchased a gift for Vangie's baby yet."

"You'll find the perfect memento to commemorate the babe's birth in Middleham," Ewan assured her.

Their coach-and-four rolled into the dusty township the third day of travel, and he directed Malcolm to stop the carriage so Yvette could shop for the baby's gift.

Peggy clambered from atop the coach the minute the vehicle stopped moving. Clutching her stomach and groaning, she tottered to an oak tree a short distance away, slid to the ground, and collapsed against the trunk.

"Peggy, can I get you anything? Some water perhaps? I can sit with you until you feel better." Yvette admired the plucky girl. Traveling aboard the coach didn't agree with her, and she'd been ill from the start, yet she hadn't complained.

Peggy swallowed and closed her eyes, waving her hand weakly. "Naw, go on with ye. I just needs to sit a spell, miss."

"Should we leave her?" Yvette arched Ewan a questioning glance.

He nodded. "I'll have Carmichael keep an eye on her. Besides, we won't be long."

Reluctant to leave the ill girl, Yvette vacillated. "If you're quite sure, Peggy?"

"Aye, miss," Peggy mumbled, already half-asleep.

Ewan's hand at her elbow, Yvette wandered the town's lanes. She stopped to admire a jewelry store's window display.

"Ewan, there toward the back. It's a silver baby's rattle. Oh, look at the scrolling on the handle." She pressed her forehead against the glass, straining to see the trinket. "May we go—?"

"Do you wish to go—?" He stepped closer, looking at where she pointed.

They'd spoken at the same time, and she giggled.

His hearty chuckle blended with her laughter.

"Yes, I would love to go inside." Nodding, she swiftly turned, plowing into him. She would've fallen if he hadn't caught her by her upper arms. Flushing, she muttered, "I'm sorry, I thought you'd moved."

"A wee bit eager to see the toy, are ye?" he murmured, his brogue unusually thick.

She peeked at him.

He smiled and gave her a playful wink. He was teasing her.

Yvette happily returned his smile, her embarrassment evaporating.

Ewan extended his elbow, and she looped her hand through it as they entered the unassuming shop.

A bell tinkled overhead, alerting the jeweler, and he glanced up from his ledger. "I'll be right with you."

She ambled to the window display and, locating the rattle, lifted the trinket from its satin nest. Even lovelier than she had first thought. An etched lamb graced the rounded surface on one side above a beautifully crafted ornate handle. Rotating it, she ran her fingertip over a rectangular, flattened area free from decoration.

"It's meant for an inscription. Perhaps your infant's name?"

The rasping voice of the stoop-shouldered shopkeeper jarred Yvette. She hadn't heard him sidle up beside her.

Startled at his incorrect suggestion, she sought Ewan.

An unabashed grin stretched clear to his ears.

Scarlet heat dashed up her face. Pretending absorption in the rattle, she dared a swift glance at him from beneath half-closed lids.

He caught the perusal and lowered one lid in a knowing wink.

Why, he seems pleased with the notion.

"It's lovely indeed. However, the rattle is a gift. I'd like an inscription, but we're traveling through." Her eyes met Ewan's over the jeweler's head.

Ewan rubbed his jaw. "How long would it take to inscribe the toy?"

"Oh, it's a simple matter. I could have it engraved and polished in under half an hour." The skinny man looked between her and Ewan, obviously unsure whom he was supposed to address.

"We've time enough," Ewan assured her.

Yvette smiled her gratitude while glancing around the charming shop. A carousel atop a shelf behind a cluttered countertop stood out like a shining beacon. The fascinating toy drew her across the compact room.

Noting her keen interest, the shopkeeper hurried behind the jumbled counter, then reached overhead to take the extraordinary treasure down.

"This is one-of-a-kind, missus."

The jeweler wound the knob on the marble base, and the carousel slowly spun. Awed, Yvette stared at the six intricately-carved miniature horses prancing before her. Meticulous workmanship had gone into adorning the rotating equines, which appeared carved from semi-precious stones.

Engrossed in the merry-go-round, she only gave Ewan a cursory glance when he moved to a display case across the room. The shop's doorbell clanked, and she veered her gaze to the entrance for a moment as a fashionable man and woman entered. Another clerk appeared from behind a faded curtain and hurried over to assist the new patrons.

As Yvette touched a silver braid affixed lengthways on the toy's base, she sensed eyes boring into her. Angling her head, she met the piercing, obsidian-eyed stare of a cropped-haired beauty. A shadow flitted across the woman's face, so fleeting Yvette almost believed she had imagined it. Her attention swerved to the man absorbed in the window display.

When she looked back at the woman, the newcomer's smoky eyes strayed to the now-silent carousel. The lady issued a throaty, "It's, how you say, *favoloso carosello*, no?"

Smiling, Yvette replied in perfect Italian, "*Si tratta di un giocattolo più straordinario musical davvero.*" True. The carousel was an extraordinary musical toy.

For an ephemeral moment, a look of astonishment appeared on the woman's face before she shuttered it under mask-like poise.

"Shall I wrap it for you, your ladyship?" asked the solicitous beanpole-of-a-gem-dealer.

Returning her focus to the jeweler, Yvette smiled her acquiescence. "Yes, please, but it's miss, not your ladyship."

His ears turning scarlet, the shopkeeper dipped his head, chagrined. "I beg your pardon, miss. You and his lordship seem so..."

His words trailed off into awkward silence.

She couldn't bear his pitiful countenance. Pray God in his goodness would forgive her for the falsehood she was about to utter. "You're not so very wrong. We're recently betrothed."

A slice of truth there—the recent part anyway.

He gleefully slapped the countertop so hard it vibrated

the span of its marred surface. Considering how frail he appeared, his strength rather surprised Yvette. His face split into a grin so enormous his beetle brows half hid his merry eyes. "It's easy to see you are *trés amoureux,* in love."

Yvette repressed a smile, for his French was appalling. As was his observation.

In love? Ridiculous.

Scandalized, the jeweler's focus dipped to her hand. "You've no ring?" His milky eyes searched hers.

A wretched ache poking her middle, she stared at the counter.

Bother it all. How utterly mortifying.

Ewan's deep voice interjected from behind her, startling her again. "I prefer the Scots tradition of presenting my betrothed with a Luckenbooth brooch."

In his hand, he held a spectacular pin—two entwined silver hearts encrusted with vibrant marquise-shaped sapphires, glistening garnets, and diamonds. A dazzling ruby graced the center.

Brows drawn together in bafflement, Yvette's attention traveled from the amazing token to Ewan's beaming face and back again. What was he thinking, for pity's sake?

A confident smile kicking up one corner of his mouth, Ewan addressed the jeweler. "I'd like this engraved too."

He doesn't need to carry our masquerade this far.

"Certainly, your lordship," eagerly agreed the gem dealer. "Hanley, please wrap the lady's selection," he said. "I must see to the inscriptions."

Excusing himself from the other couple, the clerk hurried over to do as his employer bade.

"Miss?" the storekeeper inquired. "What would you like inscribed on the rattle?

Yvette contemplated for a moment. "Gift of God."

"Indeed," crowed the scrawny man.

"Most fitting, Yvette," Ewan murmured in her ear.

Pleased by his approval, she smiled.

"And you, your lordship?" The jeweler peered at Ewan expectantly.

Yvette glanced across the room, and her breath caught, hanging suspended in her lungs for an interminable, prickly moment. The Italian creature had her gaze fixed on Ewan, and something akin to loathing laced with yearning glimmered the ebony pools.

Her swarthy companion's scowl wasn't as complex.

Pure, unadulterated distaste—aimed straight at Ewan.

Gripping the beauty by the arm, the man swung her around, hissing under his breath. Even though he spoke quietly, Yvette's ears burned. She clearly heard the last few words of their heated exchange.

"*Controllati*, Pauline."

Control yourself?

"Miss, would you like me to pack the carousel in straw to protect it?" The clerk peered at her eagerly.

Yvette tore her gaze away from the quarrelling couple, her skin crawling from their exchange. She shuddered, then rubbed her arms, suddenly chilled.

"Yes, please. I don't want it damaged during the remainder of our journey."

"Do you have far to go?" Hanley asked conversationally as he tended to the packaging.

She cast a cursory glance at the arguing pair. The woman had become so agitated, her abrupt movements threatened to send the slew of vibrant feathers on her bonnet aloft.

However, the gentleman appeared unaffected. His dark

eyes hooded, he raised a soft, white hand to smooth his mustache.

Taking care to lower her voice, Yvette answered. "A bit farther, on to my cousin's in Northumberland." She was reluctant to reveal her final destination.

Moments later, still issuing a frenetic tirade in Italian, the exotic woman flounced from the shop in a swirl of magenta skirts. Leveling Yvette an inscrutable stare, her companion followed at a more sedate pace.

The clerk finished arranging the carousel in its plush straw nest within a stout box. A few minutes more, and the jeweler returned with two wrapped parcels. He handed one to her and the other to Ewan. Once she'd tucked hers inside her reticule, she reached for the carousel. The bony shopkeep lifted the treasure and gingerly passed it to her waiting arms.

"Allow me to carry the box for you," Ewan offered after tucking his package into his coat's inner pocket.

Yvette sent him a grateful smile. "Thank you. It's rather heavy."

"What say you, rather than walking to the carriage, we first dine at that charming eatery?" His gloved finger emerged from beneath the package, pointing to the café across the street.

Yvette nodded. "Oh, yes. I'm quite hungry."

Tucking the toy beneath one arm, he extended his other to Yvette. Without hesitation, she slipped her hand into the crook.

"Vangie will be thrilled with the carousel." She stepped into the street and half-turned to face him. "Did you notice the sculpted details on the horses? I do believe one is carved from jasper and another from onyx."

"*Merde!*"

Without warning, Ewan suddenly jerked his arm away from her hand. Seizing her by the waist, he roughly hoisted her off her feet as he leaped backward.

Yvette emitted a strangled shriek as a gilded barouche, pulled by four pitch-black horses, roared past, so close the wind brushed her face.

Sweet Jesus, that was too close by far.

Surely, she'd seen a hint of fuchsia through the swaying window shades. No, no. Nothing so dramatic. Fright had her light-headed—that was all. She tried taking a deep, calming breath but an unyielding band still encircled her middle.

She surveyed her sore waist.

Ewan's crushing grip held her suspended in the air.

Yvette tapped his forearm. "You can put me down now."

He didn't respond except to let her slide down the length of his rigid body until her feet rested on the ground. Somehow he'd managed to retain his hold on the carousel too.

Trembling, she arched her neck, seeking his eyes.

His gaze remained trained on the dusty cloud obscuring the speeding carriage. A muscle ticked in his clenched jaw, keeping perfect time with a vein pulsing in his temple.

Eyes widening, Yvette gaped at him.

He was enraged—no, absolutely furious.

"Ewan?"

He swept her a calm, if somewhat veiled, look. "Come along. People are staring, and we're drawing a crowd."

A surprising number of passersby had stopped to gawk.

Mr. Carmichael plowed through the assembled oglers, making his way to Ewan's side. "Lord Sethwick, are you both uninjured? I saw the carriage from the other end of the street and shouted a warning."

Perplexed, she turned to Carmichael.

What warning?

Giving an affirmative nod, Ewan handed the package to his aide. "Please take this to the coach and have Malcolm bring the carriage round to the café, just there." With a slant of his head, he indicated their intended destination. "And, please, do join us for supper." His gaze roved the area. "You and Peggy both."

Though politely worded, Yvette recognized it wasn't as much a request as an order.

Peggy made her way to Yvette's side and clasped her hand. "Lawks, I was afeared the both of ye were done in, I was."

Unusually subdued when they resumed their journey, Yvette kept replaying the frightening incident in her mind. Having a team of horses nearly trample you had that effect. As much as she was loath to admit it, she'd no choice but to concede the runaway carriage hadn't been accidental.

More than once before darkness descended, shrouding the park-carriage in inky oblivion, she peered out the window and scanned the road behind them. How Peggy could prefer riding atop in the gloom was beyond her.

Yvette insisted on holding her hatbox, which, unbeknownst to Ewan, contained a custom-made, ivory-handled pistol, in addition to several other items she deemed essential to their safety. Tilting the lid open only enough to slip her hand inside, she ran her fingers over the cool handle.

Though she'd fired the pistol dozens of times, her target had never been human.

If the time came, would she be able to pull the trigger?

Fourteen

Early the next morning, amid the serenades of sleepy songbirds, a reticent Ewan handed Yvette into the carriage. They would reach Somersfield by nightfall, bringing an end to their sojourn.

For the first several miles of travel along the arid road, he remained uncharacteristically quiet, his countenance not quite stern but not relaxed either.

The countryside had become increasingly hot and dusty, and the carriage left a gritty cloud in its wake. Yvette sneezed, then sneezed twice more. "Please excuse me. It must be the dust."

Rummaging inside her reticule, she finally retrieved her scented hanky. A few moments later, after she'd blown her nose, she replaced the lacy bit of fabric, and her hand brushed against the wrapped rattle. Within its cozy confines, the paper crackled in protest.

Yvette removed the package and gave in to the temptation to unwrap the trinket. The morning sun's soft glow bathed the silver orb in radiant light. The bright beam deflected straight into Ewan's eyes.

"What are you attempting, to blind me?" Chuckling, Ewan took the rattle. He shook it at her before turning it over and running a finger along the engraving. "It's a most fitting inscription."

Preoccupied by the caressing strokes of his hand, she only distantly heard him.

"Do you like children?" he asked rather unexpectedly. "Large families?"

"Uh hum." Yvette nodded. "Very much, actually. I disliked being an only child. I'd have adored having a younger brother or sister." She stifled another sneeze behind her hand. "My childhood would've been awfully lonely if it weren't for the twins and Vangie."

"Twins?"

"Yes, Josiah and Isaiah Fairchild. Their father has been our family butler since I was two. The twins are like brothers to me."

Ewan rotated the rattle in his hand. "You and Vangie are very close too, aren't you?"

"Yes, more like sisters, really." Yvette rubbed the end of her nose. "She was orphaned when she was quite young. Papa wanted her to come live with us, but there was some stipulation in her father's will that prevented it." She scrunched her forehead, trying to recall the details. "Something to do with her Romani clan." She curved her mouth ruefully. "In any event, life wasn't easy for her."

"Aye, it's never easy for an orphan. My village, Craig-cutty, has several, as does Craiglocky Keep, including my stepfather's relatives." Ewan passed the rattle to her, his roughened hand trailing across the inside of her wrist.

Thoroughly distracted by his touch's lingering effect, Yvette stared at his hands. Though his nails were neatly trimmed, his palms bore calluses.

"I hope to have several children. If the good Lord sees fit, that is." Giving him a sunny smile, she smoothed her skirt across her lap. "I've always wanted a large family—should I ever decide to wed."

"You don't want to marry?" Ewan canted his head, his expression inscrutable.

Something in his tone gave her pause. "I should like to someday, but—"

She doubted he'd understand her reluctance to become a man's chattel with only the rights a benevolent husband might grant her. *Or might not.* She hunched her shoulders dismissively.

"In any event, I've yet to find the man who finds more favor with me than my father's fortune." Glancing at him, and observing the three creases lining his forehead, Yvette pointedly changed the subject. "What of you, Ewan? Do you have any siblings?"

A broad grin split his face and lit his eyes. "Aye, I do indeed. I've three younger sisters and a brother who's just seen his six-and-tenth birthday."

"Four? How wonderful." She clasped her hands against her chest. "Tell me about them."

He tossed his hat onto the seat and, once he'd removed his riding coat, unbuttoned his waistcoat before resuming his story.

"Adaira, the eldest, is two score and fiercely independent. And I might add, loath to wear skirts. More often than not, she's astride her stallion, dressed in leather breeches—much to my French mother's horror."

In the process of removing her bonnet, Yvette gaped at him, incredulous. "She wears breeches? Truly?"

"Aye, more often than skirts."

Could she ever be that daring? To ride astride and wear breeches?

No, perhaps not breeches. But could she defy convention and stay unwed if she never found love?

"My middle sister, Isobel, was eight-and-ten her last birthday and has every swain in five shires at her beck and call. She's brilliant, though, and considers them inferior intellectually."

Ewan paused in his narrative to adjust his position on the seat. "It's an immense family secret, but Isobel wears spectacles, no doubt from reading excessively." His brogue more pronounced, he lowered his voice to a conspiratorial whisper. "You have to promise not to tell."

Tell? Lord, no.

Yvette wore spectacles when she read, too. Should she tell him?

Perhaps not quite yet.

Bobbing her head in agreement, she vowed, "I'll not say a word."

"I was but teasing." He chucked her chin and chuckled, that delicious low rumble that caused all sorts of things to frolic about inside her.

Dratted man.

To hide her discomfiture, she asked, "What of the others?"

"My youngest sister, Seonaid, is a trifle bashful, with an extraordinary affinity for animals. Both wild and domestic animals alike let her tend them. She also has the second sight, a prophetic gift, not unusual in Scots women.

"Second sight." Yvette gaped at him once more. "You mean she *knows* things?"

Ewan nodded, stretching his legs before him. "Aye, and she's not often wrong."

"My word," breathed Yvette, enthralled.

"Then there's Dugall, a rascally whelp if there ever was one." Ewan laughed outright and shook his head. "He'll be breaking many a bonnie lass's heart."

As you have?

Hounds' teeth. Where did that come from?

Yvette mentally shook herself. "Your childhood must've been very happy."

His eyes darkening and taking on a far-off look, he gave a slow nod. "There's no place like Craiglochy. Scots protect their own with a loyalty and devotion foreign and incomprehensible to outsiders."

His face softened and reverence colored his voice when he spoke of his keep. He must've noticed her wide-eyed expression, because he shook his head and quirked the corners of his lips skyward. "I get sentimental when I speak of my home. Forgive me."

"There's nothing at all to forgive. I should very much like to see your home one day."

"Nothing would please me more." His subtle smile and the timbre of his voice held a promise.

Yvette bent her mouth in response. She'd done an awful lot of smiling these past days. "What of your parents. Are they alive?"

"Father drowned when I was in nappies. I don't recall him at all, but Mother says I resemble him. She eventually wed Hugh Ferguson, my father's best friend. Theirs is a sweet love story in the telling."

"I should like to hear it. Will you tell me, please?"

Ewan proceeded to do so until they stopped at Cross Keys Inn for a fresh team of horses and to eat a light repast. Several times, Mr. Carmichael rode past the carriage, and each time, Ewan's eyes shadowed further, and he became tenser with each passing mile.

Oh, a casual observer mightn't notice his edginess, but attuned to him as she'd become, Yvette recognized the signs: stiffly-held shoulders, flaring nostrils, and the familiar tick in his jaw, whitening his scythe-shaped scar. Speaking about his family hadn't caused his stress either, for he obviously enjoyed sharing about them.

Ewan appeared as anxious as Yvette to resume their travels now that their destination was near, and they didn't dawdle at Cross Keys. He escorted her from the inn to a post chaise waiting in the stable, and her steps faltered.

He looked too serious by far.

"Ewan, whatever—?"

He didn't permit her to finish. "I've arranged for a post chaise to take us the remaining leg of our journey, Evvy."

She knitted her brows. "Why must we switch carriages?"

"It's simply a precautionary measure." As he spoke, he and Mr. Carmichael transferred the smaller luggage to the hackney. This was done in the covert privacy of the inn's stables, out of public site, with the drivers standing watch at both entrances.

Her gaze traveled between the coach and hackney. "My trunk?"

"Will remain with the park carriage," Ewan said. "It's too noticeable if we transfer it to this vehicle."

Yvette observed them in silence for a few moments, her ire rising with each passing minute. Did he think to keep her in the dark?

Ewan curved his lips into a thin, forced smile before indicating the dusty hackney with a tilt of his head. "Carmichael will attend the empty carriage, which will take another more commonly traveled route to Somersfield. We shall take a shorter, somewhat bumpier road I usually use when traveling on horseback. He'll meet us at Somersfield."

Yvette crossed her arms and shook her head. "I'm not getting in that," she flung her hand in the hackney's direction, "until you tell me what's going on."

Ewan's eyebrows scampered up his high forehead, and he shot Mr. Carmichael a flummoxed glance before shifting his gaze to her once more. "I'm sure you're aware the carriage that nearly ran us down yesterday did so intentionally."

Scowling, she snorted. "I'm not bird-witted, Ewan."

"We're being followed." He handed Mr. Carmichael the boxed carousel.

"I presumed as much, but why ever didn't you say something earlier?" She eyed the carousel as Mr. Carmichael placed it inside the rented chaise.

"I didn't want to worry you." Ewan passed the aide her valise.

Yvette's scorching glare would've ignited tinder. "Are you completely daft? My parents were poisoned. I survived that attempt on my life, as well as a near-fatal riding accident, and I fought off Edgar twice. Did I tell you I stabbed him the first time?" She extended her hatbox to Mr. Carmichael.

He took it from her, an appreciative grin on his face.

"Thank you," she murmured before launching into Ewan once more. "I fled Boston in the middle of the night with scant more than the clothes I wore. I crossed an ocean —in the company of Mrs. Pettigrove, no less—and was chased on London's docks upon disembarking. Edgar broke into my chamber the very night I arrived in England, and yesterday, a team of horses nearly trampled us."

"Evvy—" Ewan touched her arm, but she shook off his hand.

"And *you* didn't want me to worry?" Her voice rose to an unladylike shout. "I'm way beyond worry, you arrogant, beef-brained dolt!"

Mr. Carmichael guffawed, and Ewan speared him a fierce scowl.

Hands on her hips, she glared at Ewan. "Just because I don't choose to be confrontational, and I find being affable much more pleasant than being contentious doesn't mean that I want to be coddled and protected. My God," she jabbed him with her fan, "I've had a lifetime of being smothered and protected."

Ewan canted his head. "Your point," his gaze sank to the fan she still brandished like a dagger, "is well taken. I promise to keep you more informed." Still grinning, he did just that. "I sent a messenger ahead to notify Ian and Vangie of our arrival today."

Peggy entered the stable and stumbled to an abrupt halt. She looked first to Ewan, then Yvette, confusion etched across her plain face.

"Why be there two?" She motioned to both conveyances.

"We will complete our journey in this one." Ewan indicated the hackney with a sweep of his hand.

Peggy vehemently shook her head. "I won't. I told ye, me stomach..." She grimaced at the hackney with something akin to abhorrence. "I ain't had an easy time of it atop ta other one." She pointed at the chaise. "And I ain't gettin' in that one."

Yvette and Ewan tried their best to persuade her, but Peggy refused to go on. Delaying their departure, he paid her and made arrangements for her return to London.

Yvette hugged the girl. "Thank you. I know you've had a difficult time of it."

Peggy wiped tears from her eyes. "I tried, miss, I truly did. I couldn't do no more." She snuffled and blew her nose in the handkerchief Mr. Carmichael gave her. "Me stomach's been turned inside-out since we left London."

"I know, and I appreciate you coming this far, as miserable as you've been." Sympathy for Peggy's plight did nothing to ease Yvette's misgivings. Now she'd no choice but to complete the last portion of their journey without a chaperone.

"Good luck to ye, miss," sniffled Peggy before she turned and walked into the inn.

Yvette drew in a deep breath. There was no help for it. Facing Mr. Carmichael as he patiently held the carriage door open, she offered a courageous half-smile. "Thank you for taking this precaution for us. I'm sure it's an inconvenience."

"No inconvenience, Miss Stapleton." Shaking his head, he cupped her elbow to assist her into the carriage, but she paused with one foot atop the step.

"How much farther to Somersfield?"

"Three hours, mayhap a bit more."

Giving a brief nod, Yvette climbed into the conveyance. Though clean, constant use had rendered the interior shabby, and the equipage lacked the luxurious padded seats and well-sprung undercarriage of the park coach. She crinkled her nose and pulled her skirts a mite higher. From the sour smell permeating the vehicle, a previous passenger had cast up their accounts on the scratched and scarred floor.

Outside the hackney, Ewan spoke quietly to Mr. Carmichael.

Yvette strained to hear. Not that she was given to eavesdropping, mind you, but she was most curious. She edged toward the doorway.

"Park the carriage before the inn and make a pretense of convincing anyone watching that Miss Stapleton and I've already boarded. I've arranged to have a basket of food sent along. Hopefully, any spectators will be convinced we are within. Put it inside, and tell Malcolm I've requested the shades drawn for some privacy with my betrothed."

More than a little flustered, Yvette drew herself up. That arrangement would surely to tarnish her character.

She snorted in self-derision.

One moment she'd determined to maintain her independence, and the next, she lamented her decisions, fearing the marks against her reputation would hinder any opportunity for a good match. Still, prudence suggested she ought to leave her options open, and therefore her reputation must remain intact at all cost.

Marriage wasn't completely out of the question, but she wasn't entering the parson's mousetrap until she was ready and the conditions acceptable.

Vangie's marriage had been forced. She and Ian had bitterly protested the union, and afterward, Vangie had run off to her Romani clan.

Yvette was determined to love her husband *before* she married him. She'd no desire to endure the heartbreak Vangie had.

She and Ewan left the inn a full half-hour before Mr. Carmichael was to follow the empty coach from the courtyard and down the road in the opposite direction. After a few teeth-jarring miles, she raised the hackney's shades and shoved a window open. She looked pointedly at Ewan.

"You're not riding in here the remainder of the journey."

Giving her a boyish grin, he canted his head. "No?"

"No." She pounded on the roof with her fist, and the vehicle lurched to a bumpy stop. "My reputation is already in shreds, but I won't willingly contribute to my utter ruination." She jerked her thumb toward the door. "Out with you.

"The devil you say." Humor danced in his eyes. "I'm to ride outside?"

"Yes." Yvette lifted her chin and squared her shoulders.

"Very well." Chuckling good-naturedly, he hopped from the carriage. After shutting the door, he poked his head through the window. "You're quite sure?"

"Quite." She tamped down her urge to smile.

A moment later, the vehicle tipped as he climbed onto the driver's seat.

Yvette breathed a sigh of relief. That had gone much smoother than expected.

The hackney lurched forward, and she clutched the carriage's shabby bench to keep from losing her seat. The coachmen's skills left much to be desired. Though inept drivers, the fellows were cheerful chaps. They sang one naughty ditty after another at the top of their coarse voices.

And Ewan's baritone accompanied them several times.

Her face flamed more than once as crude taproom lyrics echoed over the rough road. The constant jarring churned her stomach, and bile rose to the back of her throat. As the coach plunged into another large pothole, her teeth snapped together painfully. She clutched the seat once again, certain her jaw and behind would be tender for a week.

Regarding the former, she shifted gingerly. "Probably covered with bruises."

Peggy had made a very wise decision.

Almost four hours later, the carriage turned into the

lengthy drive announcing their arrival onto Somersfield's grounds. An elaborate stone archway bade them entry to the estate.

As the post chaise squeaked and protested its way down the well-tended, rambling lane, excitement and anticipation had Yvette practically bouncing on the tattered seat.

The hackney rounded a corner, and in the distance, the mansion rose resplendently into view. Leaning forward to peer out the window, Yvette spied people standing atop the manor's steps.

Vangie and Ian awaited their arrival.

The conveyance rumbled to a stop, and Yvette scooted to the seat's edge. Impatient to reunite with her cousin, she reached for the door handle, but Ewan was there first and swung the door open. As Yvette stepped from the coach, her toe caught on the hem of her gown, and she tumbled headlong from the carriage.

"Oh!"

"*Oomph.*" Ewan caught her behind her shoulders and under her knees, her hat's feather smacking him across his nose.

She sliced him a quick, mortified glance and found humor crinkling his eyes. A bit of her embarrassment eased, and she veered a glance at her cousins.

Jaw slack, Vangie gawked at them, but a scowl lined Ian's brow as his knowing gaze traveled between Yvette and Ewan.

"Pray tell me why you're still holding my wife's cousin, Sethwick?"

Yvette in his arms and a wide grin on his handsome face, Ewan faced them.

"It's all right. We're betrothed."

Fifteen

Thirty minutes later, Yvette sat sipping tea beside Vangie on a settee. Ewan and Ian relaxed in a pair of matching armchairs on either side of an ornate fireplace.

"So, you see, we'd no choice but to fake a betrothal." Yvette flashed Ewan a glance upon concluding the abbreviated and less scandalous version of why they pretended to be affianced.

He seemed completely unperturbed at her glaring chagrin or the situation's awkwardness.

Uncertainty shadowing her eyes, Vangie gave a slow nod. "Yes, I do see how it became necessary, but—"

"I take full responsibility." With a flick of his long fingers, Ewan interjected. "I should've woken Yvette the moment I saw her in my room."

"Yes, you should have," Ian snapped. "It's a deuced fine thing to have one of my dearest friends compromise my wife's cousin."

"I didn't compromise her." Ewan's tone went ragged around the edges.

"You might as well have." Ian sighed and shook his head. "But I suppose I'm the last person who should judge anyone in that regard."

He'd been wrongly accused of compromising Vangie, which lead to their forced marriage. Thank goodness they'd fallen in love.

"If anyone is to blame, it's me." Yvette offered a cheerful smile in an attempt to lighten the mood. "In any event, we've arrived safely, and my reputation is relatively intact."

Jasper, the butler, entered the room with the boxed carousel. "Miss Stapleton, your package."

"Oh, it's for Ian and Vangie's little one." Yvette waved him to her cousin. "You must open it now, Vangie."

Vangie insisted on making for the nursery straightaway once she had. She placed the carousel as a centerpiece on a small marble-topped table, rather than on a shelf already overflowing with toys, dolls, trinkets, and picture-books for her baby.

She turned the merry-go-round's knob, and the four adults watched the miniature jeweled horses dance their circles to the tinkling music.

Yvette surveyed the charming nursery, taking in the handsome carved cradle and blue-and-white cushioned rocking chair. A wave of yearning encompassed her. She wanted children.

A child with Ewan.

Merciful God in heaven. Where did *that* come from?

She sought his eyes, and a tingling shock reverberated through her entire being when her gaze meshed with his.

He'd been watching her.

His I-know-what-you-wished-for smile brimmed with understanding and simmered with an unconstrained promise.

She turned away, pretending to be absorbed in a picture book, lest the blush stealing across her face give her thoughts away entirely.

Dratted man, reading her mind again.

Yvette's attention wandered to her cousin and Ian, and she entertained a small smile.

Vangie leaned against Ian, and his arms encircled her distended abdomen as they watched the carousel complete its fanciful journey. The babe must've chosen that moment to kick, because Vangie jumped.

Ian chuckled and murmured something in her ear, which earned him a loving smile.

Indeed, what would it be like to have a child with Ewan?

Reluctant to retire and bring an end to their long-awaited reunion, the cousins sat in the middle of Yvette's bed, nibbling shortbread and giggling. A plethora of plump pillows buffered the head of the bed, and amongst these the women relaxed, chatting.

A heavy rapping caused them to face the door.

"Enter." Yvette took another bit of crisp, buttery shortbread.

The housekeeper, Mrs. Tanssen, marched in like a general about to inspect his troops. She inclined her head at a sharp angle. "Please excuse the interruption. My lady, your presence is required downstairs."

"Whatever's so urgent it cannot wait 'til morning?" Vangie sent the housekeeper a quizzical glance as Yvette assisted her from the bed.

"Mr. Carmichael is in the drawing room. He's been wounded—"

Vangie and Yvette made the doorway before the house-keeper finished her sentence. Vangie had a gift for healing—part of her Romani heritage. She called over her shoulder, "Mrs. Tanssen, please fetch my healing basket."

Feet bare, they flew down the lengthy corridor and unceremoniously barged into the drawing room. Pale but alert, Mr. Carmichael, bare from the waist up and propped against a sheet-covered settee, spoke to Ewan.

"Only a small troupe of highwaymen, and two of them had accents. The smallest, no more than a boy, really, appeared to be their leader. He was livid to find the coach unoccupied."

Ian grazed two fingers along his jaw. "No occupants means no jewels or money."

"*If* that's what they were after." Suspicion tinged Ewan's voice.

"Blade or firearm?" Vangie asked before examining the wound.

"Pistol, my lady." Mr. Carmichael flinched, his muscles bunching when she pulled away the cloths Ewan held, staunching the blood.

Vangie leaned in, peering at the injury.

Yvette tried not to.

Feeling light-headed and faintly sick, she sucked in a steadying breath.

Chin up. You're made of sterner stuff.

"Ah, it's but a flesh wound." Vangie gave Mr. Carmichael a reassuring smile as she examined his injury. "You're fortunate. The bleeding's all but stopped. You won't require suturing."

Yvette swallowed in relief. She wasn't sure she would've been much help with the task. The sight of blood rendered her queasy and light-headed.

Mrs. Tanssen arrived with Vangie's healing goods.

"Thank you." Vangie accepted the basket and then, with practiced efficiency, set about tending Mr. Carmichael's wound.

Feeling rather useless, Yvette inspected the impressive room. Her focus drifted to Ewan, to his mouth turned downward into a pair of grim lines. She raised her eyes to his, a shudder stealing through her.

What if they'd been in that carriage?

Ewan's breath stalled the moment Yvette rushed into the room. Her face milk pale, she hovered near the settee, her toes peeking from the hem of her proper nightgown. A coral and yellow fringed silk shawl curtained her shoulders, more for modesty's sake than any need to stay warm. She'd plaited her hair, and the golden rope teased the swell of her bottom.

Her attire stirred something primitive and hot within him. Was she naked beneath the nightgown? His gaze probed the chaste covering. Unlike the one she'd worn a few nights ago, the cotton fabric revealed no feminine secrets.

And by God, a good thing, too, with Warrick and Carmichael in the room. Anger mixed with a goodly portion of dread snaked along Ewan's spine and slithered through his blood. Though he'd meant Carmichael to be a decoy—and bloody good thing he had—Ewan had underestimated his friend's danger. And for that he soundly chastised himself.

His gaze met Yvette's—wondering and wistful—from across the room, and he bent his lips upward in a silent greeting.

She smiled warily before returning her attention to Vangie and Carmichael.

Had she read his uneasiness in his eyes?

Probably. Yvette was too perceptive by far.

"Carmichael, did you wound any of them?" Like a giant annoyed panther, Ian paced back and forth.

"Malcolm and I each managed to get off a round before I was hit." Jaw taut, Carmichael flinched. "Someone hid in the shadows and shot me from behind, but I'm sure my aim was true. I heard the bugger's cry of pain."

"Accent, you said?" Ewan crossed his arms and rested one against an armchair. "Mayhap Italian?"

He hoped to God Carmichael said no. Ewan checked an automatic wince when Yvette gasped and jerked her head up, searching his face in stunned surprise.

"Perhaps. I'm not familiar with the language." Carmichael grunted again as Vangie cleansed the wound.

Ewan rubbed the bridge of his nose. "There were three knights of the road?"

Carmichael sucked in a sharp breath. "Four," he hissed from between clenched teeth. "Three stopped the carriage —two blocking the road ahead and one sneaking up from behind. The other blackguard lurked out of sight, under cover of the tall shrubbery beside the lane. It's only after they found the carriage empty that things turned ugly."

"Evvy, hold this bandage in place while I secure it." Vangie gave Carmichael an encouraging smile. "Almost finished. Can you lean forward, so I can wrap the bandages 'round your back?"

Grimacing, he did as bidden.

"The short one started arguing with the other two." Eyes closed, he continued. "Half the conversation was foreign gibberish, but I'm certain they were arguing about ransom—"

He stopped abruptly, his gaze veering to Yvette.

Damnation.

Ewan shot her a guarded glance.

Accusation flashed in her sky-blue eyes.

The devil take it. He'd not meant for her to hear that particular news. No help for it now, though. The truth would out soon enough.

"There, all done," Vangie announced, offering another comforting tilt of her mouth.

Ian helped her stand.

"I'll return momentarily," he said to no one in particular. "I want to see Vangie to bed. She tires easily these days."

"I'm not an invalid, dear." Still, Vangie leaned into the arm he wrapped around her shoulder.

After she bade the others good night, Ian led her from the room.

Ewan bowed his head and pinched the bridge of his nose. He sighed and took up pacing the drawing room. "Could the small thief have been a woman?"

Shutting his eyes, Carmichael nodded. "Perhaps. If so, her hair was quite short for a woman, and she wore men's clothing. They were masked, so I can't say for certain."

Yvette's puzzled stare bored into Ewan as surely as if she'd poked him with that blade she toted about. He met her gaze head on and curved his mouth in reassurance. Intuitive and intelligent, she'd already begun putting the pieces together.

Silent to this point, she face Carmichael. "The man in the shadows... Did you get a look at him? Was it Edgar?"

～

The hairs on Yvette's nape rose. Even with her back to him, she felt Ewan's intense stare.

In three long strides, he crossed to her. Despite Mr. Carmichael's rapt attention, he lifted her hand and brushed his warm lips across her knuckles. "That's why I switched carriages. I feared something of this nature would happen."

"Do you know who they were?" She couldn't read anything in his tender gaze.

Ewan cut a glance to Mr. Carmichael. "You know Marquardt. Was he one of the highwaymen?"

Mr. Carmichael started to shrug, then winced. "I can't be certain."

"Nevertheless, I have a strong suspicion whom they may be." Ewan gave her fingers a little squeeze, which, she was positive, he meant to reassure her, but only increased her angst.

"But you won't share their identities with me." Annoyed, she shook her head, her braid bouncing against her bottom. "Why? I'm not some delicate flower, Ewan. You don't have to protect me from this unpleasantness."

He opened his mouth then snapped shut it. Why was he being so blasted secretive?

All too aware that Mr. Carmichael watched them, she withdrew her hand from Ewan's.

The smile hitching the corners of the agent's mouth brought a dash of color to her cheeks.

Oh, how she wanted to shout at Ewan, demand he tell her what he knew. And if Mr. Carmichael hadn't been present, she might've indulged the urge.

If Ewan didn't trust her, how was she to ever trust him?

Disappointment and frustration bathed her, leaving her utterly weary.

Ewan touched her shoulder. "Yvette—"

She gave her head one sharp shake, cutting him off. "Goodnight, Ewan."

Forcing a composure she didn't feel, Yvette looked to his agent. "Goodnight, Mr. Carmichael. I hope your injury doesn't prevent you from sleeping."

"Thank you, Miss Stapleton."

As she turned to leave, Ewan touched her arm again. "Please, ride with me tomorrow before breaking your fast."

Torn, Yvette studied him for a penetrating moment. The eyes returning her regard shone clear and guileless. Should she deprive herself of one of her greatest pleasures because he was an evasive clod?

No, that would be childish.

"That would be lovely. It's been too long since I've indulged in a ride."

Relief tinged his half-smile. "Is half-past seven too early?"

"Not at all." She shook her head. "Shall I expect you at the stables?"

"No. I shall have our mounts at the manor's entrance."

"Splendid. Till the morrow, then. Goodnight."

"Sleep well, Evvy."

As she departed the room, he said to Mr. Carmichael, "Tell me more about the smallest highwayman. Did he carry a knife?"

Sixteen

A week later, Yvette raced beside a buckthorn hedge, her horse's thundering hooves routing pheasants and partridges. The fowl took to the early morning air amid a chorus of raucous scolding and frightened cries. As her steed surged ahead of Ewan's, her laughter tickled the drooping leaves clustering a willow tree's curling branches.

His shout of laughter echoed across the meadow as the horse he rode cleared the hedge in an agile leap.

"Unfair." Yvette's protest sifted away on the breeze as her mount galloped up the sloping incline. "That was sneaky of you, my lord," she said, laughing, not truly miffed. "We agreed to race to the top of the hill. There was no mention of jumping the shrubbery. You know it's much more difficult to stay seated sidesaddle."

Oh, how she'd come to enjoy these early morning rides with him this past week.

Edging his mount next to hers, so close his buckskin-covered thigh brushed her linen-draped one, Ewan leaned forward until his face was but inches from hers.

Yvette's focus riveted on the carved lips framing his mouth.

They transformed into a roguish smile, and she lowered her eyes in anticipation of the kiss sure to come.

"I expect my betrothed to call me by my given name."

At the unexpected chastisement, her eyes sprang open in astonishment. "I..."

"It's apparent I've been too lax." Ewan had inched devilishly close.

So close, the gold flecks in his irises twinkled at her and his breath caressed her cheek.

Sidling nearer yet, his lips all but touching her parted mouth, he whispered, "A fitting punishment is needed. What say you? A kiss every time you don't use my name?"

In one deft sweep of his arms, he snatched her from her mount to sit across his lap.

"Ooh—!" Yvette's astounded yelp caught in her throat as she clutched his stony forearm in alarm.

His arms engaged in balancing her on his thighs, his powerful leg muscles contracted under her bottom as he used his knees to control his prancing horse.

Her added weight shifted the saddle, and the stallion side-stepped, adjusting his footing.

She gripped Ewan even tighter, positive she was about to topple helter-skelter to the ground.

His chest shook, rumbling with suppressed humor.

Brute.

"I have you." He chuckled aloud now, a wolfish grin emphasizing his darkly handsome face. "I'd never let you fall."

She tilted her head, staring into his eyes. God in heaven, she loved the color of his beautiful eyes. Like looking into the sea's most secretive depths.

His humor receded, and an altogether different emotion surged to the surface. His gaze dropped, fixing on her mouth.

She instinctively licked her lower lip.

With a groan, Ewan brought his mouth down to hers.

Yvette slipped her arms upward, looping them behind his sturdy neck. Clinging to him, she welcomed the sensual attack. She kissed him with everything budding in her heart and kindling in her soul. Their tongues jousted, igniting the flames of her passion into a rapturous inferno. Her soul sparked anew.

He lifted his head slightly, breaking their kiss, and disappointment sluiced through her. His labored breathing and tightly-closed eyes revealed how much the effort cost him.

Dazed, her head spinning, she stared at him, awed.

My goodness, what his kisses did to her.

A lifetime wouldn't be long enough to enjoy them. Only —she plucked her riding habit's heavy skirt—she didn't have a lifetime. She didn't have any time left with him. He'd delivered her to Somersfield, and their time together was at an end.

Releasing a pensive sigh, she lowered her eyes.

What of this betrothal farce?

Yvette twisted on his lap, levering her arms to lean away and look at him fully. She had tucked the worry about their sham engagement aside, pushing it to the corner of her mind. Now, she would have an answer.

Her eyes searing him with a direct look, she spoke plainly. "I'm aware you must leave Somersfield soon. What will be said when it's known our betrothal is ended?"

She could already hear the cruel barbs and waspish innuendoes. Fingering the row of silk braiding edging her jacket, she veered her attention away from his astute scrutiny.

She didn't dare look at him lest he see the pain and humiliation surely shining in her eyes. Instead, she focused her gaze beyond his shoulder, on a gnarled oak tree. A pair of mourning doves perched on a branch, cocking their delicate grayish-brown heads from side to side. Their intense black eyes studied her.

It seemed she was an object of speculation for the birds too.

She arced her lips at the incongruity. She was in a deuced difficult position, and it didn't help in the least that the fault could be laid squarely at her half-boot-covered feet. Her naïve musings about remaining unwed might prove to be prophetic in the end.

Dash it all, spinsterhood no longer held any appeal. None whatsoever.

Studying the transparent emotions in concert across Yvette's features, Ewan understood the battle warring within her. Wasn't he occupied with the same maddening conflict?

Their faux engagement wasn't widely known, thus the scandal might be minimized.

Mrs. Pettigrove.

No, the devil take it. That wasn't likely the case at all.

One might as well take have placed an advert in *Black-wood's*. Mrs. Pettigrove's notorious sister Lady Clutterbuck was a vicious gossip.

He didn't doubt both ladies had been wagging their tongues all over Town, and most likely embellishing the truth to boot. Adjusting his seat, he positioned Yvette more securely on his lap.

She gave him a brave half-smile before her dejected gaze gravitated over his shoulder again.

There'd be disgrace attached to the dissolution, no matter the circumstances. Members of the peerage didn't enter into a betrothal agreement without considering the considerable significant consequences of breaking the contract. Even an unwritten one.

The scandal might spell ruination for her.

And his honor?

It wouldn't be worth a hog. Yet he'd been desperate to remove her from London.

He scanned the green-blanketed meadow. They'd been here a week now, and thus far there had been no sign anyone lurked about. Ian had instructed several of his stable hands, mostly former soldiers, to keep a careful watch and patrol the estate borders. He'd also required Yvette and Vangie to take their daily strolls within sight of the manor.

But, if Ewan's hunch proved right, and he hoped to God it didn't, the danger wasn't over. Fear's icy fingers slithered round his heart. He'd risk all to keep Yvette from harm. He brushed his fingers over her cheek.

Without hesitation, she shut her eyes and turned her head to rub the soft flesh against his palm. Surely that meant she cared for him?

The gesture gave him hope, emboldened him.

Still caressing her cheek, he ventured, "There is another option."

She opened her eyes, curiosity in their bright blue depths.

"We don't have to end the betrothal." Taking a deep breath, he plunged onward. "We could—can—in fact, wed."

Yvette stiffened, her eyes widening, and her face draining of color.

His thumb resting against her high cheek bone contrasted vividly with her ashen face.

Tension radiated through him as he sat rigid in the saddle. How would she respond? Eyes hooded, he waited, suppressing the unease jabbing at his vitals.

She sat mute, her doe-like eyes regarding him as if he had lost any semblance of reason.

He cleared his throat and curved his hand to cup her neck.

"Would being my wife be so objectionable?"

Yvette gawked, open-mouthed. Had she heard him correctly?

Us? Actually wed?

She snapped her mouth shut. Words and reasoning failed her for several interminable moments.

She'd been in his arms and enjoyed, even craved, his kisses.

Lust or love?

She'd nothing to compare the feeling to. Bother it all. Her body said one thing and her dratted mind said the opposite.

And what of him?

Yvette peeked at him from beneath her lashes.

His chiseled face revealed nothing.

True, Ewan desired her.

She wasn't that naïve, but did he only want her body to slake his lust? Or did the lure of her wealth entice him? Men would do any manner of things for money. She searched her memory. Had he said or done anything that gave her cause to believe he harbored deeper emotions for her?

No. Not that she could recall. Suspicion and doubt niggled relentlessly at her.

He nudged her bottom with his thighs. "Would it, Evvy?"

"Ewan, I..." She swallowed against the dryness in her mouth. "It has scarcely been more than a fortnight since you rescued me from the docks."

She worried her lower lip. A marriage for financial gain was appalling, though acceptable—even desired—in polite circles. But one of unrequited love or without affection? That would be far worse. Simply intolerable.

No, she wouldn't marry unless she knew she was loved. Though how one deciphered genuine love from feigned, she had yet to determine. Men had told her they loved her before, when really it had been her father's money they lusted after.

At sixteen, Yvette had thought Theodore Willowy loved her.

After only two weeks of courting, he'd tried talking her into eloping to Gretna Green. She'd refused, and the next week he ran off with Widow Buffington, twenty years his senior. Seems Theodore had acquired a significant gambling debt, and unless he expediently found himself a rich wife, he was headed for debtor's prison.

She'd rather become an old maid than marry without love. At least she'd be a very rich tabby. She grimaced. Not such a comforting notion, really.

Yvette eyed Ewan.

He waited for her answer. His scar pulsed white against

his tanned face, and his eyes burned with an intensity that both thrilled and made her edgy.

What was she to do?

"These past few days," she ventured, "I've greatly enjoyed your company." She closed her eyes and rushed on. "But, I'm afraid I can't make such an important decision this soon. I need more time to properly know you."

~

Ewan squelched a stab of disappointment. After all, he'd known rejection was a distinct possibility.

"I... Ewan?"

He met Yvette's uncertain gaze.

"I wouldn't be averse to a courtship." A fresh bloom of color tinted her face, emphasizing her adorable freckles.

He released a pent-up breath. She wanted to be wooed. No harm in that.

"And," her blush deepened, though she pressed on, "*if* the time ever comes, I expect to receive a proper proposal." She shook her head, waving her forefinger at him. "That was a sorry excuse for one."

"Aye, it was." Jubilant, he grinned. Wrapping his arms around her, he hugged her, holding her tight against his chest.

She gasped and laughed.

Lord, he loved making her laugh.

"*Chéri*, then there can be no harm in leaving our betrothal facade as it is. I'm hopeful it will help keep Edgar at bay." Ewan spoke into the baby-soft hair at her nape. "And, my dearest, if it's a courtship you want, I'd be most happy to oblige you."

He placed nibbling kisses along the slender column of her throat.

Her breath caught, and she arched her neck.

He checked a satisfied chuckle. She was so sensitive to his touch. Breathing into her ear, he assured her, "We can take all the time you need to know me."

The last he murmured in a deliberately husky, suggestive rumble.

She shuddered against him.

Catching her demure gaze, he smiled and wiggled his eyebrows wickedly. "And now I know you're receptive to my attentions, I warn you, *ma petite,* I'll be most persistent."

"I should hope so," she retorted, arching a starchy brow.

Ewan couldn't wipe the grin from his face. Yvette wanted to be courted. And she wanted a proper proposal. *If the time came.* He hoped it would...no, he'd see that it did.

He'd wait for as long as it took to win her over. Controlling his flesh in the meanwhile—that would take Herculean strength. He wanted her—wanted her so desperately he ached. But he desired more than her luscious body, needed more than her sweet flesh yielding to him in mindless passion.

He needed all of her. He must have her heart.

Yes, he was a patient man.

He would wait.

Angling his head, he studied her profile, taking in each delicate feature, noting the sprinkling of fawn-colored freckles across her nose. *Adorable.* His heart tightened near to bursting when Yvette turned her head and bestowed a breathtaking smile on him.

Yes, he most certainly would wait.

He shifted, covertly adjusting himself in the saddle. It

would prove to be an uncomfortable wait with a near-constant erection. He gave Yvette a sideways glance. Mayhap he knew a thing or two to hurry her along.

Seventeen

Arm-in-arm, Yvette and Vangie, each attired in white muslin gowns and beribboned straw bonnets, wandered the immaculately-manicured path. Their final destination? A wisteria-covered bower at the far side of the formal garden paralleling a crop of trees. Beneath the arbor's shady, perfumed covering, sat a stone bench.

Three gardeners tending the beds near the manor nodded respectfully as Yvette and Vangie passed by.

Yvette carried a small basket with shears, gloves, and other necessary whatnots should she wish to cut a bouquet or two from the profusion of flowers in the gardens. Her gun lay tucked inside the basket as well. After the incident with Mr. Carmichael, she wasn't taking any chances.

Stopping to admire a cobalt delphinium, she remarked, "The sun is quite tolerable this time of day."

"Which is why I prefer morning constitutionals," Vangie said.

Shading her eyes, Yvette searched the cloudless sky.

"Though I fear that," she pointed to the distant, hazy horizon, "holds promise of oppressive heat later."

Vangie nodded and grimaced. "Faith, I wish it were not so. The heat is most tedious when one is this large." She looked at her rounded stomach, then Yvette's flat middle. "It's impossible to believe I was ever once as slender as you."

Hugging her cousin, Yvette assured her, "You're beautiful."

"You're a dear to say so, even if it is a taradiddle." She gave a rueful little smile. "By-the-by, how was your ride with Lord Sethwick?" Vangie gave a delicate shudder. "I've never understood your love of riding."

Yvette laughed. "That's only because you weren't placed on a horse before you could walk, as I was."

She skipped down the path a few steps before whirling to face Vangie. The shears flew from the basket, clattering to the flagstone path. She bent to retrieve them. "Something astonishing has happened."

Standing upright, she reorganized the basket's contents, then tucked the shears inside once more.

Vangie caught up to Yvette. "Do tell."

They linked arms and continued along the pathway.

"It happened when Lord Sethwick and I were riding this morning." She cast Vangie a sidelong glance, smiling at the memory. "It was most unexpected."

And terrifyingly wonderful.

She'd kept that bit to herself. How could she explain her emotional paradox?

An impish gleam lit Vangie's eyes, and Yvette twisted to look at her full on. Whatever was her dear cousin up to? Was that a mischievous smile hovering around her lips?

"This morning's event. Does it have anything to do with

how your gaze follows Ewan's every movement when he's in the room?" Vangie teased.

Stumbling to an unceremonious stop, Yvette uttered a mortified squeak and covered her mouth with her hand. "That's not so." She searched her cousin's humor-filled eyes. "Is it?"

A playful grin curling her lips, Vangie nodded.

"Oh, Lord above," Yvette groaned.

Looping her arm through Yvette's once more, Vangie tugged her along the trail. "I know you better than any person on earth, dearest. Though not apparent to others, you do indeed watch his every move."

Yvette's embarrassed groan brought on another giggle from her cousin.

Vangie patted her arm and *tsked* comfortingly. "I'm quite sure neither Ian nor Ewan have taken notice."

Stopping on an arched footbridge, Yvette leaned over the rail to watch several swans. At least Vangie would think her flushed face was due to bending over. A fat duck quacked a warning when the swans neared her quartet of downy ducklings. Several jewel-colored dragonflies flitted and dipped across the pond's glimmering surface.

Yvette straightened, and they resumed their walk.

Vangie pressed her, "So what did happen?"

Not quite recovered from her embarrassment, Yvette toyed with the basket's handle. "I agreed to allow him to court me after he said we might truly marry." It was completely backward. A proposal then courting—and no declaration of affection at all.

"Marry?" Vangie clapped her hands. "Oh, that would be splendid!" She wrapped her arm round Yvette's waist. "So...did he kiss you?"

Yvette laughed, hugging her cousin again. "Indeed, he did. Most thoroughly."

For a moment, Vangie's laughter mixed with hers then Yvette sobered.

"I worry if his affections are engaged, though. Papa's riches have caused more than one man to declare his ardent affections when it's been the money that enamored them, not I." She met Vangie's sympathetic gaze before looking away. "I'd rather not marry at all than have a man marry me for my money."

"You have to learn to trust, though the Lord knows, after that disaster with Theodore you've reason not to. Give Ewan a chance to prove himself."

But what of Lord Ramsbury's comments about her wealth and Edgar in the inn? Ewan hadn't refuted them.

Recalling the degrading morning leading to her betrothal, Yvette's mouth bent into a wry smile. "I must say, I never anticipated our betrothal ever becoming genuine." She met Vangie's warm gaze then shifted the basket to her other arm. "Ewan hopes Edgar will leave me be if he believes I am to wed soon."

She didn't voice her doubts regarding that, or her suspicions that Edgar was queer in the attic. Right up to the topmost rafter.

"I think it's wise too." Clasping Yvette's hand, Vangie gave it a quick squeeze. "I want you to be happy. As happy as I am with Ian." Pausing to bend and sniff a voluptuous, peach-etched rose, Vangie ventured, "You said Edgar found your room at the inn the day. Or rather the *night* you arrived in London. Do you think he still pursues you?"

Wrinkling her brow, Yvette thought for a moment. Should she tell Vangie her qualms about Edgar? Vangie straightened then rubbed her lower back. The movement emphasized her enormous belly. No, with the babe expected in less than a month, better not to cause her any undue upset.

The untied purple ribbons of Yvette's bonnet twirled round her shoulders when she shook her head. "I've not seen anything to indicate he does, although Ewan did take every precaution traveling here."

Indeed, her *derrière* had been sore for days after riding in the post chaise.

A wood pigeon swooped to land further along the footpath, cooing to its reluctant mate sequestered in a nearby magnolia tree. "He would tell me if anything suspicious occurred."

He wouldn't, and that troubled her.

Yvette paused when an unexpected thought took root. She was protecting Vangie from unpleasantness much the same way Papa, and now Ewan, had protected her.

"You don't think..." Vangie fidgeted with the lace on one glove. "The night you arrived and there was the commotion with Mr. Carmichael..."

Yvette's brows veered downward again. Yes, Ewan had acted odd that night. As if he hid something.

Nearing the wisteria arbor, Yvette conceded that Mr. Carmichael's shooting continued to plague her. Though it had occurred a week ago, the day she and Ewan had first arrived, she wasn't certain Edgar hadn't followed her to Somersfield. Who was the man hidden in the forest if not him? Even now, she felt he watched her.

He was the devil's own, to be sure.

An icy shiver tingled the length of her spine.

Did Ewan have reason to be suspicious of the couple they'd seen in the jeweler's shop? Was that why he had asked Mr. Carmichael if they spoke Italian and if it were possible for one of the highwaymen to have been a woman?

If they were the same pair, why would they want to abduct her?

She'd asked Ewan those same questions, rather heatedly, in fact, and he would only say he was investigating the matter. *Investigating the matter?* What did he mean by that?

Why were men forever protecting women from anything disagreeable?

"Evvy, the baby kicks." Seizing Yvette's hand, she grinned as she placed it on her stomach where the infant made its presence known.

A tiny bump pulsed against her palm. Yvette giggled in delighted surprise. "Vangie, I felt it! The babe's movement. I think I felt it kicking."

"Well, well," a deep voice droned. "What a touching scene."

Yvette and Vangie whirled toward the voice.

Two intruders stood in the garden.

Yvette smothered a gasp.

She knew them—the woman from the jeweler's and Lord Fielding. Frissons of unease prickled her skin. Why were they here?

"Do forgive the interruption, ladies." Fielding flourished a mocking bow.

"Lord Fielding?" Yvette slid Vangie a questioning glance.

The imperceptible slanting of her cousin's eyes answered Yvette's silent question, and they shifted into defensive stances. Yvette inched closer to Vangie and gripped her icy hand.

Raising her chin, sounding every bit the lady of the

manor, Vangie confronted the pair. "You're trespassing on Somersfield lands. What business have you here?"

As if conversing in a drawing room about the weather, Fielding answered with polite smoothness. "None with you, Lady Warrick. Miss Stapleton, on the other hand, will need to accompany Pauline and myself."

"I think not." Yvette sidled closer to Vangie and wrapped her arm about her waist.

Trembling, Vangie covered Yvette's hand with her own.

A throaty laugh reverberated amongst the foliage. In a sweeping arc, Pauline brandished the wicked-looking knife she had concealed in her short jacket. "I have a weapon. You have no choice. You *will* come with us."

Hurling the gardening basket at Fielding, Yvette shouted, "Now, Vangie!"

In a flurry of creamy, swirling skirts, Yvette aimed for Pauline's shoulder and fired the pistol she'd hidden in the basket. She missed, piercing the Italian beauty's hand clear through instead. The knife Pauline wielded dropped to the ground.

The small knife she'd slipped Vangie flew through the air with deadly precision.

Clutching his throat, Fielding issued a strangled groan. Scarlet streamed from the knife imbedded in his neck.

Pauline held her oozing hand, a prolific stream of Italian profanity pouring from her white-edged lips. Eyes narrowed, she vowed, "This is not over. We will meet again, and I shall finish next time."

Yvette gaped at her, speechless. Was the woman addled?

Vangie let loose with a virago's infuriated scream. She flipped up the hem of her dress and removed a razor-sharp dagger sheathed to her thigh. Neither intruder gave her the opportunity to use it. They sprinted into the woods, leaving a speckled ruby trail in their wake.

Deep satisfaction bathed Yvette. Never before had she been as grateful for the weaponry training she and Vangie had received. Though, Vangie's skill with a blade was more an element of her Romani heritage than anything else, as was the dagger she kept strapped to her leg.

A gruff bellow echoed in the distance, followed by coarse shouts.

An inarticulate sound drew Yvette's attention from the retreating intruders.

Vangie stared at her soaked skirts, a bewildered frown lining her forehead.

Dropping her pistol, Yvette dashed to her.

Her eyes glazed with pain and clutching her belly, Vangie crumpled to the ground.

"Dearest, what's wrong?" Scalding tears filled Yvette's eyes. "Is it the babe?"

Eyes closed, Vangie didn't respond but lay heavily against her. Terrified, and fearing the worst, Yvette whispered, "God, help her."

"It would seem my baby is about to be born." Vangie's lips tilted fractionally. Her nascent smile faded into a grimace as pain racked her.

"Vangie, Evvy, where are you?"

Ewan, thank God!

"Over here, on the wisteria path. Hurry, Ewan!"

She sagged in relief when Ewan, Ian, several grooms, and a stable boy drummed down the flagstone footpath.

Ian rushed to his wife. Kneeling beside her, his hand shaking, he brushed a raven lock off her pale cheek. "Vangie, sweeting?"

"My lords." Palmer, the head groom, pointed to the

discarded weapons and the blood-spattered tracks ending at the wood's edge.

"*Merde.*" Ewan's worried gaze raked Yvette and Vangie. "Are either of you hurt?"

"No." Yvette shook her head. She closed her eyes and swallowed the bile lodged in her throat. Voice quaking, she managed, "I shot one. Vangie threw a knife at the other."

Shock set in, and she clenched her hands to stop their quaking. Merciful God, she'd actually shot someone. Vangie moaned against Ian, and anger surged through Yvette. And she'd do it again. She'd been right to suspect the Italian. Lord Fielding... Now that was unexpected.

Yvette pressed against Ewan. "How did you know?"

"Ian and I were at the stables. We heard the gunfire, *ma chérie.*" He smiled at her. "Your shot alerted us. That, and a woman's bloodcurdling scream."

"Where are the men I assigned to patrol the perimeter?" Ian's furious gaze roamed the area. "Palmer, take three armed men and follow their trail. I want to know who dared to trespass on my lands and assault my wife."

Yvette laid a calming hand on his arm. "I know who they were."

He stiffened, rage spewing from his eyes. "Who?"

The single rasping word echoed ominously amongst the greenery.

"It was Lord Fielding and a woman named Pauline." Yvette's troubled gaze swung to Ewan. "It was the same woman we encountered at the jeweler's."

Vangie's guttural moan brought everyone's attention back to her. "Ian, I fear our little one is going to arrive early."

Yvette saw the terror reflected in Vangie's eyes despite her bravado. She had already lost one babe.

Please, dear God, not another.

"Sweeting, it will be all right," Ian soothed. "You there, lad." He pointed at the scrawny stable boy in tattered breeches and a threadbare shirt. "What's your name again?"

"Jimmers, sir."

"Run, quick. Have Jasper fetch Dr. Farnsworthy and Midwife Godfrey at once. Tell him to hurry." Ian cradled Vangie to him. "We need a stretcher sent here, too. Hurry, boy!"

Gulping, his Adam's apple bobbing, Jimmers sputtered, "Yes, m'lord," before bolting off to the mansion, his lanky legs churning furiously.

Ewan helped Yvette to her feet. She swayed against him.

"Evvy, you're sure you're unharmed?"

Leaning against his strong, solid maleness, she shut her eyes in relief. She breathed him in, pressing her face against his chest. His heartbeat, steady and soothing, thrummed beneath her ear. Propriety was of no account in this moment. She needed this, needed his comforting embrace.

"Yes, Ewan, only frightened."

He drew her shaking form closer, kissing her forehead, and she smiled against his shoulder.

The stretcher arrived for Vangie, and together, the anxious troupe found their way to the manor to await the Warrick heir's birth.

Some sixteen hours later, Vangie gave birth to twins—a boy and a girl. Yvette sent word to Ian and Ewan sequestered in the study with a bottle of cognac. Mere moments later, a forceful knock rattled the bedchamber door.

Grinning, she'd opened it.

A humble, unsure Ian stood there.

Ewan shifted from foot to foot, looking equally ill at ease.

Goodness, they could be lads called before the schoolmaster to be chastised.

Ian's gaze kept sliding past Yvette to Vangie lying in the bed.

"You can come in now." She looked to Ewan. His smile shifted ever so slightly when her eyes met his. Was he remembering the night of their arrival, when she'd yearned for a child of her own, too?

She stepped aside, allowing Ian to pass.

Breaking with decorum, Ewan followed his friend into the chamber.

Vangie lay propped against a pile of pillows, pale but beaming and cradling a babe in each arm. Ian maneuvered himself onto the bed beside her. Reclining against the headboard, he took his son and tenderly tucked him in the crook of his arm.

Yvette and Ewan stood at the end of the bed, his strong arm wrapped around her waist. She looked up at him, their gazes meshing in understanding.

One of the babes whimpered, drawing Ewan's attention. Grinning he said, "Careful there, *Papa*, you're squeezing the little chap."

Mrs. Tanssen slipped into the room, a pinched expression on her face. "Please forgive me for intruding and ruining this happy moment, my lord." She wrung her hands in her spotless apron. "Palmer found two of your men in the woods... Dead."

❧

The first timid rays of dawn inched over the horizon, causing the uppermost branches of the hoary oaks to glimmer with iridescent light. Yvette exhaled a contented sigh. The terrace view bordered on paradisiacal, possibly more so because her heart overflowed with gladness. Ambushed by a myriad of emotions, she felt a sense of *joie de vivre* at the birth of a new day.

It was good to be alive, especially since Vangie and the twins had come through the birth without complication.

A steady tread sounded behind her before Ewan's strong arms encircled her, drawing her against his solid chest.

"Ewan." Closing her eyes, Yvette relaxed against him. Wholly exhausted, she had yet to find her bed after the terrifying ordeal in the garden yesterday morning.

He pressed his lips to the crown of her head. The heat from his kiss remained long after he lifted his mouth.

"I thought you'd retired." She yawned behind her hand, so fatigued she could scarcely keep her eyes open.

"I'm too restless to sleep just yet," he murmured against her hair.

Jasper and Mrs. Tanssen, laden with overflowing trays, bustled to a table situated near the periphery of the patio.

"My lord, Miss Stapleton, we concluded some nourishment might be in order," Jasper said.

After lowering their burdens, Mrs. Tanssen set about distributing the contents while Jasper bowed to Yvette and Ewan.

"Breakfast, if you please? Neither of you has eaten since yesterday morn." The staid butler's mouth remained turned up in the same grin that had adorned his face for three hours now.

Even Mrs. Tanssen's mouth arced a fraction, despite the

disturbing news she'd delivered after the babes' births. "Yes indeed. The two of you've had a long night of it."

"Not as long as dear Vangie." Yvette slipped into the chair Ewan held for her.

"Or Ian." He chuckled, taking the other seat.

She giggled. "He was quite Friday-faced, wasn't he?"

A shape separated from the shadows alongside the concealing border. From the corner of her eye, Yvette caught the faint movement, and her heartbeat quickened.

Did someone watch them?

Eighteen

Five days later, Yvette eyed Vangie. "You're quite sure you're feeling well enough to be about so soon?"

This morning her dear cousin had insisted she would go mad if she had to stay in her room one more day. An exaggeration to be sure, but Vangie wasn't one to laze about.

"I'm perfectly fine."

Reaching for the steaming pot of tea Jasper had just delivered, Yvette arced a brow. "Shall I pour?" Not giving her cousin time to answer, she filled the cup. Handing Vangie the steaming brew, she prompted, "Would you like an almond shortbread biscuit or a maid-of-honor tart?"

"The tart, I think." Vangie reclined against the chaise lounge, smiling as she sipped her tea.

Choosing a pastry for herself, Yvette lifted a serviette from the tray. A piece of paper twirled to the floor. She raised curious eyes to Vangie, now sitting upright, peering at the scrap.

Vangie pointed to the slip of paper. "Whatever is that?"

Bending over, Yvette retrieved the folded paper. She

held it between her thumb and forefinger. "It appears to be a note." She turned the missive over and found her name scrawled across the surface. "For me."

Vangie giggled. "Perhaps it's a love note from Ewan."

Dubious, Yvette eyed the poor quality paper, the writing smudged and crudely penned. The missive was crinkled and grimy, as if it had been stuffed into a pocket by a dirty hand. She shook her head. "I think not."

She unfolded the note and scanned the contents.

Dear God.

Her stomach and heart flopping somewhere near the vicinity of her feet, she wordlessly passed the note to her cousin.

Vangie read the note and gasped. "Faith, who would do this?"

"I'm sure I don't know. Unless it was Edgar or, perhaps, Lord Fielding."

Yvette tried to keep the terror from her voice. She sat mute as tentacles of fear seized her. Was Somersfield not to be the haven she'd expected it to be? Remaining here indefinitely wasn't her intention. She had three mansions of her own. She'd hoped, after the Fairchilds and Pippa arrived, to make a decision about her future.

Snatching a bell from the end table, Vangie rang it insistently.

Jasper hustled into the room, his face etched with concern. "My lady, you require—" One look at the ladies' stricken faces, and the majordomo stopped short. "Whatever is amiss?"

Vangie showed him the offending paper. "This note was concealed on the tea tray. Have you any idea how it came to be there?"

Jasper drew himself up to his full height, which was not

considerable—Yvette looked him eye to eye when standing. What he lacked in stature, though, he more than compensated for with dignity.

"Certainly not, Lady Warrick. I," he raised his chin another two inches, "always present correspondences on a salver." He sniffed disdainfully, as if to imply such an act was beneath him. "*Never* on a tea service."

"Of course you do," Vangie soothed. "I didn't mean to suggest you placed the note on the tray. I only meant perhaps you saw something unusual or suspicious?"

"No, my lady." His chin lowered a fraction. "Cook delivered the prepared tray to my hands, and I walked here, directly."

Yvette's attention flicked to her cousin.

Fine brows drawn into a fierce scowl, Vangie glared at the note. The expression on her face reflected her puzzlement and apprehension.

How had the note come to be on the tray?

Had someone entered the house?

Chills raised the hairs the length of Yvette's arms. Even her scalp tingled in warning.

He swung his troubled gaze between the two women. "Might I presume the correspondence was unwelcome in nature?"

"Indeed, Jasper," Vangie admitted. "Please request their lordships join Miss Stapleton and me."

Jasper delivered a smart bow. "At once, my lady."

Moments later, Ewan and Ian strode into the room.

Her mind a cacophony of emotions, Yvette waited in silence for their responses.

"Sweeting, Jasper said you'd need of us?" Ian planted a kiss on top of Vangie's head.

Repeating Yvette's actions, Vangie transferred the paper to him without a word.

Ian accepted the note, his brows shooting into twin arches of disbelief. "Bloody hell."

Without asking permission, Ewan helped himself to the missive. His eyes narrowed, and fury darkened his hawkish features. "The devil take it."

"Ewan, the note says," Yvette paused to take a bracing breath, "I passed within inches of them in the garden today."

He grasped her hands and drew her to her feet. "Don't fret, we shall get to the bottom of this. Perhaps it's nothing more than a childish prank."

She doubted any of them believed his suggestion. She certainly didn't, but to contemplate the alternative proved far more disturbing. Someone watched her and wanted her to know it—wanted all of them to know it.

Yvette shuddered, and Ewan squeezed her hands.

His next words sent another tremor through her already chilled body. "Evvy, I think you and Vangie should refrain from venturing outdoors without Ian or me."

"Aye, I'm in agreement." Ian nodded, his mien contemplative. "It's the surest method to keep you safe." His gaze traveled to include Vangie before meeting Ewan's.

Yvette studied them. They knew something, she was sure of it. What was it, and why were they so determined to keep it a secret? "You've seen more trespassers?" She directed her question to Ewan.

"We've had reports of other intruders on the outer grounds," he reluctantly admitted.

"I'll instruct the staff again to be watchful of any strangers lurking near the manor," Ian said.

Yvette tried to stifle the fear that slithered into her mind and coiled there. She wouldn't dwell on it, she determined resolutely. Her cheeks aching from the effort, she put on what she hoped was a brave smile.

"There's plenty to occupy my time indoors. I shall help Vangie with Roman and Rowynne, and I've neglected the piano and my correspondences."

Ewan wrapped his arms about her, and for a moment, she let herself believe all would be well.

The message she discovered lying on her dressing table, bold as brass, the next afternoon brought her to her breaking point, however.

Weeping, she fled down the stairs, burst into Ian's office, and flung herself into Ewan's arms. "I found a note on my dressing table." She sucked in a rasping breath. "How could they get into my chamber?"

Moments later, a grim-faced Vangie entered the study, the now familiar grungy paper held in her hand. "Mrs. Tanssen found this on the floor upstairs."

Ian scowled. "Ewan and I've interrogated every member of this household. We've no new house servants, yet somehow the notes continue to find their way into the mansion."

Wrapped in Ewan's protective embrace, Yvette asked, through her tears, "But how?"

"No doubt a bribed hireling delivered them," Ewan murmured into her hair.

Ian took the note from Vangie. Scanning it, he exclaimed, "This reeks of Marquardt."

He handed the crumpled paper to Ewan, but after giving it a cursory glance, he rejected the notion. "I think not. Edgar hasn't been seen once since we arrived. After the garden abduction attempt, and the murder of your men, Ian, I suspect something larger is afoot."

Now he suspects? Balderdash.

Yvette didn't think so. She sniffled loudly. He'd been on the scent since they left London.

Vangie ventured, "Is it possible we've a new groundskeeper or groom? The first note mentioned the garden."

Ian moved to his wife then hugged her. "It's not impossible, sweeting. I shall speak with Palmer and see if we've any new help in the stables or gardens."

Yvette reluctantly removed herself from Ewan's embrace and accepted the handkerchief he passed her. Good Lord, she'd soaked his shirt and waistcoat with her tears. Why couldn't she cry daintily? No doubt her cheeks were blotchy, her nose and eyes red and swollen.

Dabbing her eyes, she allowed Ewan to direct her to the settee, then sat at his urging.

Vangie sank onto the matching settee.

"Evvy?" Ewan took the seat beside her, covering her hand with his.

She met his eyes, disliking the disquiet reflected in their depths. Apprehension churned in her stomach.

He didn't mince his words. "Ian and I are in agreement. It's not safe for you to remain at Somersfield."

The knot in her belly tightened, and she bit her trembling lip. "I've thought as much myself."

"It's my concern... our concern," he sliced Ian a sideways glance, "that whoever is responsible for the trespassers and notes, will use any means to gain access to you." He paused, as if seeking the right words. "We are concerned that Vangie and the twins may be at risk too."

"God in heaven." Yvette flung her cousin an appalled look. "I'd never place you or the babes in danger."

Indignation gripped her, as her outrage spiraled into

fury. "I cannot believe Edgar is so determined to have me or my inheritance that he would resort to terrorizing infants." Bolting to her feet, her gown billowing in angry waves about her ankles, she vented her frustration. "Who is doing this? Why? What of Fielding and those Italians? What is their connection? Why did they attempt to abduct me?"

The questions were hurled at no one in particular. Yvette pivoted to face Ian. She peered at him sitting calmly behind his desk then spun to glare at Ewan. She fisted her hands in her skirt.

Was that remorse in his eyes?

She pointed at him. "You know something. Something you've kept from Vangie and me." She narrowed her eyes. "Don't deny it. What is it? I have a right to know. I cannot keep living in constant fear!"

She couldn't. She was exhausted. Dear God, would she ever know peace again?

Her emotional tirade at an end, stinging tears pooling in her eyes, she slumped onto the settee beside Vangie.

Take a deep breath. Calm down. Stop behaving like a hysterical schoolgirl.

Vangie wrapped an arm around her shoulders. Leaning into the comforting embrace, Yvette scrutinized the men.

Ian's expression remained carefully bland.

Switching her gaze to Ewan, she arched a skeptical brow. "Ewan?"

He rose and, as he was wont to do when agitated, began pacing. "You're right. There's more to this situation, but Ian and I aren't sure precisely what. We've made inquiries and have strong suspicions. You'll have to trust me in this."

Yvette gapped at him. "Trust you? When you refuse to trust—"

A single knock echoed at the study door.

"Enter," Ian beckoned.

"You have callers, my lord," Jasper intoned, looking at Ewan.

Despite the sobering conversation of moments past, a broad grin lightened his features.

"Would they be well-armed and Scots?"

Nineteen

Entering the drawing room a couple of hours later, Yvette paused, taking in Ewan's happy countenance.

Five of the largest men she'd ever seen surrounded him and Ian, and Ewan had his head thrown back in unrestrained laughter.

A stunning woman wearing a white shirt, short jacket, and black breeches tucked into knee-high boots relaxed against the fireplace. Ah, Ewan's sister, Adaira.

Yvette flashed a welcoming smile, which Adaira immediately reciprocated with an impish grin.

The slight woman came toward her, pulling her cap off her head as she went. Waves of thick coffee-brown hair fell to her waist, though a ribbon at her nape constrained the mass.

"Yvette." Ian looked past her to the doorway. "Vangie isn't with you?"

"No." Yvette stepped farther into the room. "The babies were fussy and took longer to feed than she anticipated. She said she would be down shortly and sends her apologies once more."

Ewan extended his hand toward her. "Come. Meet my family."

Suddenly nervous and unsure, Yvette stopped short of him. A knot formed, then coiled somewhere in the region of her stomach. How much had he told them? Would they think ill of her?

He drew her arm through his, and rested his large, warm hand atop hers. Partially reassured, she peeped at him from the corner of her eye. Did he just wink? He had a broad smile on his face and didn't seem the least vexed.

Guiding her toward a handsome middling-aged man, Ewan introduced her. "Yvette, I'd like you to meet my step-father, Hugh Ferguson."

Yvette extended her hand. "Ewan's spoken of you, Mr. Ferguson."

"Och, call me Hugh." He bent over her hand then winked at Ewan. "She's a very bonnie lassie, son."

"Aye, she is at that."

Something in the timbre of Ewan's voice caused Yvette's heart to catch and her skin to prickle deliciously. She trembled from top to toe, and it wasn't from nerves. Ewan must've felt her tremor, because he released a rumbling, sensual laugh.

Beast.

Heat crept from Yvette's neck to the roots of her hair. Hoping to divert the attention from herself, she extended her hand to the beautiful young woman. "You must be Adaira."

Adaira grinned and nodded. "I was thrilled when Ewan sent for his kin and asked that I come too. I've looked forward to meeting you, Yvette."

Yvette cast a surprised glance at Ewan. Adaira knew of her? How? She smiled to hide her confusion. "Please call me Evvy."

"And you must call me Addy. Everyone does except Ewan." She pulled a face at her older brother. "He's so stuffy, insisting on addressing me by my given name."

"Indeed?" Yvette quirked a brow at him. "It's a wonder he deems it fitting to address me by my pet name. He was most insistent about doing so. Why is that, Ewan?"

Obviously happy to see someone challenge her brother, Adaira laughed, a naughty gleam flashing in her treacle-brown eyes.

"Be good, minx," Ewan admonished his sister with a warning glint in his eye. Switching his attention to Yvette, he gave her a speaking look. "You know full well why. We can discuss it later—*alone*—if you wish," he finished smoothly, lips tilting into an enigmatic smile.

Her pithy response flew from her brain as she gawked, her jaw slack. She tore her focus off his unnerving eyes then swallowed against a rush of sensation.

Those eyes.

Ewan introduced her to the two men, now standing on either side of his sister. "Evvy, these brutes are my cousins, Alasdair and Gregor McTavish."

All muscle and brawn, both men boasted hair as blond as Yvette's. She widened her eyes in not-so-polite surprise as she tilted her head to stare up at them.

"Good God, they're huge."

I didn't say that out loud, did I?

The chorus of masculine laughter answered her silent question.

She resisted the urge to clap her hands over her cheeks to cover the color surely sweeping them again. Didn't they grow normal-sized men in Scotland? She'd always believed Scots to be rather on the short side.

Grinning, Alasdair thumped his brother on the shoulder with a blow that would've staggered a smaller man. As if reading her mind, he declared, "Aye, lassie, our father took a liking to a verra tall, verra bonnie Norse lass. Mother sends ye her regards."

Humor shimmered in his gray-blue eyes.

Gregor elbowed his gargantuan brother aside to take Yvette's hand. As he stood to his full height, he motioned toward another Scot. "That giant yonder be our father."

Ah, that explained their size.

The giant bowed. As he straightened, she was drawn to his kind green eyes. He resembled Ewan, though he stood even taller.

"Duncan McTavish, Miss Stapleton. It be a pleasure to be sure, lass."

"Bratling," Ewan said, "stop ogling the maid and come meet your future sister." He spoke to another tall, profoundly handsome Scot flirting with the maid.

Sister?

Yvette's heart flip-flopped and skidded to a stop. She could not tear her gaze from the fragile lace on the hem of her gown. Her heart resumed beating, a hopscotching rhythm of confusion. Was her erratic pulse visible at her throat?

She daren't look at Ewan.

Whatever was he thinking? Why in the world had he said that in front of everyone? Nothing was official.

Did they all stare at her?

Did they all know he'd found her in his bed?

She took a furtive peek about the room. No one seemed

the least surprised or disturbed by his announcement. Pleasant faces smiled back at her.

The young downstairs maid giggled and left the room carrying the remnants of tea, but not before sending the other striking Scot a saucy smile, then swinging her curvy behind in invitation as she departed.

The young man approached. Good Lord, he was a living, breathing Adonis. No man on earth should be so beautiful. As much as she was smitten with Ewan, the look in the Scot's eye still stole her breath. In spite of his all-too-manly appraisal, he wasn't many years past boyhood. Straightaway, she knew who he was.

"It's a pleasure to meet you, Dugall."

His sable brows shot upward, and his wide smile exposed perfect white teeth. Sea-green eyes, a shade lighter than his brother's, danced with intelligence. "Me brother's been speaking of me, has he?"

"He has indeed." Yvette lifted her gaze to Ewan for a moment, then grinned unabashedly.

Dugall lingered above her raised hand. She swore she felt his soft, well-shaped lips caress her knuckles. Twice.

Did Ewan just growl?

Of course not.

What hogwash.

Growl indeed.

What was *she* thinking?

"The only reason Father allowed you to come, whelp," Adaira teased Dugall, "is because Callum's wife is birthing their bairn, and he needed someone to care for the horses." She edged nearer Yvette. "Callum is our cousin. He and his sister, Aubry, were raised with us after their parents were lost at sea."

Something about the way she said Aubry's name caused Yvette to pause and search Adaira's eyes.

Her chocolate brown gaze regarded Yvette with innocent humor.

Perhaps she'd only imagined it.

Ewan smacked Dugall playfully on his dark head. "Away with you, scamp. I'm courting Yvette."

He pulled her to his side, wrapping the thick band of his arm about her waist, as if to say to all present, *mine*.

She rather liked his possessiveness.

"Mayhap she be wanting a younger man instead of one in his dotage." Dugall puffed his chest and waggled his eyebrows. "What say ye, lass? Do ye want to toss him off for meself? I shall be certain to please ye."

Yvette couldn't help herself. She burst out laughing. Charming rogue. However, he was no callow youth. She hadn't a doubt he had more experience in the ways of the world—and the goings-on in the bedroom—than she.

Eyeing Ewan, she pretended to contemplate Dugall's offer. "I see your point, Dugall, indeed I do. But alas, I've given my word. And a lady must always keep her word, no matter how great or difficult the sacrifice. It's a matter of integrity."

An unwelcome thought filtered into her mind.

Was Ewan a man of integrity?

Four days later, slogging through muck, Ewan turned to survey those hunkered in their saddles behind him. They needed to find shelter, and soon. Returning his focus to the trail ahead, he peered through the dense gloom. The narrow path through the woods had become a stream of oozing sludge, forcing the travelers to slow their pace.

They needn't travel any longer at the breakneck speed they had these past several hours. They had distanced themselves from their pursuers, thanks to the storm's fury, and two hours ago their entourage had crossed the border into Scotland.

Ewan shifted in his saddle again, then slowed Shaidae's gait until the horse drew even with his uncle riding behind him.

Ewan shouted to be heard above the raging wind. "Munlocky's is but a mile yonder. What say you, Duncan?"

Standing in his stirrups, the Scot turned to look over his shoulder. Facing Ewan again, he shrugged. "Och now, Munlocky's isnae me first choice, but the wee one is done in. She be verra cold. We are well-armed. Shouldn't be any trouble if'n we keep our swords and dirks nearby and are canny."

Ewan gave a sharp nod. "Pass the word."

Duncan swung his enormous horse around, shouting to each rider in turn. "Munlocky's tonight, lads."

Kneeing his roan, he took his place at the front once more, intent on finding the inconspicuous, nearly-hidden pathway leading to the hostelry. Few reputable men knew of its existence, and those frequenting the secluded cottage preferred it that way.

Yvette summoned a miserable smile when Duncan dropped back to encourage her. "The inn is nigh. Ye can get out of the cold, though Munlocky's be a rough place. Keep to yerself, dinnae speak, and stay close to the laird. Ye ken, lassie?"

Yvette only nodded. She'd been clenching her chattering teeth for so long, she wasn't sure she'd be able to utter a word, even had she the strength.

She sneezed again.

Blast it.

There went her cap for the hundredth time. She yanked it into place, her patience at an end. The oversized cap she'd stuffed her hair into kept slipping down her rain-slickened forehead, blocking her already limited view of the trail.

Utterly miserable, she slid forward in the saddle, trying to relieve the painful chafing along her inner thighs. She'd never ridden astride before, and her legs ached, not only due to the unaccustomed hours straddling the horse, but because of the boy's breeches she'd donned. Though constructed of soft wool, the seams rubbed incessantly, leaving a ridge of irritation on the tender skin of her inner thighs.

A steady trickle of rainwater ran down her nose, plunking onto her borrowed fly plaid. Little good the woolen covering did, since beneath it, Yvette's jacket was a drenched, soggy mess. *She* was soaked to the skin, too. She sniffed at the persistent tickle in her nose and sneezed again. Swallowing the burning ache at the back of her throat, she tried to restrain another violent sneeze, to no avail.

She flinched again, adjusting her rump in the saddle. The effort proved futile. The painful pressure in her buttocks and legs persisted. So help her, she'd never complain about a bumpy carriage ride again.

Tied to the saddle, her oilcloth-wrapped hatbox thumped against her thigh, and Yvette winced. She refused to leave it behind. What if she had need of the contents? Better to be prepared. The box banged against her leg again. At this rate, she'd sport a nasty bruise.

No help for it though. The sly miscreants watching the mansion had been diligent, as if they had waited for an escape attempt—and the more she contemplated their flight and pursuit, the more convinced she became that such was the case.

She wiped an icy raindrop from her chin.

Ewan must've known it would be sheer folly to leave Somersfield without a well-thought-out plan. Why else had his enormous male relatives arrived armed to the hilt? Why else had he insisted Adaira journey to Somersfield attired as a boy? And the cave conveniently supplied with the essentials that first night? No, it didn't take a whole lot of cunning to put the pieces together.

Her upper story wasn't empty.

He'd planned every last detail.

It made sense now—the notes and the continuum of taunting intruders. Whoever was intent on intimidating her had wanted to force her hand, wanted her to take flight, and Ewan realized it.

As the horses plodded onward, Yvette huffed out a small, defeated sigh.

She was running away, yet again.

Boston, London, Somersfield.

How weary she'd grown of the calamitous events dominating her once tranquil life.

Lifting her damp face, she scrutinized the dismal sky. Only the silhouettes of the contorting trees were visible, and those only when lightning ripped a jagged path across the tenebrous firmament. The dreary charcoal sky mirrored the bleakness in her soul.

Wrapped in unparalleled weariness as she was, a mile had never seemed so far. Shivering, she sneezed twice, more miserable than at any other time in her life. How she yearned for a hot bath and soft bed. She'd barely the energy to stay in the saddle, and a headache nagged perpetually at the front of her skull. The incessant throbbing kept time with the sturdy clomping steps of her mount.

"I won't complain," she vowed beneath her breath.

Scrunching her eyes against the stinging pellets, Yvette strained to see past the tartan-draped, broad-shouldered men in front of her. She glimpsed the outline of Ewan, strong and upright in his saddle despite the wretched weather. He'd become a source of strength to her. The sight of him renewed her even as she puzzled over his feelings for her.

Three times he'd come to her aid—four, if she counted the runaway carriage. He'd seen to her protection, at some peril to himself, no less. That meant he felt something for her. Didn't it?

She sneezed then wiped her nose on her sleeve.

No mere sense of duty or honor would compel him to escort her, would it? Unless he had ulterior motives, and what could those be? Had his emotions become at all engaged as she suspected hers had? The notion weighed on her.

Wiping her face with the plaid, she crinkled her nose at the smelly, wet wool. *Ugh.* The borrowed garment needed laundering.

Her mare slipped in the muck, the movement jarring Yvette's already tender derriere. Tears pricked her eyes. *Blister it.* Would this wretched ride never end? How much further was...?

What was the name of the blasted inn?

Murdock's? Mulligan's?

Another fatigued sigh escaped her.

Even wholly, desperately in love with Ewan, she wouldn't wed him without a meaningful declaration of affection from him. She'd only marry a man who loved her for herself, not for what she brought to the marriage. Specifically, her colossal wealth.

But how did one know whether it was genuine love or not?

Yvette scraped her lip with her teeth. She ought to have talked with Vangie, told her of her growing doubts. But Vangie had said to trust Ewan.

How can I when he continues to keep secrets from me?

Uneasy, Ewan shrugged tension-stiff shoulders.

The need to get Yvette out of the elements forced him to find shelter, and little was to be had hereabouts.

A few minutes ago, Duncan had fallen in behind him and told Ewan shivers beset her and her teeth chattered.

Dammit.

If it were only he and the other Scots, he'd not worry about lodging at Munlocky's—he'd done so many times before—but reprobates frequented the unsavory establishment. Scoundrels making their living just this side of the law, and some boasting otherwise, were always in attendance. Over the years, Munlocky's had become a haven to all sorts of rabble, brigands, and the like. Several lightskirts, selling their favors to anyone with enough coin, called the inn their home too.

No, Ewan didn't like taking Yvette into their midst at

all. Yet, what choice had he? The gale showed no signs of abating, and she'd suffered in silence for some time.

Though she had pluck, she wasn't accustomed to this type of hardship.

He quirked his mouth upward.

She hadn't complained. Not once.

How many ladies of his acquaintance would've endured so valiantly? Other than his sisters, none.

He glanced skyward and pressed his lips into a hard line. He couldn't subject her to this weather any longer. *Curse this storm.* It complicated his plans and slowed their progress—and that could prove bloody dangerous.

For days, he'd plotted to remove Yvette from Somersfield. But under circumstances he could control and that gave him a strategic advantage, hence the arrival of his kin. He'd set a brisk pace, keeping them ahead of their pursuers, but intentionally leaving signs to permit those following to find their trail.

Ewan led them straight to Craiglocky.

There, his ability to protect and defend Yvette was indisputable. He'd been in high dudgeon, rage simmering within him, for weeks, and he'd use all his skills to snare and destroy those daring to threaten what he'd claimed as his.

Twenty

Yvette heard Munlocky's several minutes before the inn rose into view.

Rowdy, drunken laughter and raucous, lewd singing mingled with a plethora of foul oaths. The shrill tittering of a woman echoed dimly among the dripping trees as a ribald comment sent a wave of warmth skimming over her face.

Good Lord, Munlocky's wasn't a brothel, was it?

Ewan wouldn't dare.

Smoke rose in steamy tendrils from the partial chimneys balanced atop the building's thatched, poorly-patched roof. Light blazed from every shuttered window on the first floor, and a few on the second. Most of the ground-level casings, several hanging crookedly from rusted nails, were thrown wide open, thus explaining the boisterous sounds carrying far into the saturated forest.

She tensed as the seven riders approached the cottage and the Scots grasped their weapons. This place was dangerous. She lifted her hatbox onto her lap. Better to be prepared.

Two armed men, lounging with their booted feet on battered whisky barrels, stood at their approach. They edged their hands to the powerful swords at their waists.

"Who goes there?" demanded a surly voice.

Duncan urged his gelding forward a few paces. "It be Laird Ewan McTavish of Craiglocky Keep and his kinsman. We be wantin' a bed for the night, if'n it pleases ye. This confounded weather waylaid our journey home a wee bit."

"How many ye be?"

"Seven, with our horses and all," Duncan said.

Dugall sidled up to Yvette, and she cast him a troubled glance.

His gave her a reassuring smile and wink. Neither bolstered her confidence a jot.

A squat man appeared limned in the open doorway. Scratching his head, he stepped onto the lopsided porch. "Did I hear the name of McTavish? Ewan, be that ye?"

"Aye, Paddy." Ewan edged Shaidae frontward a bit. "Me and me brethren."

Smiling so wide his ears twitched, Paddy stepped off the porch and trundled toward the newcomers.

"Welcome to ye. Come in the house, *mon*. Get ye out of the weather."

Releasing a puff of air, Yvette turned her attention to dismounting. *Gads.* Was she capable of getting off this horse? Her backside burned something awful. And her legs...

Could she even stand?

Dugall must have sensed her disquiet, because he reached to pluck her off the beast.

Before he touched her, Ewan growled, "Nae." He nudged his brother aside with Shaidae and gave Dugall a grim look. "The *lad* can get off the horse."

Dugall's eyes rounded, but he dipped his head in comprehension. "Aye, Ewan. It's verra sorry I be."

Ewan rode his charger round the other side of Yvette's horse, away from the curious eyes of the guards. He dismounted and, tone low, said, "Evvy, I cannot help you dismount. Not without drawing attention we don't want. Can you manage yourself? They mustn't know you're a woman."

The other riders surrounded her, alighting in a flurry of distracting activity, loud voices, and waving tartans. Setting her jaw, Yvette drew her leg over the saddle. Pain, sharp as a blade, coursed the length of her leg.

"Sweet Jesus," she hissed through clamped teeth.

Biting her lower lip till she drew blood, she turned over. Lying on her stomach and gritting her teeth, she slid off the horse's side. Her legs crumpled when her feet touched the ground. She grabbed the saddle to stay upright.

Ewan's hands steadied her. "That's my lass."

Despite the frigid rain and blowing wind, the sight of Yvette's bottom—tipped upward, face level—as she sprawled on her belly across the mare caused Ewan's pulse to quicken. He sucked in a great gulp of moist air as she wriggled her delectably-rounded *derrière*.

Curling his hand into a fist, he restrained the urge to reach out and smooth his palm over the supple mounds before squeezing their tempting fullness. Though he'd forbidden his hand from enjoying her luscious curves, he allowed his mind to fully indulge.

He tilted his lips into an appreciative grin.

Gripping the saddle, Yvette rested her forehead against

it, croaking, "Lord, I feel dreadful. I can hardly stand, my legs ache so."

Her comment jerked Ewan back to reality. Bloody knave, ogling her backside when she was utterly miserable. He'd bet his finest mare her death grip on the saddle was the only thing keeping her from slithering onto the boggy court-yard. That, and his hand at her elbow.

"Evvy, this is a most unsavory public-house. Keep your eyes lowered and speak to no one. I hope to get you tucked into a room without revealing your gender. It's far from what you are accustomed to, but still better than outdoors."

Still clutching the saddle, she angled toward him. "All right. My hatbox?"

Ewan let loose of her arm. "It will look odd if you carry it in. Hugh will smuggle it in later."

Hugh nodded, his kind eyes crinkled with concern. "Aye, lass. It's not a problem to drape me tartan about the braw box. I shall see ye gets it."

Voice subdued, Ewan glanced to his men. "Look lively, lads. We don't know who may be inside this night. Keep Yvette to the middle, and watch your backs. Weapons at the ready, all of you. Dugall, you and Gregor see to the horses and find your way inside. Be quick about it."

Yvette didn't know where she found the strength to hobble unassisted into the boisterous inn. Only God could've carried her to the dismal entrance, for surely no flesh-and-blood effort would've sufficed. Ewan forged the way, Hugh and Duncan flanked her on either side, and Alasdair's hulking form brought up the rear.

She stumbled twice.

Each time, a steadying hand caught her, releasing its hold the instant she regained her footing. Yvette stepped across the grubby threshold and the light, the noise, and most of all, the women, momentarily stupefied her.

Curious, Yvette peeked upward through her lashes.

A trollop sat on the counter—or rather sprawled across the mutilated surface. She might as well have been unclothed from the waist up, so immodest was the atrocity of a gown she wore.

A disheveled man, obviously in his cups, staggered to the bar, then buried his grizzled head between the harlot's drooping breasts. The tattered kilt he wore hiked upward, exposing most of his hairy backside.

The hussy's shriek of laughter clawed along Yvette's nerves, where it clung, its sharp sting echoing in her ears.

She shook her head, trying to dislodge the din banging in her skull. The humming persisted, whether from the bellowing thunder outside, the clamorous crowd gathered within, or the stomach-churning, relentless pounding in her temples, she didn't know.

Her throat convulsed as she gulped against waves of nausea. She needed to sit.

Now.

Another wench, spying the good-looking, affluent newcomers, sashayed to them. She slapped away the many grimy hands groping her scantily-covered, but more than ample, bosom and bottom.

Cozying up to Ewan, she purred, revealing stained yellow teeth, "Are ye wantin' some company tonight? I'd be most pleased to see to yer manly needs."

Rubbing against him, the tart skimmed her hand along his inner thigh, brushing and cupping his manhood.

A wave of outraged heat blossomed across Yvette's

already hot face. Beneath the cap's low brim, she narrowed her eyes.

How dare she? The… the ladybird.

The strumpet's odor assailed Yvette, and she wrinkled her nose in disgust. *Does she never bathe?* The reeking combination of cheap perfume, whisky, stale tobacco, and another repugnant scent caused Yvette to gag. She swallowed, coughing reflexively to dislodge the bile accosting her throat.

Was she ill? Of all the rotten luck. Here and now when she needed her wits about her?

The slight cough caught the fleshy floozy's attention, and her painted mouth arced into a seductive grin. "Well now, does the laddie need to be taught the pleasures of the flesh?"

Good Lord, no.

Before anyone realized what she was about, the harlot reached around Ewan and snatched the cap from Yvette's head.

A sudden, foreboding hush encompassed the room as Yvette's mass of waterlogged curls cascaded to her waist.

"*Merde.*"

"Shite."

"Jesus, Mary, and Joseph."

Only Duncan remained silent, deftly pulling his broadsword from its leather scabbard.

Horrified, Yvette gasped, her gaze swooping to Ewan. This didn't bode well. Her gaze raked the room, and she recoiled from the leering, lust-filled, gawking men. No, this didn't bode well at all.

Where was her hatbox when she needed it?

Gregor and Dugall barged in, the door banging shut behind them. They went deathly still when their eyes met

Ewan's. Without a word, they moved to stand with their kin, settling into defensive stances.

"Damn it, McTavish, ye ken bawds be the only women allowed." Paddy's angry, blotchy face bobbed above the bar he'd been tending.

"Mayhap she's their *private putain*," a clipped, cultured voice offered from a shadowy corner at the rear of the tavern near the kitchen. "I'd be willing to pay extra for a go at her. Name your fee, McTavish. I'd welcome some fresh arse. These diseased sluts spread their thighs for any man. I've no doubt half of them are riddled with clap."

Several men chortled their agreement.

"Ye filthy plug tail," one of the strumpets screeched.

Cringing, Yvette edged closer to Ewan.

Dugall grabbed his dirk, but Hugh laid a restraining hand on his son's arm. "Easy, son, keep yer heid. Just watch the laird."

Paddy quaffed back a dram, then released a thunderous belch. "Ye mean to share her?"

Aghast, Yvette met his bleary scowl.

Share her?

Surely he doesn't mean—

"Nae." Ewan laid a hand on his broadsword.

His clan followed suit.

Shouts of outrage rang throughout the pub, the rumblings growing more threatening in volume.

The brazen tart seized Yvette's hair and yanked viciously.

"No. Stop." Yvette yelped, seizing the trollop's hand. "Let me go."

The next cruel jerk snapped her head backward, nearly tearing her hair from her scalp. Tears sprang to her eyes, and she ceased struggling.

The wench dragged her to the center of the room.

Ewan's furious growl didn't stop the infuriated harlot. She turned a belligerent glare on Yvette, shouting, "She's nae so special. Who wants her first?"

First?

Yvette renewed her struggles.

The trollop slapped her hard across the face.

Yvette's injured lip stung anew from the blow.

The tavern erupted in chaos as nearly every man present vied for the privilege of bedding her. Several fights broke out. Glass shattered, and whores screamed their outrage. Two young derelicts groped and tugged at Yvette, each trying to gain possession of her.

Terrified, she slapped at the hands accosting her. Raising her eyes, her gaze collided with Ewan's, his face a mask of unflinching fury.

She raised her hands in entreaty.

Help me.

Why didn't he do something?

One man mashed at her breast.

A tormented cry tore from her throat. "Ewan."

Ewan fired his pistol in the air, simultaneously drawing his broadsword.

Wood and straw exploded overhead.

His clan held weapons in both hands, prepared to wreak havoc.

A piece of straw, feather-light, floated from the rafters, settling on the filthy floor of the now eerily quiet room.

"Unhand my *wife*." His words penetrated to the far reaches.

Dugall inhaled sharply, and Alasdair elbowed him in the stomach.

Yvette paid them little mind, focusing her blurry gaze on Ewan.

Wife?

Was there no end to the lies Ewan would tell?

Looking like a man possessed, he glared at the men restraining her, his eyes black, rancorous pools. God help anyone stupid enough to cross him.

His voice dripping with wrath, he angled his broadsword menacingly. "Ye are touching what's mine, idiots."

Yvette tugged against their grasps, but they held tight.

Ewan stepped closer, the tip of his sword wavering between the two. "Do ye mean to die tonight?"

The culls promptly released her. Fear distorting their mangy faces and chins tucked to their chests, they scuttled out the door like a pair of insects.

Driven by fevered fury, Yvette turned on the whore. Raising her hand, she let fly with more strength than she knew she had. The impact of her palm connecting with the trull's cheek rang throughout the silent room.

"Don't—*ever*—touch me again!" Yvette clasped her stinging palm in her other hand.

Holding her flaming cheek, the taunting harlot slithered into a dingy corner to hide in fusty disgrace.

Her head swimming in dizzying waves, Yvette clutched a chair to keep from crumpling to the floor.

One of the patrons mumbled to another, "I ain't never seen a wife that beautiful afore."

Had Ewan truly said wife?

"Wife? The lass be yer wife?" Paddy paused in lifting a cup to his lips. He looked down, perplexed, apparently trying to absorb this new, confounding information. "Yer *married* to the lass, McTavish? Ye took her as yer wife?"

"Aye, I've taken Yvette as my wife." Ewan looked her, unwaveringly in the eye. "To love, honor, and cherish, till death do us part."

Paddy turned a skeptical eye on her, then sniffed before wiping his nose on his stubby forearm. "Ye'r his wife, lass? Ye exchanged vows with the McTavish?"

Even if it isn't true, what's so impossible to believe about that?

Yvette flicked a glance to Ewan, reading the concentrated message in his eyes. She nervously scrutinized the taproom. Several men still leered. She nodded, her wet curls swinging back and forth with the motion.

Ouch.

She ought not to have done that. She pressed a shaky hand to her throbbing scalp.

"Yes. I..." Her eyes met Ewan's again, and she swallowed.

Say it.

"I'm married to Laird McTavish. I'm his wife."

The world tilted around her, and not just because her head throbbed abominably and she felt perfectly wretched.

Now she and Ewan pretended to be wed. First a false betrothal, and now these people thought they were actually married. What a bumblebroth. At least his family knew the truth.

She cut a wary glance in Paddy's direction.

Lines of doubt creased his forehead, and his disbelief bracketed his downward-curved mouth.

Didn't he believe her?

He *had* to believe her, or else these men...

At the thought, a terror-born shudder shook her from shoulder to knees.

Forcing a smile to her lips, Yvette added for good

measure, "Of course we exchanged vows. We're married. For better or worse, in sickness and in health, till death do us part."

She'd never lied so much in her life.

Dugall made an inarticulate sound in his throat, and Yvette sent him a quizzical look.

Why were Ewan's relatives grinning like inebriated, oversized baboons? Did Dugall wink at her? This was nothing to laugh about.

Were *all* Scots touched in the head?

Only Ewan looked serious.

Why?

A smattering of alarm sounded in the recesses of her muddled mind.

Whatever in the world was going on?

Cackling in glee, Paddy slapped his podgy thigh before gulping the fiery liquid he held in his stumpy hand.

"If ye weren't before," he chortled, "ye are now."

Twenty-One

Yvette tottered across the room, stumbling into Ewan's waiting arms. Pressing her aching head into his chest, she begged throatily, "Please, take me away from here."

Ewan felt the fear shaking her slight figure, riddling her entire body with tremors. He cupped her hot cheek in a comforting gesture. Fright caused her trembling, didn't it?

"Paddy, is my chamber ready?"

"Aye."

Scooping her into his arms, her loose hair swishing an inch from his muddied boots, Ewan faced Hugh. "Can you acquire warm water?"

Hugh gathered Yvette's sunny locks, carefully twisting them into a rope before laying them across her bent body.

She lay against Ewan with eyes closed, face white as death.

Hugh's lips thinned. "Aye, son."

Ewan directed his attention to Duncan. "We need to eat. Bread and cheese are fine, if Paddy has naught else." He examined the grimy parlor. "Buy a round for all. Don't spare the coin. Mayhap we can avoid any more complications this night."

"I'll see to it," Duncan assured him.

Before he turned to climb the stairs, Ewan met the two older men's eyes. "I need to speak to you as soon as I've seen to Yvette."

"Is the lass verra sick?" Hugh touched her forehead.

Frowning, Ewan glanced at the bundle in his arms. *Sick?* Was that why she shivered so? He hitched a shoulder. "I don't know."

He prayed she wasn't.

Munlocky's wasn't the place to get ill. The riffraff here would kill you in your sickbed between drams of whisky and tussles in the sack.

Ewan reached his usual chamber and after sliding Yvette to the floor, supporting her limp form with one arm, he unlatched the well-worn door. Toeing it open, he left it ajar, allowing the dull light from below to lend a faint glow to the room's interior.

Lifting her again, he frowned. Heat radiated off her.

He strode to the bed, and after setting her tenderly on the rope mattress, made quick work of lighting the candle on the bedside table before lighting two more wall tapers.

He withdrew a wicked-looking knife from his boot. He might have need of it yet this night.

Too tired to attempt to remove her sopped plaid, Yvette lay on her back, her legs dangling over the edge of the bed. The drumming in her head had reached an apex, and it took monumental strength just to keep her eyes open. Lord, her head hurt.

A fine counterpane lay smoothed across the bumpy surface, and she fingered the bed covering.

If satin sheets didn't lie beneath the coverlet, she wasn't blond.

She quirked her mouth, the movement pulling at the dried blood on her lower lip, and she winced. She ran her tongue tentatively over the cut. The small abrasion was the least of her injuries from the grueling trip. Dismounting from that blasted horse had been excruciating.

She sniffed, as much because of the room's staleness as her stuffy nose. Likely, the chamber was seldom used, the air musty from lack of circulation.

Ewan strode to the lone casement. Throwing open the shutters, he spoke over his shoulder. "I'll close the window once the room has aired."

Yvette rather liked the damp, refreshing air. She remained silent though, too weak and tired to bother talking.

When she didn't respond, he frowned.

Sighing, she levered onto her elbows, regarding him through a pain-induced haze.

There, that should please him.

He crossed to the door and push it closed with a hollow *thunk*, then slide the bolt into place. He removed his tartan, hanging it on a peg before approaching the bed.

"Let's get some of those wet clothes off you."

She didn't say a word as he removed the drenched plaid. She felt remarkably light without the saturated tartan's weight.

Ewan kneeled before her and gently pulled off her boots then her soaked socks.

She didn't remember closing her eyes, but they popped open when he exclaimed, "Your feet are freezing."

Well, what had he expected? She almost laughed, but shivered instead.

He lifted one foot. "I'm going to rub your feet to warm them."

She slouched, staring at him.

Placing the foot on his knee, he rubbed the sole, forcing the blood to circulate. As her foot warmed, pins and needles galloped relentlessly through her icy veins.

Ouch. It hurts.

As he switched to her other foot, he glanced up, and his gaze fell on her mouth. "What happened to your lip?" His face hardened. "Did *she* do that to you?"

Surprise arched Yvette's brows. He hadn't noticed her lip downstairs? "No. I bit my lip to keep from crying out when I dismounted."

His rough hand lingered on her instep. "I'm sorry. I never thought—"

A light tapping interrupted him, and he set her foot down. In three strides, he reached the door and opened it to admit Duncan and Hugh.

Hugh held a bucket, a cloth, and what appeared to be crudely-fashioned soap, as well as Yvette's hatbox tucked under one arm.

The dear, he'd remembered her hatbox.

Duncan carried a shabby, one-handled tray, sporting a bottle of wine, a crusty loaf of bread, some hard cheese, and a knife.

Glancing over the tray, Ewan's face broke into a smile. "Thank ye, uncle." He slapped Duncan on the back. "Put it on the table, will ye?"

Duncan moved to the table. "Cock-a-leekie soup's about ready below," he said. "Paddy keeps his daughter hidden in the kitchen. The lass be a fine cook. Anythin' else ye need?" He looked at Yvette, a troubled vee between his full brows.

Ewan followed Duncan's gaze. "Tea, if they have it."

Oh, that would be wonderful.

"Evvy cannot drink wine. It makes her ill." Ewan took the bucket and soap from Hugh.

Duncan moved to the door. "Aye, I'll check on the tea, though I doubt they have much call for the brew."

Hugh still held her hatbox. Raising it in the air, he sent Ewan a questioning look.

Ewan slanted his head in the direction of the bedside table while depositing the bathing goods on the washstand. "Over there, please."

Oddly detached, Yvette slumped through their whole exchange. The ringing in her ears had subsided into a steady, low-pitched roar. She'd gone from shivering with cold to sweltering hot.

She swung her gaze to the window.

Yes, the window's open.

She fingered her jacket and breeches.

And yes, her clothing was soaking wet. Whyever was she so warm then?

Had she caught a fever? Bad business, that.

Ewan crouched before her again. "Will you be all right for a few moments? I need to speak to the others."

She nodded the tiniest bit. More vigorous movement sent shards of pain stabbing through her skull.

"That's my lass." Ewan patted her knee then straightened. He left the room, closing the lopsided panel behind him.

To stop the swirling in her head, Yvette clutched at the bedding. Why did her head seem so heavy? She flopped backward onto the bed, staring at the crude ceiling. It cavorted about, spinning and dipping before sucking her into a dark, comforting vortex of oblivion.

~

Ewan didn't trust Munlocky's rabble rousers. He knew their type. Those intent on enjoying Yvette's favors earlier would feel thwarted and deserving of some recompense. He wouldn't put it past some of the more daring, unscrupulous scunners to try to snatch her for ransom—or worse.

The inn's revelry would continue until the wee morning hours. Most of the carousers would sleep where they passed out, sprawled on the floor or drooped across a table. Few had sufficient coin to rent a room. The bawds lived in a small cottage behind the inn, but most nights shared a bed with a paying customer.

He'd already asked his kinsmen to take shifts guarding his door. Gregor volunteered to stand the first watch. As luck would have it, the room opposite Ewan's was vacant. The others would rest there, requiring no more than their tartans to sleep comfortably.

He took Hugh and Duncan aside, and less than twenty minutes later, they thundered from the cottage's soggy yard into the blustery night.

Upon entering his chamber, alarm sluiced through Ewan upon seeing Yvette stretched across the bed. He rushed to her.

"Evvy?" He caressed her soft cheek with his forefinger. The devil take it. Was she asleep or unconscious? He tried again, tapping her shoulder. "Evvy?"

Almost incoherent, she mumbled, "Let me sleep. I'm tired."

"*Ma petite*, you need to bathe and eat."

"*Uh-uhm.* Just sleep." She weakly rubbed her hand across her flushed face. Her bent arm plopped across her eyes. The rough fabric of her coat caught her lip, causing it to bleed again.

After dipping the washcloth in the bucket of warm water, he returned to her. As he dabbed the blood from her lip, she began shivering once more.

He tossed the cloth on the bedside table. "I need to take off your wet clothing."

"Nooo," Yvette protested. "Sleeping."

Ewan chuckled. She had a stubborn streak.

"Stop laughing, brute."

Restraining the chuckle surging to his lips, he unfastened her jacket. "Sorry, *ma petite*, it must be done."

"Bully."

A relieved grin tipped his mouth. If she was this feisty, she couldn't be too ill.

Could she?

After slipping the jacket from her shoulders, he worked the laces of her shirt. Underneath, she wore a frilly ivory chemise tucked into her breeches. The silk stuck to her like a second skin, her rosy nipples protruding, protesting the cold.

Casting the shirt aside, he then released the fastenings of her breeches. Already skintight, when soaking wet they had to be peeled from her quaking form.

As he tugged them off, Yvette groaned.

"*Merde.*" Ewan swore beneath his breath.

Telltale bruises had formed on the tender flesh of her legs, disappearing at the juncture between her thighs. No doubt, if he turned her over, the offending blotches would cover her *derrière,* too.

He lifted the fluttering candle from the bedside table.

Holding it aloft, he stood over her. The added light clearly revealed her injuries.

"Bloody hell."

His gaze lingered on the shadowy triangle from whence the marks emerged. Dozens of angry purple and red lesions lay across Yvette's satiny inner thighs. Welts to below her knees had raised in ugly protest.

Trembling, she curled into a ball, tucking her legs to her chest.

Worried, Ewan tugged the bedspread over her. He closed the shutters, then collected the items to bathe her. "Evvy, I'm going to wash you. I'll not be overly familiar, but your skin is too cold. The warm water will help rid you of the chill."

As if caring for a newborn infant, he bathed her, everywhere except where her filmy chemise covered her.

Levering her limp form into a sitting position, Ewan toweled her hair, removing much of the moisture. Her curls sprang about her head and shoulders in wild disarray. They crept round his fingers and arms like living vines. He lifted her chin, searching her cloudy eyes. "Can you manage your—"

He paused, taking a different tack.

"There's hot soup below stairs. I'll have Gregor fetch the broth, and I'll give him your clothing to dry before the fire. I want to fetch ointment for your legs too. I won't be long." He canted his head, studying her overly pale face. "If I leave, are you able to finish bathing?"

"I can manage," she rasped, averting her gaze.

Brows pinched, Ewan considered her. A blush crept across her fever-flushed skin. "I'll be but a few moments, *doucette*."

After gathering her wet clothing from where he'd

strewn them on the floor, he left the chamber. Gregor, already on duty in the corridor, looked up when Ewan left his chamber.

"Find Alasdair and ask him to take Yvette's clothing and hang it before the fire below." Ewan passed the garments to Gregor. "He's to stay with them until they dry. I cannot leave her, and she has naught else to wear." His attention flicked to the closed door. "The ruffians below will steal her garments without hesitation."

Gregor draped the wet clothing over his arm. "Aye. How be the lass?"

Ewan ran his hand through his nearly-dry hair. Sighing, he cupped the base of his neck and shrugged. "She's weak as a newborn kitten and needs to eat. There's hot soup in the kitchen. Fetch a bowl for us, would you please?"

"Of course." Gregor started for the stairs.

"Ah, Gregor." Chagrin kicked Ewan in the arse.

Gregor, paused after a half-step. "Aye?"

"Have ye yer medicines with ye? Yvette needs a healing ointment. Her legs are..." Ewan shook his head in self-condemnation. "I never should've allowed her to ride astride."

Gregor placed his great hand on Ewan's shoulder. "Ye couldnae have kent. I shall fetch the ointment."

Nodding his thanks, Ewan slipped back into his chamber. He closed the door, eyeing the lump in the middle of the bed. Better to leave Yvette be for now. Supper needed preparing anyway. After slicing the bread, he cut the cheese into bite-sized pieces. As he uncorked the wine, he searched the table for a cup.

Blast.

Nothing for it then. He took a healthy pull and shuddered. Grimacing, he re-corked the bottle.

Foul, inferior stuff, that.

A knock sounded.

Ewan opened the door, revealing Gregor awkwardly balancing a tray with two bowls of soup, a teapot, and a cup with a cracked saucer. A small jar of salve also sat upon the tray. "Here be the rest of yer meal. And the ointment too. Spread the medicine on her legs morn and night."

"Thank you." With his shoulder, Ewan shoved the door closed. He strode to the bed. "*Ma chérie*, I've hot soup. Sit up so you can eat."

A tussled blond head appeared from beneath the covers. Yvette sniffed, her nose wrinkling adorably as her stomach growled. "It smells delicious."

Ewan smiled. Good, she was hungry.

She climbed from her cocoon. Bedspread pulled to her chin, she sagged against the wall.

Ewan shook his head. "That'll never do."

He placed the tray on the chair before plucking the cover from her hands, disregarding her surprised gasp. He wrapped the bedspread about her shoulders. Head cocked and hands on his hips, he stood back and eyed his handwork.

"That's better."

Yvette stared at him, glassy-eyed.

He poured a cup of tea.

"Drink," he ordered as he passed it to her.

Yvette refrained from making a face. Only the pounding in her head and the fact that sitting upright took every bit of strength she had, kept her from doing so. He'd taken to ordering her about, and she didn't like it in the least.

He took the cup resting on her lap and replaced it with a plate of cheese and bread.

She shook her head. "I'd prefer the soup, please."

She didn't tell him her throat hurt dreadfully, and she doubted she'd be able to swallow a single bite of anything solid. Just speaking hurt.

Without a word, he handed her a steaming bowl.

Knowing he watched her, she tried to eat the tasty broth. She managed to swallow several spoonfuls before weariness overtook her. Slumping, she rested her head against the wall, fighting to keep her eyes open. They kept fluttering shut of their own accord.

She dozed off, rousing when Ewan blurted, "The devil take it!"

Yvette opened wooly eyes and tried to focus on his much-too-serious face. The bowl in her lap must've tipped, and he'd caught it in time to prevent the contents from ruining the bedding. She lowered her gaze to the bed.

Satin sheets.

Of course they were.

"You've had enough, I think." After setting her bowl aside, he showed her a small jar. "This is ointment, for your legs. The ride left you with some abrasions and bruising."

She let her eyes drift shut again. "I shall be fine. I only want to sleep."

She scootched lower into the bed, intent on succumbing to the muzzy sensation enveloping her.

"Nae, lass, I insist." The bed squeaked and dipped with his weight. "You'll be worse in the morning if I don't tend you tonight."

Ewan *was* becoming a bully. Too exhausted to argue, she lay on her stomach. "Oh fine, since you insist."

He flipped aside the coverlet and a moment later, his

soothing hands, feather light, rubbed the salve on her legs. The gentle kneading relaxed her, and within a few minutes, she was far less uncomfortable.

When the soothing strokes of his hands skimmed across her sore buttocks, she shifted restlessly. Something foreign flickered to life. She bit her lip to keep from gasping aloud. Ewan must stop or she'd be groaning in pleasure. He *had* to stop before she embarrassed herself.

Voice thick and rasping, Yvette murmured, "Thank you, Ewan. I'm much better. The salve has been helpful."

Lord, even ill as she was, she responded to his touch like a practiced wanton.

The caressing stopped, though his fingers lingered. She fought the urge to press her bum into his palms as sleep claimed her.

Mindful not to apply pressure to Yvette's tender skin or jar her overworked muscles, Ewan had gently rubbed her soft flesh. Despite her pitiful condition, he'd found her inarticulate gasps and sighs arousing, and his manhood had stiffened.

Ye gods, man, control yourself.

The defiant appendage still remained erect.

He needed a finger's worth or two of brandy or whisky.

He eyed the wine bottle.

No, not that weak swill.

Yvette sighed, turning over and wincing in her sleep.

Her restless slumber caused him to scowl and silently swear.

She was in this hellhole, in this condition, because of Marquardt, Fielding, Pauline, and the spymaster. There must be a common thread amongst that quartet, and Yvette appeared to be that thread, though how she figured into it the whole scheme, Ewan had yet to discover.

He smoothed her hair from her flushed face. Even in her sleep, her features pinched in pain.

Wasn't this what he'd hoped for? That she'd be useful in forcing the spies' hands?

Yes, but that was before he knew whom he was up against, before he realized the risk to her.

Before I'd come to care for her.

His conscience was having none of it, and it chastised him soundly.

What a Banbury story of cock and bull.

Fine. Truth to tell, he'd suspected the risk but had been confident of his ability to keep her safe. Now, even with his clan members at hand, doubt wormed its insidious way into his mind.

Yvette moaned softly.

He'd not done a tip-top job of it, now had he? The guilt simmering within flared to life, serving to curb his lustful tension as no self-denial could.

A brief rapping pattered at the door once more. Ewan tugged the coverlet over Yvette before sauntering to the entrance and cracking it open.

Alasdair stood there with Yvette's dry clothing draped across one bulging arm. In his other hand, he extended a large wooden cup, worn smooth with use.

Ewan edged the door open farther, and after sniffing the cup's contents, a grin split his face.

It might not be a crystal snifter, but he received the burnished amber floating within with exuberant thanks. "How did ye know?"

One fair brow elevated, Alasdair snickered. "If I had to

sleep with a verra bonnie lass without dipping me wick...?" He hefted his massive shoulders. "I filled the cup to the brim with Scots whisky for ye, cousin. I dinnae ken if I could keep me hands off such a temptin' armful, especially if she was my *wife*."

Ewan raised a finger to his lips and glanced over his shoulder at the sleeping bundle nestled in his bed. He nudged Alasdair out the door. In the hallway, he looked at Gregor leaning against the rough planking of the grungy wall, then shifted his gaze back to Alasdair.

"Dinnae speak of it in front of Yvette. I need time to tell her. To prepare her."

A teasing smile playing about his lips, Gregor gave a brief nod. "How be the lass?"

"Better now that she's bathed and eaten." Ewan puckered his brows. "She's not herself though." His hand on the door latch, he paused. "Duncan and Hugh?"

"Left more than an hour ago," Alasdair offered, passing over the clothing and brew.

Ewan nodded. "Excellent. Till the morrow, then."

In the chamber, he paused to take a lengthy swallow of the pungent liquid. It raced a welcome, heated path to his gut, spreading sizzling warmth throughout his innards.

"Ewan?" Scant more than a raspy croak carried to him.

Surprised to find Yvette awake, he sat on the edge of the bed.

She lay curled on her side, one hand cupping her face, the other wrapped around the pillow.

Laying a palm across her hot brow, he gave her a tender smile "What is it? I thought you were asleep."

She considered him before her gaze shifted to the candle on the table. "Is your room nearby? This place frightens me."

"This *is* my room. You cannot sleep alone here." He drew the bed covering over her shoulders. "It's simply too dangerous. My kin stand guard outside the door even now."

"Oh." She was silent for a moment. "You'll share this bed with me?"

Ewan sighed, not relishing the idea of sleeping on the floor. "I can make a pallet if the idea of sharing a bed disturbs you."

"Oh."

He stood, reluctant to leave her, even for a few moments. "I'll fetch another blanket."

"There's no need. There's room enough." To prove her point, she rolled to the far side of the small bed. Her attempt at a brave smile wrenched his heart.

"My clothing needs to dry. I'll have to remove all of it."

"Oh."

"I'll blow out the candles before undressing. Does that meet with your approval?"

"Yes." Her response was so soft, he strained to hear her.

Blowing the candles out, Ewan couldn't contain a self-satisfied smile. He took another stiff swig of whisky. The strong drink would help him sleep and also keep his mind off more carnal pursuits.

I hope.

When the bed dipped with his weight, Yvette sucked in a quick, short breath. Was she afraid? The notion didn't settle well with him.

"*Doucette*, are you sure?"

Silence greeted his question.

Well, hell. What had he expected? He scooted to the edge of the bed, halting when she laid her hand on his arm.

"Yes," she whispered.

He lay down, carefully draping the sheet over his lower body.

~

Ewan lay so close, Yvette inhaled his scent with every breath.

He smelled of strong drink, rain, and the familiar spicy scent she had come to associate with him—a pleasant, comforting aroma.

When he rolled onto his side, she knew he stared at her. She lay on her back, looking at the ceiling. Her eyes hadn't adjusted to the dark yet, and blackness loomed before her probing gaze. She'd sucked her lower lip into her mouth in a vain attempt to stop trembling.

Ewan stirred beside her. "Evvy, if you're afraid, I'll sleep—"

"No. I'm not afraid, just cold." She swallowed, then winced when her throat protested. "I cannot seem to get warm." Each word tortured her inflamed throat.

He shifted closer, drawing her against him. "Let me warm you, *petite amie*."

Oh, it did feel wonderful, snuggled next to him, sharing his body's heat. However, her conscience wasn't one to let the matter go. It railed in silent yet unrelenting protest, convicting her.

God's toenails.

She lay in bed with a naked man. Again.

Only now, she pretended to be his wife.

Twenty-Two

The storm blew by, leaving cloying air in its wake. Throughout the night, Ewan kept Yvette tucked to his side. His worry increased as the moon, like a mistress who's no longer desired, slipped away, and the sun rose in cheerful resolution.

Yvette shivered and mumbled in her sleep, striving to push the covers off her sweat-slickened body. Twice during the night, he rose and wiped her with the cooled water from the bucket.

Near dawn, she settled into a restful slumber.

He slipped from the bed and opened the shutters before dressing with practiced efficiency. Cracking the door, he poked his head out and signaled Alasdair.

His chair propped on the two back legs, his cousin relaxed against the wall, whittling.

"Have ye broken your fast?" Ewan asked.

"Nae one's about yet." Alasdair lowered the chair.

"Rouse the others." Ewan opened the door a bit farther. He rested his forearm above his head on the doorjamb. "See if you can round up some tea and perhaps porridge. Some

Scotch pies and oatcakes to take with us too. If need be, wake Paddy's daughter, and pay her handsomely. I want to depart within the hour."

"Aye." Alasdair smirked, a wicked glint in his eye. "How did ye sleep?"

Ewan's answering grin revealed nothing and everything. "Well enough, *mon*."

~

Yvette struggled awake through layers of dense mist. Her eyelids felt made of stone. With gritty perseverance, she forced them open, and immediately regretted it when blinding pain sliced through her head. Taking slow, deep breaths, she ventured a tiny peek through narrowed slits.

Ah, much better.

Ewan stood at the open door speaking to someone.

Lord, she ached everywhere.

She swallowed against the tightness in her throat. A drink of water would be heavenly. Her attention lit on the teapot from last night. Cold tea would suffice. Sitting upright, she waited until the room stopped whirling before sliding her throbbing legs off the edge of the mattress.

Gripping the mattress, she took several shuffling, sideways steps toward the desperately craved liquid.

"What do you think you're doing?" Ewan's sharp question startled her.

Yvette spun about to face him. Already light-headed and off-balance, the motion sent her flailing.

He caught her before she crashed to the ground.

Her bare limbs lay exposed to an amused Alasdair.

With a mortified squeak, she pressed her face into Ewan's chest, alerting him to his leering cousin.

Ewan shot an irritated glance behind him. "You wouldn't be ogling my wife, would ye, cousin?"

She wished he wouldn't call her his wife. It was a lie.

"Aye, I would," Alasdair answered with a low rumble of laughter.

Yvette peeked over Ewan's shoulder as his cousin sauntered down the corridor. She steered her gaze to Ewan once more.

His attention was fixated on her bosom where her chemise gaped open, revealing her breasts, complete with puckered tips, to his heated stare.

She sucked in a sharp breath, the air on her raw throat causing it to spasm in complaint. As the heat from twin streaks of crimson skated up her face, she snatched the chemise to her chest.

"Let me up." She shoved against his unyielding embrace.

"Not without my assistance. You're not well." Supporting her with his strong hands, he asked again, "What were you doing?"

Yvette shrugged, the motion sending her hair swinging. "I'm thirsty. There's no clean water, so I thought to have some tea."

He skewed a brow skeptically. "It's cold."

"I care not. I'm parched."

Ewan leaned away, studying her. "You've taken a chill. I don't want you attempting anything more strenuous than a sneeze without my assistance." He gripped her upper arms, his gaze boring into hers. "Do you understand me, Yvette? Not. A. Thing."

Yvette? What happened to Evvy?

Perhaps because she felt wretched, something sparked, then simmered mutinously within her. She narrowed her eyes to mere slits and pursed her lips in irritation.

Ewan was dictating to her—again—something he'd done almost from the moment she'd met him. She had a lifetime of suppressing her feelings, of being docile and compliant. Straightening, she shrugged from his grasp.

"You seem to forget, my lord, I am *not* your wife, nor am I one of your underlings. Necessity may have forced us to share this chamber, but that doesn't mean you can order me about."

Necessity that now had her reputation in tatters. She was utterly ruined.

Stepping behind the ramshackle chair, she clenched the back with a white-knuckled grip, essential to still her shaking and remain standing. Lest Ewan see any show of weakness, she straightened her spine and jutted her chin. "I'm capable of tending to myself this morning, my lord. As for your assistance, it's neither required nor appreciated. Do *I* make myself clear?"

He scowled. "Let me—"

"I won't delay our departure, if that's your concern." She wasn't an idiot. Pure folly to remain here. Sick or not, they must leave.

"Fine. I shall return in fifteen minutes. See to it you're dressed and prepared to eat." With that parting shot, he left her to dress.

Yvette felt awful, emotionally and physically. She flopped onto the bed. How to struggle into her clothing— well, that should prove interesting. Or entertaining. As she yanked a thick, woolen sock onto her foot, her focus fell on her marred legs.

Gads. No wonder she hurt so. How in the name of heaven would she be able to ride today?

She cringed, and her stomach dropped as her head began to spin in what was becoming a familiar turbulence. She lifted the ointment, and after removing the cap and sniffing the salve, dabbed the greasy, pungent cream on her sore legs.

She wanted nothing more than to crawl into bed and stay there for days. With grim, willful stubbornness, she refused to allow Ewan to even suspect how miserable she actually was.

Never at her best when ill—her ability to temper her rebellious tendencies proved most difficult to suppress—she didn't know why she felt compelled to defy him. Perhaps because she'd no control over her life since Ewan took charge of seeing her to Vangie's. Again a man told her what she could and couldn't do, and it frustrated her no end.

Papa had been a wonderful father, and he'd provided her with everything a woman of her status could possibly desire. But his overprotectiveness had bordered on smothering control.

She'd often wondered if the real reason he hadn't insisted she marry was because he'd no longer be able to protect her. She also suspected his obsession had begun when she'd nearly died in the carriage accident that took her mother's life.

Pausing, Yvette rubbed her oily thumb and forefinger together.

In any event, Papa had shielded her from everything unpleasant and ugly in the world. She'd adored him, so she'd never done anything outside his will—even when it meant squashing her own desires.

She wouldn't quell her preferences anymore. Her more compliant nature surfaced, and she sighed.

Was she being unfair? Ewan was only concerned for

her wellbeing, wasn't he? Why he riled her so, she couldn't begin to understand. He had the ability to infuriate her, and yet when he looked at her with those startling eyes, she turned into a quivering lump of lemon cream.

∽

Ewan marched up the wobbly staircase, wholly prepared to find Yvette in her shift, contrite and apologetic, and grateful he'd returned to assist her. Either that, or splayed unconscious on the floor.

She acted like an intractable child, the stubborn chit.

He'd seen her tumbling toward the floor, and his heart had done something painful and foreign. Though not a great fall, she was frail. In her weakened state, she might've been injured, delaying their departure, and lingering at Munlocky's was lethal. He must see her to Craiglocky forthwith, and his anxiety had caused him to speak harsher than he'd intended.

His staccato knocking rattled the door, a mite more enthusiastically than required.

"Come in," Yvette called.

Surprised but pleased, he found Yvette sitting on the bed, fully clothed, right down to her boots. Her hatbox rested beside her on the rumpled bedding, and she'd just finished tying a ribbon at the end of her long braid.

Holding another time-worn serving tray, he shouldered his way into the room.

He placed the laden tray on the table. Two bowls of steaming porridge, a small pitcher of cream, and more tea teetered on the surface. A mug held ice-cold well water.

∽

Yvette licked her parched lips. While he'd been downstairs, she'd gulped some cold tea, only to promptly gag it up. Though grayish and globby, if one didn't look at the porridge, it smelled quite good. She reached for the water, intending to thank Ewan for his thoughtfulness. "Ewan—"

"You cannot ride astride today."

Having drawn the same conclusion herself, she was unwilling to admit it to him. Instead, she tucked her hairbrush, Bible, and salve into the hatbox, then replaced the tooth cleanser and strands of ribbon. Her dagger and pistol followed.

Perversely, she argued, "Oh, my lord? How else will I travel to Craiglocky?"

Confound it. She swore inwardly when her voice cracked.

Ewan sat beside her. "Evvy, stop calling me my lord."

"*Your lordship,* unless I sprout wings and fly, my only recourse is horseback." Feeling truly rebellious, she stretched and peeked over her shoulder. She pointed to her back. "No wings, milord. It's plain I'll have to mount a horse."

"Those below believe us wed. A Scots wife doesn't call her husband 'my lord.'" Clearly annoyed but struggling to control his temper, Ewan scraped a hand through his hair.

Even disheveled, his slightly-too-long ebony hair flattered him.

Arching a mutinous brow, Yvette dared, "And just who gave them reason to believe we were wed, my lord? You're the one who continues to perpetuate that myth, and I want you to cease at once."

Ewan looked at her hard. "These people must believe us wed, else you're in grave danger."

"So *you* say, Lord Sethwick." Yvette reached for the cup,

then took a grateful swallow of the sweet water. The icy coolness soothed her irritated throat and emboldened her. "Perhaps it was only a ploy to publicly ruin me, so I'd have to marry you. I overheard Lord Ramsbury at the inn. You haven't exactly been forthright with me, have you?"

Ewan stiffened, the line of his mouth flattening and his eyes darkening dangerously.

Indignation spurring her on, she lowered her voice in imitation of the earl. "'A wealthy wife is always an asset. I'd say you've done quite well for yourself, old chap.' Sounds rather like you planned this entire charade to entrap me."

Merciful God, did I truly say that?

It must be her illness speaking.

Face granite hard, Ewan lifted the cup from her shaking hand and set it on the bedside table.

She couldn't tear her gaze off his eyes—bottomless pools reflecting to the depths of his soul.

And he was angry—in fact, livid—with her. His moon-shaped scar ticked rhythmically.

She'd gone too far. "Ewan—"

"Yvette, remember what happened the last time you didn't use my given name? I've counted no fewer than five," he held up as many fingers, "times you've intentionally defied me."

She couldn't swallow past the constriction in her throat. She'd done it up brown now. Holding her hand before her to ward him off, she shook her head.

In a movement so swift she didn't even have time to gasp, he lay atop her torso, pinning her with his weight. His gaze pierced hers before he lowered his head. She felt a soft, fluttering touch and a slight sting on her sore lip as his mouth brushed hers.

"One." Playful and tender. He nibbled at the corner of her mouth until it slackened beneath the onslaught.

"Two." Inquisitive and inviting. He traced the seam of her lips with his tongue, pulling the lower one into his open mouth, tugging gently.

"Three." Breathless and gravelly. Head angled, Ewan's open mouth and teasing tongue mesmerized Yvette until her lips parted, allowing him to take his fill.

"Four." Low and strangled with desire. Head descending, his hot mouth connected with her welcoming one.

Long-repressed passion welled forth and burst its banks. The floodgates opened, the dam broke, and she couldn't restrain her overwhelming desire. She wrapped her arms around his muscled back, tugging him ever closer, unmindful of his weight pressing her chest and shoulders into the disheveled bed.

"Blister it, I made your lip bleed."

His soft curse brought Yvette sailing back to her senses. Dazed, she lay staring at him. She weakly quipped, "That was more than five," before averting her face, coughs racking her.

Ewan propped her up before retrieving the cup of water. He held it to her lips, and she took a lengthy drink. When she was done, he set the cup down then dabbed the blood off her lip. All solicitous now, he pressed a cup of warm tea into her cold hands before standing.

"Try to drink some tea. Please."

The latter seemed an afterthought, but it delighted her no end.

Yvette smiled against the chipped cup's rim, taking a tentative sniff of the dark contents. A fragrant aroma, faintly spicy, earthy even, wafted upward. "What is it?"

As he gathering their belongings, Ewan's regard veered

to the cup. "It's a special brew Gregor prepared. It has healing qualities."

To please Ewan, she took a hesitant sip. Tart tanginess ambushed her tongue, but she tasted sweetness too. Mayhap honey? Only lukewarm, the liquid glided down her throat. A slight numbness permeated her tongue before the throbbing in her throat eased. "It's good."

She glanced at their cooled breakfast, the porridge congealed and less than appetizing. Stomach churning, she grimaced in distaste. She couldn't eat that, but she didn't want to seem ungrateful either.

"Never mind, *chéri*." Ewan approached the bed. "We'll eat along the way."

"All right."

Walking slowly, and holding Ewan's arm, Yvette left the chamber.

Dugall and Alasdair waited in the corridor to escort them below. What must they be thinking? She blushed, but summoned a brave smile. "Thank you for standing watch last night. I hope you had a chance to sleep yourselves."

Alasdair responded, "Aye, lass, we did."

Dugall's face broke into a roguish grin, and he winked. "How did *ye* sleep, *sister*?"

Her alarmed gaze flew to Ewan's.

Good God, did Dugall think...?

This time, the heat shot from her feet to the top of her head.

"Dugall." Ewan's tone held censure.

Dugall bent to speak to Yvette and, *sotto voce*, advised, "My brother's a bit tetchy in the morn. I'd better take ye below." The scamp stepped in front of Ewan and led her away by her elbow.

Yvette sent an apologetic closed-mouth smile over her

shoulder, but faltered at Ewan's fierce scowl. "You oughtn't to have done that, Dugall."

"I ken." With another unabashed wink and flash of teeth, he started whistling a ditty.

Grateful she didn't have to attempt small talk, she concentrated on staying upright on her aching legs. The effort took every ounce of her strength and determination, and when blackness threatened three times, she touched the wall to steady herself.

At the bottom of the staircase, she wiped away the moisture glistening on her upper lip.

Ewan came up behind her and expeditiously steered her through the open door. Not, however, before she noticed several prostrate bodies in the common room.

The radiant sun reflected brilliantly off the wet ground where puddles of muddy water littered the courtyard. By day's end, likely every sign of the violent torrent would be gone. Yvette squinted, raising a hand to shield her eyes against the brutal brightness radiating from the now-clear blue sky.

What met her pained gaze caused her to halt mid-step. She opened and closed her mouth in astonishment at the vivid array displayed before her. At least fifty mounted, tartan-clad Scots milled about the yard. Another dozen stood in small groups, chatting and laughing.

Hugh and Duncan conversed with two men. As she and Ewan stepped from Munlocky's threshold, the foursome approached.

A shortish man, with sand-brown hair and a jagged scar from his right eye to the corner of his mouth, gripped Ewan's arm. "It's pleased I be to see ye, Ewan McTavish."

"And I ye, Roby McIntyre." Ewan greeted his friend just as enthusiastically.

Another man, slender with solemn hazel eyes, grasped Ewan's forearm in greeting. "McTavish."

Ewan grinned. "Shamus O'Donovan, thank ye."

Yvette swayed ever so slightly before dissolving into a fit of coughing. Putting a bracing arm around her waist, Ewan drew her to his side. Though grateful for his solid form to rest against, she colored nevertheless. His possessiveness in front of this many curious men—strangers to her—disconcerted.

"Ewan, are these men all relatives?" She grasped his sturdy arm to steady herself.

She swayed again, catching herself, but only after stepping on his foot.

Take a deep breath. There, that's better.

He tightened his arm around her waist.

"Aye. By blood, marriage, or choice, these are some of my kin." The soft burr of his words wrapped around her vulnerable heart, marking her for all time.

She stared at him, transfixed.

He loves them.

He gave her waist a slight squeeze.

"These are only my kin within a couple of hours' ride of here. Were all my clan present, they'd number well over a thousand." He gazed across the courtyard, pride gleaming in his turquoise eyes. "I sent out the call, and these men," he jutted his head toward the assembled Scots, "answered without hesitation."

Impressed, and unusually touched, Yvette peered around the clearing. "Amazing."

He gave her a roguish wink. "I told you. There's nothing like the Scots' loyalty."

A moment later, Dugall brought Ewan's steed forward. Once he'd mounted his stallion, Ewan signaled his brother, and Dugall swung an unsuspecting Yvette before Ewan in the saddle.

Her face connecting with his chest muffled her startled squeak. As she clutched at him, a rumble of masculine laughter surged 'round the clearing.

Roby trotted his dappled roan over to Shaidae. "Ye haven't introduced yer bride."

Bother and rot. He'd heard that taradiddle, had he?

For a small man, Roby possessed an inconveniently booming voice, and his words carried to the ears of every curious Scot present.

Ewan sat tall and confident in his saddle. Taking Yvette's clammy hand in his, he raised it to his lips. His poignant, penetrating gaze sent her a message she didn't understand. He took a deep breath then proclaimed to all, "Kin and kith o' Clan McTavish, my wife, Yvette McTavish."

Yvette choked on a gasp, her head swimming in great undulating waves.

He did not.

A deafening roar exploded in the glen, as over one hundred eyes veered their way. A blush began at her neck and crept, unchecked, to her forehead.

God in heaven, please tell her she'd heard wrong.

Closing her eyes, she swallowed against a peculiar pain in the vicinity of her heart. Why was Ewan forcing her hand? She had only said they were married last night to keep from being ravaged. Why hadn't he made the ruse clear to his kin? Surely, with their numbers for protection, she needn't fear the Munlocky's derelicts any longer.

She tilted her head, trying to catch his eye to demand an explanation. Though certain he knew she looked at him, he stared straight ahead. She opened her mouth to rebuke him, but he dipped his dark head in a swift, quieting kiss.

She tried again. "Ewan—"

His grip tightening round her waist, he cut her off. Raising his other arm, he shouted, "On to Craiglocky."

The Scots thundered from the courtyard, their mounts tossing up great clods of mud as they left Munlocky's behind.

Yvette sat numb, disbelieving. Every few minutes she ventured a peek at Ewan then resumed worrying her lower lip, each heartbeat a painful tweak of duplicity.

What was he about?

He had claimed not once, but twice—and in front of witnesses, for pity's sake—that she was his wife.

True, she had agreed as much the first time, though the lie plagued her conscience. She might be outspoken, and even a jot rebellious, but she wasn't a liar. At least, she'd not been until she met him.

As if her engagement weren't topic enough for the latest *on dit*, now she'd a sham marriage to explain away.

Ewan looked at the woman asleep in his arms. The telltale murmurs and jerks told him she wasn't resting peacefully. When tears slipped from the corners of her eyes, he decided to wake her, despite her sick body's need for sleep.

"Evvy." He nudged her ear with his mouth. Fever heated her almost translucent skin.

"*Ma petite*, wake up. You're dreaming."

"*Hmm?*"

"Wake up. You're having a nightmare."

Her lids inched open, then shut for a moment before fluttering up again.

"I'm thirsty," she said, her voice a scratchy crackle.

He untied a leather flask from his saddle then handed it to her.

She took a sip of water before returning it to him.

Securing the flask in place, he pulled a smaller one from inside his coat. "This is more of the tea Gregor concocted for you this morning. It will soothe your throat."

Yvette didn't argue and took several swallows of the tepid liquid. "Thank you."

Studying her pale face, Ewan recognized a lingering ennui shadowing her eyes. They rode in troubled silence for a time. Though the day was fair, a persistent breeze beset them, and loose strands of her golden hair frolicked in the light wind. One tendril caught on his stubble.

He brushed the silky length aside, noticing she'd dozed off once more. She shivered in her sleep as he tucked the hair behind her ear. After wrapping his tartan around her shaking form, he settled her more comfortably in his arms.

Yvette sighed, burrowing against his chest, her face snuggled into shoulder.

Ewan's heart tugged with what was now a familiar sensation. He would do anything to make her his, had already done so, though she knew it not. Kissing the top of her head, he vowed, "I'll make it up to you, my darling. I promise."

Hours later, when he gave the order for the clan to halt to rest the horseflesh and eat, Yvette didn't stir. Duncan came alongside Ewan's mount to lift her down after his third attempt finally succeeded in awakening her. Offering a sleepy smile, she reached for Duncan, who retained a courteous but secure hold on her arm until Ewan had planted his feet on the ground.

He led Yvette to a willow tree, and there laid his tartan beneath its sheltering branches.

She promptly sank onto the plaid.

"Evvy, Hugh has food. I'll fetch you some." Handing her the flasks from earlier in the day, he urged, "Try to drink a bit of both."

She nodded, her azure eyes glazed and dull.

More than a little troubled, Ewan eyed her.

She'd grown paler and looked even weaker than she had this morning. Making his way across the clearing, he sought Gregor. "Will you come with me? I fear Yvette is worsening."

The men approached the tree and found her curled onto her side, sound asleep.

Gregor shook his head, urgency in his voice. "Nothin' more I can do for her here. We needs get her to Craiglocky, and soon."

Ewan gave the order to mount and finish eating while on the move. Lifting Yvette, he exchanged an anxious glance with Gregor. She didn't waken, even when Ewan passed her to his muscular cousin so he could mount Shaidae.

Worry caused Ewan to push his clan ruthlessly, and six hours later, the weary troop clattered across Craiglocky's drawbridge. The thundering of two hundred hooves colliding with wooden planks roused Yvette from her stupor.

The entire keep's household stood atop the gatehouse steps, evidently eager to extend a warm welcome and to meet the mysterious woman under their laird's protection.

Hugh dismounted first, then gently extracted her from

Ewan's grasp. He set her on her feet, but retained a light hold on her until Ewan slid to the ground. Her fever-bright eyes unfocused, her entire body wavered unsteadily.

Hands trembling, she licked her chalk-dry lips. She tried to straighten her mussed hair and smooth the wrinkles from her rumpled, travel-stained clothing.

"I must look a sight," she muttered under her breath.

Ewan's lips twitched.

Ill as she was, she worried about her appearance.

He came alongside her and wrapped one arm about her waist while supporting her arm with his hand.

Blinking, her expression groggy, she attempted a smile. She glanced at the steps where his family stood, and her nascent smile faded.

"Ewan?"

Something in her tone alerted him.

She couldn't climb the risers.

He scooped her into his arms, carrying her up the short flight of steps. Depositing her on the stoop in front of his mother, he retained his hold lest she topple over.

"Yvette, this is my mother, Giselle Ferguson."

"It's a pleasure to meet you," Yvette managed weakly before she fainted dead away.

Twenty-Three

Soft, feminine voices woke Yvette.

Voices, and pacing feet with an occasional, peculiar, recurring slapping sound.

What *was* that noise?

Thwack.

There it was again.

Eyes shut, she listened to the unfamiliar women's chatter.

Who are these women, and why are they in my bedchamber?

With a jolt, Yvette realized she didn't know what bedchamber she lay in or, for that matter, where she was.

The events leading to waking in this scrumptiously soft, heather-scented bed remained a blur. She scrunched her forehead in concentration. She'd left Munlocky's, riding before Ewan on Shaidae. His clansmen had been there too. And she'd been ill.

Awfully ill.

She stretched her legs. They didn't hurt anymore. She flexed her arms beneath the downy bed covers. No pain.

She started to turn her head but froze in sudden remembrance.

Ewan had claimed to two score or more Scots that they were married.

"I think she's awake." The serene-voiced suggestion came from Yvette's left.

The pacing and slapping stopped. Right beside Yvette's head.

Slitting an eyelid half-open, she gave a small closed-mouth smile. "Hello, Addy."

Adaira *whomped* onto the bed, bouncing Yvette an inch off the goose-down tick. "'Bout time, sleepyhead. I didn't think you'd *ever* awaken. I've been home *two whole* days."

Adaira gestured wildly, her hair, tied at her nape, whipping across her shoulders.

"Oh, do be still, Addy. Give Yvette a moment to collect herself. She doesn't need you jostling about on her bed."

A woman with light cocoa-colored hair—the female equivalent of Dugall's unrivaled male beauty—chastised Adaira.

Yvette had never laid eyes on such perfection of features before. Familiar turquoise eyes, filled with serene intelligence, gazed at her.

Bending her lips into a friendly smile, Yvette sat up, her thick braid falling over one shoulder. Her stiff muscles protested the movement, and she winced. She adjusted her position on the poufy mattress. There, that was better.

Her throat didn't hurt anymore. She swallowed to be sure. No, the pain had disappeared, though her mouth felt like a herd of Shetland ponies had galloped across her tongue—after romping in a miry bog. "You must be Isobel."

Isobel smiled, and Yvette blinked in astonishment.

How was it possible that Isobel was so exquisite?

"Indeed. Please excuse Addy. She's a bit of a hoyden." Isobel's affectionate, teasing tone belied any true censure.

Yvette cut her attention to Adaira, wearing her customary leather breeches, and sitting cross-legged, as she swished a riding crop through the air.

Ah, the thwacking noise.

Completely unaffected by her sister's rebuke, Addy grinned at Yvette before sticking out her tongue. "Better a hoyden than a bluestocking."

Isobel arched a tawny brow, her mien one of long-suffering patience. "You see what I mean?" Shaking her head, she declared, *"Totalement désespérée."*

Pretending to yawn, Yvette hid a grin behind her hand. Despite their bantering, the sisters were obviously close.

What would it be like to have sisters?

Another young woman, Seonaid perhaps, stood at the chamber's door, speaking to someone in the hallway. "Run and tell Mother she's awake."

The pattering of feet faded as the person hurried along the passageway.

The girl turned away from the door, a shy smile tipping the corners of her mouth. *Most definitely Seonaid.* Pretty, and greatly resembling Adaira, though her eyes were more toast-colored than treacle, she had a much more serene demeanor than her boisterous sister. She emitted a gentleness and sweetness of spirit that immediately appealed to Yvette.

"Seonaid, Ewan tells me you have a special ability with animals."

Seonaid tilted her head, her warm gaze curious, yet speculative.

Yvette hadn't a doubt Seonaid assessed her.

Evidently she passed muster, because the youngest

Ferguson daughter smiled again, this time bright and welcoming. "It's a gift the Lord bestowed on me."

Giselle floated into the room, all sublime smiles and soft eyes. She bore a hot oatmeal posset and tea, and a freckled-face lass, no more than eight, carried a bed tray with sweet gruel and custard. As she took the tray from the thin girl's hands, Giselle's maternal glance drifted from daughter to daughter to daughter.

"Thank you, Iona. Why don't you return to the kitchen and ask Sorcha to heat bathwater for our guest. Perhaps there are a few chores you can do to help Cook, *non?*"

Dipping a clumsy curtsy, the redheaded moppet pivoted to do as bidden. Spinning back around, she all but bounced on her toes. "Glad I be to see ye awake, ledy. I ken ye'd be today." With that brazen declaration, her ragged dress hiked to her knobby knees exposing dirty bare feet, Iona bolted from the room

Yvette stared after her retreating form, grinning. "She's utterly adorable. Who is she?"

"One of our many orphans, bless the dears." Giselle placed the breakfast tray on Yvette's lap, chatting the whole time. "They're another casualty of the war and two years of crop failures. We do what we can to care for them, but I fear it's not enough." Her soft, French-accented voice reminded Yvette of Belle-mére. A great wave of homesickness washed over her. She needed someone familiar nearby.

Ewan.

"Is Ewan here?" From the heat searing her face, she'd pinkened rosy as the flowers adorning the breakfast china.

The Ferguson women exchanged swift glances before Giselle answered. "Indeed. He's been most impatient, waiting for you to rouse."

He has?

Another wave of emotion bathed Yvette, this one much more pleasant. While she ate, she inspected her chamber—a stone turret containing long, angular windows within the semi-circular arc. Might this be the bower? She'd never been inside a Scots keep before, so she couldn't be certain.

She counted four thick, arched doors, and heavy, solid furniture, generations old, filled the large room. The unusual-shaped window boasted a raised window seat with an abundance of different-sized pillows.

Seonaid sat there, petting a bunny. Every so often, her fawn-like eyes met Yvette's, and each time, she felt as if Seonaid could see her soul or read her mind. Though disquieting, the impression wasn't frightening in the least.

To please her hostesses, Yvette drank the posset and ate as much of the food as her shrunken stomach would hold. Her bathwater arrived as she finished her meal. Mindful not to mention her engagement or sham marriage, gratitude filled her when none of the women did either.

Pulling aside a painted screen, Giselle exposed another door. She pushed it open, revealing a bathing room, complete with a large copper bathtub.

"Come, girls, let's help Yvette with her bath."

Yes, Yvette must be at her best when she faced Ewan. It would take every bit of her courage to insist he set things right and tell his family and clan the truth.

We are not married.

Ewan paced to the window, looking at the picturesque Highland scene for the thousandth time.

Hundreds of sheep roamed the rolling hills, their white coats creamy blots against the emerald blanket. Loch

Arkaig's waters, a glistening indigo crystal, hosted a variety of waterfowl. Across its shimmering waters, migrating cranes wandered the original castle's remains. A dense forest, edged on two sides by deceptively innocent-looking bogs, provided the backdrop to the ancient, sooty ruin.

His thoughts consumed with Yvette, he couldn't appreciate the view's beauty.

Spinning about, he strode the reverse path to his mahogany desk—for the thousandth time.

The last four days had been the longest, most nerve-racking in his memory. Hours spent sitting at Yvette's bedside, holding her hand, willing her to wake up. Finally, yesterday morning, Gregor had announced that Yvette had regained consciousness and now slumbered in a deep, restorative sleep. Ewan would be forever grateful to his cousin and the old crone who'd taught him the art of healing.

At the prospect of losing her, a fierce emptiness had claimed a portion of his soul, and his spirit still ached unbearably.

Stuffing his hands in his jacket pocket, he closed his fist around the brooch he always carried, waiting for the opportune moment to present it to Yvette. It must be soon. Determined and desperate that she learn the truth from him, he'd threatened his clan and family with banishment if anyone so much as whispered a hint before he told her.

Exhaling a gusty sigh, he slumped against the window's glass. Shaking his head in self-recrimination, he muttered aloud, "I must ask her to forgive me. Perhaps if I explain my motives, she'll understand."

Would that be enough to earn her forgiveness, though?

Hell, could I be so forgiving?

He wasn't ignorant of courtship's intricacies.

Announcing one had wed before a ceremony commenced, let alone prior to the groom proposing and the bride accepting, was definitely not *de rigueur*. Not even in Scotland.

Especially when the young woman in question had made it abundantly clear she wouldn't be forced into a union. He shouldn't be at all astonished if Yvette didn't spurn any further advances and return to London posthaste. Standing at the window, gazing at the charming landscape, Ewan hoped with every fiber in him that wouldn't be the case.

He could not—*would not*—let her leave.

"You can see Yvette now."

Ewan whirled to face the study door.

Isobel stood there, hands clasped

"How is she?" His flicked his focus to the ceiling. "Did she ask about me?"

Isobel tilted the corners of her mouth. "She's remarkably well, and, yes, she asked after you." She crossed the study to peer into his face. Her eyes rounded, and she touched his arm. "You love her."

A statement of simple truth, not a question.

Ewan angled his head. "Aye, more than I believed possible."

Isobel hugged him. "I'm happy for you, Ewan." Twining her arm through his, she tugged him to the door. "Come along then, she's waiting for you. Most anxiously too."

Yvette scolded herself for her stampeding pulse and hopscotching heart. Good heavens, why was she all aflutter at the prospect of seeing Ewan? Plucking at the printed fabric of her dress, she couldn't help her pleased smile.

Giselle and her daughters had truly outdone themselves.

She'd cast off her mourning weeds, and wore one of her favorite afternoon dresses, a pink and yellow chintz frock. Seonaid had tucked a few yellow baby roses into Yvette's hair, which was piled into a simple knot atop her head, except for a few wispy ringlets framing her face. Pink clustered pearl earrings and a dab of jasmine perfume completed her ensemble.

With Giselle and Adaira's help, she'd walked to a divan placed before the hearth. Though stiff from lack of exercise, she needed little assistance traveling the short distance. Once Yvette sank onto the seat, Giselle had tucked a knitted wool afghan over her lap.

"It won't do for you to take a chill again, now that you're mending so well."

Yvette rather liked being mothered.

Three brisk raps echoed on the thick arched door leading to the chamber, and her stomach cramped. She wiped damp palms on the nubby woolen blanket. Though her back faced the door, she couldn't mistake Ewan's velvety baritone as he spoke to one of his sisters.

Staring at her now-icy hands, Yvette remained immobile.

A swishing nearby caught her attention as Giselle bent to kiss her cheek. "We shall leave you alone. I'm sure you've much to discuss."

Indeed, not the least of which was how he intended to put things aright about their fabricated marriage. Yvette pulled in a deep, bracing breath. She'd have her answer before the hour ended.

The sisters followed suit, each bending to embrace her and place a kiss on her cheek. Even Adaira condescended to do so, but admonished as she stood, "I expect you to mend swiftly. I'm anxious to introduce you to Craiglocky and the village."

"Adaira, I'm perfectly capable of escorting Evvy." Ewan's tone, dryer than foolscap, held the merest hint of possessiveness.

Yvette peeked his way. Nothing in his demeanor suggests a speck of jealousy. Had she imagined it?

"Oh bosh," Adaira scoffed. "You're always busy with lairdly business. We go *days* without seeing you. Why, you haven't been home in months and months. You'll have much too much to do, catching up with your responsibilities. Which we all know you take most seriously."

Yvette stifled a giggle when Isobel shook her head and rolled her eyes, and Seonaid pulled an impatient face at their sister.

Ewan's deep chuckle filled the room. "Days? Indeed. You make me sound a bore."

"Well..." An impish grin lit Adaira's already jovial countenance. "You—"

"I'd like to show Yvette the library," Isobel smoothly announced, effectively curbing whatever naughtiness Adaira had been about to say. "Yvette, Ewan told me you enjoy reading as much as I."

Sensing a kindred spirit, Yvette nodded her acceptance. "I do."

Seonaid ventured, "And I'd like to show you my menagerie when you've recovered."

"I'd be delighted to see your pets, Seonaid. I adore animals. I've two hounds of my own."

The youngest Ferguson daughter's face beamed for a moment before a peculiar look whisked across her face. "Ewan?"

An inflection in Seonaid's tone caught her family's attention.

Everyone faced her, their bearing expectant, yet cautious too.

Staring past Yvette, her gaze slightly vacant, she murmured, "Have a care. All is not as it should be."

Yvette looked from Seonaid, to Ewan, and back again.

What in the world?

After her disturbing proclamation, Seonaid drifted from the room, but not before giving Yvette one final penetrating look. Her sisters followed in her wake, breaking into fervent whispers even before they exited the chamber.

Giselle stopped at the door. "Ewan, heed your sister."

"Aye, Mother, I shall."

Whatever just happened?

Yvette had the oddest sensation everyone knew a secret to which she wasn't privy. Frowning, she glanced at the closed door. Another notion took hold, pulling her musings in a different, but equally troubling, direction.

Why hadn't the door been left ajar for propriety's sake?

Under no circumstances was it acceptable for a man to be in an unmarried woman's bedchamber. True, she and Ewan had been unchaperoned in prior circumstances, but always by chance, not design.

Visions of the Banbury Inn, the Rose and Crown, and Munlocky's frolicked about in her head. By thunder, she'd been compromised so many times, she almost found it comical, like some great, theatrical parody.

For the first time since he'd entered, Yvette directed her attention directly at Ewan, and her heart danced a happy jig.

Such a dashing figure he cut today. A flint gray jacket hugged the broad planes of his shoulders, and in an unusual departure from fashion, he wore a black neckcloth, complete with an emerald-cut diamond stud. It complemented his silver-and-crimson striped waistcoat to perfection.

A delighted smile bent her lips.

She couldn't help herself.

Thank goodness she'd taken extra care with her appearance. He'd not seen her in anything but mourning attire.

What would he think? Would he be pleased? Why did it matter so much?

His gaze roamed over her, and his lips slid upward in a slow smile of approval and something much more sensual. Lord help her, when he looked at her like that—

He raised her hand to his mouth, brushing his lips across the knuckles. Turning her palm up, he pressed his lips to the pulse beating at her wrist.

"I've missed you, *mon amour*. You're recovering well?"

"Yes, I'm much better. Your mother and sisters have been most kind."

Ewan settled himself on the settee, his thigh pressing against hers. He still held her hand.

Yvette didn't mind. She gazed deep into his eyes, reading the message there. Her eyelids drifted closed, even as she tilted her chin upward in silent invitation.

An instant later, as if as eager as she, he pressed his lips to hers.

Sighing in pleasure, she angled her head to allow him greater access to the recesses of her mouth. Inhaling, she savored his spicy smell before reaching to cup his nape. She loved how his silky hair slid between her fingers.

He kissed her like a man long starved, and she relished every moment of it. She explored his mouth just as fervently, touching his tongue, retreating, then stroking it with her own once more.

Trailing feather-like kisses across her jaw, Ewan whispered into the sensitive area behind her ear. "You cause me to forget my promises."

She arched her neck as his lips skimmed along the flesh below her earlobe. He lowered his head, nipping and tasting her neck, her shoulder, the hollow where her pulse beat. She became undone. Moaning low in her throat, she pulled him closer, a love-driven need she didn't understand building within.

He returned his ravenous mouth to hers in an age-old dance of desire. An instant later, he skimmed his fingers along the bodice of her dress before slipping inside the warm confines, delving deeper. When he lowered his head, showering hot, wet kisses on her breasts, she offered no resistance

The sensations he aroused jumbled and muddled her in a most delightful way. But this wasn't the direction she'd planned their meeting to go. Wasn't she supposed to demand Ewan make right their marriage farce?

When had he laid her on the settee?

She recalled unbuttoning his shirt and yanking it free of his breeches. The hem of her gown rode high on her thighs, and her bodice had been shoved low, baring her breasts to his smoldering eyes.

Shouldn't his hot gaze roving over her cause embarrassment?

For certain, what she felt could never be defined as such.

～

Not like this.

This wasn't how Ewan wanted to love Yvette the first time, rushed, half-clothed, on a cramped divan.

By God, she'd scarcely recovered from a serious bout of ill health. Her first time ought to be wondrous, after he'd driven her half-mad with desire. And, more importantly, secure in the knowledge she was married. Cherished. Adored.

Sucking in a great gulp of air, he levered upright. He helped Yvette to a sitting position, and after assuring himself she wouldn't topple onto the Aubusson carpet, straightened his clothing.

"Ewan? Did I do something wrong?" she asked, confusion written across her face.

He kissed her nose. "Nae, it's precisely the opposite. You're such a passionate woman, I... Well, I explored much farther than I ever intended." He chuckled in self-derision. Quirking a brow as he confessed, "I only meant to give you a chaste kiss, *ma chérie.*"

And that had been no chaste kiss.

Yvette stared at him, her eyes glazed with passion and her lips swollen from his kisses. Her breasts beckoned, taunting him.

Better get her done up before his resolve faded. He turned his attention to righting her clothing. She allowed his ministrations without argument. "I'm afraid there's naught I can do for your hair."

The rosebuds adorning her hair now lay crushed against the divan or on the floor where several of her hair pins had fallen. Shiny curls spilled to her waist in golden waves.

"It's of little importance. I can arrange my own hair."

He stood and slipped on his waistcoat. Draping his cravat about his neck, he strode to the large looking glass above her dressing table. With efficiency born of practice, he retied the neckcloth then secured the stud before shrugging into his coat.

Head tilted, she watched his every move, all the while pinning her hair into a tidy coil. "Ewan, is it...? Does everybody...? What I mean is, is it like that for everyone?"

His heart set sail and his masculine pride swelled. No matter her inexperience, Yvette understood, at a fundamental level, that what they shared was unique. She hadn't even experienced *that,* and yet she sensed the unifying bond.

Sitting beside her, he took one of her hands in his and rubbed his thumb over the tender flesh. He looked into her uncertain eyes, telling her with his gaze what he feared to say with words.

"Evvy, only a fortunate few experience what we have together. I must believe it's ordained. It's far more than physical passion. It's what happens when two souls who care for each other unite with a connection more powerful and indestructible than mere carnal desire."

A delighted smile blossomed across her radiant face. She bent forward and kissed him full on the mouth.

His turn to be stunned, for he could've sworn that wholehearted adoration filled her sweet kiss. And by George, it was also the first kiss she'd ever initiated. Ewan couldn't bring himself to broach the subject at the forefront of his mind now and ruin this precious moment.

Tomorrow, he'd take Yvette on a tour of his castle and estate, introduce her to the staff and perhaps some of the locals, as well as show her some of his favorite places at Craiglocky. Then, he'd mention the worrisome matter plaguing his conscience.

"Let me help you to bed, *chérie*. I want to show you off at supper tonight, and I think a rest is in order first."

He tucked her into bed. After wrapping the coverlet round her shoulders, he placed a lingering kiss on her already rosy mouth.

She twisted her head away, her voice husky with desire. "Ewan, we must tell the others we're not married. I cannot continue to lie about it. And I won't keep misleading them."

He gave her a small reassuring smile then tweaked her freckled nose. "It's my plan to put things right tonight."

"Truly?" Her sky-blue eyes held a mixture of hope and wariness.

"Truly."

The relief sweeping her face gave him pause.

Why was she so eager for everyone to know they weren't married?

Had he misinterpreted her kisses?

Twenty-Four

Yvette stood outside the entrance to the great hall. It had taken her longer to find her way below than she had anticipated, and she feared she was tardy. From her vantage point, she observed Ewan deep in conversation with a group of men and women. Several Scots, wearing the McTavish colors and other bright tartans, lounged in the chairs and benches lining the walls.

Easily seating fifty or more, the massive table running down the center of the hall drew her attention. Bronze candelabras, at least four feet tall, stood regally along the length, a dozen candles blazing in each. Situated horizontally to the long public table, the high table atop a raised dais was reserved for positions of honor and privilege.

She laid a trembling hand across her frolicking stomach.

A rustling alerted Yvette to presences behind her.

Isobel and Seonaid crossed the stone floor, their elaborate gowns shimmering in the candlelight.

Ah, not late after all.

Embarrassed to be caught spying on those already

assembled in the great hall, Yvette shrugged and offered a guilty smile. "I'm afraid I'm having a fit of nerves."

"Whatever for, Yvette? You look ravishing." Isobel bent closer. "I don't believe I've ever seen a gown that particular shade of ivory before. It's iridescent and seems to move of its own accord. And the gold inlay is absolutely stunning."

Yvette fingered the material. "My father acquired the fabric in India." Dragging in a nervous breath, she confessed, "I thought dressing in one of my finest gowns would help boost my courage. But it hasn't. I'm aquiver inside."

Seonaid poked her head round the doorframe. "It's only kin present. Well, the Scots aren't all kin, but in Scotland, they're treated as such. There cannot be more than twenty present. Oh, and their ladies, of course, though only half are married."

Isobel linked arms with Yvette. She angled her head at Seonaid, who looped her arm through Yvette's other crooked elbow. Flashing a brilliant smile, Isobel proclaimed, "We shall enter as one."

Yvette's smile revealed her gratitude. "Thank you."

"Wait for me." Breathless, Adaira hastened down the stairs, pulling on her gloves. "I couldn't find my other glove. Found it in one of my riding boots, of all places."

Isobel's mouth curled up on one side. "Would that be because the last time you wore them you challenged Brayan McVey to a race? Mother nearly swooned when she saw you astride Fionn in your ball gown, your legs exposed for everyone to see."

"They were not. I had on my riding boots. They come to my knees." Adaira winked at Yvette. "I won the race, and Brayan had to kiss Mistress Peeble's prize sow."

Dumbfounded, Yvette stared at Adaira. "Dare I ask what Brayan's prize would've been, should he have won?"

"Why, a kiss from me, of course. That's why I *couldn't* let him win." Adaira shuddered. Leaning forward, she whispered, "He has great fat lips and smells of trout. Ugh!" She sucked in her cheeks while pursing her lips, smacking them in an imitation of a fish.

Yvette's peal of laughter echoed throughout the hall, catching the attention of everyone assembled. Smiling, she entered the room accompanied by Ewan's sisters in what could only be interpreted as an entourage of acceptance and support.

Ewan excused himself, making his way to her side.

Pride and a nuance of something infinitely more meaningful warmed his eyes. He bowed low over her hand, grazing the knuckles with his lips before tucking her gloved hand into his bent elbow.

Nodding a greeting to his sisters, he leaned nearer. "Evvy, you're an absolute vision."

Drawing her farther into the enormous room, proud as a peacock, he made the rounds with her on his arm.

The tall blonde standing next to Duncan was his wife, Kitta. And the weary-eyed couple were the new parents, Callum and his petite wife, Lilias. Ewan introduced her to several clansmen, whose names all sounded much the same to her untrained ear.

Gregor and Alasdair separated themselves from a trio of chunky matrons, and Yvette caught Alasdair's bold assessment as the twins approached.

"Ye be lookin' yer bonnie self, lass," he said, giving her a flirtatious wink.

She gave him a half-smile; the rakish look in his eye

needing no further encouragement. Yvette addressed his more reticent brother. "Gregor, thank you for tending me during my illness. I've been told that if it weren't for you and your healing skills, I may have perished."

The gargantuan man blushed, shuffling his great booted feet. "Och, ye but needed a wee bit of help, ye did, lass."

Hugh and Giselle sauntered toward the group, smiling and exchanging a word or two with several clan members as they passed.

Seonaid joined them halfway across the room and whispered to Yvette, "How are you faring?"

"Wonderfully, thank you. Yon dragon," Yvette inclined her head minutely in Ewan's direction, "is a diligent guardian."

Seonaid giggled, and giving Yvette's hand a gentle squeeze, turned to speak to her mother.

Yvette took a moment to examine the rest of the hall. A familiar unpleasant tingle skittered across her shoulders, raising the fine hairs on her nape. She angled halfway around to peer over her shoulder.

A pretty young woman and the Scot Ewan had introduced as Frasar Campbell scrutinized her. The woman's steely stare bored hostile holes into Yvette from across the room. She met the Scotswoman's eyes, and her face contorted into a disdainful smirk. She said something to her companion before turning her back on Yvette, cutting her.

Scorching heat flamed across Yvette's face. She shifted her stance to face forward once more and tightened her hand on Ewan's arm in distress. Engrossed in conversation with his cousins and Hugh, he gave her a distracted smile.

A servant signaled Giselle that supper was served.

Yvette seized the moment and touched Seonaid on the arm.

She halted, her winged brows raised in inquiry.

"Who's that woman with the saffron and green gown. The one with the reddish-gold hair?" Yvette subtly pointed her fan toward the pair making their way to the trestle table.

A shadow flitted across Seonaid's features. "Aubry."

The one word response spoke volumes.

"She's your cousin, is she not?" If only Yvette dared to look and see if Aubry still stared. From the eerie sensation clawing across her flesh, she'd wager the woman did.

"Yes." Seonaid flicked Aubry another considering glance. "She only returned to Craiglocky late this afternoon. She'd been visiting relatives in Edinburgh these past weeks."

As Ewan led Yvette to the table, she breathed a silent sigh of relief. He'd broken with tradition and opted not to use the high table for the meal. Had he done so out of consideration for her? She liked to think so.

He stood behind a chair waiting for her.

She sank onto the seat. "Thank you."

"I'd rather you sat beside me, but Mother arranged the seating. Scots dinner parties are a mite more informal than the English." He bent low. "You'll be all right?"

Yvette gave him a brave nod. "I shall be fine."

Why wouldn't she? Eating with forty people she'd only just met. No worries there.

He squeezed her shoulder before striding to his assigned seat. Duncan sat at his right and Hugh his left. Unlike the strict formality dictated by English society, there didn't appear to be any hierarchy in the placement of the guests. No one appeared to take exception to the seating arrangements either.

Yvette took a quick inventory of those around her. Seated one quarter the way down the table, she sat across from Giselle, who was sandwiched between Gregor and Alasdair. Dugall had taken the seat to Yvette's right, Isobel the chair beside him. Adaira took the place to Yvette's immediate left and Seonaid one seat farther down.

Adaira, already poking fun at Alasdair, fluttered her gloved fingers at Yvette and pointed to the other end of the table. "*Fish lips,*" she mouthed.

Yvette's attention darted to the clan member indicated, and she checked a smile. Good Lord, the man did indeed have fish lips. Her wide gaze met Adaira's mirth-filled eyes.

"*Glub, glub,*" she gurgled in Yvette's ear.

Yvette bit the inside of her mouth to keep from laughing outright. What an incorrigible and utterly charming minx. Never before had she met such a free-spirited woman. One who cared nothing for convention or what others thought of her.

Eyeing his sister dubiously, Dugall bent near Yvette. "Addy be making the strangest sounds."

Yvette placed her serviette in her lap. "Yes, it seems she's taken exception to a young man with rather large lips."

He gave a sage nod. "Ye be speaking of Brayan, poor mon. Worse yet, he be fond of fishing. Never quite gets the bait off his hands."

She cut Adaira another sidelong smile, only to realize Aubry sat next to Callum. She skewered Yvette with spiteful glares every few moments.

Yvette's smile faltered as the joy drained from her. Bewildered, she lowered her eyes to her plate. Why was Aubry so hostile toward her? They'd not even been introduced yet.

Several times throughout the extended meal, Yvette caught Ewan's eye. He winked once, and she blushed before looking away. One such look lingered. A silent message between two lovers.

"Yvette, I asked if ye play any instruments." Dugall lightly touched her forearm.

Yvette tore her gaze from Ewan and gave Dugall an apologetic smile. "I'm sorry, Dugall. Yes, I play the piano."

"What are yer other accomplishments, Yvette?" Ridicule laced Aubry's strident voice.

What an odd question.

Startled and put off, Yvette met her antagonistic stare. "I'm afraid I don't—"

"What? Nae other skills? Well then, what do ye ken of running a keep of this size?" Aubry waved her hand in the air, indicating Craiglocky.

Was she always this rude?

Yvette glanced Ewan's way.

He scowled at Aubry, his brows pinched into a tight frown.

Reluctantly, Yvette directed her attention back to the peeved young woman.

"Very little, truth to tell. The largest household I've managed with my stepmother had only five-and-thirty staff."

Dugall delivered Aubry a mocking grin before bending near her ear. "Craiglocky has but nine-and-twenty."

Making a pretense of cutting a carrot, Yvette swept a surreptitious glance round the table. Busy with their meal and chitchat, only those guests seated closest were privy to the irregular discussion.

Leaning forward, eyebrows high on her haughty forehead, Aubry persisted. "Wouldn't ye agree a lady of an estate the magnitude of Craiglocky should be well educated? Perhaps even fluent in another language?"

Expression carefully schooled, inwardly, Yvette became even more perplexed. What was the point of these peculiar questions? Another wave of unease tiptoed across Yvette's shoulders, and she dared a swift glimpse in Ewan's direction again.

His countenance downright fierce, his mouth had thinned into a line of irritation, his sea-green eyes smoldering in annoyance.

Aubry noticed Yvette's silent plea for help. Her mouth curled into a sneer as potent hatred sparked from her gaze.

Clasping her fork in a white-knuckled grip, Yvette inhaled a tight, ragged breath.

She loathes me.

But why?

As diners realized Aubry deliberately harangued her, conversations around them dwindled.

"Do ye speak any other languages, Yvette? *Comprenez-vous le français?*"

"Aubry," Ewan warned coldly.

Why such strange questions?

Yvette eyed Giselle and Adaira—both of whom looked ill at ease—before returning her consideration to Aubry. Perhaps she was touched in the upper works, but surely Seonaid would've mentioned something so significant?

"Well, Yvette, do ye?" Aubry demanded, her superior chin raised.

Yvette tilted her head, meeting Aubry's agitated, feline gaze. "Yes, several, actually. My father believed a woman should be as educated as a man."

A disbelieving laugh trilled from Aubry.

Definitely a hint of madness there.

"Several?" she scoffed. "Come now, surely ye exaggerate. I'm sure ye feel the need to impress us all, but to lie...?"

Dugall growled at the barbed insult while Isobel looked between Yvette and Aubry, a troubled frown marring her face.

More people began to take note of the discord.

"Indeed?" Yvette arched a brow. Her most reproachful one. "Should I be so inclined, I might comment on the preferred manners of ladies and the treatment of their guests. Only in languages I'm fluent in, of course."

"Please do. If ye do ken *several*." A cynical smile twisting her mouth, Aubry gestured to the gawking guests. "We're waitin' for ye to impress us."

"That's enough. Not another word." Ewan's tone brooked no argument.

Aubry glared daggers at him but fell silent. She drummed her fingers on the tabletop, clearly vexed.

A clansman approached Ewan, and, after he whispered in his laird's ear, Ewan stood. "Please excuse me. There's a matter that requires my immediate attention. I'll return as swiftly as I'm able."

Yvette swore Ewan spoke the last words to her. Her lower lip caught between her teeth, she tracked his departure.

"We're all waiting, Yvette." Aubry renewed her taunting the moment he'd disappeared from sight.

"This is utter gammon," Adaira said. "*We're* not waiting. You needn't do any such thing, Yvette."

"*Non*, of course you needn't, *chérie*," Giselle reassured her.

"Nae, ye dinnae have to do anythin' that banshee demands." Dugall glowered at Aubry.

Did they also think Yvette exaggerated?

Her gaze traveled the table. Everyone watched the

exchange between her and Aubry with perverse fascination, unable to tear their gazes away.

A smile teased the corners of Yvette's mouth as she tilted her head in acquiescence. By thunder, she'd give them something to watch, then.

"As you wish." She proceeded to do so in French, Italian, German, Latin, Spanish, and Greek.

A jubilant grin splitting his face, Dugall held up six thick fingers and wiggled them at Aubry across the table.

"And..." Yvette wasn't done yet. She'd been pushed too dratted far. "I've recently learned another. Scots."

Up sprang another one of Dugall's large fingers.

She smiled before softly delivering the *coup de grâce*.

"*Ah wid ne'er treat a guest sae awfy.*"

Titters echoed the length of the table, and Aubry's face mottled unbecomingly, her lips curling into a feral snarl.

"I'm sure you're aware, Aubry, how important the custom of hospitality is to Highlanders. After all, you're a Scot." A great deal of satisfaction thrummed through Yvette. She'd had enough of the jealous chit.

Dead silence filled the hall.

The unqualified mortification-born hatred in Aubry's glare seared Yvette's flesh. Bother and blast, she oughtn't to have done that. What possessed her to be so prideful and mean-spirited? She'd made an enemy this night.

"Aubry, please—"

"Ye..." Lips quivering, Aubry stabbed a finger at her. Placing her hands on the table, she shoved to her feet. "How could Ewan have married ye, ye bloody Sassenach?"

Desperate to diffuse the situation and calm Aubry, Yvette tried reassuring her. "We're not truly married. We only said we were husband and wife to protect me."

She wasn't about to tell them she would've been ravished otherwise. Her reputation already lay in tatters.

Someone gasped, causing Yvette to peer around the table.

Several guests averted their eyes or became engrossed with their cold food or the mounted hunting trophies.

Why did everyone look so wretched and uncomfortable?

Something wasn't right.

Her regard skipped to the door.

No Ewan.

She returned her attention to those seated near her. A crestfallen expression shadowed Seonaid's face, and Adaira muttered dire threats—and an oath or two—under her breath while flexing her fingers, no doubt aching to wring Aubry's scrawny neck.

By all the clootie pudding in Scotland, something was too smoky by far.

Did pity fill Giselle's eyes?

Even Dugall had settled into an uncomfortable silence.

Jaw slack, Aubry peered at Yvette. "Ye dinnae ken. Oh my God, this is too rich."

"Know what?" Where was Ewan?

A smile of undiluted malice warped Aubry's face. "Under Scots law, declarin' ye'r married in front of witnesses makes it a legal union. I've been told Ewan did so, nae once, but twice."

Pardon?

Yvette recoiled as if slapped.

"Shut up, ye banshee," Dugall roared in youthful fury.

Aubry didn't spare him a glance. "Ye were in Scotland when ye and Ewan professed marriage, weren't ye? Did anyone ask ye if ye were his wife? Did ye nae say ye were?"

No. No, no, no.

Yvette clutched the serviette in her lap, wadding it into a mangled knot. Her gazed searched Alasdair's then Adaira's, and finally Giselle's sympathetic gazes, seeking the truth.

Her thoughts screamed chaotically.

Oh, Lord, please tell me Ewan wouldn't do that to me? He wouldn't trap me in marriage. He wouldn't.

"Did ye agree either time? Deny it either time? If ye portrayed yerself as Ewan's wife, and live with him, the Church of Scotland recognizes the marriage." Another scurrilous laugh echoed throughout the hall.

"Shut yer mouth," Gregor growled through clenched teeth.

"I can see yer answers written on yer face," Aubry taunted.

Seonaid begged, "Aubry, hush. Have you lost all sense of reason?"

Gloating, Aubry made a jerky movement with her hand to include the others sitting in uncomfortable silence. "We all ken the irregular marriage, and ye've *pretended* to be Ewan's wife since ye arrived."

Yvette shook her head. "No, I was ill and—"

"Ye *are* Ewan's wife, ye filthy English hoor!"

If Yvette had been run through with a sword, the agony would've been less piercing. Each breath cut deeper, like a fresh lance from a double-edged blade.

God in heaven, this cannot be happening. It isn't real. This is a terrible dream, has to be a terrible dream. Is that why Ewan had the special license? Did he plan this?

"We cannot be." Yvette choked back a sob. "There's been no ceremony. No clergy officiated."

"We Scots dinnae require a cleric to perform the ceremony. Almost anybody can do it." Aubry sniggered and shoved her hair off her forehead. "Even Craiglocky's blacksmith."

It wasn't possible.

"But we haven't—" Yvette couldn't prevent the scarlet she knew blazed across her inflamed face. She twisted her tortured serviette tighter. "The marriage hasn't been consummated."

The last word was almost inaudible.

Hugh's incensed glare sliced around the table, checking several muffled snickers. "Aubry, ye've gone too far with yer malice."

Giselle stretched across the table, reaching for Yvette's hand. "It matters not, *cherie*. Though an irregular marriage, Scot's Canon Code decrees you're bound to Ewan. That is, if you vowed in front of witnesses you'd taken him to husband."

Oh, dear God, I did.

Aubry screamed, "Ye've stolen another's betrothed."

The hall swirled, zigzagging, dipping up and down, and Yvette feared she might cast up her accounts.

"Ye didnae ken that either, did ye?" Aubry dealt another calculated, spiteful blow.

"That be a lie!" Dugall pounded his fist on the table, toppling his wine goblet. China and silverware clattered as crimson stained the pristine cloth. "Ewan ne'er made a match with ye."

In a complete frenzy, Aubry wouldn't stop. "Ewan couldn't resist yer wealth. He forfeited his happiness and put true love aside to keep Craiglocky."

"It's not true. She's lying." Isobel tried to reassure Yvette.

Certain her face had blanched as pale as the gown she wore, she didn't know what to think anymore.

"Ewan would never do such thing. Ever," Isobel insisted.

"He didnae even marry nobility," Aubry crowed, her invective tirade building to a crescendo. "But settled for a merchant's lowly daughter."

Flee.

Yvette scooted her chair backward.

Aubry's next words froze her in place, transfixed by shock.

"How many times did ye spread yer scrawny legs afore Ewan decided yer money is worth the price of his sacrifice?"

Horrorstruck, Yvette felt her face drain of color, as surely as if someone had poured wine from a goblet. The room swirled faster, and she clutched at the table's edge.

Don't faint.

At Aubry's brutal viciousness and disgustingly crude innuendo, a fuzzy roaring filled Yvette's ears, and she scarcely heard the disbelieving gasps and growls of disapproval.

"The devil take ye, I'll banish ye from Craiglocky this night," Ewan roared.

Yvette cut him a damning glance and, just as rapidly, looked away.

He stood inside the doorway, rage etched across his face.

She couldn't bear to look at him, didn't want to see the treachery in his eyes.

His threatening snarl sobered Aubry. Uncertainty danced across her contorted features. Doubt lingered in her eyes, curbing her savage tongue.

Adaira leveled Aubry a scathing glare. "You nasty, jealous, spiteful... lickspittle."

"Aubry, how could you?" Seonaid whispered, her face a mask of anguish.

With calm fury, Isobel proclaimed, "You're a disgrace to the Ferguson name, Aubry. To everything that's honorable and noble in a Scot."

Escape. Now.

Yvette stood on unsteady legs, grasping the table's edge for balance. She strove for poised composure, despite feeling like a powerless pawn in a despicable game of human chess. Played for the amusement of those enjoying tragic endings at the expense of someone else's happiness—no—their very existence.

The great hall radiated silent tension, everyone's attention resting on her.

She regarded the strangers staring at her, their eyes reflecting a myriad of emotions: embarrassment, horror, dismay, pity, outrage, compassion, and yes, even a few smugly satisfied.

"You knew?" She looked at Hugh and Duncan before swinging her accusing gaze to Alasdair and Gregor.

Chagrined, they bowed their heads.

Her turbid gaze swept the rest of Ewan's family.

"You all knew?" Yvette searched Giselle's sorrowful eyes, then Adaira's tear-filled ones. "You must think me such a fool."

Her agonized whisper exposed her vulnerability. Her shame. Her absolute humiliation.

I've been such an utter gudgeon. Fool. Fribble.

Seonaid's face crumpled, a plump tear trailing over her cheek.

Ewan touched her arm. "Evvy—"

She whirled around, speaking between stiff lips, "Don't. *You*. Touch. Me."

Yvette knew her gaze mirrored her desolation when she finally forced herself to meet his eyes. "How could you?" she whispered. "I trusted you."

She'd *never* make that mistake again.

He reached for her again. "Please—"

"Don't." She slapped away his hand.

To still her quivering mouth and chin, she clenched her teeth. Shutting her eyes against the torrent of tears cascading down her face, she drew in a bracing breath.

Lord, give me the strength to walk from this room with my head held high.

On wooden legs, she stepped away from her chair.

Ewan grasped her elbow, restraining her. "Evvy, I don't know what she told you, but—"

Aubry jerked her chair aside. It clattered to the floor, skidding several feet. In the eerily silent hall, the jarring crash echoed harshly.

Yvette yanked her arm free just as Aubry threw herself into Ewan's arms, wailing her remorse. "Forgive me, Ewan. Dinnae send me away. I love ye. I always have. Say ye love me. I dinnae care ye'r married now. We can still be together."

Yvette's tormented mind couldn't bear seeing her in his embrace.

She could tolerate no more. With steadfast singlemindedness, she sought to escape this place of insufferable pain. Backing away from the table, she shoved away the restraining hands. Like a wild animal caught in a snare, she fought her way free.

She spun to face the door. She ran from the room, her heart breaking. The fresh, jagged, crack fractured further with each stumbling step, until she feared the fragile organ would shatter into nothingness. And she'd exist no more—wanted to exist no more, so intolerable was her pain.

Great sobs welled up, choking her, as streams of tears blinded her progress. She didn't know the castle's layout, didn't even know how to return to her chamber. Yet she ran.

Ran to escape the pain shredding her soul.

Ran to obliterate the betrayal clawing at her mind.

And ran to forget the love now gushing from her broken heart.

Why, oh God, why? How could you let this happen?

Twenty-Five

Hours later, standing in the great hall, Ewan raked a hand through his hair. The castle and immediate grounds had been searched multiple times, and Yvette had yet to be found. Had she ventured as far as the loch or, worse, the forest?

He released a frustrated breath.

She didn't know how dangerous the bogs were. Many a Scot, with far greater familiarity than she, had perished in their unforgiving mires.

"Gregor, you and Alasdair take some men and extend the search. I fear Yvette may have gone farther than I thought. Send word at once if you see anything suspicious."

"Aye, Ewan." Gregor gave a solemn nod.

Ewan knew those pursuing Yvette already watched the Keep. His men had spotted signs of them days ago, and he'd been given information this night that confirmed they'd been seen in the village.

What if they had her even now?

His mind shied away from the thought.

He clenched his fists and teeth until both ached, a fierce

protectiveness for his wife roiling in his gut. He'd wanted to horsewhip Aubry when his mother told him what she'd said.

Mother laid a comforting hand on his arm. "We shall find her, Ewan."

"I drove her to this, Mother. I should've told her the truth at Munlocky's, but she was very ill."

"You've only done what you believed was in her best interest, *non*? You can explain your actions to Yvette. She seems a reasonable young woman. She'll listen. Especially if you tell her you love her."

Ewan arced his brows in surprise.

She smiled. "*Cher,* one has only to look at you when she's in the room to know it's so."

He shook his head. "I'm not so sure. I've hurt her. She doesn't easily trust, has good reasons not to, and I betrayed her trust."

Raising his gaze, he took in the now empty hall. He'd had such hopes for this night.

"*Merde.* I cannot wait here, doing nothing." He cupped his nape. "I'm going to search outside again."

As he turned to stride from the room, Seonaid entered the hall. "I found her."

"Where?" Ewan rushed to her. "Where is she? I must speak with her."

He took Seonaid's arm, expecting her to lead him to his wife.

Seonaid shook her head. "No, not tonight. I'm sorry."

"What do you mean not tonight?" Ewan gaped at her, incredulous. "I have to explain—"

"Yvette's already abed. I found her with my animals and helped her upstairs." She stared at him, then shifted her doe-like gaze over his shoulder.

What did she see?

"Trust me in this, Ewan. You *must* wait until tomorrow."

Yvette sat in the turret's window seat, staring bleakly at the choppy loch as morn's joyful colors splayed across the sky. Toying with her shawl's silky fringe, she watched a couple of ragamuffins dart into the wooded area near the dock.

She'd changed into a plain black gown. The ivory one lay crumpled in a corner. She shuddered anew at the memories associated with it.

A soft knock disturbed the quiet of the room. Yvette crossed to the door, but didn't open it. "Yes?"

Giselle's kind voice responded. "I've brought you breakfast."

"No, thank you. I'd like my trunks, though, as soon as possible. And a carriage ordered, please." Not waiting for a response, she returned to her perch in anticipation of Ewan and the dreaded confrontation he'd insisted upon.

She hadn't long to wait. Less than half an hour later, knuckles rapped at her chamber.

She unlocked the door and, leaving it standing open, returned to the window seat. She could no more sit on the divan where she and Ewan had been intimate yesterday than she could mend the cracks in her shattered heart. She clutched a pillow to her middle, much like a shield, as she hunched in the alcove.

From beneath her lashes, she observed him entering her bedchamber. Attired only in breeches and a shirt, he stood in the middle of the room, warily considering her. He'd stood in her chamber similarly attired another time.

With controlled deliberateness, she forced the image from her mind.

His brows knitted together, he scrutinized her. She knew she looked tired. Standing before the dressing table mirror and securing her hair into a severe knot, she'd seen the dark circles rimming her eyes.

Yvette lifted her head and met his gaze head on.

His disconcerting eyes peered straight into her soul.

She spoke with quiet resolve. "My lord, I asked for my trunks. They've yet to be brought to me. I'm leaving as soon as I've packed."

He stiffened and pressed his lips together. "Evvy, that I cannot allow."

"You misunderstand me. I'm not asking your permission."

He heaved a weighty sigh.

She tilted her chin in defiance. "Surely, you didn't think I would remain here after last night?"

After she'd learned what an unscrupulous rogue he truly was.

Head cocked, he stood spread-eagled before her, his hands resting on his lean hips. "You're my wife, legally before God and King, whether you can accept it or not. There are those who wish you harm, and it's my duty to protect you."

Yvette narrowed her eyes to thin slits, fisting one hand into the pillow. "So, mere duty caused you to deceive me and coerce me into marriage? My substantial wealth wasn't an enticement at all?"

The glare she speared him would've singed feathers from a duck's behind. "Your eagerness to declare us betrothed at the inn, the convenient license. Was that all part of your scheme too?" She shook her head. "Did you snicker at how gullible I was? You made a May game of me, to be sure."

Suddenly she went rigid. "Was Munlocky's a ploy, too?" Her voice shaking with disbelief and hurt, she raged, "Did you deliberately take me there, knowing what the outcome would be? Did you?"

"It wasn't like that. I never intended to deceive you. I've only ever tried to protect you." With one hand resting on his hip, he rubbed his nape with the other. "And I don't need your wealth. I've accumulated my own fortune."

He extended his hand palm upward then made a sweeping gesture. "If I could undo what's been done, I would, but there's naught for it now. The blade's been forged, and there's no uncasting it."

She lowered the pillow to her lap, plucking at the tatting to release some of her pent-up fury. "Would you have me believe, because you claim your intentions were honorable, the affront you committed against me is acceptable? What of your duplicity? When were you going to tell me, Ewan?" She jerked at the threads, a sense of satisfaction filling her as they unraveled.

Much like my life.

"Out riding? Over tea? *In bed?* When, Ewan? When?" She hated how shrill her voice sounded. She calmed her hands and glared daggers at him before continuing in a mocking imitation of him.

"Oh, by-the-by, Yvette, I do hope you've no notions of acquiring a husband of your own choosing—one who has some affection for you. I dare say, it's a bit too late for that.

Gads, I believe I forgot to mention it. You're already married.

To me!"

Yvette punched the pillow for emphasis before tossing it onto the seat beside her.

"Dammit, Yvette." Ewan plowed his fingers through his hair. "I'm sorry, but there's nothing for it now. What's done is done. We're brought to Point Non Plus."

Unable to stay seated any longer, Yvette jumped to her feet. She swept past his intimidating figure, tossing a defiant challenge as she passed. "I disagree, my lord. There are other options. The marriage hasn't been consummated. It *can* be annulled."

Before she knew what he was about, Ewan snaked his arm out, twined it around her waist, then jerked her to his solid side.

Astonishment prevented her from resisting. She stood in his embrace, wide-eyed, mouth parted.

"That can be remedied, *ma belle*." His head swooped downward, his mouth taking hers in a plundering, punishing kiss.

Yvette stood stock-still, too stunned to fight him, and truth be told, not altogether unaffected by the skillful play of his lips upon hers.

He lifted her in his arms, carrying her to the bed, where he continued the gentle buffeting of her overwhelmed senses.

She felt herself slipping, caving in under his spell of practiced passion. She had to stop him before she lost what meager self-respect she had left.

Wrenching her mouth free, she gasped, "You'd force me?"

~

Turquoise eyes clashed with sapphire.

"There'd be no forcing. We both know it. But no. I want you to come to me of your own free will."

If he took Yvette now, there'd be no question of an annulment. Nonetheless he knew, with everything in him, she would never be his if he—if they—yielded to their desires now.

Oh, she'd respond.

She was a very sensual woman.

He'd tasted her sweet, hot passion. These past weeks, he'd come to know her, though. She'd feel an even deeper sense of betrayal for having that choice taken from her, too. She had to want him as much as he wanted her. He'd leave the decision to her, had to leave it to her, no matter the outcome.

Continuing to hold her, he peered into her eyes. "You're not to leave the Keep's grounds under any circumstances. You're free to roam inside the walls of Craiglocky as you please, as long as an armed escort is with you."

"So, I'm to be a prisoner then?" Blue sparks kindled in her eyes.

"For your own safety." He resisted the urge to shake her, to make her listen to reason. "Signs have been seen of those seeking to harm you."

"May I venture into the village? With an armed escort, of course?" Sarcasm riddled her questions.

Angling his head, Ewan considered her request. "Aye, but you must be accompanied by no fewer than a dozen of my clan. I shall speak with them."

"Are you sure a mere dozen is sufficient, my lord?"

Ewan clamped his jaw. "Don't push me, Yvette."

The timbre of his voice brooked no argument.

Yvette swallowed, averting her gaze.

Her slim throat convulsing brought him no satisfaction.

Merde. Now, he could add fear to her lists of complaints against him.

Disgusted with himself, Ewan released her. He rose from the bed and, needing to put some distance between them, strode to the window. Resting a shoulder against the aged stones framing the arched opening, he gazed out the warped panes. Careful to keep his expression and voice devoid of emotion, he told her, "I shall be leaving Craiglocky within the hour."

Silence met his pronouncement.

What had he expected?

Yvette to protest his leaving?

Not bloody likely, when she was hell-bent on putting as much distance between them as a well-matched team enabled.

"I've received a message from Ian. Seems the young lad who ran for help when Vangie went into labor is responsible for the notes left at Somersfield." He suppressed a defeated sigh and shifted his weight to his other foot.

Not as much as a rustle upon the mattress in response. Might as well be speaking to the stones he stood upon.

"The boy claims Fielding was blackmailing him. The lad's mother ailed and needed a doctor's care. Fielding paid the whelp to carry his threatening missives. I want to question the lad myself, and I've other business in London as well."

Still nothing.

Confound it all. He'd made a royal mull of it.

"Ian and I believe Fielding, Pauline, and Edgar are working for the same person, and I need to tell Yancy whom we suspect." Ewan intended to resign his position with the War Office too—Prinny be damned.

"I'll be gone for three weeks. Possibly more."

Was she even listening?

Ewan finally turned away from the window.

Yvette hadn't moved an inch.

"I'd have asked you to marry me, *petite amie*. I've wanted to propose to you since you tumbled headlong into my carriage that day in London." He curled his lips in a self-depreciating smile at the revelation. "One dance at Ian and Vangie's reception, and my heart became forever yours."

He gave a slight shrug. She might as well know all. "Aye, I've adored you for over two years."

Staring with unblinking, fawn-like eyes, Yvette remained mute.

"I was willing to wait for you to come to love me. And I hoped you were beginning to feel for me what I cherish in my heart for you. I've not handled things well, I'll admit it." He paused, raking a hand through his hair again.

He did sigh then, a low sound, equal parts remorse and futility.

Why do I even waste my breath?

Because, fool, you adore her.

He permitted his gaze to trail over her curves before meeting her poignant azure-eyed gaze once more. "I wanted you for my own, *ma petite*. I didn't consider your desires as I should've. It was selfish of me."

And may have cost you the only woman you've ever loved.

Lolling against the window's edge—the effort to stand on his own far too great—Ewan continued, regret coloring each word. "While I'm gone, you decide whether you're able to forgive me. If we have any chance of a future together."

He reached into his pocket and withdrew the Luckenbooth brooch, fingering the ruby in its center. "When I return, if you're wearing this brooch, I'll know there's reason to hope. That somehow, some way, I can make amends to you. I shall spend a lifetime doing so, if you only give me the chance, Evvy."

Ewan stopped his monologue to peruse the view once more. Shoulders slumping, he forced his tongue and mouth to say the words, though his heart shouted for him not to. "If you cannot forgive me, I'll petition the Kirk for an annulment. I see no reason why it shouldn't be granted. We've not been intimate. It could take years though, *l'amour de ma vie.*"

His gaze swung to Yvette before lowering to the brooch in his hand. "The Church disapproves of annulments almost as much as it does divorce."

Giving her a final searching look, he strode to the bed then placed the brooch on the coverlet. It sparkled in the morning light, inches from where his reluctant bride lay.

Bending over Yvette, Ewan kissed her smooth forehead.
"Je t'aime."
I love you.

Twenty-Six

The room was unnaturally quiet after Ewan left, taking Yvette's mangled heart with him. She lay on the bed, staggered, and incapable of forming a single articulate sound.

He loved her? Had loved her for years?

She couldn't help herself. Her hand crept out of its own accord, and she traced her fingers over the glittering jewels. She lifted the brooch, yet warm from being inside his pocket, and read the inscription.

Reading the etched words, anguished tears filled her eyes.

Love of my life.

The same words Ewan had spoken to her in French moments before.

Clutching the brooch to her heart, Yvette curled into a ball and cried. Cried until there were no more tears, the reservoir of her sorrow exhausted. Then, mercifully, she slipped into the forgetfulness of sleep.

It was late afternoon before she awoke, and the crushing memories came flooding back. Still clasping the brooch, she climbed from the bed, her movements that of an old woman. Eyes puffy and weighted by sorrow, she stared glumly at the symbol of Ewan's love. The symbol of what she now feared she had lost forever.

He loved her.

He lied to me.

Yes, but he loved her.

He tricked me into marriage.

Had he?

Or had he done what he must to protect her? Because he loved her?

She didn't know.

Nothing made sense right now. Love, betrayal, fear, fury, deceit, trust, and a myriad of other emotions tumbled pell-mell around inside her. A mixed-up, messed-up jumble she couldn't sort through.

A single tear teetered at the corner of her eye before dropping on the brooch where it glistened, taunting her.

A cheerless smile framed her mouth.

At last she had her meaningful declaration of love.

For the first three days after Ewan's departure, Yvette refused to leave her chamber.

Seonaid brought the bunny to visit, but Yvette wasn't inclined to talk, so Seonaid did the chatting.

"There are dozens of orphans running half-clothed and hungry throughout the countryside, and we've need of a physician to treat the poor and infirm." She stroked the bunny's soft fur. "Gregor and I do our best, but alas, our knowledge is limited."

Yvette, lost in her own unhappy melancholia, only half listened.

Nevertheless, Seonaid rattled on cheerily. "Do you know, most of the Scots hereabouts don't have an iota of education?"

Yvette flicked Seonaid a brief glance then returned her focus to the window she lay curled against.

"Now, don't misunderstand me. Both Ewan and Father are diligent overseers, but Scots have pride." Seonaid shook her head while petting the sleeping bunny nestled in her lap. "They'll not take charity. No indeed. Ewan's people want to be indebted to no man. Give them the means, and they'll take care of the need themselves." Her voice rang with pride.

Despite her doldrums, the tiniest smile tilted the corners of Yvette's mouth.

"Did I tell you," asked Seonaid, "I've planted some new varieties of herbs outside the east side of the castle? I do believe the rich soil and abundant sunshine on that side of the Keep might produce a heartier variety of plant life."

Yvette wrapped her shawl tighter round her shoulders and shook her head. Politeness necessitated she reply. "No, you've not mentioned it."

Seonaid's soft honey-brown eyes brightened. "I've even tried some new specimens which flourish in the wetlands." Her tone became much more serious. "Though I'm careful never to venture too near the bogs."

Other than Seonaid, Yvette refused any visitors. She spent the days lost in misery, gazing at the scene beyond the window's warped panes. She slept little and ate even less, losing weight she could ill-afford to spare.

She missed Ewan.

Her eyes misted with tears, blurring the scenery further.

She dreamt of him each night. Not the passionate, sensual dreams of weeks ago, but visions of him grinning as he handed her from a carriage or passed jam to her at breakfast. Even dreams of her riding across his lap, a tender smile on his lips and devotion in his arresting eyes.

Eventually, as the days passed, reason returned as Yvette's emotions calmed, and she recognized the truth. Ewan wasn't entirely to blame for their predicament. He'd been trying to protect her. Perhaps his methods were questionable, but if she were honest with herself, she hadn't truly objected to a betrothal to him.

Or to being his wife.

Now that she knew he loved her, wouldn't marriage have been her choice?

She exhaled a poof of air, her breath fogging the window glass. Even to her, the sigh sounded wistful and forlorn.

A movement caught her eye.

There, near the dock, two little boys and a slip of a girl skipped along. One of the poppets looked to have a loaf of bread tucked under his scrawny arm. Some goodwife had been careless and left her bread to cool where small, thieving hands could snatch it.

Yvette had noticed children scurrying into the woods on multiple occasions during her self-imposed vigil. They must be some of the war orphans Giselle and Seonaid spoke of.

A sudden epiphany struck Yvette. "The orphans, of course!"

A delighted grin split her face.

Dear Vangie had been orphaned at six and lived with a miserly aunt and uncle. They had treated her little better than a servant. It was only when she visited Yvette or her Romani family that Vangie experienced any happiness. Yet, compared to these urchins—Yvette searched the trees again, catching a glimpse of a tattered yellow skirt—Vangie had been blessed.

Something resonated deep within Yvette.

Making an impulsive decision, she wrote Mr. Dehring a detailed letter. As she reread it, a satisfied smile curled her lips. She wrote another missive, this one to her stepbrother, the Earl of Clarendon. Once she'd sealed the letters, she left her room with purposeful intent.

At the bottom of the staircase, Yvette hesitated. Where would she find Hugh or Duncan?

Voices filtered from the great hall, and she marched toward the room which only days ago had witnessed her ruination. Inhaling a cleansing breath, she determined to put that aside.

She had a purpose for leaving the bower.

Squaring her shoulders, she notched her chin a trifle higher. After all, she was the Lady of Craiglocky now— however would she become accustomed to that? Well, she would eventually, and it was within her rights to seek Craiglocky's steward and Ewan's second-in-command. At her appearance in the entrance, conversations dwindled, then ceased altogether as one by one the family noticed her.

Deuce and drat.

Except for Dugall, Aubry, Seonaid, and Lilias, the entire family had assembled for the midday meal.

Yvette hesitated. "I'm sorry to interrupt." She half-turned to leave. "I shall come back later."

"Yvette, won't you join us?" Giselle motioned to the table.

Smiling tentatively, she nodded. "Yes, thank you."

Giselle called for another place setting, while Gregor stood then pulled the chair out beside his.

"Thank you." Sending him a grateful smile, Yvette sank into the chair.

Adaira beamed and reached under the table to squeeze her hand.

Isobel smiled. "It's wonderful to see you, Yvette."

"Have ye need of something?" Hugh's warm eyes met hers before he looked pointedly at the letters in her hand.

Yvette glanced at the letters. "Yes, I sought an audience with you and Duncan."

"Lass, ye'r the lady of Craiglocky now. Ye needn't ask for an audience," Hugh said kindly.

Yvette blushed, uncomfortable with her new title. "I've a proposition I need your help with." She gazed around the table. "If you don't object, I could share my plan with everyone now."

Hugh's keen gaze roamed those seated. "Aye. We'd like to hear what ye have to propose."

As efficiently as possible, Yvette revealed her plans. "Do you think it possible, Hugh?"

Brushing his chin with his hand, he looked first to Duncan, then the other astonished faces. "Aye. It can be done, but it would be costly, lass. *Verra* costly."

She breathed a sigh of relief. "Money isn't an issue. Ewan did indeed marry an heiress." She colored when she acknowledged her marriage, but forged on. "Even he doesn't know the extent of my wealth."

Hugh raised an eyebrow. "Indeed, lass?" A touch of disbelief colored his voice.

Yvette's lips twitched. "Indeed." She named a sum which wiped the humor off everyone's faces. "And those are only my holdings in England." Her gaze skimmed their slack-jawed, astonished countenances. "I've interests around the world."

Duncan's "Holy Mother of God," smothered Alasdair's "Jesus, Mary, and Joseph."

Hugh grunted and pulled his left earlobe. "I've never kent a'body so wealthy."

The others were too quiet, and doubt raised its troll-like head. "Please forgive me. I didn't mean to sound boastful."

Giselle shook her head. "Please don't mistake our silence for disapproval. I think I speak for each of us," she paused, sweeping her hand to indicate those seated at the table, "when I say we're amazed at your generosity. You've been here but days, ill the first few, and, I'm ashamed to say, treated abominably by some thereafter, though our intent was never to hurt you. What possible motive can you have for wanting to do this?"

"You don't wish me to?" Studying their sober faces, Yvette frowned, trying to determine their thoughts.

Duncan regarded her. "Nae that, lass." He leaned forward, propping his elbows on the table. "What we're trying to ken is why ye'd do something so kind when ye've been treated so shoddily?"

Faith, they doubted her motives. Understandable, given they didn't know her.

Angling her head, Yvette folded her hands and kicked her pride to next November. "I want to do it for Ewan." Her attention circled the table, searching the faces of everyone seated there. "Will you help me?"

Hugh stood and Duncan followed suit. "Who be with us?" Hugh asked.

She watched in tearful amazement as everyone present stood in acknowledgement of their commitment. They would help her.

Lifting Mr. Dehring's letter, a triumphant smile upon her mouth, she waved the foolscap. "I've a letter drafted to my solicitor. I need a list of supplies, materials, laborers, anything and everything you can think of. I'd like to get started at once, and if possible, send a rider to London today."

"Lass, I dinnae want to spoil the moment for ye, but ye need to present yer case to the folk if yer to be successful." Duncan's sober declaration wiped the smile from her face.

Doubt kneed her in the chest again, and she cut him a troubled gaze.

Giselle laid her hand over Yvette's. "You're their laird's wife now. Tell them what's in your heart, *chérie*. Why it's important for you to do this."

Hugh nodded and picked up his knife. "We shall call for a council of the folk in the mornin'."

Tomorrow?

His proclamation wrenched Yvette's stomach, giving her the collywobbles. She pressed a palm to her upset middle.

Her face must've registered her panic, because he chuckled, not unkindly. "Dinnae fash yerself. We'll help ye."

Aubry flounced into the hall, and every muscle the breadth of Yvette's neck and shoulders tightened into hard, miserable little rocks. She wasn't prepared to speak to Aubry yet. No, that wasn't true. She never wanted to speak to the shrew again.

Yvette passed Hugh the letters. "Will you please see these are posted for me?" She smiled at the others as she stood. "Thank you. Please excuse me."

Head lowered, she made for the hall's massive carved doors.

Aubry sidestepped, blocking her escape. "Yvette, please wait. I'd like to apologize for my appallin' behavior. I was distraught and said a batch of things I shouldnae have. Intolerably unkind things."

Head bowed, Yvette clenched her fists. Did Aubry expect a polite thank you for her apology? Not deuced likely. Perhaps give her the cut direct then. Or plant her a facer. Yvette rather liked that last choice.

"I wronged ye," Aubry blathered on. "I'd like to start over, should like for us to become friends. If ye can find it in yer heart to forgive me."

Friends? I'd sooner sleep with an asp.

Adaira snorted in blatant disbelief. "And I'm a horse's arse."

"Hush, Addy, there's no need to be vulgar," Giselle chastised.

"Mere words aren't enough to undo the harm ye did, Aubry. Ewan may yet send ye from the Keep, so furious he be." Duncan made the dour proclamation in his brother's stead.

Addy muttered beneath her breath, "I hope Ewan *does* send her away. *Far* away."

Aubry's cheeks took on a rosy hue. "I'm certain I can be of help in the endeavor Yvette has suggested."

Several brows rose askance at her remark, and Yvette looked her square on for the first time.

How did Aubry know of her plans?

Yvette's gaze veered to the hall's open doors.

Seeing the direction of Yvette's focus, Aubry confessed, "I didnae mean to eavesdrop, but I was reluctant to enter. I was—I am—ashamed of my behavior." Her gaze took in the others as she waved a hand in Yvette's direction. "Aren't ye willing to help her? Then why shouldnae I be too?"

From beneath her lashes, Yvette scrutinized Aubry. She

didn't believe a word. Not one. From everyone's wary expressions, it appeared they didn't either.

Aubry flashed a bright smile. "Ye'll see how sincere I am. I shall prove myself to all of ye."

Her lower lip tucked between her teeth, Yvette considered Aubry. Her mind waged a soundless battle between her convictions and emotions. Not for a minute did she think Aubry was the least remorseful.

Yvette considered the others, waiting for her decision. *Blast it.* This was asking too much, too soon. She wanted nothing to do with Aubry. An idea took hold.

But perhaps—

Yvette suggested smoothly, "I'm sure you know where Aubry will be the most helpful, Hugh and Giselle. May I rely upon you to place her where her talents would be useful?" That way, Yvette was spared Aubry's company.

"Of course." Giselle nodded, a meaningful twinkle in her eyes, so like Ewan's.

Aubry managed to curl her mouth into a semblance of a smile, rather looking like she'd swallowed rotten fish. "Wonderful. Please let me ken how I can help. I'll leave ye to yer meal." In a flurry of russet-colored skirts, Aubry hastened from the room.

A mixture of relief and trepidation engulfing at her, Yvette watched her go. No, indeed. She wasn't so short on wit she'd believe Aubry had had a change of heart, but at least the woman had quit the room.

Ewan's family and clan forming a half-circle behind her, Yvette stood on the top step of the keep and swallowed. Fingering the Luckenbooth brooch at her shoulder, she scanned the crowd before her. Lord, would that her stomach would stop frolicking about like lambs set to pasture.

Determined to be taken seriously as their laird's lady, she'd donned the plaid and linen blouse Giselle had brought her. With her help, Yvette had secured the scarf across her left shoulder.

The Luckenbooth brooch gleamed triumphantly against the McTavish tartan, its jewels complimenting the checked cloth to perfection. In traditional Scots fashion, she let her hair hang loose with a simple blue ribbon tied across her crown.

She wiped her damp palms on her wool skirt. Taking a deep breath, she addressed the crowd, explaining what she wanted to do for the orphans and Ewan's people.

"I cannot do this alone. I've seen the sturdy homes built by the skilled craftsmen in the clan. I need your help to build a school, an orphanage, and a woolen mill. These new buildings will require all your skills and talents. And I've not forgotten the sick and elderly. I sent a missive to my solicitor asking him to retain a physician for the village.

"You don't know me and have no reason to trust me, but I ask you to do this for your laird." She lifted her hands, palm upward in entreaty. "Help me in this. I cannot do it without you. I want to make your laird, now my husband, proud."

Yvette would never forget the nerve-racking silence greeting her final words. It stretched on and on for endless minutes. Then, all at once, rousing cheers erupted, and her mouth dropped open in astonishment.

Ewan's people had accepted her propositions.

Elated, she turned to Hugh. "They've agreed."

He gathered her in a crushing embrace, lifting her off her feet. "Och, well done, lassie."

Several other enthusiastic hugs followed, and even Aubry condescended to buss Yvette's cheek.

A grand celebration followed that evening. Everyone, including Yvette, danced into the late hours. When she at last found her bed, she sank in to the welcoming softness and snuggled beneath the satiny cover's weight.

They've accepted me as the chieftainess.

Yvette and Hugh reined in their mounts. Head tilted, she proudly surveyed the building before them. "I'd no idea this much progress could be made in such a short time."

"Aye, the second story is framed, and the roof beams are in place already."

Thoroughly pleased, she grinned. "Things are shaping up well, aren't they?"

Hugh chuckled as he peered around. "Och, they are, lass."

The transformation in the village since she'd presented her idea to the McTavish Clan a fortnight ago was nothing short of phenomenal. Clan members and villagers worked side-by-side, calling cheerful greetings to passersby. A continuous stream of workers, vendors, clansmen, as well as Ewan's family traveled from the Keep to the village then back again.

A contingent of twelve Scots was her constant companion outside Craiglocky's bailey, and a half-score more accompanied her on more far-reaching outings. She was hard-pressed to remember the names of the men assigned as her escorts, for their faces changed often.

Hugh said they jostled amongst themselves for the honor.

Yvette allowed herself a small, mockery-tinged smile. Ewan would be gratified to know how diligent his men were. A trussed-up hen boasted more freedom than she.

Her heart twinged.

There had been no word from him, though given he was an agent in the Diplomatic Corps, that wasn't cause for alarm.

How her life had changed since stepping off the *Atlantic Star*. Married to a wonderful man, and she'd found something meaningful to do with the wealth she'd been blessed with.

The baker waved. "G'day, me lady."

"Good day to you too." After returning the waves of several villagers, she guided her mare to the rear of the building.

Hugh followed.

At her insistence, the first structure built was the orphanage's kitchen so the hungry urchins could eat. Two cooks had been employed to prepare meals. A crude, temporary shelter provided a place for the foundlings to sleep. Once the ragamuffins realized what was happening, they began to venture from the woods and surrounding areas, eager to help.

Whenever possible, native Scots had been hired to fill the numerous positions. Yvette retained a sweet orphan named Nessia to train as her personal maid. Pippa was getting along in years and could use an assistant. Yvette's heart wrenched, thinking of her dear companion. Surely Pippa and the Fairchilds would arrive in England soon.

Twisting in her saddle, she met Hugh's eyes. "I'd not dreamed we'd accomplish this much this fast. Mr. Dehring and Rory have been godsends. Without their influence, we'd still be awaiting supplies."

Smiling, brown eyes twinkling kindly, he agreed. "Aye, lass, it's a wonder to behold."

Yvette snagged her lower lip between her teeth. "Have I overstepped my bounds? Will Ewan be angry?"

Hugh's penetrating gaze met hers, warmth softening the corners of his eyes. "How can he be displeased, lass? Look at the folk. Ye've restored their pride, ye have." He surveyed the projects, and a grin erupted across his rugged face. "Nae, lassie, he'll nae be displeased with ye."

Twenty-Seven

"Get on with ye." Kicking Shaidae, Ewan urged the stallion on. Every mile that brought him closer to Yvette magnified his desire to see her. And, with each mile, his trepidation mounted.

Lord, he'd missed her. She consumed his thoughts day and night, and poignant memories of her replayed in his mind. Never before had he been as uncertain of anything. Nothing had ever mattered as much as her decision about their marriage.

Had she decided to remain his wife? With everything in him, he hoped she had.

As he crested the last hill before descending into the village, Ewan jerked Shaidae's reins.

The horse reared and snorted in disapproval.

"Sorry, lad." Ewan patted the stallion's neck.

From his vantage point atop the knoll, he stared dumbfounded at the landscape before him.

What the hell?

Digging his heels into the horse's flanks, he tore down

the hill. When he reached the village, he slowed Shaidae to a walk. Ewan turned his head this way and that, trying to absorb all the changes since his departure over three weeks ago.

What was going on?

A man atop a building under construction called to him. "Laird McTavish, bless ye."

An ancient crone seized Ewan's boot, giving him a toothless smile. "Yer lady be an angel, me laird."

Ewan heard, "Thank ye, laird. God bless ye and yer lady," over and over again.

At a complete loss, he stopped Shaidae in front of the two largest new buildings. He glimpsed his stepfather between the supporting beams of one. Eyeing the workers bustling around him, he waited for Hugh's approach.

Ewan required some answers.

"Good to see ye, Ewan." Hugh clasped his hand. "Ye've been missed."

Wholly bewildered, looking around the thrumming community, Ewan finally met Hugh's amused gaze. "Hugh?"

"Ye have to ask yer wife, son. She's been *verra* busy while ye be gone."

Ewan stood in his stirrups, craning his neck and peering at the commotion. "I can bloody well see that."

Yvette was responsible for this?

Chuckling, Hugh slapped Ewan's thigh. "Come, get off yer horse, and have a wee peek inside."

After a tour of the buildings, Ewan stood in the middle of the street scrutinizing the lively scene before him. Yvette *was* responsible for this. He shook his head, amazed.

"How did you... did *she* manage it?"

"She's a rich lass with powerful connections." Palm upward, Hugh extended his hand to indicate the villagers. "Yer clan is eager to please both of ye."

Ewan lifted his hat, and after wiping his brow, smoothed aside the hair that had fallen onto his forehead. "Aye, so I see."

"I want to show ye the woolen mill. It be over by the river." Hugh mounted his horse. "Duncan be overseeing its construction."

A woolen mill too?

Ewan donned his hat, then gripped Shaidae's reins and hoisted himself onto the stallion. He and Hugh trotted their mounts the mile to River Falkirk. A half hour later, Ewan stood outdoors once more.

Yvette.

He shook his head again. She'd thought of everything.

A smile started at the edges of his mouth and split into a grin of primordial male triumph. No wife intent on leaving her husband would go to this much effort. Yvette had decided to stay, to remain his wife.

An overwhelming joy filled him as he sprinted to his smoky black mount. He fairly leaped into the saddle. Though the castle wasn't visible from the hamlet, his heart's desire lay a short distance away. With one final look around the village, he trotted Shaidae to the path leading to home and a welcoming wife.

Had news of his arrival reached her yet?

Unsure of her welcome, Yvette entered the kitchen.

A large woman with well-muscled arms, her hair

hidden by a bright scarf tied about her head, smiled a cheerful greeting.

"Can I help ye, m'lady?" The look the cook sent Yvette held curiosity, though not censure.

"Yes, please. You're Sorcha?"

"Aye, lady."

"I'm looking for Iona." She raised the basket she carried. "I've something for her."

"The wee lass will return soon. She ran to the garden for some onions and carrots."

"Might I wait?"

"Of course. Would ye like some fresh bread? I took it from the oven minutes ago."

Sitting on a rough chair at the simple table, Yvette sniffed the fragrant air. "Yes, please."

Placing the basket atop the table, she took stock of the immaculate kitchen. Drying herbs hung from hooks inserted in one rough-hewn beam. Two women cut vegetables while another strained cheese.

Sorcha put a plate piled with thick, steaming bread slices before Yvette. A crock of creamy butter and a dish of fruit preserves followed. She put a hand to her rumbling stomach.

"Tea, milady?"

"If it wouldn't be too much trouble."

"Nae trouble at all."

Biting into the warm bread, Yvette grinned. "It's wonderful."

Sorcha smiled and put water on to boil before returning her attention to the large pot she'd been stirring when Yvette entered the kitchen.

Moments later, Yvette heard the clamor of childish voices

Iona and a small boy burst into the kitchen, their arms full of fresh vegetables. Upon seeing Yvette, Iona's face broke into a gap-toothed grin. Dumping the contents of her arms into the sink, she helped the boy do the same. She looked to Sorcha, but obviously wanted to go to Yvette.

"Go on with ye." The smiling cook said, waving her spoon in Yvette's direction.

Iona grabbed the boy's hand and tugged him to stand with her before Yvette.

Given the unmistakable resemblance, the lad had to be Iona's brother. "Iona, would you please introduce me to your brother?"

Looking abashed, the freckles more pronounced on her cherub's face, Iona nodded. "Yer ledyship, this be me brother, Peadar."

Yvette guessed the boy might be five or six years old. He had the same bright red mop of hair his sister sported. "I'm pleased to meet you, Peadar."

The boy hid his grubby face in his sister's shoulder.

"I've brought you something, Iona. Your brother too."

"Ye have, lady?"

"Aye." Yvette lifted the basket off the table and settled it in her lap. "Come, see what I have for you."

She tipped the top open.

Iona's squeal of delight echoed throughout the kitchen.

Yvette held a fat, fuzzy calico kitten in her hands. She transferred the bit of fluff to Iona, who buried her face in the kitten's soft fur.

Cooing softly, cradling the cat in her arms, she plopped onto the floor.

Peadar stood looking at the kitten in his sister's arms, trying to still the trembling of his distended lower lip.

"Peadar, look." Yvette held a sleepy, jade-eyed, orange and white striped tabby.

His blue eyes huge in his thin face, Peadar asked, "For me?"

Yvette smiled and nodded. "Yes. For you."

The grin splitting his face would've turned night to day had it been dark outside. He reached for the kitten, cuddled it to his neck, and talked to it in a soft, lisping whisper.

Yvette glanced across the kitchen to find the four kitchen staff staring at her, their faces beaming with undisguised approval. She suspected she'd just made four allies and happily returned their smiles.

With the corner of her apron, Sorcha wiped a tear from her eye before turning her stern gaze on the rest of the help.

They swiftly resumed their duties, whispering beneath their breaths and darting glances Yvette's way every few minutes.

"The kittens are brother and sister, like you." Yvette pointed to each cat in turn "They are your responsibility. You must feed them and take them outside." Pausing, she scrutinized the kitchen. "Sorcha, is there someplace the kittens can sleep which wouldn't be underfoot?"

"They might as well sleep with the bairns. They have a pallet in one of the storerooms."

Storeroom?

Yvette must talk to Ewan about remedying that immediately.

"Peadar, Iona, you must see that the kittens do not disrupt the work of these dear women. Can you do that?"

As one, the children answered, "Aye."

"Might I show the laird me kitten?" Brows puckered, Iona studied her kitten's face. The kitten swatted at the curls bouncing beyond her paws.

Yvette chuckled at the kitten's antics. "I'm sure he would like that when he returns."

When would that be?

It had been over three weeks since Ewan left. Yvette had been certain—well, had hoped—he'd return early, or at the very least, post a letter. But she'd heard nothing at all.

Turning the mite over, Iona tickled the cat's belly.

A sad smile touched Yvette's lips. She'd been right about the kittens, though. Iona and Peadar needed something to love and that loved them in return.

He lay on his back, holding the purring kitten across his skinny chest. "The laird be in the village, thithter. He be home soon."

"What did you say?" Yvette practically dropped her teacup in its saucer.

The clatter drew the servant's probing gazes for a moment.

Clutching the kitten to his side, his blue eyes pooling with tears, Peadar slowly sat up.

"It's all right, Peadar. You've done nothing wrong," Yvette assured him. "What's this about the laird?"

"Thom thaid he thaw the laird afore. When he wath in town."

Merciful God in heaven. Ewan is home.

Yvette took in her smudged dress and put a hand to her hair. She was a sight. Thank goodness she'd washed her hair last night.

In a flurry of skirts, she jumped to her feet. He couldn't see her like this. "Sorcha, please heat water for my bath. I know you're busy, but the laird's home. I must make myself presentable."

Before darting from the room, Yvette dashed to the cook and hugged her. "Thank you for the delicious bread.

And for allowing the children the kittens. And for the water."

Jaw slack, Sorcha gaped for a moment, then, spinning to face the other servants, hollered, "What are ye waitin' for? Ye heard her ladyship. Heat the water. The laird be home."

Yvette hurried to the stone stairs beside the enormous fireplace. "Oh, and could someone please find Nessia and send her to my chamber at once?"

Wiping her hands on her starched apron, her mouth tipped into a knowing smile, Sorcha nodded. "Aye, m'lady."

As Yvette started up the stairs, the cook spoke again.

"Did ye see the way she jumped from her chair when she heard the laird was near? She be eager to be reunited with her husband, to be sure." The women tittered in agreement.

At the cook's observation, Yvette's face burned. Hiking her skirts to her knees, she raced up the back staircase, one of the many alternate routes Isobel and Adaira had shared with her. They had taken her on a tour of the castle, showing her the seldom-used corridors and staircases, even a few cobweb-filled secret passageways.

Adaira had giggled in remembrance. "Many were the times I snuck outside the keep by way of these corridors. There are a couple of secret entrances to the dungeon too. It's said prisoners, enemy clan members, and even aristocracy were smuggled in and out through those hidden doors."

Lowering her voice to a covert whisper, Adaira had confessed. "I know where the keys to the cells are kept, too. They're hanging on a peg at the base of the stairs, in a little alcove."

Recalling the conversation, Yvette's mouth lifted in amusement. No surprise there. Adaira was incorrigible.

Yvette rounded a sharp corner and charged up more

risers. She had grown adept at using the routes in order to avoid Aubry. She drew her brows together. Aubry still made her uncomfortable. Oh, she was pleasant enough, some might even call her genial, but Yvette had seen a calculating look in her eye when she thought no one watched.

Yvette hastened around another bend and ascended a rarely used, very narrow stairwell. Enough dour thoughts.

Her husband was home.

Twenty-Eight

From the tub, Yvette called, "Nessia, hang the light blue silk with the white organza overskirt to air, please."

A gentle smile framed her mouth. The Luckenbooth brooch would look exquisite pinned at the bodice.

Lathering the sponge with jasmine-scented soap, she listened to Nessia moving about in the outer chamber. A door clicked closed. The wardrobe, no doubt. Nessia was adapting to her role as a lady's maid with considerable finesse, and Yvette was quite pleased with the sweet-tempered girl.

Resting her head against the tub's tall edge, careful not to dislodge her loosely-piled hair, she let her eyes drift closed. The warm water slipping across her skin felt wonderful.

No word had reached her yet of Ewan's return to the castle. She had asked to be informed the moment he arrived. She allowed herself these few moments to collect her wits and decide what she would say to her husband.

Husband.

The word caused bumps to rise across her exposed skin. She'd been married for a moon, yet was as jittery as a new bride. A disturbing idea flitted through her mind. What if the delay in Ewan's return was due to disapproval? Mayhap he'd not liked the changes she'd implemented in the village and was incensed at her forwardness.

Suddenly anxious, she sat up, reaching for a fluffy towel.

"Nae, stay, wife."

The water's sloshing muffled her startled squeak as she plunged into the tub, leaving only her head exposed above the bubbles.

What was *he* doing in her bathing chamber?

"Ewan, what—?" She peeped over the tub's edge, and her mouth dropped open.

Stripping off his clothing, a wicked grin on his face, he winked.

Squeezing her eyes shut, she sank even deeper into the bubbles.

Ewan's unrepentant chuckle sent shivers skittering across her sensitive flesh. She tried to swallow the nervous lump in her throat.

"Scoot forward, *mon amour*."

"You mean to join me?"

"Aye, and much more."

More? Much more?

Sweet Lord, help her.

"Nessia?" Yvette asked.

"I told her you wouldn't need her services this afternoon. Or evening."

"Ewan...?" Hesitation laced her voice.

"Trust me, *bien amour*."

Arms crossed, knees drawn to her chest, she moved up exposing her back to his gaze.

He stepped into the tub.

She sucked in a sharp breath, tensing as the water level rose, announcing her husband's presence. She waited, anticipating his touch. When it didn't come, she dared to steal a look over her shoulder.

Hair lathered with soap, he winked again. A nuance of desire smoldered in his eyes.

Whatever was the man about?

More splashing and lapping of the water stirred her curiosity, though she wasn't about to peep again. He lifted the pail of warm water to rinse his hair, but she steadfastly kept her attention fixed forward.

It's a wonder the water hasn't spilled over the tub's edge, she thought inanely.

A raspy rubbing sounded behind her. He must be toweling his hair dry.

No. She would not look.

She started in surprise when a gentle, soothing palm ran across her shoulders and backbone.

Ewan traced the ragged scar on her right shoulder with his calloused forefinger. "How did you come by this, *doucette?*"

The air wouldn't leave Yvette's lungs. She stuttered, "Ch-child, c-carriage accident, k-killed my mother."

"I'm sorry, *mon amour.*" He kissed the puckered skin.

She tensed, holding herself rigid.

"*Ma belle,* relax."

Was the man daft?

Relax?

She was an untried maid, naked in a bathtub with her

equally naked husband. Relaxing was the *last* thing she was capable of doing.

His legs grazed the sides of hers, cradling her between their muscular lengths. Taut as a bowstring, she gulped, then gulped again. Ewan trailed the lightest of caresses over the curve of her jaw and neck, then skimmed across her shoulders.

Yvette shivered.

He slipped his hands around her waist, tugging her against his chest. "Lean back, Evvy."

Releasing a pent-up sigh, she gingerly rested her stiff shoulders against Ewan's rugged width. Another low chuckle echoed in his chest. He continued to caress her shoulders, sliding his hands down her arms in an entrancing, calming touch.

The tension eased from her limbs.

Ewan's exploration moved lower, feathering across her abdomen and the tops of her thighs. He nuzzled her neck, placing light kisses across the nape and along her shoulders.

Something nudged against her buttocks. What was that?

Oh!

She dipped her head as heat seared her cheeks.

"I missed ye, wife."

That was quite obvious.

A low, rumbling purr tickled Yvette's ear. "Did ye miss me?"

Did I?

Yvette nodded, too distracted by the tender yet thorough examination of her husband's roaming hands. She gasped when he cupped her breasts, holding them above the water for his viewing.

"Beautiful." His husky breath in her ear caused all manner of delicious sensations.

He touched the mole on her breast. There was something terribly exciting about seeing her smooth white breasts cradled in his calloused brown hands.

Before releasing them to bob atop the surface, he swirled rough fingertips 'round the nipples. Desire, hot and forceful, flamed within her. She shifted her position, accidentally sitting on *it*.

Lord Almighty.

His knowing laugh rumbling deep in his chest stirred the embers of her desire even more.

Finger crooked, Ewan turned her head.

She met his burning eyes before her gaze lowered to his lips. Her own parted in expectation. The soul-shattering kiss ignited an uncontainable blaze. Fierce, hungry, and intense, it lasted several delicious moments. There was nothing gentle or subtle in the dueling tongues or gasping breaths, as she sought to breathe amid the mutual onslaught of sensuality.

Water sloshed onto the floor. She didn't care.

Yvette gasped as his exploration became bolder, daring to sweep across forbidden territory.

"The water cools, *mon amour*." Ewan kissed Yvette's shoulder. "I don't want you catching another chill."

He rose, then stepped from the tub, his hungry gaze roaming over her. Tendrils of flaxen hair framed her face. Lips swollen from his kisses, her milky skin glistened in the candlelight.

Her gaze darted to his erection and skipped away just as

quickly. She licked her lips, and desire shot straight to his groin, heavy and aching.

The temptress. Had she done that on purpose?

Of course not. She was just curious and nervous. In a trice, he toweled off, admonishing himself.

Patience, old chap. Patience.

Once he'd dried off, he helped her from the water. She stood submissive, her cheeks crimson, as he patted her dry. Turning her until she faced him, Ewan stood at arm's length, and leisurely examined every luscious curve and dimple.

Burying his hands in her silky hair, he tugged the pins loose. The bounty of curls fell to swirl around her supple hips. Pulling Yvette to him, her round breasts pressing against his chest, he took her mouth again, this time in an imitation of the act he yearned to perform with her inexperienced body.

He lifted her, never breaking their passionate kiss. She wound her arms around his neck as he strode to her bed. Earlier, he'd turned the covers to the foot, so as not to hinder his love play. Resting one knee on the bed, Ewan laid her across the sheets.

Kneeling by her side, he studied her.

The afternoon sunlight slanted through the imperfect panes, casting rainbows across the bed. "Perfection."

He grasped one thick, golden strand and drew it between her breasts to rest across her stomach.

Summoning unmitigated willpower, he forced himself to take it slowly. Generously curved in the right places, Yvette was every man's fantasy. And she was his wife. Through narrowed slits, he marveled at her voluptuous figure: small waist, rounded hips and thighs, weighty breasts, slim arms, and flat stomach.

Her siren's form begged him to make her his, though she was unaware of the sensual song her innocent's body sang, or the blatant invitation in her sultry eyes. He could smell her subtle scent, see her body's every response to his gaze.

⁓

Incapable of moving, something in the predatory, possessive way Ewan stared at Yvette stirred a primitive female response. She craved his approval, needed him to admire her body. She stole a look at her curvy hips and thighs. Always before, she'd thought she was too generous from the waist down. Given the hungry look on Ewan's face, he didn't agree.

She ran her appreciative gaze over him, relishing the thrill looking at him caused.

A strange, raw hunger simmered in her middle.

A powerfully-built man, muscles bulged in his arms and legs and across the width of his chest and torso. Dark springy hair covered the expanse, tapering to a nest of crisp, black curls from which his maleness sprang.

How could she accommodate *that*? She swallowed. She wasn't afraid. Well, maybe the teeniest bit uneasy.

Ewan trailed one finger from the pulse raging at her throat to the center of her chest to circle the taut peak of her left breast.

Breath suspended, she couldn't tear her gaze from the steady, determined progress of his forefinger. Leaving off teasing that breast, he traced a pattern of sensation to her other areola. Her nipple firmed in anticipation. Starting at the widest part of her breast, he drew an ever smaller circle until his finger scraped across the protruding tip.

God above.

She sucked in a hissing breath of incredible longing and desperate desire.

His manhood pulsed against her thigh, and her eyes widened at the single droplet of moisture glistening on her skin. Where had that come from? She'd no time to wonder further, because suddenly, he was beside her, pulling her into his solid embrace. He whispered words of love and passion, all the while assaulting her senses with his skillful mouth and knowing hands.

"Ewan, I don't know what to do."

"If you like it, *enchanteresse*, chances are, I shall too."

Holding her breath, her lower lip snagged between her teeth, she watched him close his mouth over one turgid nipple, bathing her in glorious sensation. "Ewan—" The air left her in a whoosh.

He switched to her other breast, lavishing loving ministrations on its fullness too.

Yvette pressed against him, her hands and lips exploring his broad planes and firm flesh. She floated on a sea of longing and desire, aching at her very center.

This was more than she'd dared hope. She boldly brushed her fingertips over his buttocks, relishing the feel of his taut flesh beneath her fingertips. Ready to accept him, desperate to ease the incessant, internal pressure, she wiggled her hips in frustration, seeking release from the accumulation of sensation. If he didn't do something soon, she'd burst.

"Easy, *mon ange*." He reached between them, touching her core.

She moaned. "Ewan, please." Opening her eyes, she tugged at his shoulders.

"Aye, love, ye are ready."

Ewan shifted her, pulling her hips beneath his.

She stared into the passion-darkened pools of his eyes.

At last.

He took her lips in a tender kiss. "I'm sorry, *mon amour*, there's no help for it. I'm a large man."

In one swift, powerful movement, he surged forward, penetrating her.

Yvette choked on a cry of pain. For the love of God, why had no one told her of the pain? Was there supposed to be pain?

"*Shh, doucette.* The pain will ease. I promise."

It seemed there was.

Ewan lay still atop her, his elbows bearing most of his weight, except where his hips were locked with hers. Bit by bit, he moved, pushing deeper into her before withdrawing part way.

She bit her lip against a guttural groan. What was he doing now?

He moved again.

The stinging discomfort ebbed, replaced by another fluttery feeling. Stretched to the ends of her endurance, she tilted her hips, seeking succor. Sharp little darts of pleasure pricked her where he remained fully sheathed.

His strong body joined with hers was beyond anything she'd ever imagined. She was awash in sensation. Losing all sense of time, of awareness, their physical union was secondary to the melding of their souls. All that remained was the two of them in an age-old, glorious communion.

She ascended, faster and faster, striving toward she knew not what, until she reached the pinnacle and crashed over the top. At her peak before reality shattered and she plummeted into nothing but pulsating sensation, she cried, "Ewan."

He absorbed her sobs of ecstasy in his open mouth. A

moment later, he stiffened in her arms, followed by a low growl of fulfillment.

Yvette lay in the aftermath of their joining, incapable of moving. Ewan had collapsed atop her, his head buried in her shoulders as potent tremors convulsed his body. She hadn't understood how extraordinary, how powerful their union would be. He had brought her to heaven and back. She lay under him, stunned.

She almost cried out when he withdrew.

He rolled onto his side, carrying her with him. Her head rested on his solid shoulder while he strummed a soothing rhythm across her curves.

His embrace tightened. "I love you."

Smiling, Yvette tilted her head, gazing into his heavy-lidded eyes. Raising her hand, she traced his scar. "I... I never imagined it would be like that."

Why didn't she tell him she loved him? Why did she still hold back? Fear? Pride?

A shadow darkened his eyes before his sculpted mouth tilted into a grin and something else entirely glittered in their depths. "Lady McTavish, you need to expand your imagination."

Sometime later, after he sat her atop him and taught her a new way of cresting the wave, Ewan rose from her bed, pure male confidence, not the least embarrassed to stand nude before her. Faith, but he had a gorgeous body.

His tender gaze bathed her. "Wait there, *amour*."

He disappeared into the bathing chamber, returning moments later with a wet cloth and soft towel. Sitting on the edge of the rumpled bed, he stared at her thighs. Her gaze followed his, noting the streaks branding her as his. He moved to wipe the smears from her legs. She closed them, as much against her own self-consciousness as his probing gaze.

"*Petite amie*, let me wash you." He bent and kissed her, effectively diffusing her resistance.

A single knock rattled the door.

"One moment," Ewan called.

He wrapped his tartan around his glorious masculine hips before snatching the bedding from the foot of the bed.

Yvette grasped the coverlet and yanked it to her chest. A smile teased the edges of her mouth when he tugged the bed curtains closed on the door side. Protecting her again.

She couldn't see who knocked or hear what they said.

The door softly clunked shut, and a moment later, Ewan returned to the bed, bearing a large tray laden with food and drink. "I took the liberty of ordering us supper." He smiled his naughty schoolboy smile and twitched his eyebrows. "In bed."

"You were that confident of your success, my lord? I wasn't wearing the brooch." Yvette's teasing tone belied any real disapproval.

"Aye, lass, I was sure. No wife does what ye did while I was gone unless she cares for her husband." The smile on his handsome face skewed wickedly. "I'm most grateful you weren't wearing the brooch. I much prefer what you were wearing. Nothing at all."

His raffish gaze traveled across her bare shoulders, lingering on the valley between her breasts.

"Ewan!"

Yvette pressed her hands to her hot cheeks. The coverlet slipped down, exposing her nipples. She grabbed at it, but stopped when Ewan leaned across her.

He closed a palm over her breast, his mouth capturing

hers in a searing, toe-curling, bone-melting kiss. Forgotten, the counterpane slithered to her waist.

Her stomach growled, and he chuckled, raising his head. "Seems my wife needs to eat." He chucked her chin with his crooked finger. "Ye'll need yer strength for our bedsport."

She'd hoped there'd be more of that splendidness tonight.

They nibbled on the light supper, Ewan sneaking kisses between bites. Halfway through their meal, a hunger of another sort began to build in Yvette. She licked her lips when Ewan's eyes darkened with sensual promise.

He set the tray aside, and her pulse quickened in anticipation.

He pounced on her, rolling her, giggling, onto her back. Her laughter died in her throat at the profound intensity in his eyes.

"Yvette, I love you. Mere words can ne'er express how much."

"No? So then show me, my lord."

As Yvette drew his head lower, she kissed him, pouring her adoration into the single, focused act. Long moments later, she convulsed with pleasure. Whatever had she done to deserve this happiness?

As the last shudder rippled through her body, she felt his pinnacle. Arching her hips, she savored the sensation of his release pouring into her intimate depths. She gasped, her loins coiling tighter with each of his hot spurts, hurtling her over the edge once more.

Long after slumber claimed Ewan, his rhythmic breathing whispering softly against her neck, Yvette lay awake, unable to sleep.

A peculiar, inexplicable, yet persistent unease taunted

her. Today, as she and Seonaid had tended the herbs by the wetlands, her skin had prickled in the same disturbing manner it had on the dock, at the inn, and at the jeweler's.

She would've sworn someone watched them.

Seonaid paused in her digging. Dirty spade raised, her eyes had taken on the far-off expression Yvette had become accustomed to. Her brow creased and gaze troubled, Seonaid tossed aside the tool and climbed to her feet.

"Danger lurks."

Twenty-Nine

The gallery clock chimed noon as Yvette and Ewan left their chamber. Dawn had tiptoed across the horizon before she'd drifted into an exhausted sleep, a smile of contentment on her face, a prayer of gratitude on her lips.

She'd lost track of the number of times Ewan loved her yesterday afternoon and last night, lost track of the many ways he'd loved her. She'd responded eagerly, and reached degrees of satisfaction she'd not dreamed possible.

She flushed in remembrance, fingering the shimmery ruffled overskirt of her scarlet gown. An intricate lace fichu added a degree of modesty to the gown's low bodice. The Luckenbooth brooch held the fichu in place, its fiery rubies reflecting the dress's brilliant red. Nessia had dressed her hair in a simple Grecian knot, securing a crimson ribbon across the crown.

At the bottom of the stairway, Yvette bit her lip in nervous embarrassment. Tugging at Ewan's arm, she slowed her pace. "Ewan, does everyone know why we missed supper and stayed abed this late?"

"I do hope so." He skewed his lips into a mischievous grin. "Only imagine how jealous they are."

Yvette gaped, scandalized. "Surely you're not serious?"

"Don't worry, *mon amour*, they'll pretend they don't."

That's so much better.

"Come along, wife. I'm hungry." With a reassuring peck on her forehead, he strode into the great hall, holding her hand.

Relieved to find only Giselle, Adaira, and Isobel present, Yvette exhaled the tense breath she held, and relaxed her taut shoulders. Seated at a smaller, less formal side table, they enjoyed a simple meal.

"Ewan, Yvette, do join us," Giselle bade, signaling a maid for the necessary place settings.

After pushing in Yvette's chair, Ewan trailed his fingers across her nape.

Stifling a moan, she resisted the urge to arch into his warm hand.

She glanced across the table.

Giselle's eyes twinkled, and she was smiling, her gaze shifting between Yvette and her son.

She knows.

Of course she does. She's been married twice and birthed five children.

Somehow, that eased Yvette's embarrassment.

After taking a seat, Ewan unfolded his serviette. "Where are the others?"

Passing Yvette a bowl of strawberries, Giselle laughed. "All working in the village, except Seonaid and Lilias. Seonaid's doctoring a dog that injured its shoulder yesterday. Poor Lilias is napping. Bethia fussed most of the night."

Having eaten little yesterday and nothing today, Yvette

was ravenous. She helped herself to a generous portion and dove into the meal with gusto.

Ewan's meaningful grin gave her pause. Bending near, he whispered, "Built up an appetite did ye, *ma chérie?*"

The heat climbed her face, inch by inch, to her hairline. Arching a brow, she forked a strawberry. "I find invigorating physical exercise always increases my hunger."

She suppressed a smile at Ewan's discomfort when he at last became aware of his sisters' gazes vacillating between him and her, puzzlement in their naïve depths.

Yvette did indulge in a wide grin when Giselle's amused, perceptive smile had him flushing and pulling at his neckcloth.

Taking a bite of her chicken pie, Yvette's attention fell on Adaira.

Except for a quiet hello, she'd not said a word since Yvette and Ewan sat down. Adaira picked at the flaky pastry on her plate, not at all her usual vivacious, precocious self.

Yvette eyed her. "Addy, is everything well with you?"

"*Hmm?* Oh yes, everything's fine." Her chocolate gaze flicked to Yvette's before darting away. "I'm simply trying to behave with a mite more decorum. I need to be an example for my sisters. I know I've been a hellion... uncouth and all that. I've not demonstrated the behavior of a lady of quality."

Fork in the air, Yvette furrowed her brow and cut Ewan a puzzled glance.

Adaira sounded like she repeated an oft-heard lecture.

Isobel snorted, the first unladylike behavior Yvette had ever observed in her. "And a zebra can change its stripes to spots."

Adaira lifted a shoulder and continued to pick at her food. Her lack of reaction alarmed Yvette even more.

Evidently it did Isobel too, for she probed her sister with a searching look.

"I think I shall take my luncheon with me. If you don't mind, Mother." Adaira began gathering food. "I've an idea for the woolen mill I'd like to ask Father about."

Giselle waved her away. "Go, dear, but do be careful. With the construction in town, there are an unusual number of wagons and carts on the roads, not to mention strangers hereabout."

"I shall, Mother."

No one said a word about the large amount of food Adaira piled on her serviette, though Ewan quirked a brow.

Excusing herself, she left the room, munching on a hard crust of bread.

A frown marring Isobel's forehead, her serious regard never strayed from Adaira until she disappeared from sight.

A short time later, Ewan scooted from the table. "Evvy, Hugh promised me a thorough tour and detailed accounting of your projects. You, wife," he tapped her on the nose with his forefinger, "have been most industrious in my absence." He helped her to her feet. "Would you care to accompany me? I'd be grateful for your input."

Yvette wasn't sure she would be able to sit a horse. That region was most tender. She cut him a flirty smile. Not that she was complaining, mind you.

"Would you mind terribly if I cried off? I need to respond to a letter from my solicitor, and Rory wrote two weeks ago asking to visit." She faced Giselle. "Would it be an inconvenience to have the earl underfoot for a few days? I've not seen him in three years." And it was past time to tell him Edgar had poisoned their parents.

"*Cher*, you needn't ask me." Giselle patted Yvette's hand. "You're the lady of the keep, though I appreciate the consideration you've shown me. By all means, write the Earl of Clarendon and ask him to pay us an extended visit."

"Thank you." Yvette bent and hugged Giselle before taking Ewan's extended arm.

"There is one thing I'd ask of you, Yvette."

Yvette turned halfway around. "Yes?"

"It would please me no end if you'd call me *Mére,* or, if you prefer, Mother."

Yvette blinked against the tears surging to her eyes. She embraced Giselle again. "I'd like that too, *Mére.*"

Ewan bestowed a kiss on his mother's cheek. "Thank you, Mother." He clasped Yvette's hand in his big palm. "See me to the door, will you, *bien amour?*"

Fingers entwined with his, Yvette strolled to the castle's entry.

Iona attempted to dust the vast area, though from the myriad particles floating about pell-mell, her success appeared dubious at best. She bobbed an unsteady curtsy to Ewan then Yvette.

"How's your kitten?" Yvette asked her.

Face splitting into an adorable grin, the child exclaimed excitedly, "She already catched a moussy in the storeroom, m'ledy. Sorcha be pleased."

"Wonderful, dear. Perhaps you and Peadar can show his lordship your kittens after supper tonight."

"Aye. I'll go tell Peadar." The moppet skipped from the foyer.

"Kittens?"

"Oh, Ewan, the poor dears have nothing of their own, and Iona so desperately wanted a kitten. Isobel knew of a litter in the hamlet, and I took two. One for Iona and one for her brother. I hoped they'd be mousers in the kitchen. Oh, and Ewan, the children sleep in a storeroom. I'd like to move them to the nursery, if you don't object." Teeth scraping her lower lip, Yvette raised reluctant eyes to his. "Have I overstep—"

"You amaze me, wife." He wrapped her in his arms, hugging her to his wide chest and lifting her off the floor.

"You're not angry?"

"Because you care for others? Nae, anger's not what I'm feeling." Ewan looked pointedly at his pantaloons, a revealing bulge most evident.

She giggled, peering around the grand entrance. "Ewan!"

"Now give your husband a proper kiss goodbye, *wife*."

Yvette was happy to oblige. Ewan left her with a kiss which made her weak in the knees and eager for the day to be over. Nessia descended the stairs as she turned from shutting the door.

"Nessia, I'd like to wear the pink and white muslin tonight. Can you see that it is aired and pressed if need be?"

"Ye mean the one with the double row of lace and pink and blue roses?"

"Yes, that's the one."

"Aye, I shall see to it." Nessia dipped a curtsy and continued on her way.

Humming, Yvette headed for the library, a contented smile curving her mouth. Ewan's homecoming had been everything she'd hoped it would be and more. Settling herself at her tidy desk, she penned an invitation to Rory. She'd no sooner set the seal and addressed Mr. Dehring's letter when Aubry barged into the room.

Panting, face pale and eyes wide with alarm, she gasped, "Seonaid's hurt. Come quickly. She's askin' for ye."

Dear God, no.

Dropping her quill, Yvette jumped from her chair.

Dizziness engulfed her for a moment, no doubt from standing suddenly. Yanking her spectacles from her face, she dropped them on the desk and dashed to the door. "What happened? How seriously injured is she?"

"I dinnae ken." Aubry shook her head. "Aunt Giselle didnae say. She and Isobel ran to the lower levels for it's the quickest way to reach Seonaid."

"Who brought word?" Should Yvette send for Hugh and Ewan? Had someone already'?

"Oh, I dinnae ken." Aubry blinked, her face crinkling in puzzlement. "A gardener perhaps? I'm only fetching ye like Aunt Giselle asked me to."

Hurrying through the seldom used hallway at the rear of the Keep, Yvette worried. Did Seonaid need a stretcher? A doctor? Good Lord, she didn't even know if the newly-hired physician was nearby today. "Shouldn't we notify the others? Gregor will be needed."

"Help has already been sent for." Her worry obvious, Aubry forged ahead of Yvette. "Aunt Giselle said ye were in the library and to take ye to Seonaid at once."

Yvette lifted her skirts to keep up with Aubry. "Where is she?"

"She was tending her herbs." Aubry peered over her shoulder and gestured impatiently. "Hurry, there's a tunnel below which exits almost where she lies."

A heavy wooden door stood cracked open, no doubt from Giselle and Isobel's hasty passage through.

"Here." Aubry handed Yvette a lantern.

Making quick work of lighting it, Yvette stood at the threshold. Black as the Earl of Hell's waistcoat down there.

Urgency in her voice, Aubry coaxed, "Come along then, quickly."

Yvette stepped onto the landing, peering below at the

steep, narrow steps wending into the castle's bowels. "You're sure this is the quickest way?"

"Aye, otherwise we have to exit the gatehouse and go through the bailey." Aubry made a sweeping arc with her free hand. "The wetlands are on the other side of the Keep. We'd have to go halfway around the castle again. This route's much faster."

The door clunked shut with a portentous *thunk*.

"Follow me, Yvette. Watch yer step. These stairs are slippery from disuse."

The two women edged down the narrow steps as speedily as their slippered feet allowed. More than once, Yvette extended a tentative hand to steady herself, coming in contact with slimy, damp stone walls and thick cobwebs. Shuddering, she didn't allow herself to think of the hairy creatures calling the webs home. She loathed spiders.

At last, she and Aubry reached the final riser. A flight of stairs had never taken so long to descend. A complex labyrinth lay before them, but Aubry obviously knew the way and hurried across the passageway. Several other door-ways and corridors led from the one they rushed along.

Ears and eyes straining, Yvette followed Aubry, almost at a run. Rustling sounded to her left, and Yvette inhaled a choking breath. A creature scuttled across the floor, and she bit her lip to keep from crying out. A moment later, when something hairy brushed her foot, a noise did escape her.

Aubry tossed an impatient glance over her shoulder. "Only rats. The dungeon's full of them."

Only rats?

Yvette shuddered again. To keep her mind off the sharp-clawed inhabitants scurrying near her toes, she questioned Aubry. "Did you ever use these passages to escape the schoolroom?"

"Pardon? I... um, nae."

"Adaira told me she used to sometimes sneak from the keep through these tunnels."

Aubry replied with a non-committal grunt.

They turned a corner onto another corridor, and Yvette shivered. The farther they went, the colder and more confused she became. She'd never be able to retrace her steps.

"So a gardener told you Seonaid was hurt?"

"Nae. I already told ye, Aunt Giselle told me. A gardener must've told her."

Uneasiness sifted the length of Yvette's spine. "But weren't you in the village?"

Aubry nodded. "Aye, I only just returned."

"And Seonaid was tending her herbs in the wetlands?"

"Yvette, really! All these questions." Aubry's voice rang with irritation. "We can discuss all this later."

Aubry turned another corner, and they came to an arched door constructed of heavy, crudely carved wood. It stood ajar, evidence that Giselle and Isobel had come this way moments before.

"Nae much further, Yvette. Just at the end of this tunnel."

Thank goodness. Yvette didn't like the dark or confined spaces. She peered down another eerie corridor and shivered. She could get lost in this creepy maze. Was there a dungeon down here? There must be. Adaira had said enemies and prisoners were smuggled in and out.

"We're here," Aubry said. "Help me push this door open."

Yvette shoved against the slab. It inched outward, groaning in protest. She glimpsed grass a few feet beyond the door.

Where was the loch?

Something was wrong. She sensed it with everything inside her. Striving to appear calm, she asked, "Who went to the village for help?"

Aubry continued to press her shoulder into the stone door. "Aunt Giselle said Adaira did. She's the fastest rider."

God help me.

Adaira had left for the village hours ago.

Yvette gave Aubry a mighty shove before swiveling to run from whence she'd come. Better to be lost in these fusty corridors than risk staying with Ewan's insane cousin.

Aubry's outraged shriek echoed loudly, bouncing off the walls, the sound magnified in the small enclosure.

Yvette took no more than a half-dozen steps before someone struck her on the back of the head.

Thirty

Whistling no particular melody, Ewan took the gatehouse steps two at a time. His afternoon in Craigcutty caused him to admire his wife even more. It turned out, she could add skilled diplomat to her ever-growing list of accomplishments.

He had offered time and again to help his clan, but obstinate Scots pride prevented them from accepting his charity. Yet Yvette had persuaded the clan to allow her to help. She'd claimed it was her way of convincing their laird that she was devoted to him and his people. And as the improvements in the village proved, they'd believed her.

Sauntering into the hall, he exchanged meaningful grins, nods, and a bold wink or two with the few men present. Good thing Yvette wasn't there to see it. She'd blush pink throughout the evening. Seated at the smaller table before the hearth, the women visited as they busily sewed or embroidered. Everyone except Aubry, tapping her nails on her chair's worn arms in what appeared to be boredom.

Ewan surveyed the room.

Where was Yvette?

Upstairs dressing for supper, no doubt.

His mouth pulling into a rakish smile, he decided to offer his assistance. He ran up the stairs, and once he reached her chamber, didn't bother knocking, but entered unannounced.

"Evvy?"

A gown lay across the bed, but she was nowhere in sight.

He peeked into the bathing chamber and the wardrobe.

No Yvette.

Her maidservant was absent too.

Perhaps Yvette was yet cloistered in the library. Tripping down the stairs, his boots ringing a sharp rhythm on the stone floor, he headed for the library.

The heavy door's hinges squeaked when he opened it. "Evvy?"

She wasn't here either.

Moving to her desk, Ewan noted the letter to her stepbrother and one started to her solicitor. Quite a large blot of ink marred the page where the writing ended. She hadn't written much. Had she been interrupted?

A pair of spectacles lay beside the letter, and he grinned. She wore spectacles? What other secrets did his delightful wife have?

Turning away from the desk, he trod on something. Bending over, he retrieved a quill pen.

He scanned the room. Nothing appeared out of order, yet his nape hair stood on end as if electrified.

Where the blazes was she?

Ewan tried to curb his unease as he returned to the hall. "Mother, have you seen Yvette?"

Giselle lifted her focus from her sewing, shaking her

dark head. "Not since luncheon. She's been in the library since you left."

"No. She isn't. Where's Seonaid?"

"With her animals." Giselle tied a thread off. "She's been caring for a hound all day."

He met Hugh's eyes across the hall. Slanting his head, Ewan jutted his chin, issuing a silent order.

Hugh tapped Duncan and Dugall on the arms.

The three men crossed to Ewan's side.

"Dugall, please find Seonaid. Tell her I need to see her at once."

"Aye." Dugall hurried from the hall.

Ewan placed his hand on Isobel's shoulder. "I need Nessia too. Would you locate her for me?"

"Certainly." She promptly set aside her embroidery and, expression concerned, hurried to the kitchen.

He searched the hall again. "Where's Adaira? She hasn't returned from the village yet?"

Giselle looked troubled. "Why, no, now that you mention it, she hasn't."

Hands on his hips, he met everyone's gaze in turn. "Has anyone seen Yvette this afternoon?"

He strove to remain calm. Someone must've seen her. His men had strict orders to guard her if she went to the bailey or left the Keep.

A cat-like smile twitching the corners of her mouth, Aubry quipped, "Mayhap she decided wedded bliss wasn't her cup of tea after all, and she sneaked off while ye were away."

Ewan speared her a frosty glare.

"I was but teasing." She sank further into her chair, a pout upon her face.

"I suggest you refrain from speaking of my wife at all, Aubry. I've not decided what recourse to take against you."

Isobel returned with Nessia.

"Nessia, have you seen your mistress this afternoon?" Ewan silently prayed she'd say yes.

"Nae. She told me what gown to air this morn. I haven't seen her since."

Seonaid, with Dugall at her side, hurried into the room, wiping her hands on a soiled apron. "Ewan, you have need of me?"

A small, quickly-stifled child's gasp flitted across the room.

"Have you seen Yvette today?" Ewan dreaded her answer.

"Nae." Meeting the worried eyes of those assembled, her eyebrows peaked. "Whatever is wrong?"

"I'll search upstairs. Yesterday, Yvette told me she wanted to redecorate a few of the bedchambers." Scrutinizing the looks of disbelief directed at her, Aubry challenged, "It's as good as any other place to begin looking."

Ewan spotted Iona peeking around the dais, clutching her kitten to her gaunt chest.

Her regard kept shifting between Aubry and the others.

He beckoned her forward. "Iona, did you have something to say?"

Watching Aubry leave the room, she nodded her head warily.

Giselle extended her hand toward the waif. "Come. You've nothing to fear, *cheri*. Did you see Lady McTavish today?"

"Aye, in the entry this morn."

Ewan sighed in frustration. He knew that already.

Lip trembling, fat tears squeezing over the rims of her

flower-blue eyes, Iona whispered, "And when Lady Aubry took her below stairs."

Dead silence met her rasping words.

"Below stairs?" The menacing tone in Ewan's voice didn't bode well for Aubry. "To the dungeon?"

Bawling full-on now, Iona bobbed her head up and down, her wild curls bouncing with the motion. "She said Lady Seonaid was hurt and needed her ledyship."

"*Merde!*" Ewan swore, rage ripping through him.

Already vaulting into action, Duncan and Hugh seized tapers from the table.

"Nae," Ewan said. "We need torches. They're stored in the undercroft."

Dugall bolted from the room, returning moments later laden with tarred torches. A score of McTavish clansmen followed on his heels.

Voice riddled with suppressed fury, Ewan strove for a degree of composure. "Alasdair, ye and Hugh find Aubry. Bring her here. The rest of us will search the Keep's bowels. We don't know where Aubry may have taken Evvy."

"I ken."

All gazes flew to the quaking waif. Iona bravely squared her small shoulders, and met Ewan's intimidating gaze. "She be taking a tunnel that leads to the outside by the loch."

Ewan knelt on one knee, placing one hand on Iona's thin shoulder. "Thank you. You've proven yourself a brave Scot this day."

Rising, he sent a message to his men with his eyes. "Arm yourselves. Gregor, fetch my scabbard and broadsword. Meet me here in five minutes."

As the men hastened to do Ewan's bidding, a grim-faced Hugh and Alasdair returned to the hall. Hugh broke the news. "She's flown. Aubry ne'er went upstairs but fled the Keep. Mistress Peebles and Shamus saw her riding over the drawbridge."

His mouth drawn into a tense line, Alasdair slapped his fist into his palm. "She wasn't alone either. Frasar was with her."

Shocked gasps rang out in unison.

Merde.

Aubry had absconded with Campbell. She'd planned this, then. A chill raked Ewan, shaking him more than any covert assignment he'd performed for the Crown.

What had the jaded wench done with Yvette?

Countenances somber, the clansmen moved to leave, but halted abruptly and stared dumbfounded at the irregular pair entering the hall.

A wholly disheveled nobleman stood before them, several days' growth of beard on his angular face. And he held Adaira's arm wrapped in his steely grasp.

Eyes swollen from crying, her hair was a tangled mass, hanging to her waist.

"What be the meaning of this?" Hugh reached for his dirk. "Unhand me daughter."

"Clarendon?" Ewan's eyebrows arched first in total surprise—he'd never seen the earl so angry before—then descended into a dark scowl. "Where the hell did you come from?"

Clarendon's mouth skewed as he gave Adaira a slight shake.

She protested not in the least but stared mutely at the floor.

Ewan stiffened and narrowed his eyes. "Here now, that's my sister you're shaking about."

Hugh and Dugall growled dual warnings.

Clarendon sliced a coldly infuriated glance at the woman he restrained. "What, you've nothing to say now? You've been blathering non-stop for the past three days. You'd plenty to say then, most of it imprecise and illogical. Now you're tongue-tied?"

He jostled her again.

"Three days?" Ewan looked from Adaira to Clarendon then back to Adaira.

She looked guilty as Satan in heaven.

Damnation, what has she done?

"For the past three days, your sister," Clarendon leveled Adaira a blistering glare, "has kept me as a forced guest in the dungeon."

Taken aback, Ewan narrowed his eyes. "Why, Adaira?"

"I thought..." She peeked at him, then Clarendon. Shoulders slumping even more, she mumbled, "I thought he was the other one—the one who wants to harm Yvette."

"What made you think that?" Ewan didn't have time to sift through this mess.

"I met him in the village. His horse had gone lame, and he was asking for directions to the Keep."

Ewan's gaze collided with Clarendon's. A challenge simmered in them.

"I often leave off my title when traveling." Clarendon hitched a shoulder. "I find it eliminates a lot of, shall we say, undesirable attention. Surely *you* understand."

Ewan gave a crisp nod. He did understand. But to the matter at hand.

Adaira wept softly, tears streaming from her eyes as she struggled to speak. "I saw Yvette below with Aubry. I was taking him," she dared another peek at Clarendon, "some food."

That explained the enormous mound of food she'd taken with her at midday.

"I tried to follow them until I could decide what to do. Yvette heard me though. I stopped, afraid Aubry would also realize I was there." Adaira sobbed full on now, her eyes pleading. "I lost them, Ewan. I didn't know which passage Aubry took. Then I heard a scream."

Ewan sucked in a breath through clenched teeth.

A scream?

Fury pummeled him, searing his veins. By God, if Aubry had harmed a hair on Yvette's head, kin or not, he'd see her punished. With his own two hands.

"My lord, release my daughter."

Ewan's gaze shifted to his mother. Though her tone remained modulated and polite, it was also hard as granite and every bit as unyielding.

Mouth pursed, Clarendon released Adaira.

Crying loudly, she ran into Mother's arms.

Ewan scowled again. They didn't have time for this.

"To your sister's credit, she's *not* unintelligent," Clarendon said.

Ewan's gaze swept over Adaira huddled in their mother's arms then shifted back to Clarendon. "No, she's not."

"She reasoned if Yvette was in danger from another source, I *might* be who I claimed I was. It took a great deal of persuading, but when I suggested that the delay might mean the difference between life and death for Yvette, Miss Ferguson released me."

"You're absolutely right. We cannot afford to delay any longer. Clarendon, will you remain in charge here? I need every man I can muster to search for Evvy."

"With all due respect, Sethwick, she's my stepsister. I should assist in the search for her."

"She's my wife."

Stunned surprise registered on Clarendon's face. "Wife? I heard rumor of a betrothal, but...

"She didn't inform you?" Ewan gave the earl a lingering look.

"No. Yvette wrote she had something to discuss with me. I was curious why she asked for my help procuring so many supplies, and why there was such a rush about it. I determined a visit was in order."

"I haven't the time to discuss the particulars, just now. My wife's life may be in danger. I'd be grateful if you'd concede to remain here in the event I need your support at this end."

Clarendon angled his head. "As you wish, Sethwick. I would like to bathe and change my clothing, if it can be arranged."

Ewan glanced at his mother.

"I'll see to it," she assured him.

He turned to Adaira. "I expect a full accounting of your actions. Stay in your room 'til I return."

"Aye, daughter, I expect the same." Hugh's scowl held little mercy.

Gaze glued to the stone floor, Adaira simply nodded in response.

"Duncan, take half the men to the cellars. The rest of ye, follow me." Sliding his broadsword into his scabbard, Ewan strode from the room.

Was Yvette even alive still?

Thirty-One

Yvette struggled upward through a blanket of thick blackness. Eyes shut, she struggled to remember what had happened. Awareness and paralyzing fear gripped her simultaneously.

Aubry had tricked her, the wretch.

Yvette remembered running, but what occurred afterward? Try as she might, she could recollect no more. At least she was alive.

For how long?

The base of her head throbbed something awful. She cracked an eye open a hair's breadth.

No!

Though their backs were to her, Yvette nonetheless recognized the two people sitting at the broken table.

Fielding and Pauline.

Without moving, she took stock of her surroundings. She lay in a dilapidated cottage, a large portion of the thatched roof missing. The fading afternoon sun filtered into the hut's single room where she sprawled upon one of three mussed pallets. The door hung askew, light visible through its shrunken planks.

She shifted her attention to the two shutterless windows. Their decaying sills provided a glimpse of the numerous tall trees without. Two pistols and a nasty looking knife lay atop the warped table. A cluster of what looked to be whisky bottles sat beside them. From the condition of the interior, she guessed her abductors had been here for days, if not weeks.

Why?

"At last, she is awake."

Yvette didn't pretend otherwise. Struggling to a sitting position, she gingerly touched her head. She encountered an egg-sized lump and a mass of matted hair. Her hand came away smeared with drying blood. The ribbon gone, her hair billowed about her shoulders and back. "How long was I unconscious?"

Pauline shrugged indifferently. "A couple of hours."

Mouth chalk dry, Yvette swallowed. "May I have some water, please?"

Fielding poured water into a none-too-clean cup and brought it to her. He stood looming over her, watching as she drank the entire contents. Without a word, she handed him the mug.

Directness was the best approach. At least she'd know what to expect. "Why am I here?"

Pauline turned a hostile glare on her. "I want Sethwick. He will come for you, no?"

What did she want with Ewan? Was that why they had tried to abduct her at Vangie's too? It didn't make sense. She and Ewan had barely known each other then.

"Why do you want Ewan?"

Anger contorted Pauline's face. "He killed my brother."

"Not exactly, Pauline." Fielding's smirk earned him a hate-filled glower. "He captured your brother, and when you tried to help him escape, he got shot." Fielding's reptilian eyes slithered over Yvette, and she resisted the urge to scuttle as far into a corner a she could. "Pauline gave Sethwick that scar on his face."

"It should've been his throat," Pauline sneered.

Yvette frowned. "Why didn't he recognize you at the jeweler's then?"

"It was pitch black that horrible night."

"Which is precisely why you failed to kill him, isn't it, Pauline?" Fielding sniggered. "I do believe Sethwick's the only one of your victims to ever escape with his life."

Pauline glared at Fielding, fury spewing from her dark as night eyes. "Shut up or I'll—"

"What? Kill me? I think not. You need me." Fielding ambled to his chair. He sank onto the rickety piece of furniture, clasping his hands across his midsection and crossing his ankles in a relaxed pose. Staring at Yvette, a lewd spark gleamed in his weak, insipid eyes. His watery gaze kept dropping to her bosom.

She glanced downward. Her fichu was missing. The Luckenbooth brooch, where was it?

Yvette glowered at Fielding, crossing her arms over her breasts as crimson swept across her cheeks. A lascivious smile teased the edges of his pudgy mouth. She shuddered, repulsed.

The door creaked open, and a man entered, carrying two dead rabbits.

Yvette couldn't keep her eyes from widening.

The man from the jewelry shop.

He favored one arm, keeping it tucked to his side. Was he the man Mr. Carmichael had shot?

She covertly examined Pauline's hands. A bright red scar puckered the surface of one.

Not sparing Yvette as much as a glance, the man set about skinning the rabbits before the crumbling fireplace.

"How long do you think we'll have to wait?" Fielding posed the question, his eyes never leaving Yvette.

"I don't know. By now, he knows she's missing, no?" Pauline crossed to the window. "Did you see anything, Alanzo?"

"No." His face pinched in concentration, he expertly tended the unfortunate rabbits.

Yvette's mind raced. She was meant as bait for Ewan. But why?

What if they believed he would not come? Would they release her?

"Ewan mightn't come."

Even Alanzo stopped to stare at Yvette with his peculiar, emotionless eyes.

Pauline turned from the window, a trace of alarm in her husky voice. "What you say? Of course he will come. You are his wife."

So, they knew that too. That complicated things a bit.

"Not by choice. I was unaware we were married. I didn't consent to the union. The marriage will be annulled." Trying to appear outraged, Yvette ranted, "Ewan tricked me into marriage using an obscure Scottish law. A ceremony wasn't even performed."

Pauline leveled Fielding a furious scowl. "This is true?"

"I've no idea. I'm English, remember?"

Yvette cringed as his calculating gaze roamed over her again.

A lascivious smile contorted Fielding's mouth. "The chit could be lying."

"But I'm not." She forced herself to stand. There, that wasn't so bad. Only slightly dizzy, she snagged her stocking on the rough floor when she leaned against a chair for support. Where in heaven's name were her slippers?

Deuced hard to escape without shoes.

"You've been watching the castle." She considered each of them in turn. Emotion skittered across Fielding's face. Ah, she was on to something. "You know Ewan was gone for weeks."

That explained why they'd not acted sooner. They'd waited for his return.

Pauline and Alanzo's gazes met for the briefest of moments.

Yvette notched her chin higher. "At my insistence, Ewan's been in Edinburgh, requesting an annulment."

A sly gleam appeared in Pauline's eyes. "Why you stay? Why you no leave?"

"Why? Because I cannot. Ewan is my husband. Until the church grants the annulment, I'm bound to him by law. Besides, his clan watches my every move. They don't allow me to go anywhere without armed guards. An annulment could take *years*, though."

Forcing her mouth into a moue of exasperation, she met Pauline's skeptical gaze. "There's *no* love between us. He was only after my fortune."

Yvette's heart wrenched at the lie.

She did love Ewan, and she'd never told him she did. Not even last night when he'd introduced her to passion and her heart had felt near to bursting. Stubbornness, pride, arrogance... all had kept her from telling him how much she adored him.

A nasty smile curled Pauline's lips. "See, Fielding, you're not the only one that lusts after her money."

Fielding banged his fist on the table causing a bottle to teeter before it crashed and shattered on the floor. "He *has* to come. I cannot marry the wench if her husband's still alive."

Marry me? Dear God above.

"Why would I marry you?" Contempt crept into Yvette's voice.

With ill-omened intent, Fielding angled to his feet, covering the distance between them. Snatching her by the hair, ignoring her cry of pain, he crushed her to him, snarling into her frightened face. "You won't have a choice."

"I'd rather die."

"That is an option," Pauline said. "As for your husband not knowing where you are, that is what he does best, no? He will find you." She hefted a shoulder before adding, "We made it easy for him."

She looked pointedly at Yvette's exposed chest. Her vapid gaze traveled to Yvette's hanging hair, and finally rested on her stockinged feet.

So, that was where everything was. They'd left a trail. Yvette's stomach coiled in renewed trepidation.

Oh, Ewan, be careful.

Pauline veered her attention to Fielding. "Roland, take a look around. See if anyone comes."

"The sun's setting. Sethwick mightn't be able to find her." Fielding sent a significant look in Yvette's direction. "In the dark."

"He will find her, *idiota*. You don't know him as I do. There is *no* doubt."

"Fine." Casting Pauline a peeved glance, Fielding opened the decrepit door, and seconds later, the violent impact of a gunshot blew him backward into the cottage. He slumped to the floor, lifeless.

Yvette slapped her hands over her mouth, stifling her involuntary scream. A combination of relief and horror simultaneously thundered through her.

Thank God, Ewan's here.

Prepared to do battle, Alanzo, knife in hand, and Pauline, armed with both pistols, pivoted toward the entry.

The yawning entrance stood void of human form. Another horrendous blast reverberated through the cottage, this one coming from one of the wide-open windows. Struck between the shoulders, Alanzo toppled face-first onto the floor.

Yvette jumped and yelped as she slung a glance to the window.

And he's brought help.

"Nooo, Alanzo, no." Pauline's shattering scream slashed Yvette to her soul.

She stood horrified as the signora slammed the door and latched it before falling to her knees beside her dying lover. The pistols clattered uselessly to the floor, as Alanzo's life blood saturated the packed earth.

Hysterical, Pauline begged, "Alanzo, *il mio amore,* do not leave me."

Vowing her love as she pleading with him not to die, she frantically rolled him over. Ragged sobs shaking her, she pressed her face to his cheek.

His eyes had already begun glazing over. Death wasn't far off.

Nausea roiled in Yvette's belly.

She crept forward, snatching the forgotten knife off the table. She concealed the blade in the folds of her skirt before stealing a glance at the window again.

Nothing.

The sun had set, and dusk hovered in the forest. Night would soon claim her due.

Yvette harbored no doubt help was without. Cautious by nature, Ewan wouldn't risk harming her. Even now, he might have Pauline within his gun's sights.

Yvette trembled, swallowing another wave of queasiness. Inch by inch, she crept to the door, her focus riveted on Pauline the whole while.

With supreme effort, Alanzo touched Pauline's face. Wheezing through the blood gurgling in his throat, he choked, "*Addio, caro mio amo...*"

He released a shuddering sigh, and breathed his last. His hand flopped to the floor with a sickening thud.

Nearly past Pauline, Yvette went rigid.

Pauline lurched to her feet, her obsidian eyes spewing hatred. She waved one of the discarded pistols in her blood-smeared hand. "You..." She advanced on Yvette, her eyes mad with grief. "You *puttana*. This is your fault." Pauline's crazed gaze fell on the lifeless Alanzo, and she waved the gun over his body. "You did this."

She laughed, an insane shrieking cackle that ended in a rasping sob. Lifting the pistol with both hands, she aimed it straight at Yvette's heart.

With a sharp, practiced flick of her wrist, Yvette instinctively hurled the knife. A scarlet blotch spread across Pauline's chest. Aghast and pressing both hands over her mouth, Yvette stumbled backward until she bumped into the shoddy table.

Sweet God in heaven, she'd actually knifed someone. Years of practice hadn't prepared her for the reality of the violent act. Bile rose to her throat. Spots swam before her eyes.

Gaze incredulous, Pauline quirked her mouth into an unsteady smile. "You are full of the surprises."

The pistol dropped from her hand, its discharge deafening. The sound resonated uncannily, almost as if the lead ball protested, disappointed not to have found a home in tender, human flesh.

Pauline crumpled to the floor beside her lover.

Edging around the bodies, frantic to get outside this place of death and reach Ewan, Yvette grasped the door. Fingers shaking, she fumbled with the latch. Finally, it slipped free. She stumbled into the shadowy clearing.

"Ewan?"

Where was everyone?

A figure separated itself from the cottage's stone side.

"Not Ewan, Evvy."

No! It can't be Edgar. Please. Don't let it be him.

But it was.

Yvette ran.

A faint glimmer shimmered in the distance.

The loch.

She had to reach the loch. Someone searching for her might see her.

Edgar crashed after her, his oaths and threats spurring her on.

She raced onward, dodging rocks and trees. Gnarled branches snatched at her flying hair. Stones shredded her stockings. Such was her terror, she felt no pain.

In which direction should she run? Which side of the loch would she emerge on?

Please God—not the bogs.

~

Ewan's men discovered Yvette's fichu less than five hundred yards from the castle, and a quarter mile farther on, they found one of her slippers.

He was being led into a trap. A trap set by practiced assassins.

Nevertheless, the report of gunfire spurred him and his loyal clansmen forward. Lying low across their mounts, they circled the loch, headed for the long-deserted crofters' cottages.

Using hand signals, Ewan sent men on foot to investigate each ramshackle building. He slid from Shaidae and, leaving the well-trained horse where he'd dismounted, cautiously approached a cottage, its door hanging wide open.

He peeked around the doorframe.

Standing to his full height, Ewan whistled, calling the other clansmen. He surveyed the gruesome scene before him.

Devil and damn. Yvette wasn't here.

A low moan caught his attention. In a trice, he assessed the bodies on the floor and crossed to Pauline.

His men filled the doorway.

In the dim light, he knelt beside the fatally injured woman.

Pauline's eyelids fluttered open. "I told her you would come, no?"

"Where's my wife?"

She shut her eyes, the lashes inky against her ashen cheeks. Barely audible, she rasped, "She left after she did this to me."

Ewan bent closer. "Were you working with Marquardt?"

"*Sì.*" Her chest rattled from the effort to speak. "Fielding was blackmailing him too."

So, Ewan had been right about the blackmail. He touched Pauline's shoulder. "Who gave you your orders?"

Her lips moved, but no sound emerged. She coughed and was silent.

Ewan tucked his chin to his chest. He'd been so damned close to uncovering the truth. He sighed and started to rise.

"The earl," she whispered with her last breath.

Moments later, Ewan strode from the cottage. Glancing at the brooch in his hand, he clenched his fist in barely suppressed anger. Pauline's revelation had come as no surprise. He'd suspected as much, though he'd been loath to believe it.

He now understood the connection between Marquardt, Fielding, and Pauline. They spied for the same spymaster. Because of her brother, Pauline had harbored an irrational, personal vendetta against Ewan as well. And he'd no doubt Fielding had planned on killing Marquardt. Once Ewan was eliminated, Fielding intended to gain access to Yvette's fortune by forcing her to marry him.

Little did he know Yvette. She'd have died first.

Lifting his head, searching the surrounding area, Ewan sucked in a deep, calming breath. That could wait.

Yvette was out there somewhere, probably terrified out of her mind, and Edgar hunted her. Night was almost fully upon them. They needed light.

"We can attend to the bodies in the morn. Right now, I intend to find my wife."

Thirty-Two

Yvette almost wept in fear and frustration when her feet began sinking in the quagmire. She was in grave trouble. The bog's unstable moss couldn't sustain her weight. Frantic to escape Edgar, she'd been intent on reaching the loch and had accidentally ventured straight into the marsh.

Terror urging her on, she slogged forward a few more feet, desperate to find a solid surface. She turned this way and that, trying to get her bearings in the ever-darkening swamp.

Which way should she go?

She must find stable ground and a place to hide from Edgar.

Shivering, she tapped the ground with her foot then gave it a tentative push. She pressed harder. Firm.

Oh, thank goodness.

The first star of the evening winked at her as she looked to the sky. The forest had become an obscure wall of irregular shapes and the loch a murky, oversized looking glass.

Edgar continued to chase her, though he had stopped

trying to entice her to come to him. He had been silent for several minutes now.

How close was he?

A splash and curse alerted Yvette to his presence. How had he crept up on her so quietly? She squinted into the growing gloom. No more than ten feet from where she crouched, he thrashed about.

He'd fallen into a bog pool.

"Evvy, please help me. I'm stuck in the bog. You can't let me die. You're my sister."

Damn him for making me feel guilty.

Perhaps she could help keep him afloat. Yvette looked around for a branch, but she was too far from the trees and none lay nearby. Even Edgar shouldn't die like that.

Sunk to his armpits, terror leeching into his voice, he begged, "I'm sinking. You must hurry."

No help for it. She'd have to go to him. "Edgar, I'm coming."

"Yvette! Do. Not. Move."

She spun round. There, near the forest's perimeter, she made out Ewan—tall and oh, so welcome—and a dozen of his clan members, their phantom-like forms limned by the torches they bore. Their horses stood behind them, apparitions in the nebulous shadows.

"Ewan, thank God. Edgar's caught in a bog. He's nearly sunk under."

"Evvy, whatever you do, don't move from where you are. Do you understand me? How you arrived there without the marsh claiming you is nothing short of a miracle. You're surrounded by unstable ground."

"What about Edgar?"

"I have a rope. I'll try to reach him."

Ewan and three of his men began inching across the treacherous ground.

Familiar with this marsh, they knew the safe path through it. But it was dark now and almost impossible to discern between solid land and the spongy surface capable of sucking a man under. What if Ewan...? No, she wouldn't think of it.

"Be careful, Ewan, please."

"Evvy, he won't reach me in time," Edgar whimpered. "You must help me."

Yvette cast a frantic glance at Edgar then Ewan. "What should I do?"

"I can only save one of you, Yvette. If you move, he stands no chance whatsoever."

"Oh, Edgar." Only his chin and hands remained visible above the insidious, glugging muck.

"I'm throwing you a rope, Marquardt. It has a loop in the end. Try to grasp it." Ewan tossed the rope, but it fell short by several inches.

His hopelessness evident, Edgar called to her. "I'm sorry, Evvy. Please forgive me."

Weeping, Yvette pressed her fisted hands to her mouth. Even as wicked and horrid as Edgar had been, she couldn't bear to witness his death.

Ewan threw the rope again.

Edgar managed to graze the loop with his fingertips, but the movement plunged him further into the fetid goo. "I don't want to die knowing you hate me, Evvy. Please forgive me."

Her voice clogged by tears, she managed, "I forgive you."

Two of Ewan's men ventured a few feet beyond him and

held their torches high, permitting him to see better. One final time, Ewan slung the rope. It landed on top of Edgar's hand. With his other, he latched onto the lifesaving line.

"You did it, Ewan! He has it." Tears of relief leaked from Yvette's eyes.

The men towed Edgar from the oozing slime and promptly placed him under arrest. In no condition to resist, he docilely permitted them to lead him away.

She clutched Ewan's hand as he guided her from the bog. Once on solid ground, she threw herself into his arms. "Ewan, I thought I'd never see you again."

She stood on her tiptoes and kissed his jaw and chin and neck, half hysterical from her ordeal.

"I thought I was going to die and..." Tears spilled from her eyes and trailed over cheeks. "And I never told you that I love you."

Ewan hugged her to his wide, comforting chest. "You're safe now, *mon amour*." He kissed the top of her head. "Marquardt will never terrorize you again."

They both turned to look at Edgar. He stood defeated, caked in filth, surrounded by four Scots.

"I do love you, Ewan. I think I have since you rescued me off the wharf." She rested her cheek against his chest. "I'm sorry I didn't tell you sooner. Sorry I was afraid to love you. Sorry I didn't realize sooner."

Ewan tilted her face up with a crooked finger.

In the dim light, she searched his eyes.

"Ye have dirt on your face." He brushed her cheek with his thumb. "And, lass, ye did tell me."

He chuckled at her confused frown.

"I never told you."

"Aye, ye did. Last night. Ye talk in yer sleep."

Jaw slack, Yvette gaped.

Chuckling again, Ewan pushed her mouth closed with the same crooked forefinger then wrapped her in a woolen tartan.

Grinning, Gregor led Shaidae to them. "It be good to see ye safe, lass."

After Ewan mounted, Gregor lifted Yvette and placed her before him on the saddle.

She snuggled against her husband, feeling safer and more content than she'd ever been before.

"And I'll be thanking you not to be misplacing this again so soon." Ewan held the Luckenbooth brooch in his open palm.

"Ewan!" Throwing her arms about his neck, she kissed him soundly. The laughter of his clansmen didn't deter her in the least. "How can I ever thank you?"

The entire journey to the keep, Ewan whispered an assortment of clever ways she could show her gratitude.

Yvette was most grateful for the night's darkness for her cheeks were in high color by the time they arrived home.

Once at the castle, Ewan ordered a bath for Yvette, and after kissing her on the forehead, sent her to her chamber. He went straightaway to his study, Hugh and Gregor in his wake, Marquardt secured between them. After requesting Clarendon be sent to his office at once, he sat at his desk and penned two missives.

A single tap announced the earl's arrival.

"Come."

"You requested..." Clarendon's voice trailed off upon glimpsing his brother standing stiffly, covered in drying filth. Cocking a brow, the earl quipped, "Ah, in addition to your wife, Sethwick, I see you've located my wayward sibling."

"Clarendon, I have a request to make of you."

The two sealed letters in his hand, Ewan rose. "First thing in the morning, will you depart for London and deliver these? Six of my men will accompany you. Your brother is under arrest."

Leveling Ewan with an expressionless gaze, Clarendon asked, "May I ask on what charge?"

"Take your pick. Treason, murder, attempted murder, abduction, extortion."

"Murder?" Clarendon faced his brother full on. "Whom did he murder?"

"Do you want to tell him, Marquardt, or shall I?" Ewan skirted the desk, still very much wanting to punch him to London and back.

Marquardt curled his lip. "You should've let me die in the bog."

Ewan cocked his head. "Aye, I should've. It's what you deserved. Alas, Evvy's kind heart couldn't bear it. She would've been haunted by the image the rest of her days. I rescued you for her."

"Whom did you murder, Edgar?"

Given the deadly calmness of Clarendon's voice, Ewan suspected the earl had already arrived at the truth.

Marquardt's demeanor changed to that of a sniveling wretch. "It wasn't my fault, Rory. She wasn't supposed to drink... What I mean is, it was meant for—" He faltered then mashed his lips together, refusing to speak further.

Ewan finished Marquardt's sentence. "Yvette. The drink was meant for Yvette. He tried to kill her on more than one occasion."

Silence, heavy and thick, filled the study.

Ewan heaved a sigh. "Roark, I'm sorry to be the one to tell you." His gaze flicked to Marquardt, glaring daggers at him. "He's suspected of poisoning your mother and stepfather, though Yvette was his intended victim, not your mother."

His expression shuttered, Clarendon turned his back to his brother. "I'll take your letters. I presume they're classified? Yes, I assumed as much. Rest assured, I'll see *he* is delivered to Newgate."

"Rory, you cannot."

Not sparing his brother the briefest of glances, Clarendon shifted toward the door. "I shall leave at first light."

Ewan met his gaze.

Rampant agony reflected deep within the earl's blue eyes.

"Please return to Craiglocky when you've finished. Yvette expressed her desire to have you stay for an extended visit, and you'd be most welcome." Poor sot. Ewan reached to shake his hand. "It's comforting to have family close at hand in times such as these."

Clarendon replied with a curt nod. He left the study without ever looking at his brother again.

A small, gratified smile lingered on Ewan's lips. Yes, it would be most enjoyable having the earl as a houseguest.

He was especially curious to see Adaira's reaction.

Thirty-Three

"How is she today?" Yvette peered over Seonaid's shoulder.

Seonaid spared Yvette a glance. "Frail, but improving."

On the straw lay a bitty, days-old calf, her mother dead of milk fever. The baby suckled the improvised bottle Seonaid had created for her.

Squatting, Yvette rubbed the animal's silky head.

Large, trust-filled brown eyes shifted to meet hers, though the calf never stopped her ravenous gulping.

Yvette stepped from the stall, Seonaid behind her.

One of the keep's many dogs barked outside. The barking grew louder, more frantic, somehow familiar. Yvette cocked her head.

Could it be?

Hurrying to the shed door, her heart beating in anticipation, she threw it open. Hastening outside, she skidded to a standstill at the wondrous sight meeting her eyes.

God in heaven, it was.

Two carriages lined the courtyard, and a rotund woman

dressed in a vivid red traveling ensemble descended from the first. She resembled a great ladybird beetle.

"Pippa!"

Yvette tore across the courtyard, tears streaming from her eyes. Apollo and Artemis spotted her and began high-pitched yapping, running in frenzied circles about their mistress's skirts.

Pippa bustled over to her. "My child. My dearest." The women clung to one another, tears of joy flowing freely.

Yvette pulled away first, laughing and wiping her face with her hands. "Pippa, I've missed you so."

"What about me, minx?"

"Siah!" Yvette launched herself into the twin's arms.

Yvette clasped sapphire earrings onto her ears and then the matching choker. Taking one last look in the mirror, she bent her lips into a pleased half-smile. Pippa had outdone herself. Jewels sparkled throughout Yvette's elaborately coiffed hair.

Her cobalt gown hugged her bosom before falling away in numerous layers. A glittering beaded overskirt—the intricate lace as delicate as a spider's web—split at the middle and was secured on each side, hip high, with blue ribbon roses. The Luckenbooth brooch, nestled at the lace between her breasts, proclaimed her allegiance to Ewan.

He sat on the divan, watching her finish her *toilette.*

My, but he looked splendid in his formal attire. He approached her from behind, and she met his sultry gaze in the mirror. Lowering his head, he placed a kiss on her shoulder.

"*Mon amour,* I'm not sure I approve of the current fashion." His focus dipped to the generous portion of her breasts exposed above her bodice, and he touched the mole on her breast.

"You've not objected before, my lord." A teasing smile bent her mouth.

"Aye, but I find I've become much more possessive of certain *charms* now that we're wed."

She turned in his arms. Running her hands over his chest, she grasped his broad shoulders, and rose onto her tiptoes. Pulling his head toward hers, she whispered against his lips,

"That may be, my lord, but remember, those charms are reserved for your exclusive use." She gifted him with passionate reassurance lasting several luscious moments.

Ewan wiggled his eyebrows, slanting his head toward the bed. "Perhaps we could delay supper?"

Yvette swatted him on the arm. "Heavens no. I promised the twins a full accounting since I saw them last. And Pippa worked so hard on my hair. She'd have an apoplectic fit if I disturbed a single curl." Sauntering to the door, she tossed a provocative glance over her shoulder. "Besides, husband, anticipation makes the prize more desirable."

"Minx."

She loved the way his eyes darkened and his nostrils flared when he was aroused.

Dinner proved a lengthy affair, boasting twelve courses. As Yvette looked down the table's length, her heart skipped a happy beat. How different this joyful gathering was from her first in the hall. She cut Ewan a sideways glance.

As was his habit, he watched her. "*Mon amour*, you're not eating very much."

She gave him a bemused smile. "It's impossible to eat

large portions of each course. And honestly, Ewan, I'm not fond of trout. It tastes of weeds." Yvette laid her hand on his arm. "Besides, I intend to dance until the wee hours. If I'm stuffed like a goose, it will be nigh impossible."

Running his hand along the top of her thigh, he whispered, "Nae, not 'til the wee hours, *ma belle*. I've other plans."

Certain a blush flared across her cheeks, Yvette dipped her head. Delicious sensations spread outward from where his fingers still brushed her leg. There was something to be said for seeking one's bed early.

The instrumentalist struck the first notes, and Ewan stood. "Would you honor me with this dance?"

"Of course."

They danced alone for several moments, the eyes of those assembled trained on them. Twirling across the floor, Yvette forgot everything but the feel of her husband's arms —his waltz a reminder of a fortuitous day long ago. Unlike their first dance, this time, their gazes tangled and held in an unspoken pledge. Other couples made their way onto the floor, and soon, it was a swirling mass of color.

The waltz ended, and he led her to the dais.

What is he about?

Gazes followed their progress as the room settled into a hush of anticipation. The musicians stopped playing. Conversations ceased. A suspenseful lull descended on the hall.

Whatever is going on?

Yvette tilted her head, searching his eyes. "Ewan?"

"Trust me, *petite amie*."

~

Holding her hand, Ewan turned to face the crowd.

"Kin and kith, I'm a man blessed beyond measure." He looked at Yvette and kissed her fingertips, smiling into her confused eyes before addressing the guests again. "Yvette has honored me these past weeks in her role as my wife. However, I promised her a proper proposal. One she never received."

She stared at him, her eyes wide and wondering.

He scanned the guests' faces.

Pippa wiped tears from her eyes. The Fairchild twins grinned like buffoons. Adaira and Isobel hugged each other. Dugall winked, and Mother and Hugh nodded their approval.

Drawing a deep breath, he swallowed before plowing on.

"I never asked Yvette to be my wife. My viscountess. My chieftainess. My life's partner. Circumstances, destiny, fate, divine providence... whatever you wish to call it, compelled us into marriage."

Ewan turned to look straight into Yvette's stunned eyes, burrowing into their luminous depths. Taking a knee, in the presence of those whom he had authority over, he raised her hand, and removed her elbow-length glove. "I want to give you your proper proposal, and the wedding you always wanted. Yvette Alexandra Clarisse Stapleton McTavish, will you marry me?"

Stealing a glance at the enthralled onlookers, she whispered, "Ewan, you needn't do this."

"Nae, love, I must."

It was as if it were only he and Yvette alone, the world closing in on them, erasing everything else. It became the pair of them, in this public place, their two souls reaching across a chasm, meshing, joining.

"Will you marry me, Evvy? With all the ceremony and fuss? With dozens—hundreds, I don't care—thousands in attendance? With clergy and bells, flowers and veils? Will you pledge yourself to me for now and always? I want to give you this choice, because, *mon seul amour*, you were never given it."

Head bowed, he humbly asked, "Will you *choose* to marry me?"

Yvette tugged at him until he stood, facing her. Tears loomed in her eyes. "Aye, Ewan, Laird McTavish, Viscount Sethwick, keeper of my heart. I shall wed you."

He lifted her left hand, and after pressing his lips to the back, slipped a ring onto her finger—a ruby framed by four sapphires.

"The sapphires reminded me of your eyes, *ma chérie*. One for each corner of the earth, and the ruby is my heart. There's nowhere on earth you may go where you'll not carry my heart with you. It's wholly, now, forever and always, yours.

Epilogue

On a glorious September afternoon, Yvette and Ewan exchanged wedding vows in Craiglocky Castle's private chapel. With only their closest family and friends present, the wedding was intimate and private. As they'd planned since childhood, Vangie was Yvette's matron of honor, and Ian acted as the best man.

The celebration afterward was a lavish affair, and would've been considered garish if not so tastefully done. As the newlyweds stood on the dais, the great hall resounded with cheers from the hundreds of well-wishers. The grand ball that followed was unequaled in Craiglocky's history. Not only did they celebrate the laird's wedding day, it was Yvette's first-and-twentieth birthday.

Even the scandalous arrest and imprisonment of Edgar Marquardt couldn't dampen the extravagant festivities. The Earl of Rothingham, at last exposed as the War Office traitor, was summarily arrested for high treason. Within a matter of hours—less than twelve, to be precise—he'd bribed his way out of Newgate and was reported to have fled to the Caribbean.

Since it was impossible to prove he'd murdered his mother and stepfather, Marquardt was spared the hanging he deserved. With Rothingham's disappearance, and the deaths of Fielding and the Italians, no one was left to testify to his treasonous behavior. Rothingham's systematic elimination of every witness and accomplice spared Marquardt the most extreme consequence of his actions. He departed England in disgrace.

True to his word, the Earl of Clarendon returned for an extensive holiday. Adaira's reaction to the Earl's presence proved confounding at best.

That night as Yvette lay satiated in Ewan's arms, she revealed a secret she had kept as a hidden treasure, in the deepest recesses of her heart. In late spring, she and Ewan would welcome their own bairn into the world.

Yes, she reflected as she drifted off to sleep. When a heart is filled with love, there hope abides, and one can embrace love fearlessly.

~

I hope you enjoyed
THE HIGHLANDER'S HEIRESS
If you'd like to leave a review, I would be grateful.

Keep reading for a free preview of
THE EARL'S ENTICEMENT
Book 3
Highland Heather Romancing a Scott: Castle Brides Series…

Free Preview
©Blue Rose Romance® LLC

THE VISCOUNT'S VOW
Highland Heather Romancing a Scot: Castle Brides
Book 3

Craigcutty, Scotland
Scottish Highlands

Late June 1817

Roark, Earl of Clarendon, led his limping horse toward a partially constructed building at the edge of the bustling village. The mare, the only horse available for hire at the inn he'd lodged at last night, had gone lame a half-mile back. He rubbed her velvety muzzle, and she blew into his hand.

The gentle, loyal creature had done her best.

He should've taken his coach the last leg of the journey

from London. Yet, he loathed confinement. Enclosed spaces stirred childhood memories better left buried. He arched his spine, wincing as familiar tautness twinged from shoulder to hip.

A man, his words indistinguishable, called to a lad standing in the building's doorway.

The boy glanced over his shoulder. "Aye, I shall."

He bounded across the porch, then down the steps in front of the structure. A piece of straw poked from his mouth, and he wielded a riding crop in one hand like a sword.

"Young chap." Roark waved, as with long strides, he closed the distance between them.

Ducking his head, the lad yanked the knitted cap lower on his brow. The Scottish bonnet was far too big for the boy. And tugged nearly over his eyes, he looked rather like Roark's one-eyed Old English sheepdog, Guinevere.

The crop stilled mid-air. Shoulders hunched and eyes lowered, the youth removed the straw from his mouth. He tossed it onto the packed earth. "Are ye speakin' to me, sir?"

"Yes, I need direction to a livery stable." Roark brushed his hand down the horse's warm neck. "This nag's gone lame."

The youth was taller and older than he'd first thought. Mayhap as much as five and ten. "What's your name, lad?"

"Ad—er—Addy, sir." Addy's voice was soft, and his brogue rather melodic for a lad that age. He appeared painfully shy, or perhaps, embarrassed at being caught pretending swordplay. He had yet to lift his gaze from Roark's dust-covered Wellington's.

Trickles of sweat trailed down Roark's back as he scanned the busy street, searching for a stable. "Where might I find a horse for hire?"

His gaze trained on the mare, Addy approached the horse instead of answering the question. He stood with his head cocked, assessing the horse. Rubbing the bridge of his nose, he leaned forward a fraction.

Ire pricked at the lad's audacity, but Roark swiftly stifled his irritation. It wasn't as if someone anxiously awaited his arrival. In fact, truth be told, he wasn't expected. It was gauche to come for a holiday unannounced, but there was nothing for it.

Whispering something unintelligible, Addy tucked the whip beneath one arm before running his hands along the mare's right shoulder. He squatted and trailed fine-boned fingers to her ankle. "I'd bet my sainted grandmother, a bowed tendon is causin' her pain."

Roark quirked a half-smile in grudging admiration. Addy was right. "You know something of horseflesh?"

Eyeing the tip of the crop peeking from beneath the youth's arm, Roark tensed, and his smile faded. He never took a whip to his horses. Or other animals for that matter. He had no respect for anyone who did.

Addy shrugged, still hunkered over the mare's lower leg. "Aye, a wee bit."

Roark scrutinized him. He'd originally thought the boy a village urchin. The well-made breeches and fine boots Addy wore belied that assumption. His jacket hung loosely but was of the highest quality. And, unless he toted the whip around for amusement, he had a horse.

Was he local gentry?

Weren't the only aristocrats in the immediate area the McTavishs and Fergusons, both of whom resided at the castle?

Roark rubbed his brow. Was this boy one of them?

Ewan McTavish, the Viscount Sethwick, had a brother about six and ten, and sisters, too, didn't he?

Blast. Roark couldn't remember precisely what his stepsister, Yvette, had written. Except that McTavish's mother and stepfather, Hugh Ferguson, along with a throng of other family members, lived at the keep.

Removing his hat, Roark lifted a crisp, white handkerchief from his coat pocket. He dabbed his sweaty forehead. With one last wipe across his face, he folded the handkerchief before tucking it back inside his jacket. His fingers brushed the irregular scar on his forehead—one of many marring his body—as he swept his hair backward. He donned his hat once more.

Despite his cap and coat, the lad didn't appear the least affected by the rising temperature.

Lifting his gaze, Roark examined what he could see of the flourishing township. No doubt Addy was the son of a prosperous merchant, and the structure was a—

Roark angled his head, studying the odd two-story building with its L-shaped additions. The new lumber glowed wheat-gold in the sunlight. The pleasing scent of freshly cut wood permeated the air. He had no idea what the odd structure was.

An inn, perhaps?

"Where are ye headed?"

Addy's question reined in Roark's musings. He swung his attention to the boy, still gently kneading the mare's leg. The lad made low, crooning noises in the back of his throat.

"Craiglocky Keep if I can acquire a horse."

And even if Roark couldn't, blister it. He didn't relish a lengthy trudge in this infernal heat. He gestured to the building. "What is this meant to be?"

Addy's hands stilled. "An orphanage."

Keeping his back to Roark, the lad slowly stood and grasped the crop once more. He edged around to the other side of the nag, caressing her with his free hand. His nails were clean and square. "Ye are a stranger to Craigcutty. What business have ye at the keep?"

Irritation surged through Roark at the lad's dawdling. He was anxious to see Yvette. Why hadn't she contacted him prior to returning to England? Why did he have to learn of her homecoming by way of the gossipmongers and the letter she posted from Scotland?

Scrutinizing the top of Addy's head, all that was visible above the horse, Roark suppressed his exasperation. He exhaled a long, controlled breath before answering coolly. "My stepsister, Yvette Stapleton, is in residence there."

The mare heaved a gusty breath and shifted her weight.

Before Addy dipped his head behind the nag again, Roark caught a fleeting glimpse of deep brown eyes framed by thick sable lashes. Was that surprise or alarm in the lad's gaze? He still hadn't answered Roark's question about acquiring a confounded mount.

"*Ye* have a stepsister? At the keep?" Skepticism riddled Addy's voice. He stopped patting the mare's neck, then twisted to look at the building. "I canna..."

The boy slapped his crop against his boot.

Meshing his lips together, he flicked Roark a contemptuous glance. The lad stared at the structure while tapping an irregular rhythm on his palm with the whip, frowning all the while.

What was he thinking?

"Yes, I'm—" By God, why was Roark explaining himself to this impertinent whelp?

Rivulets of sweat trickled between his shoulder blades. He examined the hamlet once more. Occasionally, he left off his title when traveling—especially when he wanted to remain anonymous. He'd found it very useful in determining peoples' genuineness.

He wasn't about to tell this cub his title.

"I'm Mr. Marquardt." Marquardt was his surname, although everyone addressed him by his title, Clarendon.

A snort followed by another muffled oath greeted his words. "Blast it to Hades."

"Pardon?" Roark skirted around the ancient horse's head.

Addy stood near the mare's rump, his nose crinkled in distaste. "Nothing. I stepped in—"

A small footprint was clearly visible in the middle of a steaming pile of horse droppings. Roark set his mouth against the grin that threatened. He patted the horse to hide his smile. Instinct told him the lad wouldn't appreciate his amusement.

Roark turned his attention to the well-used forked road. Parallel ruts, formed by innumerable wagon wheels, lined the parched earth. One lane led directly into town, and the other hugged the village perimeter. Most likely, the latter was the route to Craiglocky. "Does this village boast a livery?"

"Aye, there's a livery, but nae horses are available to ye."

Roark swung his gaze to Addy. He seemed to have overcome his bashfulness and stared intently at him now.

"And why not?" Roark tightened his grip on the reins. The mare jerked her head sharply. "Shh." He rubbed her neck. "It's all right."

"Look around." Addy waved the whip in the air. "Ye

can see the building and carts and all. Every beastie is already in use."

From where Roark stood, he observed three other buildings in various stages of construction. Hammering, sawing, boards banging, and calls from the workmen carried to him on the inadequate breeze. At least four wagons had rumbled into the hamlet while he'd spoken to the boy.

"Perhaps one of the wagons is continuing on to the keep?" Roark spoke more to himself than Addy. Another laden wagon creaked by. "Mayhap I could share a ride?"

"Nae likely." Addy shook his head, his cap promptly sliding to his nose. "Bugger me," he muttered, shoving the cap up his forehead.

Roark grinned.

Taking a couple of steps backward, Addy settled the bonnet higher on his head. It still obscured the top portion of his narrow face. "The castle's within walkin' distance."

Roark didn't relish a trek in this heat.

The lad pointed the crop at the outlying road. "It's a wee bit more than a mile along there."

He spun on his heels and started to dash away, but after a few strides, he slid to an abrupt halt. Little puffs of dirt spiraled around his ankles. Half-turning toward Roark, he said, "Take the horse with ye. There's someone at the keep who knows how to treat the animal."

He turned away and took no more than a dozen more steps before stopping again. He faced Roark, staring past him with impossibly dark eyes.

Roark arched a brow. "Was there something else?"

Addy's unnerving gaze met his for an instant, then flitted to the road behind Roark.

"Aye. When ye come to the fork, 'bout half-mile yonder, make sure ye keep to the right. Ye canna miss it. A monstrous old willow tree splits the path." Addy shook his right forearm back and forth for emphasis, and his short jacket rose and fell with the motion. "If ye dinna, ye'll find yerself sinkin' in the bogs."

Something akin to antagonism glinted in the lad's eyes.

Curious.

Beneath winged brows, they were unusual eyes, too: oval, not round, and coffee-brown, almost black.

A Highlander's coloring, to be sure.

Addy stood, hands on his hips, tapping the toe of one boot. He peered at Roark expectantly. Even with a few feet between them, Roark could see flecks of citrine in the boy's pupils. Impatience also glimmered in their depths.

"Ye un—der—stand?" Addy spoke slowly as if speaking to a simpleton. "Keep to the right. Nae. The. Left." He made three sharp jabs with the whip in Roark's direction.

Roark clenched his jaw.

He typically kept a tight grip on his temper, yet this slip of a boy had managed to rouse his displeasure four times in less than ten minutes. And that damn whip. If Addy pointed the crop at him one more time, Roark was going to snatch it from him and—

Roark gave a curt nod, his patience at an end. "Yes, I understand. Stay to the right at the fork in the road."

"Aye." With that, Addy flicked a cocky salute. One hand holding the oversized cap atop his head, he tore off down the street as if the hounds of hell nipped at his heels.

Roark released a frustrated sigh. From the sting biting on one heel, he'd sport a blister or two by the time he arrived at the castle. That was what came of hiking in new boots with the leather not broken in.

He didn't mind the walk.

He did, however, very much dislike the sweltering

temperature. Besides, the nag worried him. The mare was far too old to have carried him this distance. She should've been put to pasture long before now.

Roark shook his head as a new wave of guilt assailed him. He'd caused her lameness, albeit unintentionally, and remorse left a bitter taste in his mouth.

They both could use a drink.

Cool water for the faithful horse and something significantly more substantial for himself. Dunderhead. He should've heeded the innkeeper's offer of a flask of wine when the man suggested it this morning. Roark's stomach rumbled. He smiled ruefully. He'd also skipped breakfast—a decision he now regretted.

There was nothing for it, then.

He'd have to take his time leading the mare. Likely, there was some fresh water along the way. Addy mentioned nearby bogs. No need to hurry. Yvette wasn't expecting him. He'd come without an invitation, but his visit was warranted.

"She was only wearing a filmy chemise. And he was naked as a robin under the toweling when my sister discovered them in his chamber at Banbury Inn."

Roark shook his head to dislodge Lady Clutterbuck's shrill gossip from his memory.

What *had* Yvette been doing in McTavish's chamber?

A shout, followed by cursing, drew Roark's attention to the village center. Addy had plowed straight into a Scot carrying an armful of boards. In the ensuing turmoil of waving arms and crashing wood, the cap slipped from the lad's head.

A cascade of long, chocolate-colored curls, tied at the nape with an emerald ribbon, tumbled free.

Collette Cameron®

I hope you enjoyed this free preview of
THE EARL'S ENTICEMENT
Book 3
Highland Heather Romancing a Scott: Castle
Brides Series.
If you'd like to keep reading scan the QR code
below.

https://tinyurl.com/TEEccampr

From the Desk of Collette Cameron®

Dearest Reader,

It's hard for me to believe I'm releasing the second edition of ***THE HIGHLANDER'S HEIRESS!***

I've added the prologue back that was cut when the story was first published. I don't normally include prologues, but in the case of Yvette and Ewan's story, I thought it included important back-story that my readers would find helpful later on.

Many of the characters in my Highland Heather Romancing a Scot: Castle Brides series also appear in The Honorable Rogues® series. You can read the first chapters of all my books for free at **collettecameronbooks.com**.

Hugs,
Collette Cameron®

~

If you haven't joined Collette's exclusive mailing list click on QR image to sign up! You'll get access to exclusive content, sneak peeks, contests, giveaways, and more…
(P.S. No spam!)

https://collettecameronbooks.com/freegift

Collette loves to hear from readers.
You can contact her via her website:
collettecameronbooks.com.
Or email her directly at
collette@collettecameronbooks.com.

You can also follow Collette on social media:
Facebook: https://www.-facebook.com/ColletteCameronNovels/
Instagram: https://instagram.com/collettecamero-nauthor/
Goodreads: https://www.-goodreads.com/collettecameron

Social Media

Book Bub: https://www.bookbub.com/authors/collette-cameron
Pinterest: http://www.pinterest.com/colletteauthor/
YouTube: https://www.youtube.com/@ColletteCameronAuthor

Giggles are Guaranteed
Collette's Cheris Reader Group

https://www.facebook.com/groups/CollettesCheris/

If you love to chat about all things romance-book related and enjoy taking part in fun and engaging live events, contests, and giveaways join **Collette's Chèris VIP Reader Group, https://www.facebook.com/groups/CollettesCheris/,** my exclusive private book group on Facebook.

Giggles are guaranteed!

Hope to see you there,
Collette Cameron®

About the Author

COLLETTE CAMERON®

USA Today Bestselling author Collette Cameron® is renowned for her captivating, humorous, and heartwarming Scottish and Regency historical romance novels. With over 65 published titles, over 1.6 million books sold around the world, and multiple writing awards to her credit, Collette is a well-known author in the world of historical romance.

Readers love her witty and relatable characters including daring rogues, dashing scoundrels, and the strong and spirited heroines who capture their hearts. From the rugged highlands to the refined drawing rooms of Regency

England, Collette's novels will transport you to another time and place, where love and adventure are just a page away.

Collette's Sweet-to-Spicy Timeless Romances® are the perfect escape for readers looking for romantic escape, poignant inspiration, engaging humor, and entertaining stories.

Based in the Pacific Northwest, Collette is surrounded by the lush greenery and rainy skies that inspire her writing. She dreams of one day splitting her time between the Pacific Northwest and Scotland. In the meantime, she indulges in her love of all things cobalt blue, dachshunds, chocolate, and of course, crafting her next historical romance.

Blue Rose Romance® LLC
collette@collettecameronbooks.com
collettecameronbooks.com

Also by Collette Cameron®

BLUE ROSE ROMANCE® LLC
COLLETTE CAMERON'S® COMPLETE BOOK LIST

CHRONICLES OF THE WESTBROOK BRIDES
A Romantic Opposites Attract Mystery & Suspense
Family Saga Regency Romance

Midnight Christmas Waltz — Book 1

Mission at Midnight — Book 2

The Midnight Marquess — Book 3

Holly, Mistletoe, and Midnight Snow — Book 4

The Wallflower's Midnight Waltz — Book 5

Minuet at Midnight — Book 6

Kiss a Rake at Midnight — Book 7

Unmasked at Midnight — Book 8

Memories Made at Midnight — Book 9

Once Upon a Midnight Dream — Book 10

∼

LADIES OF OPPORTUNITY
A Bluestockings and Rogues Opposites Attract
Regency Mystery Christmas Romance

The Wallflower's Wild Wager — Book 1

~

SEDUCTIVE SCOUNDRELS
A Sensual Marriage of Convenience
Regency Historical Romance

A Diamond for a Duke — Book 1

Only a Duke Would Dare — Book 2

A December with a Duke — Book 3

What Would a Duke Do? — Book 4

Wooed by a Wicked Duke — Book 5

Duchess of His Heart — Book 6

Never Dance with a Duke — Book 7

Wedding Her Christmas Duke — Book 8

The Debutante and the Duke — Book 9

Loved by a Dangerous Duke — Book 10

How to Win a Duke's Heart — Book 11

When a Duke Desires a Lass — Book 12

My Dearest Duke — Book 13

~

FOR THE LOVE OF AN EARL (Wicked Earls' Club)
A Humorous Aristocrat and Wallflower
Regency Romance Adventure

Earl of Wainthorpe — Book 1

Earl of Scarborough — Book 2

Earl of Keyworth — Book 3

~

DAUGHTERS OF DESIRE (SCANDALOUS LADIES)
A Romantic Class Difference Forced Proximity
Regency Romance with Aristocrats

~

THE CULPEPPER MISSES
A Humorous Wallflower Family Saga
Regency Romantic Comedy

The Buccaneer and the Bluestocking — Book 4

The Lieutenant and the Lady — Book 5

❧

THE HONORABLE ROGUES®
A Second Chance Redeemable Rogue
and Wallflower Regency Romance

A Kiss for a Rogue — Book 1

A Bride for a Rogue — Book 2

A Rogue's Scandalous Wish — Book 3

To Capture a Rogue's Heart — Book 4

The Rogue and the Wallflower — Book 5

A Rose for a Rogue — Book 6

'Twas the Rogue Before Christmas — Book 7

A Rogue Worth the Risk — Book 8

www.ingramcontent.com/pod-product-compliance
Lightning Source LLC
Chambersburg PA
CBHW060424310726

48977CB00001B/43

9 781966 087175